IMMORTALS: The Awakening

JOY NASH

LOVE SPELL NEW YORK CITY

LOVE SPELL®

August 2007

Published by

Dorchester Publishing Co., Inc.
200 Madison Avenue
New York, NY 10016

ISBN-10: 0-505-52695-6
ISBN-13: 978-0-505-52695-3

Visit us on the web at www.dorchesterpub.com.

RAVE REVIEWS FOR JOY NASH!

THE GRAIL KING

"Not since Mary Stewart's Merlin trilogy has the magic of Avalon flowed as lyrically off the pages. Nash captures the myths of the Druids in a fresh, exciting approach delivering a tale that grabs hold of your heart and reaches deep into your soul bringing forth joy and a belief in the old ways bound with the new."

—*RT BOOKreviews,* Top Pick, 4 1/2 stars

"*The Grail King* is a magnificent journey filled with adventure, magic, friendship, and honor that will make it difficult to put down until the end. It's a brilliantly written tale...with its strong undertones of conflict between good and evil....Beautifully written with dymanic lead characters and several equally potent secondary players, *The Grail King* will put readers into its magical hold right from the beginning. Don't miss this terrific novel!"

—Romance Reviews Today

"Make sure you have plenty of free time before starting *The Grail King* by Joy Nash because you will not want to stop reading until reaching the stunning conclusion, which hints at what is to come in future books."

—CK's Kwips & Kritiques

"*The Grail King* turned out to be a rare jewel of a book, which grabbed my attention from the beginning and kept me enthralled until the very end....wonderful, complex characters, an exciting, adventurous plot, and a great romance...I don't know how I've missed reading Ms. Nash's work before now, but be assured she goes on my auto-buy list. Do yourself a favor and read *The Grail King*."

—Once Upon a Romance Review

MORE RAVE REVIEWS FOR JOY NASH!

CELTIC FIRE

"Nash creates suspenseful, haunting and high-tension romance...a top-notch read."

—*RT BOOKreviews*

"Joy Nash has created a lush world for senses of all kinds....This is a wonderfully fast-paced read full of romance, love and fantasy that will continue to burn in the hearts of readers after the last page is turned."

—Fresh Fiction

"Joy Nash is definitely one to be watched. She has great world-building skills, and her own personal magic with the pen is guaranteed to make hers a very strong name on the market in the not too distant future."

—Love Romances

"Wonderful! [*Celtic Fire*] contains everything one could want in a romance and even a touch of the paranormal."

—A Romance Review

"Brimming with sexual tension and enhanced by a touch of humor, *Celtic Fire* is a good book."

—*Affaire de Coeur*

FAILURE IS NOT AN OPTION

Kalen was at her side, dressed in a plaid tartan kilt and nothing else. He stood motionless, arms crossed and legs spread wide. *Goddess.* Christine had seen him in her vision—she thought she'd known what to expect. But that tiny glimpse through space had in no way prepared her for the reality of an Immortal Warrior in the flesh.

This man—no, scratch that—this *demigod* was every inch a warrior, rough and deadly. Even standing motionless as he was, he possessed a taut, coiled energy that marked him ready for swift action. Christine had no trouble at all picturing him with a sword, or ax, or halberd, or rifle, or semi-automatic machine gun—*any* weapon, for that matter. Her determination to recruit him to the Coven of Light's cause grew. With this warrior on their side, the human world had a fighting chance for survival. She couldn't fail to bring him to the Coven's home base in Seattle. She *wouldn't* fail.

ACKNOWLEDGMENTS

There are so many people I'd like to thank for making this book possible. First and foremost, Jennifer Ashley, whose fertile imagination created the world of Immortals. I'm also deeply indebted to Alicia Condon for offering me the opportunity to be part of the series, Leah Hultenschmidt for working so hard to make the books great, and Robin Popp for being such a wonderful companion on the wild journey. As always, hugs to my friends in the Romance Writers of America, whose constant encouragement and example never fail to inspire! And last—but not at all least—a big kiss to my husband and kids for always, always understanding.

IMMORTALS: The Awakening

CHAPTER ONE

There was one big problem with practicing magic naked, Christine Lachlan thought sourly.

It made her horny.

And not just an "it would be nice to get some action tonight" kind of horny. No, skyclad-induced lust, at least for Christine, was more along the lines of "Goddess, I need it so bad I'm gonna go crazy if I don't get it right *now*." In other words, the kind of lust she hadn't felt in two years.

Since the last time she'd done *this*.

Starlight cast a sharp, sweet thrill through the high branches of the Roman pines, piercing the night shadows. Inside the circle of crushed sea salt Christine had sprinkled in the ancient dirt of Rome's Palatine Hill, she knelt with head bowed, palms upraised.

The night breeze raised goose bumps on her bare arms and sent an all-too-vulnerable shiver down her naked spine. Her baggy jeans and oversized sweater lay in a heap a few yards away, but they might as well have been two miles away on the floor of her cramped, rented room—on top of the rest of her dirty laundry—for all the good they did her.

Right now, Christine's entire world existed inside her circle, where she knelt before the Goddess with no covering on her body, no deception on her soul.

Pin-sharp pine needles and fragments of crushed marble bit into her knees. Her hair, freed from its braid, brushed the length of her spine. In the distance, the water-rush of traffic, punctuated by staccato splashes of horn, flowed along the Via dei Fori Imperiali, circled the Colosseum, and faded into the distance.

The prickle of restless desire tickled her thighs.

Goddess, how she loathed this.

She hated practicing magic while skyclad—the sensations it roused were too vivid, too *real. Too dangerous.* After Shaun's death, she'd sworn she'd never attempt it again, no matter what was at stake. Turned out she'd lied.

It hardly mattered that she didn't want to be here. That she'd rather be home, kneeling before a wobbly table spread with the beautiful square of indigo silk that had cost more than she'd earned in two weeks of hawking watercolors to stingy tourists. Within walls, protected by rune sigils, she could claim a small amount of safety. Here, amid Rome's most ancient ruins, naked under the sky, she was defenseless against her own magic.

The sensual lick of her power was as seductive as a man's tongue on her bare skin. Christine could do nothing but endure it. Her breasts grew heavy, the tips hardening. Her belly tightened with sweet fire.

If an Old One found her like this, she'd be in big trouble.

There was a very real possibility that could happen, despite the wards and the carefully drawn circle. An ancient vampire would have no trouble breaking her protections. Even the weaker undead—zombies, golems, and the like— were stronger and bolder than they'd been a few months ago. Not to mention more numerous. It seemed everywhere she looked, she saw another newly made vamp or recently resurrected zombie lurking in the shadows. And while she could defeat Young Ones singly, or even in pairs, she didn't want to think about what could happen if a horde attacked.

And then there were the demons.

She shut her eyes. Oh, Goddess. The demons. Tonight could end like the last time. . . .

She was insane to attempt this. No, not insane, just out of options. For Christine, skyclad magic was the strongest she could summon. Tonight, she needed every last drop of her power.

The thin breeze stirred again, rustling dry branches. Italy was caught in the grip of the worst drought in its long history; the profusion of spring flowers that normally blanketed the Eternal City this time of year had died on the vine. Even the ancient pines and hardy olive trees were withering. Perversely, in the north, England and Scotland were enduring record rainfall. Their farms were drowning.

It was yet another sign death magic had gained frightening dominance over life magic. Christine had been watching the grim, inexorable tide advance for almost a year now. Drought in some places, floods in others. Famine and anguish everywhere. Death magic creatures were multiplying with alarming alacrity. Violence and vandalism were rampant. Even museums had been attacked, priceless works of art destroyed.

There was no end in sight—the living earth was fading, shriveling before a fierce, unrelenting onslaught of soul-withering darkness. Life magic—the source of all goodness—was draining from the world like water from a cracked sieve. Witches of the Light, like Christine, were trying to stem the tide, but it was a frantic, futile endeavor. Too many holes to plug, too many fissures to seal.

But this morning, she'd been given an unexpected reason to hope. A sudden cloudburst had poured life-giving water onto the drought-stricken city. Christine had heard it pounding on the roof of her attic apartment. She'd run up the twisted stairs to the terrace with every container she owned to collect as much of the rainfall as she could. Every drop was precious, even more so on this particular morning. It was the first of May—a Beltane rain held deep power.

It couldn't be a coincidence rain had fallen on the very day Christine had needed her deepest magic. The Mother Goddess blessed her mission. She was sure of it.

She splayed fingers on hard ground. The crusted surface was still damp, but underneath, the ground was as hard and unyielding as concrete. Drained of life, as the world was draining of magic. What could one witch do to stop the horror? Very little. But she wasn't alone. Not any longer.

Christine had always been a solitary practitioner of the Craft, but in the past months panic had driven her to an Internet café to search online for other witches as disturbed as she by the rising evil. The worldwide Coven of Light had accepted Christine into their fold. She wasn't sure she felt comfortable being part of a group—artists tended to be very independent—but what choice did she have? She had magic, strong magic, though she'd avoided using the deeper aspects of it these past two years. No more. The stakes were too high. The Coven of Light needed her. So here she was, naked, preparing to call up forces she knew damn well she couldn't control.

She pressed her hands more firmly into the moist earth. She slowed her breathing; searched the deepest part of herself. Shifting, she nudged her knees apart. The magic of the fallen rainwater flowed into her fingertips, up her arms, and down her torso in a sparkling wave. The breeze rose again, seeking the exposed feminine flesh between her thighs. A mortifying heat rushed through her stomach . . . into her breasts . . . to her neck and face. Her nipples tingled and drew tight.

She inhaled sharply. Goddess, how she hated this.

The urge to bolt toward her clothes was strong. She wanted to cover herself with her hands, bend forward to cloak her body with her hair. Anything to stop this feeling of being so exposed and vulnerable.

She forced herself to remain motionless. She was beyond pride. There were no choices left: last night, disaster had struck the Coven. An American witch had very nearly been killed during a spell designed to bring help to the world. Christine had to achieve the failed spell's purpose now, on her own. Because the alternative—a world ruled by demons and death magic—was a reality far too horrible to contemplate.

With a shaking hand, she reached for the wine bottle near her right knee. Every drop of Beltane rainwater she'd collected was inside. Working the cork free, she poured the precious liquid into the shallow brass bowl that lay between her spread knees.

Power rippled over her skin. Her breasts responded with an ache. A tremor coursed through her belly, pooled low. Water splashed over her fingers; her mind sank into a light trance. The city, the night, the outside world—they all faded. There was only her sacred circle, her carnal hunger, the sense of drifting, helpless, on the edge of the world.

Unsteadily, she set down the bottle. Splayed her right hand over the scrying bowl. Slowly, reverently, she dipped her finger in the water and traced a single rune.

Kenaz. Revelation.

"Uni." She spoke the name of the Mother Goddess in her guise as Goddess Queen of the Etruscans. Uni had been the first deity recognized by humans in this ancient land. Her name meant "The One," and Christine knelt atop the buried ruins of a temple erected long ago in her honor.

"Mother," she prayed. "Show me."

Power rippled across the water. It slipped into her fingers and pulsed into her veins. The consuming surge of magic released a panicked flood of adrenaline. Christine knew only too well that power this elemental, once unleashed, could not be stopped. Like any living thing, once born, it sought its end.

Power rose, demanding Christine's complete honesty, her

complete faith. Her complete submission to the will of the Goddess. Christine had thought she was prepared. But it was hard, harder than she'd remembered. Because of the past. Because of Shaun. Because the magic required she do something she'd not dared in two long years.

Feel.

An urgent whisper rippled over her soul. A tremor claimed her body in an automatic response that was stunning in its blatant sexuality. A throb sprang up between her legs. An unwanted moan escaped her throat.

She needed to move. The compulsion shamed her—she didn't want to feel this way, needy and out of control. Didn't want to surrender to the urge to rock her hips in a pathetic parody of the sex act. But she couldn't stop herself from doing just that.

This was why she'd shunned her deepest magic since Shaun's death. She couldn't bear to remember what it had once been like, performing the sacred rituals with the only man she'd ever loved, before his greed and her own misplaced faith had destroyed him.

Another wave of sensation. More control lost. She closed her eyes. A mistake—with her sight gone, she felt the magic all the more acutely, in every part of her body. She forced her shoulders to relax, knowing she had no choice but to accept what she'd started. *Be careful what you ask for.* Her fingers sank deeper into the shallow water. She stroked a second rune on the surface of the brass bowl.

Naudhiz. Need.

She bowed her head. "Uni, show me. Show me your son."

Opening her eyes, she lifted her hands from the bowl. Abruptly, the water's surface went silver-still, like a mirror. She leaned forward, letting her focus go soft. A roar like ocean surf sounded in her ears. A wave of giddy delight washed over her; a surprised gasp spilled from her lips. Her body felt light, too light, as if it were floating into the sky, or falling from above. Her spirit-essence thinned, rippled almost painfully in its freedom.

The water glowed silver-bright, reflecting the spatter of stars overhead. Christine's spirit-essence drifted toward the light. Sank into it.

Mother, show me your son.

A shiver flashed over her exposed skin. Her breasts grew heavy, weighted with need. Desire spiked, drawing another gasp from her lips as power swirled through her circle. She shuddered. The magic was strong, too strong. This aching feeling of yearning, of wanting something so bitter and so sweet—it was more than she could bear. But to stop now would mean abandoning her last chance to find him.

Kalen, Immortal Warrior.

He was one of five Immortal protectors, created from the union of an aspect of the Mother Goddess and her human priests in the years when humans had been new to the earth. The forces of death magic had been incredibly powerful in those dark years. It had been Kalen and his brothers who had guarded the infant human race, defending them against evil. Trained by their goddess mothers, gifted with godlike strength, possessed of magical weapons and powers, including immortality itself, the Immortals had been invaluable allies to those early human settlements struggling to stay alive.

The five Immortal brothers—Kalen, Adrian, Darius, Hunter, and Tain—were an enigma. Created of life magic, they meted out death. Demons, zombies, golems, vampires, sorcerers—none could stand against them. Championed by the Immortals, those first human settlements thrived. Eventually, men and women learned to fight their own battles and the Immortals appeared less frequently. Finally, during the Middle Ages, they disappeared for good.

Now they were needed again. Desperately. Just a month ago, an American witch named Amber Silverthorne had been investigating the death of her sister, a member of the Coven of Light. Dark forces had been involved. While pursuing a lead, Amber had encountered Adrian, the oldest Immortal, and together, the pair had discovered the truth behind the recent surge of death magic. The rise in evil was the work of Tain, the youngest Immortal. Insane and emotionally enslaved by an ancient and powerful demon known to Adrian as Kehksut, Tain had vowed to drain every drop of life magic from the human world.

Using death magic doorways known as demon portals, Tain was able to move freely between human and demon realms, appearing instantly in any location he desired. His spies were legion and his power vast. Demons and the undead all over the world were eager to aid Tain's evil vision.

According to Adrian, only the other Immortals could stop their brother. And so last night, on the Eve of Beltane, the Coven of Light—witches on six continents—assembled in spirit to speak the words of the Calling, the ancient spell that summoned the Immortals to battle. But something went horribly wrong and the magic shattered, very nearly killing Amber. The missing Immortals had not appeared.

Christine had discovered that the Immortal Warrior Kalen was the son of the Mother Goddess in her guise as the Etruscan Goddess-Queen, Uni. As the only Coven witch dwelling in the Etruscans' ancient homeland, it was up to Christine to call on Uni for help. Surely the Goddess knew where her son was.

Her gaze lost in the silver-still surface of the rainwater, Christine willed her body to go soft. She allowed the sensuality that entwined so deeply with her magic to take control of her body. "Goddess," she whispered. "Great Mother . . . Uni, Queen of Etruria . . . Show me your son."

The throbbing between her legs intensified, quickly becoming unbearable. The exquisite knot of desire in her belly tightened. Her lungs grabbed for oxygen, taking too much. Her head grew light. It took all her effort to focus on the bowl. On the sacred water.

"Show me. I beg you."

A thought dropped into the still pool of Christine's mind. *He is here, daughter.*

The shimmering surface shifted. Shadows moved like clouds across its face. Silhouettes deepened, sharpened.

Images formed.

She leaned close, not daring to blink or hardly even to breathe. The fleeting impression of a cliff, steep and rugged, a broad, rocky island separated from a coastline by a narrow swath of angry gray sea.

Like a fairy-tale dream, a castle clung to island cliffs. Its somber gray walls and the intricate crenellations of its battlements traced a large square around a high central tower. There were several garden courtyards inside the castle, formed by the lines of lower buildings spanning the distance between the central tower and the perimeter walls. A gray shroud of rain cloaked the scene.

Her corporeal body seemed to dissolve as she slipped deeper into her trance. The castle drew closer; the walls melted away. A new scene formed in a cavernous room lit only by a large, leaping fire. Christine's eye was drawn to movement amidst a pile of furs and cushions spread before the generous hearth. A man and woman lay there, limbs entwined.

Clothing had been discarded in a heap nearby; she caught a glimpse of tartan plaid wool, the gloss of black leather. The lovers were nude, the man clearly dominant, the woman spread beneath him. He was as dark as she was fair—the man's tawny skin and dark hair contrasted sharply with the woman's pale complexion and red hair. Her vivid locks were cropped short and slicked with gel around her delicately pointed ears.

She wasn't human, Christine realized with a start. The

beautiful woman was Elven. Or Sidhe, as Christine's Scottish grandmother had called the race of sensual Celtic life magic creatures. Christine experienced a stab of something very like jealousy. Of course an Immortal would choose a magical lover. What human woman could satisfy a demigod?

She shifted her attention to Kalen. He looked like a human man, but—*more*, somehow, in a way that robbed Christine of breath. Normally she couldn't see auras—she sensed magic by touch—but in this vision, aided perhaps by Uni's grace, Kalen's magic was boldly apparent. Living energy flickered around him, blending with the firelight to dance on his flexing muscles. A blue tattoo, a pentacle inscribed in a circle, was etched high on the back of his right thigh. Each Immortal, she knew, had a similar tattoo somewhere on his body.

Kalen's head dipped to his lover's generous breasts. It was impossible not to feel a pang of inadequacy as the large globes filled his hands. A smile quirked his beautiful lips as he bent his head and sucked a pink, distended nipple into his mouth.

His lover's supple body arched upward, a deep purr of satisfaction vibrating in her throat. She flung her arms overhead, lips parted.

A sudden, sick twist wrenched Christine's stomach. Her chest contracted so tightly she could hardly gulp her next lungful of air. When she did manage to breathe, the rise of her chest was sharp and painful.

She wanted to be that woman.

Her trance slipped, cracked by her irrational anger. *Damn.* This lust was just an effect of the magic—she didn't truly want Kalen that way. All she wanted was to find him and explain the grave danger the world was in. Enlist his aid in the Coven's fight.

And if she didn't get hold of herself long enough to find a clue in her vision that would lead her to him, her quest would fail before it even started.

Drawing a deep, cleansing breath, she calmed her roiling emotions with a chant of the rune mysteries.

Uraz, Gebo, Isa.

Strength, Sacrifice, Challenge.

She could not fail in this.

Jera, Eihwaz, Teiwaz.

Hope, Faith, Honor.

She *would* find him.

Mannaz, Dagaz, Inguz.

Self, Clarity, Peace.

She would *not* let her irrational jealousy shatter her vision.

Thurisaz. Hagalaz.

Conflict. Destruction.

She couldn't lie—she wanted him for herself.

Her body was on fire for him, her vagina empty and aching. Her gaze caressed him, taking in his powerful torso, lean hips, and long limbs. She saw him with her artist's eye, as if she were preparing to capture him on canvas. His hair was dark and shining, his muscles rippling with strength, moving beneath smooth olive skin. Masculine grace, strength, sensuality—all had found a home in the body of this Immortal. But Kalen's most sensual feature was not his strength, nor his beauty.

It was his magic. Christine could feel it, see it. A pulsing, shimmering cocoon encircled Kalen and his lover, blazing hotter as their urgency grew. His knee nudged the Sidhe's pale, slender thighs. With a growl, she accommodated him with parted legs. Her hands clutched at shoulders, ran down his flanks in fevered urgency. Her fingers pressed into his buttocks. Their bodies weren't joined yet, but they soon would be.

The realization put a bitter, metallic taste in the back of Christine's throat.

"*Greas ort.*" The Sidhe's voice was low and inexplicably angry, as if the words had been torn from her unwillingly. "*Tromhad a-steach.*"

Christine's heart thudded. Kalen's lover was speaking Scots Gaelic. Christine had learned snatches of the language from her grandmother. *Hurry. Come inside.*

"*An-dràsta!*"

Now.

But Kalen didn't seem in a hurry to oblige. He lingered at his lover's full breasts, sucking and kneading while the Sidhe's expression darkened like thunder. She twisted her fingers in his hair and gave a savage jerk. She arched her hips, trying to draw him in. He shifted languidly, accommodating her only slightly as he continued to lavish attention on her breasts. But the foreplay couldn't last much longer. Soon enough he'd slide inside.

Lust and jealousy, twin edges of a merciless sword, knifed through Christine's chest. She felt as though someone had sliced her open and ripped out her heart. The savage pain brought a rushing sound to her ears. Her breath went; the ground under her knees seemed to dissolve. She scrabbled to brace herself with her hands, but her palms met . . . nothing. Pitching forward, she tumbled into a dark void.

And then, suddenly, she was *there*.

No longer a spectator. *She* was the woman stretched out on the furs before the fire. It was *her* body caged by hard, male limbs, *her* legs held open by powerful masculine thighs. Kalen's dark head was bent over her breast, his lips pulling rhythmically on her nipple.

Streaks of fire raced through her body like stars shooting through a night sky. Magic and lust—opening her, claiming her, rendering her helpless. Her fingers entwined the silken locks of his hair. Her hips arched. Tears sprang to her eyes— if he didn't enter her *now*, she was sure she would die.

Heat consumed her. She was wet and ready, dying for him, but still he tortured her, the rough hair on his legs scraping the inside of her thighs as he nudged her legs wider. She squirmed, panting, the musk and sweat of his body in her nostrils. She wanted to lick his skin, taste him, but she couldn't reach him with her tongue. So she shut her eyes and concentrated on his touch, squeezing every drop of bliss from the sensation of his damp, slick skin sliding over hers.

His lips left her breast, traveled in a slow, hot line up her body, to her neck, her jaw. His weight pressed down, his body covering hers, the broad, hot head of his erection prodding her slick, swollen folds. His power flared, enveloping her. Yearning burned a path into her soul. Her hips arched in supplication.

"Kalen . . ."

At the sound of his whispered name, his head lifted. Christine stared up at him, drinking in his features. His eyes were the deepest charcoal gray, his hair even a darker black. His forehead was high and proud, his cheeks sharp and angled. He possessed a bold, slashing nose and firm, mobile lips.

He was vital, supreme, *Immortal*. And Christine knew the deepest magic she possessed was nothing compared to the magic he *was*.

The corners of his beautiful mouth tugged downward as he stared at her. His body went still; his brows drew together. His eyes captured hers and did not let go.

A frisson of unease shot through her—like she'd been caught in a lie. He felt it; she could tell in the sudden sheen of moisture that appeared on his brow. His eyes glinted like chips of onyx, his breath came on a sharp inhale.

"What the—"

She gripped his shoulders.

"Kalen . . . please . . ." But she didn't quite know what it was she was asking.

Confusion played across his features. His body went rigid, as if he was struggling with some inner question. With a muttered curse, he seemed to resolve the dilemma. He lifted his hips and positioned himself for the joining thrust.

Christine hung, suspended in time, rigid with anticipation. One heartbeat passed . . . two . . . three . . .

Crack!

With a sound like a firecracker snap, the scene collapsed. Kalen, the hearth, the castle—it was all, abruptly, simply, *gone*. As if it had never existed.

And Christine was left kneeling under the night sky on the hard-packed dirt—naked, cold, alone, and wanting.

"By all the magic in Annwyn, Kalen, *get on with it!*"

Kalen came back to himself, a sound like a thunderclap ringing in his ears, his body taut, his cock poised at the entrance to Leanna's body.

Bloody hell. What in Hades had happened?

A moment ago, Leanna had been so frantic for him to enter her that she'd cried out in Gaelic, the hated language of her childhood. That always put her in a mood. He blinked down at the Sidhe's pale, frowning eyes. Perspiration plastered her hair to her forehead like wisps of crimson seaweed. Her black eyeliner had smeared horribly, painting dark half-moon circles above her cheekbones. Her normally pouting red lips were pressed into a thin, angry line.

And still, she managed to look alluring.

He closed his eyes and dragged in a breath, trying to recapture the sensations of a heartbeat earlier. For a single, breathless moment, he could have sworn another woman lay beneath him. A woman so unlike Leanna as to be laughable. A scrappy, sharp-angled female with small, pointed breasts and scrawny hips.

But her eyes . . . they had been startling. A wide, deep blue, so intense his breath stalled in his lungs. Her nose had been small, her cheeks flushed. Her hair . . . He frowned, trying to remember. Ah yes. Her hair had been pure black, a dark cloud sensuously framing her face. The locks had been thick, like heavy skeins of silk—and long, as a woman's hair should be. But there had been something else about it . . .

His frown deepened. *Blue.* That was it. A single long lock

of hair falling from the woman's left temple had been colored a brilliant indigo. He gave himself a mental shake. Why would he dream such a thing? Unnatural hair dye was yet another entry on Kalen's long list of twenty-first-century abominations. And it had to have been a dream. His home was far too heavily warded for the vision to have been magic.

Leanna shifted beneath him, her disapproval growing more apparent by the second. Her patience—what little she had of the commodity—was obviously almost depleted. He felt her hand reach between their bodies. Her fingers curled around his phallus. She tugged and teased like a clever milkmaid.

Tantalizing zings of electricity shot through his shaft. All thoughts of the dream woman fled.

"Now, Kalen. I want it *now*."

Her breathing grew ragged as she twisted beneath him, her fingernails digging into his flesh as she tried to jerk his hips forward. No doubt such maneuverings worked with her human lovers; with Kalen the effort was useless. Her physical strength didn't begin to equal his.

But she had other powers. Powers Kalen craved.

Her magic pulsed into his being, raw with emotion, ripe with promise. Insatiable in its demands and lush with the promise of paradise. It was part of Leanna's unique essence—a magic human men willingly died for. Could it show him the path to salvation? Kalen wasn't sure, but he hoped it could.

He hoped.

Leanna's fingers tugged on his shaft, guiding him to her slick woman's flesh. "*Now*, Kalen."

And still, he hesitated, a nagging sense of disquiet again buzzing in the back of his mind. Leanna made a warning sound deep in her throat. Mentally, Kalen swatted away his vague unrest and slipped easily into her body. It was an act he'd performed a thousand times in the decade they'd been lovers. Ten years—an instant in his overlong life. He'd had countless other women, both Sidhe and human. Even so, Leanna's magic was like nothing he'd ever felt.

He moved within her. A surge of imminent freedom overtook him, like that first glorious instant when an eagle takes flight. He drove hard; there was no need to hold back, as with a human lover. Sidhe were a hardy race, far more possessed of stamina and lust than their human cousins.

He bit back a groan as Leanna bucked beneath him, her hot sheath contracting around his rock-hard shaft. Her long nails scratched pain across his back, but he barely felt it. His pleasure, his being, his *life* was focused on a single, elusive spark— the magic Leanna alone could create. The magic that could open his soul, absolve his sins, make his life bearable again.

She twisted beneath him. "Turn over. I want to be on top."

With a single smooth roll, he accommodated her. Leanna had strong preferences when it came to sex—generally, it was easier to give her what she wanted than to force his own wishes on her. And in any case, Kalen enjoyed watching a woman ride him. He steadied her hips in his hands as she flung her head back, cupping her breasts.

A sudden mental image of the woman with the blue-streaked hair, performing the same act, flashed into his brain. Her hair had been very long—he was sure it would pool in a luxurious swirl on the tops of his thighs if she were atop him, arched in just that same way. He hardened even further as he pictured it.

Leanna purred, obviously taking full credit for his phallus's sudden increase in enthusiasm. Her writhings turned urgent, her lithe body moving in a creative combination of back-and-forth and circular motions. Her magic gathered, again crowding thoughts of the dream woman from Kalen's mind. Green sparks showered around him—he concentrated on one, brighter than the others, zinging just beyond his reach. He saw, as he always did, how he might capture it. Make it his own. Feed upon it with his soul.

This time he would not fail. This time, *now*, he would

claim the elusive prize for which Leanna's human lovers willingly died.

The spark flared, flashing bright and new as the first instant of creation. Leanna hummed, her body drawing power from the living core of the universe—the font from which all life and all life magic sprang. She took the seed, saw it blossom, shaped it into a soul's center flame—a hot, burning ball of creative power. And Kalen could only gaze at it in awe.

No wonder men—and some women—traded body and soul for this instant of blazing triumph. The moment of creation—who would not die for that?

His fingers dug into her flesh. He jerked her hips down, hard.

"Oh yes!" Her body jackknifed forward, her pelvis bucking against his palms.

Their combined lust exploded, its magic raining down on their joined bodies. *"Yes!"*

Kalen's climax broke, and with it, the full force of his own magic. With a roar, he threw himself into the sparkling green stars. Snatched them, one by one, letting them pass through his skin and into his body. At the same time, he felt Leanna busy at her own game—soaking up Kalen's Immortal life essence. He didn't care. She could take what she wanted, and welcome to it. It was only fair, after all.

The sparks coalesced, emerald light contracting inside him, brightness intensifying, filling every corner of his being. A rush of elation, of power, of triumph. Inspiration, in a blinding flash. With stunning clarity, he saw the path to the heart of the universe.

It was a woman—the woman from his dream. Her features were muted, rendered in charcoal on a sepia background. Every line, every shadow, every stroke and smudge of the pencil was revealed to him. Wide eyes, delicate cheekbones, subtly pointed chin. Heavy, dark hair falling over bare shoulders. He was glad there was no color in his vision—the blue streak of the woman's hair was barely noticeable.

She was magnificent, incredible. A goddess, a Madonna, equal to any painted by the masters. As mysterious as Leonardo's *Mona Lisa*, pure as Michelangelo's *Madonna*, alluring as Botticelli's *Venus*. But she was to be Kalen's own. *At last.*

Leanna abandoned his softening phallus. She wasn't one for afterplay; once she had what she wanted she was quick to withdraw. Kalen didn't care; in fact, he barely noticed. The vision of the dark-haired woman was already wavering, the soft charcoal lines blurring. As always, time was of the essence.

He shoved himself off the furs, strode to the easel he'd set up nearby. His hand shook a bit as he grasped the slender charcoal pencil. With a deep breath, he placed the tip against the virgin page.

The first strokes came easily, flowing with exquisite delight. Dimly, he was aware of Leanna padding to the cabinet where he kept his store of single-malt whiskey. The Italian marquetry door opened and closed; glass clinked against glass as she poured. Blocking the sounds, he bent his head to the easel, his hand moving across the paper with fevered urgency.

The dream woman was fading from his mind like scratches in the sand before the tide.

He was desperate to capture her features before she disappeared completely. The long, graceful line of her neck. The hollow at the base of her throat. The haze of lust in her eyes. He worked as the image faded from his memory. Finally, his hand slowed. The stump of charcoal fell from his fingers.

She was gone.

He exhaled a long breath. Suddenly, he became aware of Leanna, his muse, watching him. His gaze took in her naked hip, propped casually against his mahogany sideboard. Her palm cradling a glass—his best Macallan, he'd wager. He'd paid twenty thousand pounds sterling for a single bottle.

She could drain it, for all he cared. If only he could grasp the prize he craved.

For several seconds he stared at the Titian hanging above the sideboard, unwilling to shift his gaze the few inches to the left that would place his own finished drawing in his line of vision. Had he grasped Leanna's magic? Had he given birth to a work of true art? Had he at last reclaimed the spark that had been taken from his soul? He'd felt nothing but glorious inspiration as the lines flowed onto the paper. But Hades himself knew Kalen had felt that way many, many times before.

Leanna cleared her throat, but didn't speak. Even she wouldn't dare to intrude on this moment—she, better than anyone, knew what it meant to him. Steeling himself, he turned his gaze on his creation.

Disappointment burned a rancid hole in his gut.

To use the vernacular of this gods-forsaken century—his drawing bloody sucked.

CHAPTER TWO

Christine threaded the medieval warren of Roman streets in a daze, her body thrumming with unfulfilled arousal. Her senses were raw. Exposed. The cobblestones under her feet were uneven, the night breeze too cold, the odor wafting from a murky corner too pungent. The bluster of a group of human teenagers irritated her profoundly. Testosterone-fueled idiots, shouting into the night, daring vamps and demons to come and get them. It was lunacy. They should be on their knees praying no death creatures had them in sight. She watched them disappear down an alley known for its vampire clubs. They'd get high on sex and blood, and a couple of them would be dead—or worse, *undead*—come morning.

She halted, suddenly light-headed with the sexual feelings left over from her scrying spell. She steadied herself with a palm spread on a peeling stucco wall. She had to get hold of herself. Rome wasn't safe at night—and stupid teenagers were the least of it. Vampires, zombies, ghosts, and demons lurked in every shadow. Christine could fight, but she'd rather avoid it. Especially now that she had a better idea where Kalen might be. She couldn't risk getting herself killed before she found him.

Stay aware. Avoid confrontation. Get home in one piece. She couldn't afford to screw up. She had a job to do. A journey to make. Kalen, Immortal Warrior, was in Scotland. At least, she thought he was. She'd seen a rocky island, a gray sea, a stone castle. Rain. A tartan plaid. And his lover had spoken Gaelic.

At the thought of the red-haired Sidhe, Christine's stomach went sour. Angrily, she pushed her jealousy aside. She couldn't afford to have irrational feelings distract her from the task at hand. Find Kalen and tell him about Tain. Convince him to travel to Seattle, where Amber and Adrian were assembling an army of humans and magical creatures dedicated to the Light.

The most difficult step was surely the first one: finding Kalen. Once the Immortal knew of the grave threat to the human world, there was no doubt in Christine's mind he'd put aside any . . . *distractions* . . . and join the fight.

She pushed away from the supporting wall. Erotic need still pulsed between her thighs. She strived to ignore it. As if *that* were possible. Drawing a steadying breath, she chanted rune mysteries. *Jera, Uraz*. Hope, Strength. The throbbing faded.

She concentrated on a burgeoning plan of action. She'd be on the first morning train traveling north from Rome to Britain. She'd sketch a picture of the castle from her vision; once she reached Scotland, she'd contact a group of Coven of Light witches based in Inverness. They were witches of only average power, but surely one of them could point her toward the castle. If necessary, she could scry again, but she really hoped she wouldn't have to.

The strap of her backpack bit into her shoulder—her scrying bowl wasn't light. She adjusted the pack, her eyes scanning the street. It was late—past 2:00 a.m. Everything seemed quiet enough, but she didn't trust it to stay that way.

Shaking off the last remnants of her trance, she headed toward home.

Her path took her past the front door of deLinea. The elite art gallery fronted on a secluded piazza. She was surprised to see the building's second-story windows flooded with light— she'd forgotten a new show was launching tonight. A month ago, Jacques Artois had been a penniless sculptor waiting tables in a Paris café, his art unknown and unappreciated. By tomorrow he'd be the hottest of commodities. All because deLinea's elusive, idiosyncratic owner—a billionaire investor known simply as *"il direttore"*—had plucked the struggling artist from obscurity and set him on modern art's highest stage. Artois would be a millionaire by morning.

The *eleganti* who could afford to make Artois's fortune were definitely in attendance tonight. Ferarris and Lamborghinis flocked like brilliant swans around the piazza's fountain. The gallery's arched entrance was flanked by two men in black, unsubtly armed with automatic weapons. No doubt they had a formidable arsenal of magical defenses, too. You couldn't be too careful these days.

Safe from the evils of the night, the gallery's rich patrons partied. A buzz of animated conversation wafted through the open upper-story windows. Laughter, excitement, exhilaration. And, of course, the music deLinea had made famous . . .

Pulsing, haunting—a mixture of instrumental, techno and natural tones. Christine sighed as the melody washed over her. It was the most magical sound on the planet . . . the lilting harmony of the elusive Celtic musician Manannán.

A slender woman and her tuxedoed escort glided in front of a window, then disappeared just as quickly beyond a wisp of lace curtain. Christine closed her eyes and allowed herself a brief fantasy. Dressed in indigo silk, she stood in the center of the party, the delicate stem of a champagne glass twirling lightly in her fingers. Her own watercolors graced the elegant easels . . .

She exhaled. Nice try, but she couldn't make the image

stick. It was too far from reality. One glance at her wrinkled jeans and hiking boots was enough to clue her in. Who was she kidding? She was a nobody, an American vagabond who hawked watercolors on the sidewalk and could barely afford a new paintbrush. DeLinea's sleek mahogany doors were closed to her. She should know—she'd tried often enough to get through them. The gallery manager had firmly shut the door in her face each time. *No, il direttore* was not in Rome. He was at his Paris, Prague, or London gallery. *Si, il direttore* handpicked each new artist. *No, il direttore's* schedule did not permit a meeting.

Christine's obsession with the gallery had become a bitter lesson in futility. There'd been a time when she'd been sure her magic and talent would take her to the top of the European art world. All she had to do was work hard and make the necessary sacrifices. But that'd been when she and Shaun had just gotten together and his music career was soaring. Life had been bright; anything had seemed possible. Now . . . what did dreams matter? If the death creatures had their way, art and music would die along with the rest of the good in the world.

She turned and trudged a tired path home, keeping a sharp eye out for foes. She breathed a prayer of relief when she arrived at the peeling door of her apartment house. She even smiled when Nero and Caligula, two strays who had taken to showing up on her doorstep for regular handouts, leaped out of the shadows, purring and weaving between her legs. She reached down and scratched behind Nero's ears. Local legend claimed the souls of the ancient Roman emperors were reborn in the stray cats of Rome. The notion appealed to her.

"Begging for breakfast so early?" she asked the former tyrants. "*Andiamo, ragazzi.* I guess I have enough for one last meal. But after tomorrow, you're on your own again." She scraped the key in the lock and pushed open the door.

"I'll be gone."

* * *

"Well." Leanna leaned over Kalen's shoulder, raking a long, red nail down his arm. "It's not . . . *bad*."

Kalen sent her a sardonic glance. "Good enough to sell on the street, perhaps." Crumpling the offending sketch in his fist, he threw it into the fire. "But not what it should be. Your magic must be off."

Her husky laugh conveyed her amusement. "There's nothing wrong with my magic." Straightening, she swirled her whiskey in its beveled glass. "My human lovers can't thank me enough for my inspiration. Why, just last night, a certain young sculptor in Inverness showed his appreciation by—"

"Spare me," Kalen muttered, making for the sideboard. He poured himself three fingers of single malt—she *had* been into his Macallan—and drained it in one draught. The obscenely expensive liquid blazed a path down his throat to his stomach, spreading like fire in his veins. He glanced at the bottle. Definitely worth the investment.

Leanna's glass clinked on the sideboard. Kalen was aware of a slight tension in his shoulders as she came up behind him. The hard points of her nipples rubbed against his bare back.

"Let's try again," she whispered.

"No." One failure per evening was more than enough.

Leanna chuckled, fitting the length of her body against his spine and buttocks. He didn't move, not even when her hands skimmed his hips. She reached for his phallus and discovered it soft. He really wasn't interested.

She jerked away. "Most men would jump at the chance to have me again."

"I'm not most men."

"You're not most artists, either." When he made no reply to that, she went on. "In my experience, the greater a man's talent, the more he wants to fuck. Take Mozart, for example. Now, he was a prize. At sixteen he could do the deed for hours, dash off a symphony or two, and come right back for more."

Her fingertips grazed Kalen's buttock, a barely-there whisper of magical sensation. "Caravaggio? The man liked to screw as much as he liked to fight . . . and paint." Her hand slipped around to his stomach in a slide of tingling stars.

"Leanna . . ." he warned.

Her tone turned dreamy with reminiscence. "Byron? Now, there was a man who was always ready. Wrote *Don Juan* after a particularly brilliant shagging. And the Americans . . . all that energy! James Dean was down and dirty, Kurt Cobain would do it *anywhere*, but that Jim Morrison . . ." She sighed. "That last time in Paris was *incroyable*."

Her fingers danced between his legs. Kalen sucked in a breath as his shaft, against his wishes, started to lengthen.

Leanna chuckled. "Even that Joplin bitch showed me a good time back in '69, after her concert at the Albert Hall. . . ."

Kalen snared her wrist. "I told you, Leanna. No."

Leanna huffed her annoyance. "Showing your age, Kalen?"

He turned, putting some distance between them as he did so. He refilled his glass. "I've had enough for tonight."

She watched his eyes. "If that were true, you'd have drawn something *magnificent*. Not that piddling hack of a sketch."

His annoyance must have shown, because she scowled and continued her harangue. "Don't heap your failures at my door, Kalen. I'm *leannan-sidhe*. If my muse's magic hasn't taken with you, it's not my fault. My human lovers get what they want . . . and they give *everything* in return. Heart and soul . . ."

"And life."

"Yes." She crossed her arms. "And life. They give their lives for the sake of their art. What do you give?"

"I can hardly give you my life."

She bit her lip. "No, but . . ."

"I give you my Immortal essence. It feeds your own power. That should be enough."

"It's not, apparently, or you would have gotten what you want by now." She frowned. "You're a special case, of course. I've never acted the muse to an Immortal before. If it's any consolation, I don't like this failure any more than you do."

He took a sip of his whiskey, wishing she would just *go*.

"You know," she said casually, "I've been giving this some thought."

"Oh?"

"And I think I've come up with a solution."

Something in her tone made him glance up sharply. "How so?"

She touched him again, stroking his hip, up and down, smiling a little when his cock jerked. "You could give me a child," she murmured.

"You've got to be joking." Leanna wasn't anyone's idea of the motherly type.

She scowled. "I'm serious. I want a child, Kalen. You could give me an Immortal one."

"I could impregnate you, yes." Immortals controlled their reproductive capacities—if he wanted to create a child, he could do so by simply willing a woman to conceive as he made love to her. But in nearly three millennia, he'd never seriously considered it.

"There's no guarantee the child would be Immortal," he told her. "There's a small chance it would have a Sidhe soul."

"No. I've been studying conception spells. I've discovered an obscure one that ensures the babe will attract the most powerful aspects of its parents. If I cast it within one of the ancient circles, the magic of the stones will enhance its power. Our child's immortality will be certain."

Kalen raised his brows. "And where did you find this spell?"

Leanna waved a dismissive hand. "What does it matter? The point is, it will work. It's a small request, Kalen, and nothing at all to you. You wouldn't have to even see the child after it's born."

A baby. To his surprise, the notion held a deep, visceral appeal. A child of his own flesh, one he would never have to bury.

"And giving me a child would give *you* what you want," Leanna continued. "Your masterpiece."

He met her gaze. "How could getting you with child do that?"

Instead of answering, she took two languid steps and retrieved her glass from the sideboard. She brought it to her lips and sipped, then looked up with a frown. "You know, Kalen, it's damned cold in here. And bloody dark besides. When are you going to bring some proper heat and electricity into this sodding castle?"

Kalen plucked the glass from her hand and put it aside. "No evasions, Leanna. Answer me."

She extended her arm along the edge of the sideboard. One sensual leg slid forward. His gaze dropped before he could stop it; when he raised his eyes, her smile was smug.

"Art requires surrender," she said. "An artist must give up control of his soul—a true master is driven to sacrifice himself for his art. But you, my love, have never completely surrendered. Oh, I understand you *can't*—your Immortal soul won't allow itself to be sacrificed. But if you were to give a part of your soul to form a new life . . ." Her lashes swept downward. "The spark of that creation would spill into your art. I'm sure of it."

He stared. He felt the truth of her words, but didn't trust her sincerity. Leanna was exceedingly vain about her flat stomach and small waist. He found it extremely hard to believe she'd ruin her figure to bear a child. "What's in it for you?"

"Kalen. You're cruel. Why does any woman want a child?"

"Come now, Leanna. You're not precisely 'any woman.'"

She laughed. "Thank the combined population of Annwyn, Valhalla, and Olympus for *that*."

"That's not an answer. Why?" He held up his hand as her mouth opened. "The truth, Leanna. Nothing else."

She shut her mouth and looked away. When she spoke, her habitual bravado was absent. "I want to give it to Niniane."

At last he began to understand. "You seek your mother's approval."

Leanna scowled. "No. Not her approval. Her acknowledgment. It's my due. You know how difficult it is for Sidhe women to conceive, how fragile our children are. Niniane will be overjoyed with an Immortal grandchild. She'll welcome it in Annwyn."

"And welcome you as well?"

Leanna's gray eyes glinted like chips of pale ice. "I wouldn't live in the same realm with that bitch. No, I only want her to admit to the Sidhe Council that I'm her daughter. I don't have to tell you what that would do for my status."

He nodded. Sidhe society was extremely clannish and strictly regulated by rank. Despite Leanna's powerful magic and Sidhe soul, her position was lowly. Her father had been human, a dirt-poor eighteenth-century Highlander whom Niniane, Queen of the Sidhe, had found amusing. She'd never expected his seed to take. As soon as the babe was born, Niniane had dumped it on its human relatives and fled.

Unacknowledged, Leanna was able to associate mainly with other half-breed and outcast Sidhe. If Niniane were to claim her as her daughter, her position would rise dramatically.

"An Immortal baby would benefit both of us," she said.

He regarded her seriously. He didn't love Leanna, and she

didn't love him. But he did feel a reluctant sort of protectiveness toward her—he couldn't help it. His essence was that of a guardian, after all. And an Immortal child, even one with Leanna as its mother, would be a treasure. He wouldn't leave the babe to Niniane, that was certain. He and Niniane were friends of a sort—he'd once done the Sidhe Queen a great favor. She wouldn't object to Kalen raising her grandchild.

"I'll give you a baby," he said slowly, "under one condition."

"What is it?"

"You'll have no lovers, human or otherwise, while you carry my child."

"Except you, of course," she said coyly.

"Of course."

"Oh, Kalen, thank you!" In a rare display of exuberance, Leanna flung her arms around his neck and kissed him on the mouth. Her eyes flashed with excitement. "You'll attend tonight's tour to the stones. We'll make love in the circle afterward."

Kalen disentangled himself from her embrace. "No. Absolutely not. You know how I feel about your tours, Leanna. I won't be part of one."

"But, Kalen, you have to! The sex energy unleashed during the tour ramps up the power of the circle. We'll need every bit of that magic to be sure of the outcome."

It was a compelling argument, but there were lines Kalen just would not cross. Engaging in public sex was one of them.

"I'll beget our child in private or not at all."

Leanna pouted. For a moment he thought she would argue, but then she shrugged. "All I ask is that you attend the tour as a spectator. After everyone's gone, we'll make love inside the circle. Alone."

He hesitated. Attending one of Leanna's Sidhe Sex Magic tours was beneath his dignity. But he supposed he could tolerate it for one night. It was, after all, for a good cause.

"All right," he said. "I'll be there."

* * *

Travel was a freaking bitch these days.

Christine's train ground to a stop somewhere between Frankfurt and Paris. Trouble on the line. Again. *Damn.* She'd just finished her last bag of potato chips.

She was sick of this. Two nights ago, a crude spell had exploded on the tracks near Verona. The next day, a pack of rabid werewolves attacked her train in the Austrian Alps near Innsbruck. Later that same evening, a power failure left Christine stranded in Munich. And now . . . she sighed. She didn't want to know. She just hoped the conductor took care of it, and soon. She could have walked to Scotland more quickly.

An hour later, a jerk of the train on the tracks indicated the problem had been dealt with. Twenty hours later, after a canceled train in Paris and a dark ride through the Channel Tunnel that left Christine feeling faintly ill, she arrived at London's King's Cross Station. Where *finally*, she encountered something good.

It was raining.

Pouring, actually. Hard. She sprinted down the concourse, all the frustrations of the last two days forgotten. Bursting out the doors leading to the street, she came to a halt and let the water soak her. It'd been *months* since she'd been in a deluge like this.

A thousand splashes struck her body. Big, powerful drops pounded the street, forming a river along the curb. The sky was nearly black with fury.

And Christine loved it.

Rain pelted her wholly inadequate sweater, drenched her jeans, poured into her boots. She sighed and opened her arms wide, trying to capture as much of the storm as possible. What did she care if passersby shot her odd glances from under their umbrellas? They'd been dealing with too much rain for months, while she'd been languishing under sunny skies in drought-stricken Italy. To the Brits, the rain was a curse. To her, it was a miracle.

She lifted her face to the sky. Beautiful raindrops splashed her forehead and cheeks, tickled her chin, dripped past the neckline of her sweater. And all she could do was laugh.

Most witches had an affinity for one of the four elements: fire, air, earth, or water. Water was Christine's element. Water magic was life magic, flowing around her, inside her, through her. Even surrounded by the drab gray of a suffering city, despite the anxiety and distrust emanating from every human Christine had encountered on her trip, a sense of rightness filled her now. As long as there was life, there was magic. And hope.

A homeless man huddled under the station's overhang didn't share her joy. Muttering something about sodding idiots and bloody loons, he retreated into his cardboard shelter. The station door swung open, discharging a handful of surly passengers. They scattered into the storm, darting in various directions. Christine sighed. Eventually, she'd have to inquire about a train to Glasgow or Edinburgh, but not just yet. Turning into the wind, she shut her eyes and reveled in the sensation of raindrops pelting her face.

A scant moment later, the rain on her face stopped. Someone—or something—had moved directly in front of her, blocking it.

Frowning, she opened her eyes.

And lifted her brows. A teenage boy stood in front of her, the beginnings of a smile tugging at the corners of his mouth. He couldn't have been more than sixteen, seventeen tops. Like Christine, he didn't have a raincoat. The collar of his black leather jacket was turned up—not that it was doing him much good. He was as soaked as she was. What was curious was that, like her, he didn't seem to mind.

He was tall and wiry, with a thick mane of blond hair and

a scalloped blue tattoo on his left cheek. His sea-green eyes held a bemused expression. Three tiny silver rings dangled from his left earlobe. A backpack was slung over one shoulder, a guitar case over the other. White earbud wires snaked down his neck and into the collar of his jacket.

He was just too cute.

He smiled and spoke. "Like a bit of water, do you?"

Christine blinked. The kid had a Scottish accent—she hadn't heard vowels so rounded since her grandmother's death. His question was close to a shout. She wasn't sure if it was because of the rain or his earbuds.

"Yes," she said with a smile as they stood there with the rain pouring over them. "It's wonderful."

He frowned. "What's that, love? Speak up."

Chuckling, Christine pointed a finger at her ear. The kid looked at her blankly for a moment, then, with a sheepish grin, tugged out his earbuds. They dangled over his collar, the music pulsing from them at an incredible decibel level. With a jolt of pleasure, Christine realized he was listening to her favorite musician.

"You like Manannán?" she asked him.

His green eyes sharpened. "Do you?"

"I'm his biggest fan!"

"He's an all-right bloke, I reckon."

"A lot more than all right, I'd say. The man's a genius."

The kid snorted. "Not sure I'd go that far, love." His gaze ran over her. "So. You enjoy rain?"

She laughed. "Yes, and so do you."

He answered with an engaging grin. "Aye, I suppose I don't mind it." He paused. "I'm Mac, by the way."

"Christine."

For a brief second, some instinctive understanding seemed to pass between them. A thoughtful look flashed through his eyes; it was gone so quickly she thought she must have imagined it. He offered a hand. Without pausing to think, she clasped it. She didn't mean to do what she did next—she rarely used her magic in such a forward way. But there was something about this kid . . .

She cast out her senses, her brows drawing together as she sent a question through their joined hands. In return . . . *nothing*. She let out a breath, disappointed. She didn't know why—maybe it was his choice of music, maybe his incredible green eyes—but she thought he might be a water witch, like her. But she'd felt nothing. Not only no water magic, but no magic of any kind.

She took back her hand. The kid was obviously just a mundane teenager, doing his best to ruin his hearing before he was old enough to drink.

"Where d'you come from, love?" he asked, shoving a hank of wet hair from his eyes.

A sudden shift in the wind drove the rain into her face. Reluctantly, she looked back at the station door. "If we're going to chat, maybe we should go inside."

He shrugged. "It's just water." He gave her a probing glance. "American?"

"Yes."

"On holiday, are you?"

"Not exactly."

"Business?"

"You might say that."

"I'm in London on a bit of business myself." For a brief moment, a shadow dimmed his eyes.

She wondered what kind of business a teenager could have. Surely not drugs—Mac didn't look the type. But then again, you never knew.

"It's almost noon," he observed. "I won't be in town long, but a bloke's got to eat." He flashed an engaging smile. "Buy you a bit of lunch?"

Christine smiled. It was like being propositioned by a little brother. "Don't tell me you have a thing for older women," she teased.

For some reason, her comment amused him. His green

eyes danced. "Older women? No, can't say as I've been with one of those."

"Well, I'm afraid I can't be your first. I'm not sticking around. I'm headed to Scotland."

"On business." He sounded dubious.

"Yes, I . . . you're Scottish, aren't you?"

He shrugged. "Came into the world there, anyway."

"Then maybe you can help me. Here, let me show you something." She retreated to the overhang; he followed readily. Unshouldering her backpack, she reached inside for her sketchbook. She flipped it open to one of the many drawings she'd done on her painfully long train ride.

"I'm looking for a certain castle. I'm pretty sure it's in Scotland, but I don't know exactly where. Maybe you've seen it?"

He glanced down at the sketch, then went still. He glanced back up at her, a new shrewdness in his eyes. "You're looking for *this* castle?"

"Yes. Do you know it?"

"Aye."

She felt a surge of elation. "Where is it?"

He frowned slightly. "Near Nairn."

"That's pretty far north, isn't it?"

"About as far north as you can get, apart from Wick and Orkney."

"How do I get there? By train, I mean."

He was looking at her as if she were a puzzle he couldn't quite figure out. "London to Edinburgh to Perth. Then on to Inverness. Nairn's a bit east from there, and the castle's on an island off the coast a little farther on. But I have to warn you, no one goes out there. If you think you can just—"

A cell phone chime interrupted, a few bars of Manannán's "Midsummer Bells" serving as the ring tone. Mac unclipped his mobile from his belt, checked the caller ID, and scowled. "She can bloody well call back later," he muttered, shoving the phone back on its clip without answering.

Girlfriend? Christine smothered a grin. Any significant other of Mac's probably had good reason to worry about him—he was an incorrigible flirt. She slid her sketchbook back into her pack. "Thanks," she said, hoisting it onto her shoulder. "You've been a big help. You've probably saved me days of searching."

He eyed her. "If you don't mind my asking, love, what's a pretty Yank like you want with a gods-forsaken gloomy castle like that?"

"I'm . . ." She caught herself just in time. Not such a great idea to broadcast her mission to a stranger, even one as cute and harmless as Mac. Tain and Kehksut could have spies anywhere. "I . . . I saw it in a book."

His brows rose. "A book."

"And I . . . I'm just . . . curious about it, I guess."

"Curiosity." He paused. "A dangerous notion, that."

She made a noncommittal sound and hiked her backpack onto her shoulder. Now that she had a firm destination in mind, she wanted to get going. But Mac shifted his position slightly, taking up the space between Christine and the train station door.

She cleared her throat. "I've got to get going. Nice meeting you."

"Until the next time, love." With a nod, he started toward the street. As he sauntered past, he skimmed a finger along her forearm.

His touch shot through her like a raging river over a dam. Magic—*water* magic—its force so intense it nearly knocked her legs out from under her. She staggered against the station door, grasping the handle to keep from falling.

Mac was already halfway across the street. Glancing back at her over his shoulder, he gave a parting wave before continuing to the other side.

Holy Goddess. What in the universe was *that?* She'd never felt anything like it. Magic, certainly—but power *way* out of her league. When just a few minutes before, she hadn't felt anything. Mac had blocked her magical probe so subtly and completely she hadn't even been aware he'd done it. Could he be a demon? No, no way. Demons had no water in their bodies, so they didn't have water magic. But he might be spying for a demon. Or for Tain.

She glanced back to the street. He was gone.

"Not wise, birdie," a voice rasped.

She spun around. The homeless man she'd seen earlier had emerged from his cardboard home and was standing so close she could see the dirt clogging the monstrous pores in his nose. He opened his mouth, displaying three rotted teeth. Christine gagged on a fetid mixture of onions, grease, and alcohol.

She backed away. "I . . . I'm sorry. I didn't hear you—"

"No, not wise at all. He looks harmless, that one, but I tell you, he's not."

"Do you know who . . . *what* he is?"

Bloodshot eyes darted toward to street and back. "Oh no, you won't get me to say more," the man muttered. "I'm no bloody fool."

CHAPTER THREE

There were wrinkles at the corners of her eyes. Humans called them laugh lines. Well, Leanna wasn't laughing. She stared at the creases, harshly illuminated in the dressing room mirror of her suite at Inverness's Palace Hotel. A shudder vibrated down her spine. *Wrinkles.* Horrid.

The bags under her eyes, slight as they were, were no better. Sharp, curved lines bracketed her mouth, and there was a soft look to her chin that hadn't been there a few years ago. And her neck . . . She tilted her head back.

Sagging. Definitely sagging.

Damn it all to Uffern, she looked like she was pushing thirty. A sharp, angry breath expelled from her lungs. This was Niniane's fault. If Leanna had been raised in the Celtic Otherworld like any full-blooded Sidhe child, she would have absorbed a good measure of Annwyn's magic. Things wouldn't be so dire. As it was, the Queen of the Sidhe hadn't wanted her king to find out she'd been slumming in the human world. It must have been a colossal shock when a brawny Highlander's seed took root in Niniane's womb. She couldn't get rid of the baby fast enough. Leanna had grown up in a miserable hovel with a drunken father, a bitter step-mother, and fifteen starving half siblings.

Her childhood had been a blur of hunger, backbreaking labor, harsh winters, and terror at the hands of English soldiers. It was a wonder she'd survived until her fifteenth year, when, suddenly, her woman's blood had flowed, her rounded ears had sprouted points, and her magic had blossomed. That was when she'd realized what she was. A *leannan-sidhe*. A love muse.

Her magic had been her ticket to freedom; she wasted no time in gaining a human lover who'd taken her to France. When he wore out, there'd been another lover. And another. Artists all. Each had drawn inspiration from her, creating masterpieces while she fed on their life energy. Soon exhausted, each had succumbed to an early grave, while her own life span had lengthened.

But it wouldn't last forever. The proof of her mortality confronted her daily in the mirror.

Faigh muin. As always when her emotions overwhelmed her, she reverted to her childhood tongue. The language she'd tried so hard to forget. But it was a part of her, too deeply ingrained to ever be rid of. Like her human blood.

She gripped the edge of her dressing table. It took a full minute for her emotions to settle enough to allow her to raise her glamour. And even longer before her anxiety faded.

Her magic-enhanced image was lovely, of course. She looked no older than a human woman of nineteen. Which was as it should be. The Sidhe race was outstandingly long-lived. At a mere two hundred and sixty-two years old, a full-blooded Sidhe female was little more than an adolescent.

She pushed away from the mirror. It could be worse. Ten years ago, when she'd felt her magic waning, she'd returned to the Highlands to be closer to the Gates of Annwyn, the source of all Sidhe power. She'd discovered Kalen then. If she hadn't, she might look . . . she shuddered . . . *forty*.

Bathing her soul in his Immortal essence had held back the decay.

Now Kalen would help her another way. He'd give her a child. A child with an Immortal soul, because a Sidhe child would be useless.

She gave a tight smile. An Immortal child would secure her future. All she had to do was find the courage to summon magic powerful enough to make it so. Dark magic. Blood magic.

Murmuring a lock-release charm, she slid open her vanity's center drawer. An iron-bladed knife lay amid a jumble of cosmetics. A crystal bottle lay in a velvet case beside it.

She eased the cork stopper from the bottle's neck. The bottle was already three-quarters full. Setting it upright on the table, she picked up the knife. The iron irritated her skin; Sidhe abhorred the metal. She tested the edge.

Sharp. But of course it was. She'd honed it herself.

Nausea burned in her stomach. She hated bloodletting, especially when her own blood was involved. But it was necessary. Ruthlessly, she pressed the tip of the knife against the center of her palm. Delicate skin broke; blood welled. She pressed her palm over the mouth of the bottle. The precious drops fell, forming a thick pool inside crystal. When it was done, her head was spinning, both from the sight of her blood and the anticipation of what she would do with it.

The exhilaration she felt while contemplating her goal was like a chemical-induced high. Like the rush humans got in the vamp clubs, or the bliss Leanna's human lovers found in the hours before their deaths. The irony of her plan wasn't lost on her. Full-blooded Sidhe were pure life magic creatures—they couldn't perform death magic. It was Leanna's human blood that enabled her to draw up darkness. Now that human blood would ensure that she gained her rightful place among her mother's people.

Light-headed, she pressed a ball of cotton against her wound. The bottle was full. It was time.

She tipped the vial. Blood dripped on the marble tile, crimson on white. Tainted blood. Blood not worthy. Ruby light flashed; the death rune sprang into being. She spoke a Word, and the image of a snake appeared to weave through the sharp angles of the sigil. It bent back on itself. When mouth reached tail, the snake's jaw unhinged to devour its own flesh.

Ouroborous. Life and death and life again. To the ancients, it had symbolized regeneration and rebirth. The essence of living magic. Life without end. A symbol of immortality.

But everything good possessed a shadow side; each life magic sign and rune had a counterpart in the realm of death. With a flick of her wrist Leanna invoked the dark essence of the Ouroborous.

Her spilled blood responded immediately. The snake rose, twisting and writhing. The unending circle turned back upon itself. Decay rose like a delicate bouquet.

The symbol of unending life had become the sign of unending death.

She gazed on the dark beauty of what she'd wrought. She felt alive. Invincible. Strong enough to do whatever was necessary to gain the prize she craved.

"By the power of my blood, I summon you."

She ended with the demon's name—not its true appellation, for no demon allowed that to be known. Among humans, a demon could be known by several names—the more ancient the demon, the more numerous those names were. The entity Leanna sought had many names. The one she spoke now was a name given in terror by humans who were long dead. Humans who had once called themselves the Etruscans.

The demon would hear it. If the entity was intrigued, it would answer.

"Culsu. Come to me," she whispered.

For long moments there was only silence. Leanna spoke again. "I call you to this place, this time. Show yourself."

It began with a hiss. A rip in the fabric of the world sprang from the death rune. Black oily smoke seeped from the void, accompanied by the odor of brimstone and sulfur.

It coalesced slowly, gathering strength, drinking power from the blood Leanna had spilled. The entity took the form of a woman: tall, regal, garbed in clinging black. Glossy black hair writhed about her perfect face. Black, fathomless eyes regarded Leanna unblinkingly.

The entity surveyed her surroundings, gaze flicking disdainfully over the jumble of cosmetics on the table. Her attention turned at last to Leanna.

The demon inclined her head. "I am here."

Her tone was imperious. No subservience infected her demeanor, no deference sounded in its voice. Yet Leanna knew that in responding to her call, Culsu consented to do Leanna's bidding. *If* Leanna agreed to the price the demon set.

"Why have you summoned me, half-breed?"

Leanna swallowed the surge of anger the offensive label provoked. "There is a man . . ."

The demon threw back her head and laughed. "Of course. Man is the root of all woman's problems. Human?"

"Not precisely."

The entity's expression sharpened. "Go on. What is this man if not *precisely* human?"

Leanna drew a breath. "Immortal."

"One of the Five?"

"Yes."

The demon's eyes glowed red. "Which?"

"You know him," Leanna said softly. "You've battled him before. That's why I've called you, and not another."

"*Kalen.*"

"Yes."

There was a moment of silence. When the demon spoke at last, her question had the tone of a threat. "What do you want of me?"

"Kalen has agreed to give me his child. I want you to ensure that the child has an immortal soul. And show me how to take that soul for myself. Afterward, Kalen is yours."

"And in return for this service? What will you give of yourself?"

"*Anything*," Leanna whispered.

The demon's gaze raked over Leanna's body. "Disrobe, so I may see if you are worth my trouble."

A tingling sensation sprang up between Leanna's thighs. She'd known what the demon would ask . . . and she was prepared to give it. She wore nothing but a thin white silk robe. With a shrug, she let it slip from her shoulders and puddle at her feet, veiling the splatters of blood on the floor.

Culsu's red gaze traveled a hungry path over Leanna's body. Her lips curved. "Your form pleases me, half-breed. And your magic is strong. It will be done as you wish. Set the death rune before the joining and I will be there."

Smoke swirled around her feet. The portal to hell glowed red. When the demon stepped through it, it closed with a wrenching squeal.

Leanna stared at the place where the portal had been, heart pounding. She'd done it! She'd summoned an Old One. Kalen's ancient enemy. Gained the demon's promise.

Surging triumph brought an exultant laugh to her lips. She would be immortal. Soon. Very soon.

With a glance at the clock on the vanity, she stowed the bottle and blade in the drawer. It was past three o'clock. She'd told Galen Munro to present himself at her hotel suite at noon. She had no doubt he was waiting in the hallway, too scared to leave even to take a piss. The death metal guitarist was on the verge of his first recording contract and was desperate for inspiration. Filled with dark energy from her interview with Culsu, Leanna was looking forward to giving it to him.

Luckily, she was already naked. It was tedious, sometimes, stripping off her clothing. Turning, she padded through the bedroom and sitting room and into the small foyer. She opened the door. Munro leaped to his feet, his face flushing scarlet.

"I . . . I . . ."

She took in his ripped leather pants and vest with one glance. "Strip," she told him, already turning away. "And go to the bedroom."

He followed her like a dog, ripping off his shirt and hopping on one leg, then the other, as he tore off his pants. He stumbled into the bedroom, white, hairy, and naked.

"Mistress," he choked. "What is your pleasure?"

His face paled as Leanna opened a tall polished cabinet and surveyed the implements inside. She ran her fingers over the handle of her favorite whip.

"My pleasure?" Her tongue swiped her upper lip. "Why, bring me your handcuffs and I'll show you."

As exhausted as Christine was when she boarded the train to Inverness, she found it impossible to sleep. Transferring in Edinburgh without a hitch, she chose an empty compartment at the farthest end of the train. She sank onto the ratty upholstery, her backpack wedged between her knees, her nerves humming with fatigue. But even after the train groaned out of the station, she still couldn't close her eyes.

Her encounter at King's Cross Station had set her on edge. Was Mac a demon spy? She prayed not. She'd been looking over her shoulder ever since London. He'd blocked her witch senses and that had truly scared her. There'd been only one other time in her life she'd been wrong about magic, and that mistake had ended with Shaun dead.

Don't go there. And she wouldn't. In the past two years she'd elevated *not* thinking of Shaun to an art form. If she dredged up those memories now, she'd go insane.

The train cleared the city and passed into a soggy countryside. Christine had just decided she was going to have the compartment to herself when the sliding door jerked. A small, elderly woman in a fuzzy pink sweater and plaid wool skirt was trying to wrestle it open, with little success. So much for privacy. Christine sighed and went to help.

"Oh, thank you, dearie," the old woman said in a pleasant Irish brogue. She ventured into the compartment. "Are all these seats taken, I ask ye?"

"No, it's just me."

"Well, then." She tugged a paisley carpetbag over the threshold. Christine backed up to give her some room.

The train lurched and the woman stumbled.

"Watch out!" Christine put out a hand to steady her.

"Oh! So clumsy of me. Thank you so much."

"No prob—"

Christine's throat went dry as her fingers tingled and her witch senses flashed. Sudden, fierce revulsion flooded her. But, strong as her disgust was, it didn't completely blot out an accompanying jolt of raw pleasure.

A demon.

For one long, sickening moment, Christine couldn't speak, couldn't move, couldn't even breathe. Her chest was numb, her hands ice cold. Her field of vision started to go a blotchy red. She sent a wild look past the demon to the door. No. She couldn't flee—if she made a dash for it, the entity would know she'd recognized it.

Somehow, she managed a polite nod. She backed up, sank into her seat, and tore open the zipper on her backpack. She yanked out her water bottle. A small measure of calm returned as her fingers tightened on the plastic. The bottle contained the last of her Beltane rainwater.

The pucker of a frown appeared above the demon's silver wire-rimmed glasses. "Is something wrong, my dear? Goodness, but you're pale! You look like you've seen a ghost!"

Not a ghost. *A demon.* "No," Christine said tightly. "Just a little motion sickness. I'll be fine."

"Well, then. It's a good thing I'm here to look after you."

Christine might have laughed if she hadn't been so

freaked out. She slid a trembling hand onto the seat cushion and traced a surreptitious rune.

Algiz. Protection.

The demon froze in the motion of settling her suitcase. Stiffly, she turned and peered at Christine. Christine slumped into her seat and pretended to stare out the window. The demon cast her a sharp glance before taking a seat on the bench opposite. Extracting knitting needles and yarn from the carpetbag, she started to knit.

Wonderful. A knitting demon. Christine forced herself to keep her body relaxed. She was overreacting, as she always did when a demon was in sight. This demon wasn't Shaun's demon. She sensed it was just a minor entity, a Young One, despite its choice of human guise. As long as she kept a modest distance, she'd be fine.

But her head felt too light to hold on to that thought. Panic rushed back. Her breathing ran shallow. Sweat chilled her temples. Red blotches crowded the edge of her vision, and her hands were so cold she couldn't feel her fingertips. A faint odor of sulfur made her stomach roil.

The demon looked up from her knitting. She glanced at Christine. Then, deliberately, she extended her knobby, stockinged legs, ankles crossed, across the narrow space between the seats. The toes of her orthopedic shoes touched the opposite bench. The message was clear: *I know you know what I am. I dare you to try and get past me.*

The red blotches multiplied. *Breathe, damn it.* She had to *breathe.*

Feigning nonchalance, Christine turned back to the window, keeping the demon in her peripheral vision. Green countryside slid past as she concentrated on inhaling and exhaling. Knitting needles clicked. Miles of track clattered away, the train swaying from side to side. The scarf or sweater or whatever it was the demon was making grew longer. Where was the conductor? If he popped in to check tickets, Christine could use the opportunity to duck out of the compartment. But the conductor didn't show.

The train stopped briefly to discharge a lone passenger into the rain. It had just started down the track again when the demon folded her knitting and slid it neatly into her suitcase. At that exact moment, Christine's rune protection dissolved.

She jerked to attention, adrenaline careening through her body.

The demon smoothed the wrinkles on her plaid skirt. "Yes, dear, that's right. I burst your pathetic little spell."

Christine rose so abruptly she nearly lost her balance. She grabbed the edge of the overhead rack, clutching her water bottle like the weapon it was. "Get out of here. Now."

The demon uncrossed its ankles. "Perhaps I might move, given the right incentive. One kiss. That's all. You know you'll like it. All humans do."

Christine sent a desperate glance toward the sliding door. Only a few feet away, but it might as well have been a mile. The demon wanted a kiss. All it would get from Christine was a fight.

It was at times like this she felt the limitations of her magic most keenly. Another witch would be able to conjure a magical shield, or shoot witchfire from her fingertips. Not Christine. Her magic only worked with water, or if she had physical contact with a foe whose body contained water. Which demon bodies did not. They were entities of brimstone, fire, sulfur, and illusion.

She clutched her water bottle. "Get out."

The demon began to change. Grandmotherly wrinkles faded, white hair darkened. Shoulders widened, legs lengthened. Its chin roughened with masculine stubble. Pink sweater and wool skirt transformed into black turtleneck and charcoal pleated trousers. The demon was male now: tall, dark, and sinfully handsome. He rose, his form filling the compartment.

His voice was a rough, erotic caress on Christine's ears. All trace of the Irish lilt was gone. "Such a pretty little human. I'll make it good for you."

The train lurched. Christine locked her knees to compensate.

The demon held out his hand, palm upward. Black sparks, accompanied by a curl of oily smoke, seeped from its fingers. Power gathered, intensifying the odor of sulfur. "Come, my sweet. It's just a kiss." His smile broadened. "Nothing you haven't known before."

Goddess help her, he *knew*. Knew how close she'd once come to turning demonwhore. But at least she'd survived Shaun's betrayal. Shaun hadn't.

"No," she said. "No."

"You refuse?" Far from being disappointed, the demon looked amused. He shrugged. "Then we will duel. That will be nearly as satisfying."

A snap of red demonfire flickered along the outline of his body. Christine popped the nozzle on her water bottle. The demon's gaze tracked the movement, its infinite black pupils ringed with red.

The only warning of his attack came with a sudden white flash of his teeth. The creature lunged, arm outstretched, demonfire crackling. Christine leaped back and slammed against the window. The train went into a curve, sending her sliding across the glass. She landed heavily on the bench as demonfire shattered against the window in a shower of sparks.

She gathered her magic and muttered a quick defensive spell. Leveling her bottle, she sent a sharp stream of water at the demon, striking him squarely between the eyes. He recoiled, shrieking, clawing at his face. Blue sparks sizzled on his skin; long gashes of flesh ripped away. A thick black substance, like molten tar, oozed from the gashes and dripped to the floor, sizzling.

A mangled mass of boiling muscle and bone occupied the

place where the demon's face had been. Christine's stomach turned. The entity's eyes alone remained recognizable. They'd gone completely crimson.

"*Fucking bitch.*" The snarling words spat from the gaping hole that was now the demon's mouth. A scream fought its way up Christine's throat. The sulfur odor thickened. The train compartment filled with a thick black haze.

Choking, eyes streaming, she could barely see her foe through the smoke. The demon seemed to move to the right, so she sprayed water in that direction. The next instant he lunged from the left. She dodged and leaped back, banging her head hard on the overhead rack. She saw stars as she fell to one side, avoiding the entity's grasp by scant inches. She managed to land a spurt of water on his black, curling skin.

The demon snarled. "Human whore."

"I told you to get out." She trained the nozzle on the demon, praying the entity couldn't tell how badly her hands were shaking. Or that her bottle was nearly empty. "Had enough?" she taunted with a confidence she in no way felt. "I can make it hurt worse."

Smoke swirled, stinging Christine's eyes. She couldn't help but inhale; acid seared the back of her throat.

The demon's mangled lips drew back in a hideous snarl. "Who are you? You're far too powerful to be an ordinary witch." His red eyes flared with sudden revelation. "You're one of *them*. The troublemakers. The Coven of Light."

"I . . . I don't know what you're talking about."

"I think you do."

She squeezed her bottle. The last of her precious Beltane water spurted, hitting the demon square in the chest. An explosion of blue burned a hole straight through its torso.

The entity let out a foul curse. He looked down at the wound, then back up at Christine, eyes dripping rage.

His voice was like a screech of fingernails on a blackboard. "If you and your witch friends imagine the Immortals will save you, you're sadly mistaken. My master will crush all of you."

"Don't count on it," Christine said tightly.

The demon gave a harsh laugh. The lines of his body grew indistinct, its limbs folding back on themselves. "Oh, I assure you, I *can* count on it. The Immortals will die, one by one. Tain will see to it. And when they are gone, my master will rule."

The entire train shuddered; a moment later the air ripped in two, opening a slice of black void. The demonfire and sulfur in the compartment poured into the rift. The demon dissolved in a curl of black smoke and disappeared.

CHAPTER FOUR

Hatred froze Gerold's eyes.

Kalen advanced slowly, not daring to take his eyes from the knife in the monk's hand. The child. He had to save the child. The tiny female meant everything.

He was too late.

Gerold's arm slashed. Sharp iron connected with pure, innocent flesh. Blood spurted. The infant's wail abruptly ceased.

Absolute horror paralyzed Kalen's limbs. A low roar sounded in his ears, growing louder and louder until the buzzing filled his brain. It expanded until the pressure could not be contained by mere flesh and bone. White-hot rage exploded. The crystal tip of Uni's magical spear went deadly cold.

He thrust the weapon into Gerold's chest. It pierced his coarse brown robe just above his plain wooden cross. Kalen had been given to believe the cross was a symbol of love. How had its message been twisted so utterly?

Kalen jerked his spear from the dead man's body. Gerold toppled forward. A harsh shout of triumph sounded. Kalen spun. Father Iacopo was laughing.

Kalen stared as the old abbot's robes turned to smoke. As his *body melted and reformed as a female. Red demon eyes glowed in a beautiful, pale face. Glossy black hair sifted around her head like writhing snakes.*

Culsu.

Kalen should have known this hell was her creation.

He should have known.

The nightmare, the memory—whatever he wished to call it—woke Kalen with a start and left a hollow feeling in his chest. Seven hundred years could not begin to erase the horror of that cursed night. He lay in his bed for a long time after the sun rose, wondering why in Hades he should get up. And yet, eventually, he did.

He dressed in a kilt and a white linen shirt. The garments were the closest the modern world came to the tunics he'd worn during the time of Etruria and Rome. Loose, comfortable, no restriction on his bare legs. Why mankind had felt the need to invent hose, breeches, pantaloons, and then trousers was a complete mystery to Kalen.

A glance out the window told him it was well past noon. It was hard to believe dawn had once been his favorite hour. He would have been content to remain unconscious until evening. His heart should have been lighter today, contemplating the changes a child would bring to his life. Instead, his nightmare had cast a pall over his senses.

He strode down the passageway outside his bedchamber and ascended the twisted stair to the tower room. The windows of his sanctuary faced north, so as to cast a diffuse light on his collection. He entered the space, skirting his older acquisitions until he came to a halt before the most recent addition to his treasures. A truly great work of art. Genius frozen in marble.

The subject was simple enough: a man and woman, nude. The figures were seated, the woman's arms entwined around the man's neck. The man's hand rested on the outside of her hip. Their lips were scant inches apart, poised in that breathless eternity that existed only in the instant before a kiss.

The statue was the work of the nineteenth-century sculptor Auguste Rodin. Kalen had wanted *The Kiss* for some time, but had only just secured it from the Musee Rodin in Paris. The museum trustees should have kicked him into the Rue de Varenne when he put the proposal before them. Fifty years ago—no, even ten years ago—they would have done just that. This time they'd taken his money and offered him his pick of the rest of the museum's collection. Kalen shook his head in disgust. Humans had always been greedy, but in the last year the race had sunk to a new low.

He walked a slow circle around the sculpture. Though the man and woman were on the verge of consummating their love, there was nothing at all lewd about the piece. The woman glowed with virginal innocence. She offered her body in complete trust.

The man was not so pure. Tense, sexual awareness infused his body. He rose above the woman, as if about to press her onto her back and enter her with one hard thrust. And yet . . . his hand on the woman's hip seemed hesitant, as if it had hovered for a long moment before the man had dared to touch his beloved. There was reverence in that touch. Honor. Love.

Kalen had had many women in his long existence—more than he cared to count. Each one had been eager; all had given him pleasure. But none had aroused the emotions evident in this pair of stone lovers. Leanna had brought him close, with her muse's magic. Yet, try as he might, he could not grasp Leanna's magic fully. Would her plan to conceive truly make a difference?

He'd hoped a visit to the tower room would soothe the unease left by his nightmare. It didn't. Still unsettled, he descended five levels to the kitchen. There, amid the whitewashed walls and crockery, he found the only female he'd ever fully trusted.

Pearl Hornblower stood on her stool before her long worktable, flour dusting her muscular forearms. Her dull hair was tucked neatly into a pristine white mobcap that only served to make the gray tinge of her skin more pronounced. The ruffles on her white apron were freshly starched and pressed, as was the plain gray dress she wore beneath it.

She looked up and scowled as Kalen entered her domain. Efficiency was Pearl's passion, and Kalen's presence in the kitchens was detrimental to order. Kalen's housekeeper came by her fastidiousness naturally. Her father had been a gnome, a race fanatically devoted to tidiness, especially in their gardens. Pearl's mother had been a halfling, a people who horded and catalogued everything.

Pearl's bristling brows drew together. Kalen knew his housekeeper's current mood went beyond fear for her tidy kitchen. She was always like this after one of Leanna's visits.

"So. Ye've dragged yer bones from bed at last," she said.

"A good morning to you, too."

She made a derisive sound. "Morning? 'Tis past noon."

"Then it's no wonder I'm hungry." He lifted an oatcake from a platter by his housekeeper's elbow and slathered it with clotted cream and jam. He did enjoy Pearl's cooking.

Pearl sniffed, pride clearly warring with displeasure. Pride won. Pulling her fingers from the dough, she wiped them on a dish towel. "Let me fix ye a proper meal, at least."

"No need. I have business in Edinburgh this afternoon. Tonight I'll be in Inverness."

"Inverness. Bedding that Sidhe *luid* again, I reckon."

Kalen was silent.

She shook a stubby finger. "I know ye doan' want to hear it, Kalen, but I'll say it true: that one has no respect, what with her dancing and fornicating inside the ancient stones. Mark my words, she'll come to a bad end. It canna be otherwise."

He took a bite of oatcake. Pearl frowned at the shower of crumbs. "Leanna's tour may be outrageous," he said, "but there's no harm done. It's just a show for the tourists."

"That female preys on human weakness, Kalen. Sooner or later some human is going to be hurt on that tour."

Kalen occupied himself with a second oatcake. He didn't approve of Leanna's tourist shows, but she made a fortune on them. She was too proud to take a lover's money. If she were accepted by Niniane, she'd have no need to support herself in that way. She'd have a steady supply of gold and silver from Annwyn, as any full-blooded Sidhe did.

He washed down the oatcake with a swig of fresh milk. "You worry too much. Every one of Leanna's tourists signs a waiver. No one's misled about the magical risks. Whatever damage idiot humans do to themselves is no concern of mine."

Pearl gave him a hard look. "It used to be."

His lips twisted. "Perhaps. But those days are long gone."

The confrontation with the demon left Christine feeling bruised all over. She was on Tain's radar now. So much for her hope of traveling unnoticed. She only hoped the rogue Immortal and his demon captor didn't stop her from reaching Kalen.

Drained, she fell into a fitful sleep that lasted until the train pulled into the station at Inverness. After stumbling onto the platform, she located the scrap of paper on which she'd scribbled the address of a local Coven of Light witch, Maired MacAuliffe. Maired lived in a farmhouse a few miles out of town. Christine had sent her an e-mail from an Internet café before leaving Rome, but hadn't seen a computer since. She hoped the Scottish witch didn't mind a stranger appearing on her doorstep.

She left the platform to find a store clerk or a friendly pedestrian who could tell her the quickest way to get to Maired's farm. She found the main drag easily enough—two roads on either side of the river Ness, lined with a haphazard mix of old and new buildings. The rain had stopped for the moment, but the clouds were still ponderous, giving the city an air of dejection. Even the magnificent hilltop castle seemed depressed.

She trudged down Bank Street. A few pedestrians passed, heads bowed and shoulders hunched. Not one person made eye contact. Christine sighed. It was the same in Rome, and, she suspected, all over the world. Death magic had gained the upper hand. People were wary, and rightly so.

"Lovely day, no?"

The cheerful, lilting greeting belied her dark musings. She turned toward the speaker, and saw nothing. Her gaze dropped.

A little man, standing no taller than her waist, grinned up at her. He was dressed completely in green, the fabric of his shirt and pants cut to resemble leaves. No, wait a minute. She looked more closely. His clothes *were* made of leaves. His hat, which sported a jaunty point at the top, was constructed of tree bark. Curling hair and pointed ears protruded from under the rim. Delicate gossamer wings unfurled from his back.

A faerie. She couldn't believe it. Faeries lived in country meadows and glens. She'd hardly expected to be accosted by one on a city street.

"Lovely day," the faerie repeated.

Christine glanced at the menacing sky. "Most people wouldn't think so."

He grinned. "Rain's stopped for a spell. These days, ye take what ye can get. On holiday, are ye?"

"Um, yes."

He rubbed his palms together. "And fresh off the train, I'd wager. Ye'll be needing a place to stay? And a hot bath and a meal? If ye doan' mind my saying so, ye look right knackered."

She couldn't deny it. After four days of traveling, she felt gritty inside and out. She was about to drop from fatigue. She wanted to reach Maired quickly, but the prospect of a quick bath was too tempting to pass up. And she had to eat, right? Salt and vinegar potato chips were all very well and good, but even Christine knew she needed something more nourishing.

"Well?" The little man beamed. "What is it?"

"I guess I could use a room."

The faerie snatched his bark hat from his head and sketched a bow. "I'm your man, then. Gilraen Ar-Finiel, at your service. The missus and I run a guesthouse here in town."

"Is it warded?" she asked.

"Aye, of course. With the strongest life magic spellcraft in the Highlands. The missus has a fine hand with magic."

The place was sounding better by the minute. "I don't have much money."

"Ah, then, but ye're in luck. We don't ask for much." He shoved his hat back on his head. Wings fluttering, he rose a couple of feet off the pavement and hovered at eye level. "Follow me, if ye please."

Christine hiked her backpack higher on her shoulders, wincing. Her scrying bowl felt like it was made of stone. "All right, then, but . . ."

He looked back at her, brow cocked. "But what, lass?"

"If you don't mind my asking, what are you and your wife doing in the city? I thought faeries preferred the country."

Gilraen's expression tightened. "Ah, so we do. But the mountains and glens are too dangerous these days."

"Worse than the city?"

"Aye. 'Tisn't safe in the countryside. Why, just last night . . ." He nodded grimly at the news kiosk just ahead. "An entire coven of witches were foully murdered. Slaughtered inside their sacred circle."

"No," Christine whispered. A sudden, sick dread assaulted her. She made a beeline for the newsstand and grabbed a copy of the *Inverness Courier*. WITCH SLAUGHTER screamed the headline. Underneath the stark two inch letters was a picture that turned Christine's stomach. She focused on the accompanying article.

> Local witch Maired MacAuliffe and her coven sisters were found murdered last night after neighbors reported a paranormal disturbance at her farmhouse outside Inverness. Parapolice rushed to answer the call, only to discover a grisly scene: thirteen witches brutally murdered, their bodies drained of blood. A foul odor hung over the corpses.
>
> There were no survivors or witnesses to the atrocity. Inverness vampire overlord Johnny Guthrie indignantly denied any involvement by local vamps. "The undead are not mindless thugs," he declared. "We unequivocally decry this kind of senseless brutality." Leering, Guthrie added, "Besides, we don't need to hunt humans. They come to us." Para-inspector Constable Brian Tilton was not convinced, however. Two local vamps, Timothy Hadley and Geoffrey Dugget, have been detained for questioning . . .

"That'll be fifty pence," the newsstand clerk said irritably.

Christine shook her head and handed the paper back to him. "I don't want it."

"Move along, then. I'm not running a bloody charity here."

Gilraen sighed as they continued down the sidewalk. " 'Tisn't the first tragedy, either. It's been happening all over the countryside. And I'm thinking the para-inspectors are wrong. These murderers are something worse than vampires. Keep to town, that's my advice. Ye'll be safe in my home, I promise ye." He started across a bridge spanning the river. Christine followed, her mind still reeling with shock.

The sluggish waters of the river Ness smelled of death. An oily sheen floated on the surface and clusters of rotting zombies loitered on the banks. Christine shuddered. She'd hoped for help from Maired's coven, Goddess rest their souls. Now she was on her own.

Tourist shops crowded the road on the opposite bank. The buildings had clearly seen better days, but somehow the shops still managed to look festive. Christine's eye took in a jumble of tartans, postcards, and shortbread, and a bin filled with stuffed Loch Ness Monsters. She was almost past the row when one shop caught her eye. It was closed, but there was a large, colorful poster in its window.

SEX MAGIC: THE ULTIMATE THRILL! proclaimed bold red letters. Below that lurid promise was a photo of a stunning red-haired Sidhe. Christine stopped dead. It was the woman from her vision. Kalen's lover.

The Sidhe's skin was white and delicate, her eyes a clear, pale gray. Her figure could have stopped traffic—enormous bust, tiny waist, lush hips. She wore an outrageous silver and black leather corset that left her rouged nipples exposed. Lower on her body, a matching black thong left very little to the imagination. Black stockings encased her long, shapely legs; her tiny feet were shod with silver and rhinestone stilettos.

> *Bored with vamp clubs? Thirsting for something different? Take a midnight tour with Leanna and experience the ultimate in Sidhe Sex Magic. A night you won't soon forget!*

Gilraen, who had flown on ahead when Christine halted, turned back when he realized she was no longer at his side. When he saw what she as looking at, he sped back, wings buzzing furiously.

"Come along, lass. Ye don't want that."

Christine barely heard him. She was too appalled. *This* was Kalen's lover? A woman who peddled sex magic to tourists? Just what kind of life did the Immortal lead?

Gilrean tugged on her arm. "Please, lass. Leave it."

She looked at him. "What do you know about this?"

He flew in close, pitching his voice low. "Enough to know ye should forget ye ever saw it. The Sidhe who leads the tours . . . some say her blood is tainted. She's a bad one. I'd rather face a zombie horde."

"She's very beautiful," Christine said quietly. *And probably incredible in bed.*

"'Tis a deadly beauty, to be sure. She has lovers all over the city. Artists all. Doesn't take long before they're dead."

"She kills them?" Christine asked, aghast.

"No. Not that. At least not outright. They die by their own hand, or from sheer exhaustion. A human male canna satisfy a Sidhe female."

But an Immortal could.

Gilraen gripped her elbow. "'Tis a sordid business, I tell ye. The tour takes place at a cairn. An ancient burial site," he amended as he caught Christine's puzzled expression. "Ringed with standing stones. It's a sacred spot, and she defiles it for her own purposes."

Christine swallowed. Selling sex atop a grave site, inside an ancient circle? Who would be so bold as to taunt the gods that way? The price for the tour was outrageous: one hundred fifty pounds for a green spectator pass. Almost twice that for a red participant's ticket.

"Is the tour popular?" she asked Gilraen.

"Oh, aye. Verra popular." His expression darkened. "There be no shortage of fools, especially in these dark days. The world has gone mad." The little man wrenched on Christine's arm again, this time with enough force to make her stumble. "Let's be on our way. The missus will tell ye of sights a nice human lass like yerself would be interested in. Inverness Castle. Museums and kirks. That kind of thing."

Christine let Gilraen lead her away. But not before she noted the departure time of the next sex magic tour.

That night at eleven.

CHAPTER FIVE

The Faerie Lights was a squat graystone building with a somber facade that was entirely at odds with its fanciful name. Gilraen's wife, Arianne, had done a competent job with the wardings. Christine's room was small, but clean. After a bath and a bowl of vegetable soup—to which Christine added several generous shakes of salt—she felt strong enough to face her problems again. Alone in her room, she pulled out her scrying bowl and scried for Amber Silverthorne, an American witch who'd been working with the Coven of Light since her older sister's death. Not wanting to alert any demon spies who might be lurking about, Christine used tap water and only a weak spell. Luckily, Amber was at home and answered her call. The image in the bowl wasn't the clearest, but it would do.

"Where are you?" Amber demanded. The Immortal Adrian's broad form was just visible behind her. "When I didn't hear from you, I thought—"

"I'm in Inverness," Christine interrupted. "I'm pretty sure Kalen is nearby. But something horrible has happened." She related the facts of Maired's murder.

"Goddess," Amber said. "Are you all right?"

"I'm fine," Christine replied tersely. "Although I did have a close call on the train ride here." She recounted her run-in with the demon. "So I'm keeping a low profile in case Tain is looking for me."

"You'd better track down Kalen quickly." Amber's tone was grave. "Do you know where he is?"

"Not exactly. But I have some very good leads." For some reason, she was reluctant to tell Amber about Leanna and her Sidhe sex tour. "Don't worry. I'll find him. I'll get in touch once I do." She paused. "Any leads on the other missing Immortals?"

"Nothing yet about Hunter," Amber replied. "But there's been news about Darius. A witch named Lexi Corvin spotted him in New York City."

Christine exhaled. "Thank the Goddess. Hopefully, I'll have something on Kalen soon."

"Be careful," Amber said.

"As careful as I can be. Blessed be."

"Blessed be."

She blinked as Amber's image dissolved. Rising, she poured the water, which now carried a magical charge, into her water bottle. Dressed in a clean pair of jeans and a bulky sweater, she anchored the water bottle's strap firmly across her shoulder as she descended the guesthouse's narrow stairway.

Arianne was as chatty as her husband; a half hour was gone before Christine managed to duck out the low doorway of the guesthouse, the shrill protests of the faeries following her.

" 'But—'tisn't safe!" Arianne exclaimed, wringing her hands.

"Be back afore dark," Gilraen added. "Please."

Christine gritted her teeth. "I'll be fine." If only she believed it.

Drawing a determined breath, she retraced her steps to

the tourist shop displaying Leanna's poster. The door was propped open, revealing a small, brightly lit room with a long counter along one side. Various tourist trinkets were displayed on the shelves opposite. A male with pointed ears, the shop's only occupant, sat behind the counter. He wore a blue and white football jersey sporting the slogan "I'm for Scotland and anyone playing England." His head was bent over the sports page of the *Inverness Courier*.

He didn't look up. Christine approached the counter and glanced down at the article that had the Sidhe so engrossed. Inverness vs. vampires united: can the highland lads dodge the bite? Christine didn't know, and frankly, she didn't care. She cleared her throat. "Excuse me."

The Sidhe looked up with a scowl. "Aye?" His voice was gruff and though his features were handsome, his skin had a decidedly green cast. His dark blond hair was coarse and his shoulders far bulkier than a Sidhe's should have been. He was half-breed, Christine realized. Part ogre. *Goddess.*

She fumbled for her wallet. "I'd . . . I'd like a ticket for tonight's tour, please. If you don't mind." It really wasn't wise to get on the wrong side of an ogre.

The half-breed's mud-colored eyes appraised her frankly. "Red ticket or green?"

Participant or spectator. "Green," Christine said quickly. "Definitely green."

He grinned, showing a row of yellow ogre teeth. "Are you sure? Red's worth the price."

"No, thanks, I'll stick with green."

He snorted. "Of course you will."

Her eyes snagged on the twin gauntlets he wore on his wrists. The dull gray metal caused the fine hairs on the back of her neck to stiffen. Worse, the bands were engraved with mirror images of the runes Christine used in her own magic. Such inscriptions invoked the shadow powers of the sacred symbols.

She swallowed hard as the half-breed scribbled on a pad

and ripped off the carbon duplicate below. "That'll be two hundred fifty. Oh, and you'll have to sign this waiver."

Two-fifty? "But—the poster in the window says one-fifty."

"Aye, well, and that's the regular price, innit? Tonight's a special."

"What do you mean?"

He grunted. "Leanna's bringing a friend." He shoved a picture across the table with the waiver. "This bloke. Take a look and ye'll see easy enough why she'd jacked the price."

It was a picture of Kalen. Christine was horrified. "This . . . *This* man is part of the special tour?"

The Sidhe gave a humorless laugh. "Aye. You're lucky there's room left. We're almost sold out." He must have read Christine's shock as lust, because he added, "Sure you don't want red? It's only four hundred."

"No," Christine said in a strangled voice. "Green is fine." She scanned the waiver, which basically said if she was injured or worse on the tour, it was her own damn fault. She scribbled her signature on the line and dug two hundred fifty pounds out of her wallet. There was precious little cash left once it was gone.

She pushed the money across the counter. The half-breed caught her forearm, holding it against his as he extracted the bills from her fingers. His gauntlet made contact with her bare skin. The metal burned like a hot brand.

She jerked her hand back with a cry. Lead. Her magic couldn't tolerate the metal, and the shadow runes made it even worse. She rubbed her arm. No marks, but the pain lingered.

The half-breed gave her an evil smile. "Ah well," he said in a conversational tone that belied his sharpening gaze. "Greens have a good time, too. You won't be allowed inside the stones, but any action you want to take with the other greenies is your own business." He shot her a speculative look. "Ever do it with more than one man? Or with a woman?"

"No!"

"Tonight might be your lucky night, then," he said, dangling her ticket in his thick fingers.

She snatched it away without touching him and crumpled it in her fist. "Don't count on it."

"Suit yourself." His tone turned brisk. "Tour leaves from the middle of the Young Street Bridge exactly one hour before midnight. Don't be late, not even by a minute. Leanna doesn't wait for anyone, and there are no refunds."

"I'll be there," Christine muttered, shoving the ticket into her pocket. She hugged her water bottle as she turned to leave.

"Oh, and sweetheart?"

She turned back. "Yes?"

"Get rid of that bloody awful sweater. Trust me, you're not going to need it."

By five minutes to eleven, Christine had been standing in the middle of the Young Street Bridge for a good half hour, water bottle anchored to her side, all her energy focused on keeping a healthy distance from the fourteen London Goths who were her tour mates. Dressed in leather, vinyl, and steel, they were accented with studs in their noses, eyebrows, tongues, ears, navels, and probably a few other places Christine didn't want to know about. They were passing bottles of whiskey and a few fat joints, their deep swigs alternating with pungent drags. Someone had brought a CD player—death metal blared loud enough to actually wake the dead. Which Christine sincerely hoped it would not do. She'd already dodged one zombie earlier that night. She could do without these idiots attracting another one.

"Hey, love," one male slurred in her direction. He held up his bottle. "Care for a sip?"

"No, thanks."

A somber church bell tolled eleven. Minutes ticked by uneventfully. At eleven-twenty, the Goths started muttering. By eleven-forty Christine was wondering if she'd thrown away her money. At eleven forty-five, a couple of the Goth females started their own show. Jumping up on the roof of their illegally parked van, they wrapped their arms around each other and joined mouths in a deep, full-tongued kiss. Their men hooted with approval.

Christine plastered herself against the guardrail on the opposite side of the roadway, keeping as much distance between herself and the Goths as possible. It was rotten luck this tour had been almost completely booked by a single group. There was only one other tourist who wasn't participating in the Goth preshow games —a stunningly handsome dark-eyed man with silky brown hair and velvety eyes. Not a chain in sight. He wore simple drawstring pants of brown linen and a flowing ivory poet's shirt. He kept glancing her way with a commiserating air.

The church bells started up again in an intonation of the midnight hour. The Goth's apparent leader—a pale, vampiric man weighted down with enough chains to give even Marley's ghost a pause, slapped an open palm on the bridge railing.

"Buggering Sidhe." He took a messy swig of whiskey and wiped his mouth on his leather gauntlet. "Can't trust 'em farther than you can fart. It'd be just like the sodding buggers to leave us standing with our wanks hanging out."

"Now, Nigel." A small, vinyl-clad female ran a soothing palm down his flank. "They'll come. They always do, you know that."

"I'll fucking believe it when I fucking see it."

The last bell cast a somber note across the city. As the tone faded, an inhuman scream rent the air.

One of the women atop the van shrieked, arms flailing. A man caught her as she fell, then dumped her on the sidewalk with an unceremonious thud. The blare of death metal abruptly stopped, plunging the night into silence.

Christine's heart slammed against her chest. Another

wild screech, vaguely equine, assaulted her ears. In the next instant, a horse and cart appeared at the end of the bridge, galloping toward the crowd. With a collective gasp, the tour group scattered from the center of the road and pressed against the bridge guardrails.

The wooden vehicle careened down the narrow roadway, sparks spitting from its iron-rimmed wheels. The cart lurched violently as the horse reared up in the center of the span. The driver was the half-breed who had sold Christine her ticket.

"Finally," Nigel muttered. He drained the last drop from his bottle and tossed it over the railing.

The driver had discarded his football jersey. Despite the chill of the night, he was naked to the waist, displaying an impressively muscle-bound torso. A pattern of intricate mirror-image rune tattoos covered his shoulders and chest. He wore the lead gauntlets at his wrists. Tight black leather encased his powerful hips and thighs.

He was the cart's only occupant. All his considerable strength was given over to controlling his magnificent equine, which was straining against a harness that seemed far too fragile to contain it. The beast was easily twice the size of any horse Christine had ever seen. Its pure white flanks and wild mane glowed like moonlight, giving it a ghostly aspect. It snorted, nostrils flaring, red eyes flashing, huge hooves smashing against the roadway, fracturing asphalt.

She gasped as majestic white wings unfurled from its powerful back. One beat of those wings was enough to lift the horse and front wheels of the cart right off the ground. It took several cracks of the driver's whip to settle the beast down.

Goddess above. A phooka. In her wildest dreams, Christine had never thought to see one. They were extremely rare. She darted a glance at the Goths. They were staring at the phooka, mouths hanging open. A couple of them looked like they were reconsidering the whole tour idea. As well they might—phookas were known for their wild rides through the midnight sky. Often, their human riders didn't survive.

Christine was on the brink of abandoning the tour herself. Only one thing stopped her from bolting—the phooka was her fastest, surest route to Kalen. She couldn't afford to let that cart leave without her.

The half-breed jabbed the handle of his whip over his shoulder. "Get in."

The Goths obeyed. Christine followed in their wake. As she grasped the cart rail to pull herself aboard, the languid, dark-haired man she'd noticed earlier touched her shoulder.

"Allow me," he murmured in a voice that recalled the tumbling silk pull of the tide on the sand. Without waiting for an answer, he placed his hands on either side of her waist and lifted her easily into the cart. With a smooth smile, he settled himself on the straw beside her and slipped an arm behind her back.

Christine contemplated moving away, but the cart was crowded, and the pale, pierced Goth on her left reeked of whiskey and vomit. She stayed put.

"Ho!" At the driver's cry, the cart jerked. The masculine arm around her shoulder tightened as the phooka sprang into a gallop, the cart whiplashing behind it. The vehicle bounced hard, once, twice, a third time. With a violent lurch, it took to the sky.

The lights of Inverness fell away in a sickening drop. The phooka careened toward the stars. Christine gripped the cart's rail, her heart in throat. Goth females shrieked; the men shouted. Nigel cursed and demanded the driver slow down. The driver laughed and cracked his whip over the phooka's back, causing the creature to let out a hideous shriek. The cart surged, then dipped and spun. Christine closed her eyes and hung on for dear life.

The dark-haired man's arm anchored her. "Dinna worry. I've got ye."

The phooka dove sharply into pitch-darkness. The strap on Christine's water bottle went taut. The next instant, it snapped; she made a grab for it and missed. The cart went into a spin. The water bottle hurtled into the night. Christine swore under her breath. *Shit.*

The cart plummeted. The phooka's hooves struck ground, the cart followed with a splintering bounce. Christine's bottom lifted, then slammed hard against the cart's decking as the vehicle thumped to an abrupt halt.

She stood on shaky legs, too upset over the loss of her water bottle to protest when the dark-haired man lifted her from the cart. Once on the ground, he slid her down his body, whispering soothing syllables in her ear.

The unmistakable bulge between his thighs brought Christine up short. Once her feet were firmly anchored on the ground, she murmured a quick thanks and took a step away. The dark-haired man's sultry gaze tracked her, his lips curved in a faint smile. When she moved again, he followed. *Not good.* She sidestepped and turned her back.

The half-breed led the group down a narrow, tree-lined road. Gentle hills rose to the left and right. The rain hadn't returned; there was even a scatter of stars, partially obscured by charcoal clouds. They rounded a corner. A dozen torches sprang into view, illuminating a ring of tall standing stones. A circular mound built of smaller rocks stood in the center of the circle. The top of the structure was about head height, leveled and covered with wide wooden planks.

The ancient burial cairn Gilraen had spoken of was set up like a stage. The disrespect of such an arrangement raised Christine's ire. Where were the actors in this farce? She scanned the clearing, but saw no sign of Leanna. Or of Kalen.

The half-breed advanced to the nearest stone. "Red tickets advance into the circle. Greens stay outside."

The tour obediently divided—six of the Goths—three men and three women—passed into the circle, four couples stayed outside. The half-breed collected tickets; each slip of paper vanished in a burst of green flame at his touch. To Christine's dismay, her dark-haired admirer also held a spectator's ticket. He smiled and moved closer. She shifted away.

Somewhere beyond the trees, bagpipes began to play. The haunting, mournful melody wound through the clearing, lifting and falling in counterpoint to the flickering shadows. From the treetops, an owl called.

The music grew louder. Shimmering forms appeared at the edges of clearing—six Sidhe garbed in hooded white robes. Were Kalen and Leanna among them? Christine couldn't tell.

Silently, the figures advanced, passing through the curved line of standing stones. Halting at the edge of the central cairn, they arranged themselves in a circle around the burial mound. Green mist obscured the stage. Christine couldn't say when the fog had begun to gather; she'd been too busy watching the Sidhes' approach. Suddenly, two figures—one large, one slender—appeared behind the green veil. They must have come up through a trapdoor in the stage.

On the ground, the six white-robed figures raised their arms, chanting in a language Christine didn't recognize. Their hoods fell back; she glimpsed three men and three women, all with blond hair and pointed ears. The chant strengthened. The green mist thinned, revealing Leanna, her red hair as bright as a flame. Her perfect body was molded by the same corset she'd been wearing in the tour poster.

Kalen was at her side, dressed in a plaid tartan kilt and nothing else. He stood motionless, arms crossed and legs spread wide. *Goddess.* Christine had seen him in her vision—she thought she'd known what to expect. But that tiny glimpse through space had in no way prepared her for the reality of an Immortal Warrior in the flesh.

He was well over six feet tall. Dark, broad-shouldered, and vital, he commanded a presence that could only be described as breathtaking. At least, Christine was having distinct trouble breathing. It was as if all the oxygen had suddenly gone out of the air.

He was simply and utterly *gorgeous*. His face, especially, was an artist's dream. Its harsh, angular beauty had Christine's fingers itching for a pencil. She'd capture his eyes first. Dark as sin, fringed with thick, charcoal lashes—she could gaze into them forever. His thick hair, pulled back from his face and tied with a cord, was just the same dark coffee color. The severity of the style accentuated his angular cheekbones, his straight nose and strong chin. His mouth, perhaps, was the only soft feature he possessed. Mobile and sensual, it enticed Christine to run a finger along its upper and lower contours. Press kisses at its corners.

This man—no, scratch that, this *demigod*—was every inch a warrior, rough and deadly. His chest looked as though it might have been hewn from solid rock. Even standing motionless as he was, he possessed a taut, coiled energy that marked him ready for swift action. Christine had no trouble at all picturing him with a sword, or ax, or halberd, or rifle, or semiautomatic machine gun—*any* weapon, for that matter. Her determination to recruit him to the Coven of Light's cause grew. With this warrior on their side, the human world had a fighting chance for survival. She couldn't fail to bring him to the Coven's home base in Seattle. She *wouldn't* fail.

The strains of the unseen bagpipe continued. The six robed Sidhe drew the red ticket holders into a swirling dance around the cairn, moving and weaving in a pattern reminiscent of a Celtic knot design. Leanna surveyed the scene with a regal air, her lush body swaying, her pale eyes gleaming. Kalen stood silently beside his lover, staring at a point in the forest outside the circle. He looked bored. Or irritated.

"Would'ye look a' tha' one?" a woman standing nearby

said, pointing at Kalen. "Wish I'd have bought me a red ticket."

"Me too, love," her friend replied. "Me too."

Me three, Christine thought. She couldn't tear her eyes from him. Her body responded, tightening in some places, growing soft in others. She remembered how his touch had felt in her vision. His hands had been warm and sure, his lips and tongue clever. They'd only had a mental connection, but oh, Goddess, it'd felt more physical than anything she'd ever experienced. She'd been close to orgasming, just from his mouth on her breast. And now he was here, standing so close, in the flesh.

Heat flooded her insides, liquid fire pooled low in her belly. Her magic flowed toward him, seeking him like water seeks its own level. A hiss of air ran through her teeth.

As if he'd heard her, Kalen's gaze shifted. Narrowed. His dark eyes surveyed the swirling, dancing figures inside the stone circle, searching, his brows drawing together in a frown. Christine caught her breath as his gaze passed over her, then snapped back to her face. She stood staring back at him, unable to move, unable to look away.

His eyes widened slightly, surprise flashing in their obsidian depths. His arm came up, as if reaching for her. Then Leanna touched his arm and murmured something Christine couldn't hear. Kalen shot Christine one last, piercing look before bending his head to his Sidhe lover.

"Oh. My. Effing. God," the woman at Christine's elbow squealed. "Did y'see that? 'E *looked* at me!"

"Not at you, you sodding idiot," her companion replied. She jabbed a finger at Christine. "At *her*. From the looks of it, she's no stranger to 'im. Must've been on the tour before."

Christine swallowed hard.

She hadn't imagined it, then.

Kalen had recognized her.

* * *

His dream woman was real.

Real, and here, on Leanna's tour. Kalen could sense her, smell her, almost taste her. She was reaching for him with a tantalizing mix of lust and magic.

His body responded, violently.

Leanna's rich, throaty voice lapped at Kalen's ear. He missed her question entirely. He murmured what he hoped was an appropriate response, but in reality, he didn't much care if she was pleased or not. The stones, the tourists, even the air he was drawing into his lungs seemed very, very far away.

His dream woman was real. His vision hadn't been a dream. Her magic had to be strong, to have slipped past his castle's magical defenses. She was a witch, he was sure.

Interesting.

Who was she? He captured her gaze again, and held it several seconds too long. She was the first to look away, her cheeks reddening. He wondered what she was after, casting herself into his lovemaking, then appearing *here*. She was hardly dressed for a sex tour. With her long bulky sweater, baggy jeans, and heavy boots, she was better prepared for a winter cruise on Loch Ness. Definitely not one of Leanna's usual clientele.

She didn't look happy about being here, either. He'd have described her as pretty if her expression hadn't been so grim. She held her spine rigid, her arms hugging her midriff. Her beautiful long hair wasn't loose as it had been in his vision, but pulled back into a long, thick braid. The incongruous blue streak was visible at her left temple.

Kalen took note of the man standing behind her. He narrowed his gaze. No, not a human man—a Selkie shapeshifter in human form. Dressed in a flowing poet's shirt, the seal-man exuded the raw sensual magic his kind used to draw humans of the opposite sex into their power.

Kalen watched with undisguised interest as the Selkie eased into place behind the witch. When he placed his elegant hands on her shoulders, she jumped and swatted him away. The Selkie smiled, unperturbed, and drew her back. The witch stepped to one side, scowling.

Kalen snorted. Few human women could resist the lure of a Selkie. Few women wanted to. Selkies were one of northern Scotland's hottest tourist attractions—females from all over the world traveled here in hopes of bedding one. The creatures were beyond arrogant and didn't tolerate rejection well. The witch was playing a coy game, pretending disinterest in order to inflame a Selkie's lust.

He pivoted, keeping her at the corner of his vision as Leanna started her ceremony. Tonight, in addition to the regular program, Leanna would be casting a fertility spell to stir the power of the stones in preparation for their lovemaking.

Leanna descended from the cairn, gliding like a queen among the red-ticket tourists. Her ogre lackey, Dougal, hung back at the fringe of the forest. Kalen was glad; he didn't like the half-breed brute. The Sidhe in the circle were no better, and far less predictable. Outcasts and rogues, they tended to look out for themselves. Leanna controlled them only through generous payments from the tour proceeds.

Tonight the Sidhe were playing their parts to the hilt. Leanna began a slow, sensual circuit, weaving between them, her musical voice chanting the spell that would increase her chances of conceiving an Immortal. Kalen watched her as she moved. Her tight corset thrust her reddened nipples forward in a blatant invitation to sex. His body should have been tight with anticipation, but it was not.

Because of the witch. She'd been foremost in his mind ever since his pathetic attempt to capture her features in charcoal on paper. And now he knew she wasn't a dream. She was real.

His eyes sought her as the Sidhe formed twosomes and threesomes with the red ticket holders. Beyond the circle, the spectators were forming their own pairings, and, as

Kalen had expected, the witch had ended up with the Selkie. Kalen frowned as the shapeshifter lifted a hand and stroked her cheek with the back of his fingers. The witch jerked away. Her braid was beginning to unravel. The strands were dark and heavy, the thin blue streak shining with reflected torchlight. The Selkie moved close, whispering something in her ear. The witch stiffened and pushed the Selkie away.

Kalen gave a tight nod of satisfaction.

Then the Selkie bent his head and nibbled the side of her neck just below her ear. A sensitive spot on any woman's body. The witch started to resist again, but a moment later she closed her eyes. A visible shudder went through her. She all but melted into the Selkie's arms.

Hades. Irritation streaked through Kalen, though why he should care, he didn't know. It hardly mattered if the witch spread her thighs for a Selkie lover.

But he couldn't seem to take his eyes from her. He silently applauded when she fought her way free of her admirer. He couldn't believe she didn't desire the Selkie—it was impossible. She was playing a dangerous game. The Selkie was growing agitated. The shapeshifter pressed his lips to her neck and pulled her roughly against his chest. The witch struggled.

Then, with a sigh, she surrendered.

Kalen turned away, scowling. Restless, he looked around the circle. The show had hardly begun, but already he wished it over. His gaze flicked over the Sidhe rutting with their human partners. Disgusting.

The hairs on his nape prickled. Pivoting, he found the witch had disentangled herself from the Selkie and was watching Kalen once again. A current of awareness passed through him, that same electric feeling he'd felt five nights earlier during the brief moment when he'd covered her naked body. She'd been soft and yielding then, but it had been a dream, a vision, a moment out of time. Like this very moment.

The Selkie wrapped his arm around the witch from behind. Sweeping aside the fall of her hair, he pressed his lips to her shoulder. Kalen's witch turned in her Selkie lover's arms.

And Kalen's moment was lost.

"Cut. That. *Out!*"

Christine ducked under the Selkie's arm, trying to break free. No luck. The shapeshifter matched her movements with a fluid grace, a smile in his expressive brown eyes. She'd known what he was the second his magic had swirled around her, making her knees go weak. She'd heard the tales, but hadn't realized until now how potent a Selkie could be. This one was a gorgeous, sensual creature, with hands and lips that promised the best sex she'd ever had.

And Goddess help her, part of her wanted it. Selkie magic, like hers, was born of the sea.

"Relax, little witch." His voice was like velvet. "No woman refuses a Selkie. Pleasure beyond your dreams is yours tonight."

Christine nearly groaned out loud. If the sensations already coursing through her traitorous body were any indication, the Selkie was telling the truth. If she couldn't raise the will to reject him once and for all, she was going to be in big trouble.

He stroked her neck, his fingers skating over her collarbone and hovering perilously close to her breast.

"I don't want you," she gasped.

He flashed his beautiful white teeth in a smile. " 'Tis nae possible. All women want me."

The statement was made wholly without conceit. Christine had a fair notion it wasn't an empty boast. What woman *wouldn't* want such a beautiful creature? Dimly, she realized the other green ticket holders had paired off and were in various states of undress. Inside the circle, the red ticket holders and the Sidhe were already rutting. One threesome was grappling in the dirt, two others were using a standing stone for leverage. There was a loud, wailing gasp from one of the Goth women as a Sidhe male thrust into her.

Kalen and Leanna? Christine's gaze darted to the cairn. The Sidhe leader was back on the stage, but she and Kalen weren't touching. Not yet, anyway.

The Selkie kissed her again, this time tugging the neckline of her sweater down to get at more sensitive territory. Christine's breasts tightened in response. She felt a moment of trembling hesitation before she blocked his advance. He pulled away, his beautiful forehead etched with anger and confusion.

On the cairn stage, Leanna gleamed like a goddess. Arms raised, she undulated in a seductive dance. Green lightning burst from her fingertips. Arcing overhead, it struck the standing stones and zipped around the circle.

Elfshot. Christine had read about the green lightning while pursuing her studies of all things magical. It was the natural weapon of the Sidhe, similar to the blue witchfire some witches could command. But far, far more deadly.

The Selkie redoubled his efforts, bending his head and nipping at her shoulder. Christine's ire surged. *Enough* already. Witch senses flaring, she reached past their superficial physical connection to the water hidden in his body. From there it was a small matter to find his magical essence. Mentally, she touched it, whispering a rune mystery as she did so.

Algiz. Protection.

She held her breath, hoping the simple spell had worked. She really didn't want to go deeper, not in this situation. But it seemed her surface magic had worked. The shapeshifter's next kiss was less potent. The one after that was barely more than an irritation. Thank the Goddess. She pushed him away.

The Selkie stroked her arm. "Dinna be afraid, little witch."

"I'm not afraid. I'm just not interested."

"That canna be true."

"Believe me, it is."

She dared a glance at the cairn. To her great relief, Kalen still stood apart from Leanna. Her relief faltered, however, when she realized the Immortal's dark, angry gaze was fixed on her. There was desire in his eyes, and a good dose of possessive ire.

She stood cat-still, desperately trying to suppress an overwhelming surge of lust his mood summoned. Fantasies, born of the connection they'd shared in her vision, rioted in her brain.

Kalen, rising above her.

Kalen, pressing her down.

Kalen, sliding inside . . .

The Selkie, encouraged by Christine's sudden lack of protest, grasped the hem of her sweater. Before she quite knew what had happened, he'd jerked the garment up over her head and tossed it away. Cool, moist air struck her bare skin like a lash. Startled, she gasped and stumbled backward, her arms coming up to cover her plain white bra.

The Selkie tugged her hands away. "Ye are mine this night. Ye know it, ye want it. There's nae need to be coy."

"Of all the vain, conceited —"

With a swift, fluid motion, the Selkie reached around her back and unhooked her bra. It was gone before she'd even finished telling him off.

Her open palm connected with his cheek. "What part of the word 'no' don't you understand?"

The Selkie gathered her against his chest, her bare breasts rubbing his shirt, his arousal hard against her stomach. His eyes were puzzled. Wounded. Angry. He truly didn't understand her rejection. "Why would ye refuse the pleasure I offer?"

She inhaled sharply. "I just do, okay? It's nothing personal. Now let me *go*."

He didn't.

Damn. He left her no choice. She couldn't risk her deeper magic, but that didn't mean she was defenseless. She'd have to go with her most potent nonmagic: a good, swift kick in the balls.

"Oof!" The Selkie crumpled to the ground.

Christine was feeling distinctly unsympathetic. "I warned you."

"Ungrateful bitch." The Selkie curled into the fetal position and rolled away, groaning. Staggering to his feet, he muttered a few more choice curses before melting into the forest.

She was hunting for her sweater and bra when a flash from the direction of the cairn caught her eye. Leanna was tracing lines of light in the air. Christine froze, her sweater slipping from nerveless fingers, her attention riveted on the motion of Leanna's fingers. She knew that spell.

Berkana . . . renewal. *Laguz* . . . growth. *Othala* . . . heritage. It was a Celtic fertility spell, very ancient, very powerful. It was the spell Shaun had taught her, the one she'd cast on the night they were to have conceived their child. The same night Shaun had opened their circle to his demon master.

She watched Leanna's movements intently. She laid the runes and spells for fertility; then, instead of closing the spell, she traced two more sigils with a subtle flick of her left wrist.

Shadow runes.

Wunjo—fellowship. *Jera*—hope. Inverted, they meant slavery and death. They were the sigils Shaun had traced two years ago.

It had been his first step. His opening gambit in a game that was to end in hell. Unknown to Christine, Shaun had turned demonwhore. He'd invited his demon master to enter their circle and make Christine his well. Two years ago, Christine hadn't known enough about death magic to recognize Shaun's deception. Now she did. The runes were only the first part of the spell. The second involved human blood.

Her gaze darted to Kalen. He was standing far to Leanna's right, looking bored. He must not have seen the sigil, or if he had, he didn't know what they were. Christine couldn't afford to wait until he noticed something was wrong. She watched in horror as a small vial of red liquid appeared in Leanna's hand.

She catapulted into action, flinging herself headlong into the circle. Lurching up onto the stage, she threw herself at Leanna. Somehow, she managed to grab the Sidhe's wrist.

"Stop!" She punctuated the command with a flash of blue energy.

Leanna snapped her wrist from Christine's grip, her gray eyes flashing with astonished rage. "Who the bloody fuck are you?"

"You can't cast that spell," Christine gasped. "I won't let you."

"You *dare* to give me orders?"

"I won't let you summon a demon."

She felt a strong hand clamp on her shoulder. Kalen. She twisted, looking up into his grim face. "You!" she panted. "How could *you* be a part of this?"

Kalen shoved her behind him. "I don't know who you are, but I suggest you get out of here. Now."

"No. Not until you destroy that vial of blood."

"What vial?"

Leanna spread her fingers. Her hands were empty.

"But—"

"Let me handle this, Kalen." Leanna shoved past Kalen and grabbed Christine by the arm. She glanced toward the stones. The Sidhe and tourists had stopped their rutting to gawk at the drama playing out on the stage. Leanna's spine stiffened; her bloodred nails dug into Christine's skin. "This little human witch needs to know who's in charge here."

Kalen's voice was cutting. "No. Let her go." His hand clamped on Christine's opposite wrist.

"She needs to be taught a lesson." Leanna's voice rose shrilly. An excited murmur ran through the audience. "She can't just barge in here and wreck my tour!"

"Leanna . . ."

Kalen and Leanna's exchange faded to a low buzz as Christine concentrated on Leanna's hand on her arm. She had to put an end to this, *now*. Reaching inside, aided by the open sky overhead and the fact that she was half naked, she called up a surge of pure, deep magic. She let it rise until it filled her. Her body trembled with the effort to keep it under control.

"Kalen," Leanna whispered furiously. "She climbed up here. I can't let her get—"

Whatever else Leanna might have said was lost. With a gasp, Christine released her magic.

CHAPTER SIX

Power exploded in a blast of pure blue light, breaking Leanna's contact with the witch. Kalen watched in shock as Leanna's body sailed through the air, tracing a perfect arc over the heads of the Sidhe and humans. His lover and muse slammed into one of the standing stones and flopped forward onto the ground.

By all the souls in Hades. He couldn't believe it.

Leanna's half-breed thug reacted first. Darting from the edge of the circle, Dougal rushed to his mistress's side. She'd be unhurt, of course. Adult Sidhe, even half-human ones, were notoriously hard to injure.

Kalen shifted his attention to the witch. The blast had recoiled on her. In his shock, his grip on her arm had loosened and she'd staggered backward. Her expression was dazed, as if she could hardly believe what she'd done. The woman possessed powerful magic—was she a talented actress as well? Kalen didn't for a moment believe she hadn't known the strength of her attack.

Bloody hell. The tourists were certainly getting their money's worth tonight.

And it wasn't over yet. Dougal was helping Leanna to her feet, and Kalen could almost see the waves of anger radiating from her. Pure rage distorted the Sidhe's beautiful face as she advanced on the witch. But did the foolish little human do the prudent thing and flee? No, she did not.

Kalen sighed. He'd caught the witch's accent—she was American. Americans, in his experience, were trouble.

The tourists, some still half naked, were getting into the spirit of things. "Give it to 'er again!" one sloppy red-faced man yelled, while a second man rooted for Leanna. "Show the Yank who's boss!" No doubt they thought it part of the show.

Leanna's complexion went deadly pale, a clear sign she was about to explode with rage. No, Sidhe weren't easily wounded—except in the realm of pride. Struck down by a human? Unforgivable.

Leanna's lips twisted. Her hands came up, fingers poised to launch a barrage of elfshot. And still the witch held her ground, blue eyes flashing, bare chest heaving. Kalen found himself momentarily distracted by her small, perfect breasts.

"I won't let you do it," the witch told Leanna quietly. "I won't let you open a door to hell."

She was serious. And truth be told, Kalen had felt a flicker of something dark just before the witch had charged the cairn. But a door to hell? Impossible. Leanna was Sidhe. Sidhe abhorred demons.

"*Beacharn*," Leanna spat. She was truly enraged if she was speaking Gaelic. Green energy crackled; Leanna flung it at the witch with a snap of her wrists. With a subtle motion, Kalen sent a burst of white energy to intercept the elfshot. The green missile fizzled.

Leanna gave a cry of rage. *Hades*. She thought the witch, not Kalen, had countered her attack. Before Kalen had time to react, Leanna launched another shot. The little witch dodged neatly, then, incredibly—against all sanity—she dove in Leanna's direction.

Landing hard on the stage, she grabbed Leanna's ankles

and spoke a spellword. The syllable called up an incredible surge of magic. It streamed from the witch's hands and surged up Leanna's legs, freezing the Sidhe in a nimbus of brilliant blue light. An instant later, Leanna collapsed.

She wasn't dead—or even unconscious—but her body was rigid. She struggled to move, her face mottling with rage. Her lips, as tightly sealed as her limbs, worked furiously.

For a moment, Kalen stood as gobsmacked as the rest of the onlookers, Sidhe and tourist alike. Holy fuck. The little witch had cast a sudden binding spell. Where in Hades had she learned that? It was an ancient curse, and one that took no small amount of power to raise. Not lethal, but often used as a precursor to murder. Once a spellcaster's enemy was bound and helpless, it was a simple matter to end the battle permanently.

Kalen readied himself to intervene, this time on Leanna's behalf. But the witch didn't complete her attack. Once again she looked dazed, as if she couldn't believe what she'd done.

Dougal was the first to move. "Kill her," he barked to the other Sidhe.

The unpredictable crew obeyed, rushing the stage. The witch's eyes widened. *Little fool.* What did she expect? Humans didn't mess with Sidhe, especially en masse. The number of spells a human witch could summon that would be effective against seven enraged Sidhe was exactly zero.

Kalen was already moving, snatching up the witch and shoving her behind him. Spinning around to face the Sidhe, he made a low, threatening sound in his throat. The Sidhe drew up short, exchanging glances among them.

"Move aside, Kalen," Dougal grunted. "She's ours."

Kalen regarded Leanna's half-breed lackey dispassionately. "No. This ends here."

"The hell it does."

Dougal lunged for the witch. Kalen caught the half-breed with a burst of white light and flung him on his ass, hard enough to hurt. But not hard enough to do any real damage.

He struggled to his feet. "Kalen. Give us the human. This is no concern of yours."

Behind him, the witch was trembling like a rabbit. "I've made it my concern," he said. "Take your mistress and go. I'll deal with the witch."

Dougal spat. "We don't let insults lie."

"In this case, you will."

"Why should we? She's only a human."

Kalen didn't answer. Leanna groaned, her head lolling to one side. The binding force was already loosening. The spell, though powerful, was meant for humans, not Sidhe.

"Kalen," Leanna moaned. *"Dougal."*

Her lackey was at her side in an instant. He lifted Leanna's head and cradled it against his broad chest. The human tourists watched with wide eyes, unsure if the scene was scripted or not. Leanna went wild, straining against her invisible bonds, grunting and moaning in rage.

No good would come of Kalen's lingering here.

Taking advantage of the distraction Leanna provided, Kalen pivoted slightly and drew the witch into his embrace. Her small, trembling body offered almost no weight in his arms. Keeping one eye on the tight knot of Sidhe around Leanna, he allowed his power to drain into the earth until he was as defenseless as any mundane human. Luckily, Dougal and the other Sidhe were occupied with Leanna's increasingly violent thrashing.

One second. Two. Three. His magic reached its nadir, gathering in a tightly coiled spiral. With a nod of his head, he released it. Power exploded, opening a rift in the fabric of space.

Lifting the witch into his arms, Kalen stepped through the portal and was gone.

Every molecule of air vacated Christine's lungs in one wild, heart-stopping rush. A whistle like shrill winter wind blowing through an attic crack screamed in her ears. The earth fell away, stars spun to black, her stomach heaved. Panic turned her throat raw. For a split second, she thought she was dead.

And then . . .

Silence.

Her feet hit something solid. She gasped, sucking in air, her legs collapsing like overcooked spaghetti. But she didn't fall. Strong arms encircled her, keeping her upright.

"Well," a man's voice said with an air of grudging admiration. "It's been a long time since I've seen a female do something that stupid."

Kalen.

She inhaled a shaky breath, but couldn't quite work up the nerve to open her eyes. Her other senses were drowning in him. His voice? That alone could drive a woman halfway to orgasm. It was low and rumbling, a vibration in his rib cage. His lips grazed her left ear—too close. His arms, hard as steel bands yet not at all bruising, surrounded her completely. His scent was a heady mix of spice and sun-heated earth.

His wool kilt rubbed her bare stomach, and his chest, tempered by a slight abrasion of crinkly hair, heated her naked breasts. But the physicality of him—the meager information gathered by her mundane senses—was nothing compared to what her witch's senses told her about his magic. Teasing sparks of it skated over her skin, dipping and swirling in all her intimate places. Goddess, was she in trouble! With full sensory overload so imminent, she was afraid that if she opened her eyes and actually looked at him, too, she'd climax in his arms. And wouldn't *that* be mortifying!

Fully anchored against him, skin to skin, she felt his power as if it were her own. Except she was sure if such magic ever resided inside her all-too-mortal body, her bones and muscles would shatter with the sheer stress of it. Kalen's magic was as wide and deep as the sea, as broad as the sky. Immortal magic, born of the Etruscan mother goddess. Magic that, perhaps, could save the world.

He was holding her much as the Selkie had. But where the Selkie had been all fluid, seductive motion, Kalen was as solid and sure as the earth. His skin was warm, almost too hot. But his touch was gentle and strangely comforting. Christine found herself wanting to believe in him. Cling to him forever.

The thought caused her to stiffen. If Shaun's death had taught her anything, it was that misplaced faith led straight to disaster. And judging from what she'd seen of Kalen so far, he didn't deserve her trust.

She eased from his arms. Surprisingly, he let her go immediately. Turning away from his heat, she drew a deep breath and opened her eyes.

She was facing the sea.

She was so startled she nearly fell, and would have if she hadn't gripped the low stone wall in front of her. She stood on the battlement of a castle. There was a steady breeze, inexplicably warm. Some magical effect, perhaps? Now that her senses weren't filled with Kalen, she was free to smell the tang of salty air, to hear the angry pounding of the ocean against the base of the steep cliff upon which the castle was perched. The first hint of an early dawn laid a shifting trail of light across the water.

"Where am I?" she breathed.

"My home." Kalen's voice came from above and behind, too close. She sucked in a breath as the front of his body covered the back of hers. His warm, heavy hands settled on her shoulders, massaging heat into her chilled skin.

"But . . . the cairn . . . the tour. We were miles from the sea."

"Yes," he said, stroking up and down her arms. Magic tingled. She couldn't help it—she began to relax into his heat. "We've traveled about twenty miles. Northeast," he added as an afterthought.

This was the castle from her vision. She turned and looked up at him. "But how did we get here?" A sudden, horrifying thought nearly gagged her. "Not . . . by demon portal?"

He scowled at her. "Hardly. It was a simple translocation."

She stared at him. "I . . . don't understand."

"I opened a portal between two locations in the human world . . . *not* a demon portal, mind you—my passageways go nowhere near the death realms. We stepped through and emerged in a different place."

She searched his eyes. They were dark, and told her nothing. "You mean . . . you can just *do* that?"

"It's a bit more involved than 'just doing,'" he said. "But yes. I can."

No wonder she was still shaking. And her stomach didn't feel so great, either. She took a few steps away, out of range of his unsettling touch. She gripped the battlement, as if wrapping her fingers around rough stone would keep him from whisking her away again.

"That was horrible," she muttered. "Just horrible."

"It's not bad once you get used to it."

"I can't imagine that ever happening." She looked back at him, then tensed when she realized the movement had drawn his attention to her chest. Her *bare* chest. Her sweater and bra were twenty miles away. Abruptly, she crossed her arms.

He chuckled.

She turned away. "What's wrong with traveling by car? Or boat?"

"My way is quicker."

It was that. It had also been disorienting, nauseating, and horrifying. In other words, sheer terror. She rubbed her bare arms, though she wasn't at all cold. The friction settled her nerves somewhat. She looked past Kalen toward the center of the castle. The rocky island was separated from an unevenly lit coastline by a dark slice of sea. The castle proper consisted of a high central tower of somber gray stone, and longer, lower buildings constructed of the same material.

She was standing atop the perimeter wall that enclosed the complex.

She took a few steps along the battlement, aware of Kalen's eyes on her. Even though she was no longer in physical contact with him, her body still hummed with the echo of his power. It made it very hard to think. Especially given the fact that she was half naked, and he was looking at her so frankly. His eyes told her he wouldn't mind at all if she dropped her arms. Goddess help her, she almost considered doing it.

"I . . ." She stopped and swallowed. "Thank you for getting me out of there. The tour, I mean."

"Ah yes. The tour. Would you mind explaining what the hell you were doing, challenging a band of Sidhe half-breeds? I can think of few better ways for a human witch to get herself killed."

"I . . . I wasn't thinking of that."

"That much was obvious."

She scowled. "I wouldn't have had to act if *you* had stopped Leanna. How could you just stand there and watch while she summoned a demon?"

"She wasn't summoning a demon," he said tightly. "She was casting a fertility spell."

"At first, yes, but then she added shadow runes at the very end . . ." She broke off, frowning. "You were planning to get her pregnant tonight?"

His expression abruptly closed down. "I don't wish to discuss it."

He took two strides toward her, his fingers closing on her elbow. The sudden, firm touch sent a shock of awareness reverberating through her body. Magic—*Immortal* magic—surged through the connection. Her knees went weak. Her thoughts—what she could remember of them—scattered.

"Come."

Blessedly, he didn't seem to notice the effect his touch had on her. It wasn't a deliberate spell, then. She tried to pull discreetly away, but his grip wouldn't relent. He drew her toward a narrow door set in a corner turret. Once inside, he propelled her down a dizzyingly steep circular stair.

Round and round they went, down what must have been at least five or six stories. At last, Christine stumbled out of the stairwell and onto level ground. Still gripping her elbow, Kalen changed directions, striding purposefully down a long, dark passage.

"Wait . . ." she stammered, trying to break free of his grip. No luck. The hallway was so dark that Kalen was little more than a shadow in the darkness, yet he walked as quickly as if the passageway were flooded with light, dragging her along behind him.

"Where are you taking me?"

"You'll see soon enough."

He paused at a portal that led to a large room, his large frame nearly filling the arched opening. Finally, *finally*, he released her. Christine sucked in a breath as the shock of his withdrawal ran through her body. She pressed her back to the cold stone wall of the corridor and crossed her arms, anchoring them once again across her bare breasts. When his gaze didn't move from her face, she didn't know whether to be relieved or insulted.

"So, tell me," he said. "Are all American witches as foolhardy as you?"

"I . . ." She inhaled. "I'm not foolhardy at all. In fact, I'm the dullest witch I know."

"I find that exceedingly hard to believe."

"It's true. I never would've challenged Leanna, except for that demon portal."

He gestured impatiently. "I told you, it was a fertility spell. That's all. Sidhe and demons do not mix. Tell me—did you *feel* any death magic?"

She sucked in a breath. Of course she hadn't. But that was because she could only sense magic through touch, and she hadn't been touching Leanna when she cast the spell.

Still, a niggling doubt assailed her. Could it be possible she'd only imagined she'd seen Leanna trace the same runes Shaun had drawn? Had she overreacted? She knew she wasn't the most rational person when it came to demons.

"You didn't feel anything, did you?" Kalen said quietly.

"No," she admitted. "But that doesn't mean—"

"What it means is that now you have a problem. There's no grudge like a Sidhe grudge. Leanna's going to be looking for you."

"But I didn't really hurt her! I just stopped her spell."

"You think that matters? You've made a powerful enemy. Leanna's no ordinary Sidhe." He paused. "She's the daughter of Niniane, Queen of Annwyn."

Christine felt the blood drain from her face. "But . . . I don't understand. If Leanna's Sidhe royalty, what's she doing leading sex tours for humans?"

"Unfortunately for Leanna, her father was human. Her mother never acknowledged her, so her rank is very low among the Sidhe. Her power, however, is too strong for them to dismiss her entirely. So . . . she does as she pleases."

"And what about you? Does it *please* you to play gigolo for her?"

The sudden, harsh expression in Kalen's eyes told Christine she'd gone too far. When he spoke, the quiet anger in his voice made her stomach clench.

"You've made one enemy tonight, little witch. I don't suggest you make another."

She knew she should drop the subject, but somehow, she couldn't back down. Not from this—it was too important. "I'm only speaking the truth," she said. "I can't believe you would stoop so low as to participate in that disgusting tour. It's a betrayal of everything you are."

His jaw tightened. "And what, pray tell, is that?"

"You're Kalen, Immortal Warrior. Son of Uni, Mother Goddess of the Etruscans. Bane of demons. Defender of mankind."

The expression in his black eyes was inscrutable. "And who, exactly, are you?"

"Christine. Christine Lachlan. I'm . . . nobody, really. Just an ordinary witch."

"Well, Christine Lachlan, ordinary witch, I see you've done your research. I suppose I should have expected that. In my experience, witches are nothing if not thorough."

It didn't sound like a compliment.

"It hardly matters," he continued, more to himself than to her. "You're here now, and here you'll stay, until I say otherwise."

"You're keeping me prisoner?"

"I'm protecting you from Leanna. You're a pretty little thing. It would be a shame to see you get killed."

"Killed! Don't you think that's a little extreme? I didn't even hurt her."

"You humiliated her, and pride is everything to Leanna. She'll be out for your blood. But you'll be safe enough in the castle. No one comes or goes without my permission."

"So I *am* a prisoner."

"Call it what you like."

She regarded him for a long moment, wishing the passageway was better lit. If she could study his face in light, instead of shadow, she might get a better idea of what kind of man he really was. Was he really concerned for her safety? Or did he have some other purpose in keeping her here? It was impossible to tell.

Finally, she sighed. She'd come to Scotland looking for him, after all. Now she had his undivided, if irritated, attention. She could work with that.

"All right," she said. "I'll stay. But I have some things at a faerie guesthouse in Inverness. Do you think you could get them for me?"

He frowned. "What kind of things?"

"Just a backpack. Clothes, mostly." And her scrying bowl, but she wasn't about to tell him that.

"Clothes." The word encompassed a universe of disdain. "Are the rest of your garments anything like the ones you wore this evening?"

She was suddenly acutely aware of her bare breasts under her crossed arms. "Mostly, yes. Why?"

He made a dismissive gesture. "Not worth retrieving, then. We'll leave them to the faeries."

"But they're mine! And I need something to wear!"

"I'll provide you with garments."

"No."

"But—"

"I said, *no*."

She glared at him. He didn't seem to notice. He stepped through the archway and into the cavernous room beyond. It was some kind of medieval great hall. With a gesture of one hand, he set at least a hundred candles in three huge iron-wheeled chandeliers ablaze.

Shadows vanished. Christine blinked at the sudden light. She blinked again when she caught sight of what was in the room. With a sense of burgeoning unreality, she passed through the doorway.

And stared, openmouthed, at a statue of a beautiful young man. Carved from pure white marble, his form loomed over her. His right hand rested on his powerful thigh while the left held a slingshot over a lean shoulder. Thick curls crowned his head, His expression was serious, his eyes clear. His young body, a study in sheer magnificence, was completely nude.

Christine's heart clenched tightly, and for a moment, she couldn't breathe. It just wasn't possible. It was like looking at a ghost. She half feared the figure would disappear in a puff of smoke.

"Michelangelo's *David*," she breathed. "It . . . it's a very fine reproduction."

"I don't own reproductions."

She spun around. "But . . . that's not possible! *David* was hacked to pieces by a madman with an ax last spring." Not two days before she'd arrived in Florence. The destruction of the crown jewel of the Renaissance had sent the city into a frenzy of mourning. "This can't be the real *David*."

"I assure you, it is."

"But . . . I saw the surveillance video of the attack on CNN. The whole world did."

Kalen's lips thinned. "Given a few more months, no doubt *David* would have been destroyed in truth. Have you been to Florence lately? It's a cesspool. Zombies rotting on the steps of the Uffizi, vampires draining their victims in the shadow of the Duomo. But no, fortunately the *David* you saw destroyed on television was only a reproduction. The original was already here. I'd taken it out the day before the attack."

She put out a hand, realized it was trembling, then let it drop to her side. "But how could that be?"

"How do you think? Money. The Museo dell'Accademia sold its greatest treasure for fifty million Euros."

"Fifty mill—no. *David* is irreplaceable. The museum wouldn't have sold it for any amount of money."

He gave a harsh laugh. "Think again, my love. Nothing is without price. Not for humans. The museum directors knocked each other over grabbing for my money."

"But the man with the ax . . ."

"A thug. Hired to hack at a copy. Far better for public relations—not to mention for insurance purposes—to have the piece believed destroyed rather than sold."

"Or stolen," Christine said hotly. "By a thief with a pile of cash."

"Fifty million Euros is hardly the tool of a thief."

"Please." Outrage churned in her gut. "Don't try to justify what you've done."

He stiffened. "I wouldn't dream of it. I've no need to answer to humans. If your people wish to sell off their artistic heritage, I'm more than happy to accommodate them. Look around you, my love. *David* is hardly alone."

He swept an arm to one side. Christine's gaze followed, her eyes widening in shock. Not far from *David* stood the serene figure of a woman, her upper body nude, her arms lost to the centuries. A little farther on, a headless female figure with graceful wings appeared poised for flight.

"*Venus di Milo*, too?" she choked out. "And *Winged Victory*? But . . . they were both irreparably damaged in a fire at the Louvre."

"No. They're here."

She made a sound of distress. Pivoting slowly, then moving in a daze among the maze of marble figures, she took in the rest of Kalen's collection. The masterpieces spread out before her like an art history curriculum. Classical and Renaissance Art 101.

From ancient Greece: *The Discus Thrower* . . . *The Laocoon* . . . a caryatid from the Acropolis. From Roman times: *The Dying Gaul* . . . *Hercules and Diomedes* . . . *The Belvedere Torso*.

The Middle Ages were not represented. There were no stiff saints depicted in stilted, lifeless form, heads topped with dinner plate halos. No, after the Fall of Rome, the history lesson skipped a thousand pious years, picking up again at the precise point in time when man once again discovered the glory of the human form. Rosetti's *Madonna and Child* . . . Michelangelo's *Pietà* . . . Bernini's *Ecstasy of St. Teresa*.

All were pieces reported destroyed or stolen in the last two years.

She turned to face Kalen. He'd propped his hip against a pedestal supporting a Roman charioteer. She was struck by the fact that his large body, draped only in a kilt, was fully as beautiful as any of the marble gods and heroes on display.

"You . . . you have to give these back."

He gave a harsh laugh. "Not likely. They're bought and paid for."

"That doesn't give you the right to own them! You can't keep the entire history of Western sculpture to yourself!

These pieces belong in a museum, where everyone can admire and learn from them."

"I think not. They *were* in museums, and their human stewards saw fit to dispose of them. I have to admit, it surprised me these treasures could be had so easily. Human honor has diminished greatly in the last century. And all but disappeared completely in the last year."

Christine sucked in a breath. That last was true, and she knew the reason why. It had to do with Tain and Kehksut.

"Maybe that wouldn't have happened," she said shakily, "if the Immortals hadn't disappeared. The human world needs you now more than ever. That's why I came here looking for you."

"I'm not interested in why you're here. Humanity's trials are none of my concern."

"That's a lie. You're an Immortal. Sworn to answer the Calling."

"If I'm not mistaken, the Calling has been forgotten."

"No. My coven cast it a week ago. But the spell was broken by dark forces. Did you hear it?"

"No. But that means nothing. The Calling no longer has any power over me."

"Adrian seems to think differently."

Kalen started visibly, pushing away from the charioteer's pedestal and pacing toward her. When he spoke, his voice held the first hint of real emotion Christine had heard him utter. "What do you know of Adrian?"

"He's the oldest Immortal. Your brother. You were raised with him in a place beyond the human world. A place called Ravenscroft."

"And you've seen him? Recently?"

"Well, not in person. He's in the United States, with another witch from my coven. We call ourselves the Coven of Light."

"Adrian, consorting with witches? I find that hard to believe. He never liked them."

"He's a . . . friend . . . of the coven leader. He's been working with her to track down the source of the surge in death magic. He said you, Darius, and Hunter would fight for us."

There was a flicker of something deep and cold in his eyes. "Ah yes. Adrian has a penchant for giving out assignments. I cannot speak for Darius and Hunter. As for me, it's out of the question. I'm no longer bound by the Calling."

"But Adrian said—"

"Adrian doesn't know what the hell he's talking about. Not where I'm concerned. I'm no longer a warrior. I will not answer any Call."

"But you don't know what's at stake! It's bad, Kalen. Very bad. The human world needs the Immortals desperately."

"They do not need me."

"But—"

He took an angry step toward her and caught her wrist. She drew in a sharp breath at his touch. Heat flooded through her body, pooling in her belly and in the tips of her breasts. Her naked breasts. Goddess, with the shock of seeing all those lost masterpieces, she'd forgotten she was topless.

He yanked her past the statuary toward a steep stone staircase hugging one side of the great hall. Christine stumbled, trying to keep up with his long stride.

"Wait—you can't just *refuse*! I won't take no for an answer. You have to help."

He hauled her up the stairs with a decisive tread. As they climbed, the candles in the great hall winked out, leaving the room once again shrouded in shadows.

"I don't have to do anything," he said. "Mankind's gotten along fine without me—without any of the Immortals, in fact—for the last seven centuries. I'm amazed a coven of twenty-first-century witches would even have heard of the Calling. The spell was lost long ago. No." He checked himself. "Not *lost*." His tone deepened dangerously. "The Calling was declared blasphemous by the very humans it was designed to protect. Do you know how many witches were burned at the stake just for knowing that spell?"

"Believe me, I'm well aware of the history of the Craft. A lot of people mistrust witches even now."

He halted on the landing midway up the stair. "How did you learn the spell?"

"Adrian told us about it, but he didn't know the exact words. The Coven of Light searched all over the world for it. I got lucky. I've been living in Rome, and I found the spell inscribed in Latin on a fragment of medieval parchment in the basement of a small museum there. Adrian was able to verify the spell as the real thing."

"Adrian again." The way Kalen spat out his brother's name made Christine wonder what trouble stood between the two Immortals. Amber hadn't mentioned anything, but then again, maybe Adrian hadn't confided in her.

Kalen reached the top of the staircase and released her at last. Turning to the right, he strode down another long, dark passageway without so much as a glance in Christine's direction. Evidently, he was so sure she would follow that he no longer felt the need to drag her along.

Christine hesitated, glancing back down the stair to the gloomy hall below. He was right—where else was she going to go? Even if she could find her way out of the castle, Kalen lived on an island and didn't need boats for transportation.

She'd come a long way to find him. He might not be the hero she'd expected, but he *was* an Immortal. If there was a shred of a chance she could convince him to add his vast power to the Coven's cause, she had to try.

She rubbed her bare arms, suddenly chilled. And maybe, just maybe, she could convince him to lend her a shirt, too.

She padded after him into the cool darkness. The corridor was punctuated by tall doors on either side, all closed. Kalen stopped before one of the arched portals. When she reached his side, he lifted the door latch.

The burnished panel swung inward without so much as a

creak. The room beyond was as dark as the hallway, allowing Christine to sense only vague shadows of its furnishings.

"Can you turn on a light? I'm afraid I don't have your night vision."

"Of course." A subtle wave of Kalen's hand summoned the soft glow of a dozen candle flames twinkling from an elaborate iron candlestand.

Kalen held the door open and gestured for Christine to enter. The first item that caught her eye was a tall mirrored wardrobe, easily big enough to hide a half dozen people inside. A marble and mahogany dressing stand stood nearby. From there her gaze passed over an enormous four-poster bed, a claw-footed secretary, and a matching chair. The wall covering was golden and looked like silk.

A graceful statue of a Greek nymph stood in a domed alcove, but the sculpture wasn't the only artwork in the room. Apparently, Kalen's artistic sensibilities reached beyond statuary. The chamber's high walls were hung with oil paintings in heavy gilded frames, displayed in tiers five paintings high. Artwork completely filled the space between a low wainscoting and a high, ornate cornice.

Christine took in the pieces, dazed. She recognized most of them. Giotto. Caravaggio. Rafael. Rembrandt. Titian. Each work had been mourned as stolen or destroyed.

She gripped the edge of a marquetry table. The treasures in this room alone were beyond imagination. She'd seen the vastness of Kalen's castle from her perch on the battlements. The place was beyond huge. Was every room crammed with masterpieces?

Kalen's hand lifted again. A fire sprang to life in a hearth on her left. She turned, her gaze snapping to the painting hanging above the baroque mantel. She jumped as if scalded.

"Goddess. The *Mona Lisa*, too?"

"Of course."

"Then the one hanging in the Louvre . . . ?"

"A copy."

Really, she should've guessed. "Every painting in this room was done by a master."

His brows rose. "You're knowledgeable about art?"

"I studied art history in college. And . . . I paint."

She pivoted slowly, trying to take it all in. Finally, her gaze returned to Kalen. With a sickening twist of her stomach, she realized he wasn't looking at his collection, but at her. At her naked breasts, to be exact. With a good dose of pure, masculine interest.

Abruptly, she recrossed her arms. "Do you have a shirt I can borrow?"

He chuckled. "For what purpose?"

"To *wear*."

He moved closer, his gaze all too intent. "In my opinion, you're somewhat overdressed as it is."

She took a step back. "I don't think so."

He advanced as silently and as slowly as a large cat. "I do."

She matched each of his forward steps with a backward one. "Don't get any ideas. I'm not going to have sex with you."

"Oh no?" He smiled, but the expression didn't reach his eyes. "I don't believe you. After all, you placed a vision of your naked body in my arms. Now that you're here . . ." His gaze raked her body. "I find I'm quite ready to finish what you started."

CHAPTER SEVEN

Kalen watched with some amusement as alarm sparked in Christine's clear blue eyes. He should have been angry she'd interrupted his plans with Leanna, but truth be told, he was relieved. He didn't think Leanna had been casting death magic, but in truth, he couldn't be sure. She'd been up to *something* in that circle she hadn't told him about ahead of time. He'd been a fool not to pay closer attention. He felt as though this little witch had given him a last-minute reprieve.

"That . . . that night you saw me here," Christine stammered. "It wasn't on purpose. I didn't mean to put myself there. In your arms." She cleared her throat. "With you."

"No?"

"No. It just . . . happened."

"You were spying on me."

She swallowed, her delicate throat moving convulsively. "No. Not spying. Scrying. Watching."

He lifted his brows. "Please enlighten me as to the difference."

"The scrying . . . it was necessary. I needed to find you. I've already told you why—the human world is in danger."

He snorted. "The human world is perpetually in danger. I told you, it's no concern of mine."

"It used to be."

Pearl had told him the same thing just the day before. But neither Pearl nor this human witch understood the constraints he was under. He sent Christine a dark look designed to silence her. But when she flinched, he felt a stab of guilt.

He felt driven to make her understand, though he knew he wouldn't be able to adequately explain. "I'm no longer a warrior. I have a different life now."

"And that's what, exactly? Putting on sex shows for tourists? Pilfering the artistic heritage of Western Civilization?"

"That was the first tour I'd ever been on," Kalen said curtly. "And as for my collection, I will not apologize for it. I take my pleasures where I may."

He eased closer to her, drawn by the scent of her burgeoning awareness of him. Her chest rose sharply beneath her crossed arms. He wasn't sure what it was about her that fascinated him so completely. Her modesty, perhaps? It put him in mind of women from days long gone. And her hair was especially beautiful. The tangled dark locks were thick and glossy, falling to her waist. He'd wager it had never been cut in her life—a rarity in these modern times. He was even starting to get used to the blue streak at the temple.

It took very little imagination to picture her naked, clothed only by her unbound hair. His phallus tightened at the thought.

"Tonight," he told her. "*You* will be my pleasure. And I will not apologize for that, either."

"Oh no." She took another futile step backward. "I don't think so—"

"I do. I know." He stalked her, his slow steps muted by the thick Persian carpet. He was herding her toward his bed, though he doubted she realized it. "Why so shy? You weren't shy the night you intruded on my interlude with Leanna."

The back of her thighs hit the edge of the bed. She put out a hand to steady herself. Panic—and arousal—flared in her blue eyes when she realized her hand was spread on a high, soft mattress.

"I told you, that night was an accident." The upper swell of her breasts went pink, the color spreading swiftly upward to her neck and face. "I didn't mean to put myself in Leanna's place. It just happened."

He halted a bare inch in front of her. "A witch of your power would never allow such a thing to 'just' happen. You must have done it for a reason."

"But I didn't! You don't understand. Yes, I have strong magic, but certain kinds of spells make it . . ." Her cheeks deepened to scarlet. ". . . hard to control myself."

He gave her a slow smile. "That sounds interesting."

He caught her gaze, then deliberately let it drop in a frank and thorough appraisal of her body. Her breasts were small, but exquisitely shaped—even the defensive spread of her hands couldn't hide that. Her stomach was flat, her hips slim, her legs too well hidden by her shapeless denim pants. They were singularly ugly; he couldn't imagine why any female would wear such a garment. Not for the first time, he cursed the last hundred years. Before the twentieth century arrived, women dressed like women.

No matter. Christine's jeans would soon be gone.

He reached for her.

She gasped and scrambled up onto the bed, the only refuge available. "Don't touch me."

Too late. His hands clamped on either side of her slender waist. He watched her eyes flutter closed, heard her breath hitch. Her muscles went taut, then soft. One arm lowered;

he caught a glimpse of the pebbled tips of her breasts. The sweet musk of feminine arousal drifted toward him.

"Stop it," she said weakly, shutting her eyes. "Just stop whatever magic you're using on me. It's not fair."

She opened her eyes and looked up at him. Her eyes were out of focus, the blue of her irises a narrow ring around wide, dark pupils.

"I'm not using any particular magic." He released her wrist and ran one hand up her arm. She trembled. "I can feel yours, though. It's interwoven with your arousal."

"I don't want you to feel it." Shaking herself as if rousing from a dream, she scooted across the mattress and dropped to the floor on the other side. But, really, there was nowhere for her to go.

"Christine. Get back on the bed."

"No. You don't understand. I didn't come here for this."

"You bought a ticket for a sex tour," Kalen pointed out. "That generally means you want to have sex."

"The only reason I bought that ticket was that I recognized Leanna on the poster. I thought the tour might lead me to you."

"And so it has." He rounded the bed with a few quick strides. She was no match for his speed. In seconds, he had her lower body trapped between his hips and the edge of the high mattress.

She strained against his entrapment, wriggling her hips and making his already rigid phallus go even harder. She must have felt it because her eyes widened with alarm. She laid her palms on his chest and shoved. But the gesture was weak. The scent of her arousal strengthened. Kalen had almost three thousand years of experience with human women. He knew when one wanted him, and he knew when one did not.

Christine wanted him. Badly.

His body tensed with the anticipation of having her. No

human woman had ever excited him as much as this one did. It was her magic, he realized. Strong and deep as the sea. It drew him to her in a tide of longing.

He brushed his finger across her cheek, tucking a stray lock of hair behind her ear. "Why fight? Your body knows what it wants. It's already surrendered."

"You're wrong. I don't want you. Not for this. I only . . ." She shoved at him again. When he moved not at all, she sagged against him, trembling. A small, utterly sensual moan escaped her lips. "I only wanted to talk to you. About the Calling."

"That subject holds no interest for me." He lifted her hands and placed them on his neck.

She blinked, clearly struggling to keep her mind focused on the conversation. "It should."

"It doesn't." He released her hands and felt a sharp spike of satisfaction when she didn't jerk away. He allowed himself the pleasure of cupping the underside of her breasts. They were much smaller than Leanna's oversized globes, and more delicately formed. Her waist firm and muscular, wider than Leanna's, which was so dainty he could span it with his hands. He liked Christine's body very much. It was a genuine woman's body. He'd always suspected Leanna enhanced her figure with glamour.

He stroked up the outer curve of her torso and traced a line along her collarbone. Buried his fingers in the tumbled black silk of her hair and unraveled the last of her braid. Separating the strands at the back of her neck, he brought two sections over her shoulders and let it fall over her upper body. Her breasts all but disappeared behind the sensual veil.

He lifted her chin with one finger. She drew in a breath and tried to look away. He didn't allow it. Their eyes locked as their combined heartbeats counted off a private eternity. He nearly lost his own breath then. Her eyes were extraordinary—he could have drowned in them. They held the color of the sea—not the angry gray of the frigid ocean beating the cliffs below the castle walls, but the fine, deep blue of the Mediterranean. The Sea of Tyrhennus. The ocean of the people he'd guarded so fervently for so many centuries.

He threaded the fingers of his right hand through her hair while he plucked softly at her nipple with his left. Her beautiful eyes flared and her breath hitched in a more rapid rhythm. For the briefest of seconds, she arched forward, pressing her breast into his palm. Kalen felt as though he'd won a prize beyond price. Then, too soon, she remembered herself and jerked back with a cry.

He lowered his hand, but didn't lessen the pressure of his thighs on her hips. She struggled, then stilled, no doubt remembering how her resistance had affected him earlier. Her breath was ragged. He almost laughed when she drew as far back as she could and recrossed her arms over her chest.

"No." He grasped her wrists and tugged her arms apart, holding them gently against the edge of the mattress on either side of her hips. "Let me look at you."

"I . . ." She colored. "There's not much to see."

"I disagree." His gaze lingered on her ruby nipples. "Beautiful."

She must have felt the sincerity he'd breathed into the single word, because a fine tremor seized her.

"I want you," he said. "Now."

"I . . . I can't."

"No?" He released one wrist and lifted his hand to her breast, grazing the hardened peak with his forefinger. She shuddered. He touched her other nipple, then used both hands to draw them together. Dipping his head, he flicked the tip of his tongue over both sweet pearls at once.

"*Goddess.*" Her eyes closed, her hands flattened on the embroidered coverlet.

Grasping her hips, he lifted her onto the bed. She didn't struggle as he settled her in the center of the mattress, puffs of silk billowing gently around her. She stared up at him with round eyes, making no move to resist as he untied and removed her boots, then tugged off her socks. He unsnapped the horrid denim pants and started working them over her hips. Then, reconsidering, he tore the zipper open, rending the seam all the way to the waistband.

"Hey! You ripped my pants."

"Good riddance."

"They're my favorite pair!"

"They're hideous."

"Comfortable."

He snorted, his fingers slipping under the elastic of her white cotton panties. These he tore as well, ignoring her protests.

She lay naked beneath his gaze. He lifted her, gathering her long hair. For a moment, he just played with it, first wrapping the length around his hand, then sifting his fingers through the glossy strands. He loved the heavy feel of it. Soft, luxurious, sensual. The blue streak glittered in the candlelight. He arranged the glorious tresses over her body, veiling her breasts.

When he was done, she presented an incredibly erotic picture. If he were a true artist, he would paint her exactly like this: clothed in nothing but her hair, face flushed, lips parted. Eyes fogged with arousal.

He felt her thighs quiver, her belly shudder. The silken musk of her arousal flowed around him. Her magic flowed with it, rousing the memory of how perfect she had felt in his arms during that brief moment when she'd replaced Leanna atop the furs in his library.

He touched the peak of her breast, just visible through the curtain of her hair. She shut her eyes and groaned, turning her face to one side.

"No," he murmured. "Look at me, Christine."

After a moment's hesitation, she obeyed.

Christine. Her name sparkled like champagne on his tongue. He eased up off the bed, his hands moving to his kilt. She watched him, eyes wide, as he dropped the garment to the floor and stepped out of it. His phallus sprang toward her. His stones were heavy, aching with a need he'd not felt in centuries.

It took all his strength not to fall on her in a rutting, sweating heap. Despite the fact he didn't completely trust her, and certainly wasn't going to answer her Call, he found he wanted her to experience deep pleasure in his bed. Even more than he wanted to take his pleasure of her.

He reached for a stray lock of hair that had fallen across her cheek. It slid through his fingers like a faerie's wing. She was as enticing as a faerie, but, he knew, not nearly so fragile.

He eased onto the bed, crawling over her on all fours like a stalking predator. The mattress dipped under his weight, creating a depression around her body. He settled the cage of his limbs around her. She lay quiescent, blinking up at him with those beautiful indigo eyes.

He fitted his palm to the curve of her jaw and stroked her lips with his thumb. She closed her eyes and let out a long, shuddering sigh.

She had one last protest to make. "This isn't right."

"Isn't it?"

"No."

He leaned over her. "Then tell me to stop—and I will."

She looked up at him with wide blue eyes. Her lips parted, but no words emerged. He read her answer in the darkening of her pupils, the soft catch of her breath, the downward sweep of her inky lashes.

And lowered his lips to hers.

She should have told him to stop. The words had been on the tip of her tongue; all she had to do was find the strength to say them.

But she didn't. Couldn't. Her magic had slipped from her control and all she could do was follow its lead. When Kalen draped her hair across her nude body, she'd felt his hands trembling—*trembling!* His beautiful eyes had transmitted such a raw, overwhelming need that her heart had contracted with the desire to give. She felt the pull of his arousal, as strong and sure and inevitable as the tide, and she couldn't stop herself from responding. And now, with his mouth claiming hers, his lips moving in erotic possession, his tongue sweeping inside to stroke and tangle with her own, she was good and truly lost.

He covered her body with hot, open kisses, his lips moving with an all-consuming urgency that stoked her own excitement. He kept moving, shifting, never keeping to one rhythm or one place on her body long enough for her to catch her breath. First, it was the corner of her mouth that seemed to fascinate him, then the line of her jaw and the long column of her neck. He nibbled and sucked, nipped and soothed all the way to the upper swell of her breast. Each spot he kissed tingled with his magic.

She lifted her arms and encircled his neck. He murmured soft encouragement, pressing her down into a soft cocoon of mattress, shifting up to kiss her lips deeply again, parting them and claiming her mouth with a slick, erotic glide of his tongue. He was almost brutal then, seeming to demand the very breath from her lungs. She gave it willingly. She didn't have the heart, or the desire, to fight his possession of her body. On the contrary—her own need had grown to a fever pitch. She felt so incredibly empty inside. He had to fill her soon—if he didn't, she was going to have to beg.

"This is crazy," she gasped.

He chuckled against her lips, torturing her with the pulsing slide of his tongue. The rhythm evoked an answering throb between her legs. She was wet there, slicked with longing. She groaned and clutched at him, trying to tell him without words what she wanted.

He understood, she was sure, but he had other ideas. "No need to rush," he murmured.

He scattered kisses over her face, touching her cheeks,

her nose, her eyelids. He nibbled her ear, swirling the tip of his tongue around the outer shell. A river of liquid fire poured through her veins, igniting lust and passion in a need so great it threatened to consume her. It was her magic taking over, splintering out of control as it did during her deepest and most powerful spells. Kalen had awakened her power and now it tossed her into an ocean of emotion, all mooring lines cut. There was nothing she could hope to do to save herself, except cling to the one anchor she could reach.

Kalen.

His lips were hot on her breast. He sucked her nipple into his mouth. She gasped, arching forward, her fingers entwining in his hair, pulling hard. If he felt any pain, he didn't show it. She gasped. The reality of his mouth on her breast was so much more potent than the same act performed in her vision, and that had been incredible enough. He tortured her that way for what seemed to be an eternity, until she was sobbing his name.

"Kalen. Please . . ." She could feel his erection—hot, hard, and enormous—pressed between their bodies.

"Shh . . ." His hand covered her breast, his thumb flicking over the pebble-hard tip. A bolt of molten heat zinged from her nipple to her belly, where it twisted like the blade of a hot knife. Christine sucked in a breath and writhed beneath him.

"Now . . ." she pleaded.

"Soon." His hand left her nipple and drifted lower, leaving trails of sensation in its wake. His knee insinuated itself between her legs, opening her. The slide of his hair-roughened leg abraded the soft inner skin of her thigh.

He kissed her jaw, her neck, her breast. His lips closed once again on her nipple. It had been two long years since Christine had made love, and even during that first exhilarating year with Shaun, it had never been like this. Sensation streaked through her. Overwhelmed her. It was too much, too vivid. She twisted and arched against him. Tears collected behind the dam of her closed eyes.

She clung to him. The broad head of his cock slid against the inside of her thigh, prodded her swollen feminine flesh. Her inner muscles started to clench. Instinctively, she lifted her hips, offering him the cradle of her thighs.

"Yes, love. Like that."

Somewhere in the back of her mind was the dim thought that she shouldn't offer him *everything*. That she should keep some small part of her soul hidden. But that was impossible. Her magic ran wild, plucking the decision from her. She could do nothing but give Kalen every part of herself, every nuance of her body and her magic.

She placed her hand over his heart and closed her eyes, casting her witch's senses into his Immortal essence. The sheer potency of it nearly took her breath away. She'd known Kalen was strong in living magic, had felt it every time he'd touched her, but now, with his body poised to claim her, she found she hadn't come close to imagining the vastness of his power. It was power inherited from his goddess mother, Uni. Power ancient and impenetrable. Power that could save mankind.

He held himself still, his sex heavy at the entrance to her body. Her thighs were slicked with wanting, her body trembling in anticipation of his intimate invasion. The wide, blunt head of his cock nudged her wet folds. Just that small contact set off fireworks in her womb.

"Christine . . ."

Her name was a rasp in his throat. Dazed, she blinked up at him, at the shocking need that once again haunted his eyes. She wanted so much to banish that emptiness. Fill him as she longed for him to fill her.

Eyes locked, breath rising and falling in tandem, they moved together. He rocked his body forward; she lifted her hips. Her body opened and he slid inside, stretching her with his thickness, his length. Claiming her fully.

She felt his possession in every cell in her body. Felt her magic rise to meet him. A streak of panic raced through her—she'd lost control over her magic, her body, her very *soul*. And she didn't care. She wanted to give all of herself to him.

He rocked forward and touched a fathomless chord inside her. Glided back, leaving her bereft. Again and again he filled her; emptied her. Made her ache, made her beg for more. She wrapped her arms around his neck, sought his lips. He kissed her deeply. He lowered his body, resting on his forearms, his hands bracketing her head as he pinned her to the mattress. She reveled in his weight atop her, shuddered with each hot slide of his cock deep inside her.

It was impossible anything should feel this good. This was potent magic, his and hers together, entwined. Rising on rigid arms, he angled his body and thrust deep, touching a part of her soul she'd never even guessed existed. A hot coil constricted in her belly. Each flex of Kalen's hips wound it tighter. And tighter.

Her pelvis rose to match his relentless rhythm. He groaned; his movements became harder, faster. Her world narrowed to the reality of their bodies' joining, a place of sharp bliss and swirling sensation. His sweat was on her skin; her fingers splayed on his back. He was slick and hot, broad and hard. Everything a man should be.

He captured her mouth in a drugging kiss, moving deeply inside her, urging her toward the precipice. Her magic gathered, readying for the fall. An odd, timeless sensation came over her, the world suspended. It was the same timeless clarity that possessed her whenever she touched watercolors to paper.

But *sex* had never felt this way before. Not with Shaun. She'd imagined she loved him—he'd been her first, and she'd thought he'd be her last as well. Now she realized the passion they'd shared had been a dim spark to the fire consuming her now. Kalen's Immortal essence was overwhelming, waking every drop of magic inside her. Turning her inside out. Demanding everything she had to give. And she gave it. Freely.

The coil drew taut inside her. Tightened unbearably. She cried out as it broke, shattering her soul into a million tiny fragments. The world dissolved in a blur like paint drenched on canvas.

Kalen's fingers bit into her hips, jerking her up hard as his body convulsed. She felt him harden and spasm inside her. The last sound she heard before she lost consciousness was his voice, calling her name.

CHAPTER EIGHT

The hideous creature had to be an Unseelie. There was, Mac thought, nothing else it *could* be.

Mac had spent the last week— except for the one morning he'd stopped in London and ran into that intriguing American witch—following rapidly fading trails of rumor and gossip through the English countryside. Niall and Ronan, his well-meaning but slightly inept cousins, had been making the rounds in Scotland and Wales.

All three of them had arrived at scene after scene of grisly slaughter and blood-draining only to find no survivors and no witnesses. A human coven near Inverness had been attacked in the midst of a circle ceremony. Selkies had been slaughtered on the shore near Aberdeen. A halfling village in Wales had been wiped off the map, and here in England, faeries were running scared. The parapolice, predictably, had fingered the vampire community, but Mac didn't think vamps were involved—the undead generally stuck to the cities and rarely attacked magical creatures. Now he had proof of his theory, in the form of an Unseelie corpse.

The thing made him ill.

He fought to control his revulsion as he hunkered down beside the body. It lay in a puddle of putrid green slime, its five limbs twisted and broken, its greenish-gray skin already starting to rot. Its batlike wings were torn—he supposed that was what had caused the creature to be brought down by faeries from the village it had attacked. It was a bloody good thing Mac hadn't nipped into the full English breakfast his hotel had offered him this morning. The stench radiating from the corpse—something midway between week-old garbage and fresh dung—was enough to make any bloke lose a meal.

But the dead Unseelie was nothing compared to the carnage in the faerie village a half mile to the east. Gods, there'd been small bodies strewn across the meadow, ripped in two and drained of blood. The villagers had fought valiantly for their homes, but faeries weren't warriors, and there'd been more than a dozen Unseelies. It was amazing enough that a mother and her children had survived the attack. They were the first ones who had.

He rose. He was all too well aware of the battered survivors huddling a short distance behind him. Their expressions were grim, their eyes hopeful. Clearly, they expected Mac to *do* something. If only he knew what that something was.

How in the *hell* had the Unseelies escaped Uffern? They'd been trapped in that underground realm for the last seven centuries, since the great battle with the Immortals had ended their reign of terror. They were supposed to have been banished forever. Clearly, someone had been overly optimistic when they'd announced that verdict.

The shrill intrusion of a car horn drew his attention to the highway, where traffic on the M20 whizzed by on its way to the Channel Tunnel a few miles to the east. The Unseelie activity had been scattered across England, Scotland, and Wales, presenting no particular pattern, except here, near Folkestone, where there'd been five attacks within ten miles of the tunnel's entrance. Coincidence? Mac didn't think so. He rejoined the faeries.

"What are you planning to do now?"

"We're for Cornwall," a plump female replied, tightening her grip on two female children. Two older males hovered behind her. Her face was etched with grief, but there was a determined cant to her chin. "We have kin in Penzance."

"Gather them and go north," Mac told her with uncharacteristic grimness. "To Scotland." He gave her the location on the shores near Nairn. "My cousins will meet you there. Travel by barrow, and spread the word as you go. There's something very evil in the air. I want every Celtic life magic creature under my direct protection."

The faerie woman searched his eyes. "Is it as bad as all that, then?"

He sighed. "Aye. It is."

Her arms tightened on her children. "Then we'll do as ye say, Mac."

With a few more parting words, he took his leave of the faeries. He might have used a barrow as well, but his preferred mode of transport was a mundane one—a vintage Norton Commando. His heart clenched every time he caught sight of the motorcycle's minimalist black-and-chrome beauty. Despite their shortcomings, there were some things humans did very, very well.

His backpack and guitar were strapped into panniers. Straddling the soft leather seat, he was just about to gun the motor when his cell rang.

"Bloody, bloody hell," he muttered. He snapped the phone open. "I'm busy, Mum."

A sound of pure disbelief puffed through the earpiece. "Too busy for your own mother? I don't think so, Mackie."

He gritted his teeth. Damn, he hated when she called him that.

"I hope you're on your way here," she added.

"I'm not," he informed her tersely. "Something's come up. I'll call you back later."

"But—"

"Bye, Mum." He shut the phone and shoved it back on his belt clip. A few seconds later, he was speeding toward Folkestone.

He left the Norton in the tunnel car park, veiled himself with a simple look-away spell, and hopped on the back of one of the passenger shuttles. The southbound span was solid, but he found what he was looking for midway through the return trip on the northbound side. A breach in the tunnel lining. It looked new. No water seeped through the crack—only the stench of rotted garbage and dung.

Damn those human engineers. They'd constructed their long-coveted underground link between Britain and France with no thought of the magical consequences. They'd dug too close to Uffern. Now the Unseelies, caged for seven centuries, had escaped. Mac didn't believe for a minute that they'd done it on their own. Unseelies were brutal, but stupid. No, someone had helped them out. But who?

He sealed the rift. *Too little, too late.* How many of the things had escaped? A dozen or so, he could handle. Hundreds—or, gods forbid—a *thousand*, well, that was another matter entirely. He pinched the bridge of his nose. If there were thousands of the creatures, what the bloody hell was he going to do?

Christine woke with the bulky arm of a softly snoring Immortal Warrior draped over her naked body. For a moment, she lay still, clinging to the memories of the night before. Kalen's lovemaking had been . . . well, she didn't have a word for it. Incredible, multiplied by awesome, multiplied by so very, very good.

But now it was the morning after, and doubts and self-recriminations were scurrying across her afterglow like dark, furtive spiders.

What in heaven's name had she done? Jumping into bed with Kalen had *not* been a good idea. For one thing, it wasn't why she'd come to Scotland. Her mission was to gain Kalen's aid in the battle against Tain, and she'd done exactly nothing to move the Immortal's inclinations in that direction. For another, she hadn't just had sex with Kalen, she'd let him have *everything*. There wasn't a part of her body or her soul she hadn't let him touch. How was she ever going to face him once he woke up?

She needed some distance—*now*. But with his muscular arm pinning her to the mattress, that was easier said than done. Cautiously, she raised her head and looked around the room. The candles in the iron stand were all gutted. The light filtering through the windows told her dawn was long gone. Kalen's body took up an amazing percentage of the huge bed. She lay very close to one edge—another few inches and she would drop over the side of the mattress and onto the floor. Her frayed emotions were even closer to a different kind of edge.

She took inventory of her body. Her thighs and back were sore. Kalen's night beard had left abrasions on her shoulder; a love bite stung the upper curve of her breast. No doubt she had bruises on her hipbones, where he'd gripped her so tightly as he poured himself inside her. Her soul was similarly bruised. She felt raw, pulled open, exposed. Uncertain. But at the same time, a sense of vitality lifted her. She recognized a spark of Kalen's Immortal essence, bolstering her human soul.

He shifted in his sleep, rolling more fully onto his stomach. She froze, holding her breath as his arm slid down her torso, his forearm brushing her sex. She stifled a groan as a jolt of desire flashed through her. Despite her conviction she'd done the wrong thing, despite the soreness in her muscles and the bruises on her skin, she wanted him again. Now.

This was not good.

She had to get out—away from his touch, preferably away

from the sight of his large, unclothed body. She had to think clearly, figure out what step to take next.

She eased out from under his arm, slipping over the edge of the bed and onto the thick rug, wincing at the twinge her contortions brought to her muscles. She froze in a half crouch, heart pounding when he stirred and muttered. For an instant she thought she'd been found out. Then he flopped over onto his back and settled back into a soundless sleep.

She straightened and stood still for a moment, looking down at him. Even when he was unconscious, his power was evident. Not one soft line alleviated his harsh features. Dark stubble peppered his jaw, accentuating its uncompromising forward jut. His brows were heavy and slanted in a slight frown, as if he were dreaming of something unpleasant. Even his long, thick eyelashes, dusky black against his olive complexion, lent him no innocence. How could they? He was nearly three thousand years old. Any innocence he'd once had was long gone. He'd seen more bloodshed—had *caused* more bloodshed—than Christine could begin to comprehend.

There were no scars to tell the tale, however. His tawny skin was perfect, as smooth and unmarked as a young man's. No doubt another effect of his Immortal magic.

He was so powerful, so vital. Possessed so much magic. Surely, *surely,* when Kalen truly realized the grave danger the human race was facing, he would consent to use that power for the good of humanity.

A shiver passed through her. She rubbed her arms. Kalen's bedroom was chilly. The fire had gone out, and other than his large body, there didn't seem to be another source of heat. No radiators, no vents, no electric space heaters. Nothing.

She searched the floor for her pants, but found them ripped beyond repair. Ditto for her panties. And her sweater and shirt were lying in a valley near Inverness. Damn. She'd have to pilfer something of Kalen's.

Softly, keeping one eye on his sleeping form, she padded across the carpet to the ornate wardrobe. She barely recognized her reflection in the mirrored door. Her skin was flushed, practically glowing. Her lips were swollen and there was that hickey on her beast. Her hair was a wild, sexy mess. The thought of Kalen's reverent expression as he'd played with it sent heat rushing to her face. With a grimace, she untangled it enough to form a tight braid. Her fastener was long gone, but she managed to wrap a thinner strand of hair around the end of the braid to keep it from unraveling.

She opened the wardrobe. Inside hung an incongruous mix of modern and old-fashioned men's clothing. There were flowing white shirts, some with lace on the cuffs. A dozen modern kilts and a number of old-style tartan plaids, the kind a man just wrapped around his body and belted. In between those hung a number of twenty-first-century business suits, along with shirts and ties. There were belts, old and new. Shoes—modern hand-tooled leather, and quaint, older ones sporting shiny buckles.

Unfortunately, there were no T-shirts or sweatpants. Or even jeans or golf shirts. She decided on one of the old-fashioned shirts, done up at the neck with laces instead of buttons. It hung to her knees. The sleeves were ridiculously long, but she managed to roll them to an appropriate length. She grabbed a tartan sash and looped it twice around her waist before tying it in a tight knot.

Decently covered at last, she tiptoed across the room, pausing only once to gaze at Kalen's slumbering form. With a tight feeling in her chest, she let herself out the door.

The passageway wasn't as dark as it had been the night before—windows at either end let in a fair amount of light. She went to the closest one and found it provided a view over a wide courtyard. The battlements and the mist above the sea formed an eerie backdrop. The sky was a clear, brilliant blue, but she could see rain clouds aligned in the distance, as if they'd come up against some invisible barrier. Kalen's wards were impressive, to say the least.

Turning, she started the long trek down the corridor, pausing to ease open some of the closed doors she'd seen the night before. They were unused bedchambers, the furniture draped with white sheets. Did Kalen live alone? It didn't seem likely. A home this large had to have an army of servants.

She found a small room she supposed was a bathroom, though it didn't look like any bathroom she'd ever seen. The toilet was carved from stone. A small alcove contained a waist-high table with a pitcher of water and a bowl for washing. A neat stack of linen towels lay to one side. To her surprise, the water in the pitcher was warm. Magic? Or had someone refreshed it recently?

It wasn't exactly the hot shower she craved, but she made do. When she was done, she poured clean water into the bowl and traced a rune on the wet surface. *Kenaz*. Vision. She had to contact Amber.

After seven tries, she gave up in frustration. The water remained lifeless, showing not even the faintest image. There some kind of magical interference or counterspell at work. Kalen's doing, she was sure.

With a sigh, she continued down the corridor to the stairway she'd climbed with Kalen the night before. The straight stair descended to the great hall, but another stair, a narrow and twisted spiral, continued on to an upper level. Up or down? She'd already been down, so she might as well try up. The treads were cool and smooth under her bare feet.

The spiral ended in a single large room with a high, peaked ceiling. It had to be the upper level of the tower she'd seen from the battlement the night before. Clerestory windows, faceted with dozens of diamond glass panes, admitted a clear, strong light.

There were no shrouds here, no sign of disuse. This was another gallery room, adorned with statues, paintings, and rare manuscripts. Each piece was professionally displayed, as it would have been in the finest museum. Christine advanced slowly, unable to quite believe her eyes. Unlike the artwork in Kalen's bedroom, the pieces in this tower room were united by a single theme.

Each one depicted an act of love in exquisite, graphic detail.

Kalen woke alone. And for the first time in almost three thousand years, he wasn't happy about it.

He shoved himself to a sitting position, cursing under his breath. Christine's unique scent, a combination of sea mist and moss roses, lingered in the air, on the bedding, on his skin. The woman herself, however, was nowhere to be found.

For a brief moment, something very much like grief assaulted him. He felt as though he'd lost something precious. But that was absurd. Christine wasn't gone—there was no way for her to leave the island without his knowledge and permission. If he wanted to see her again—*have* her again—he only needed to track her down.

And he did want her again. Soon. His phallus rose at the thought. The lovemaking they'd shared the night before had been exceptional. In fact, he couldn't remember sex ever being so fulfilling. The experience had been wholly unique. And for a man who'd lived three millennia, novelty didn't come along every day.

Never in his life had any female—human or magical— satisfied him so completely. Afterward, he'd fallen into the deepest sleep he'd had in a long, long time. Despite his high-handed maneuver in ordering her into his bed, in the end she'd not only surrendered, but surrendered sweetly and completely. She'd laid herself open, denying him nothing, giving him everything she was.

He'd tasted her essence. Her unique magic that sprang from the power of the earth's waters. He'd discovered her power was intimately linked to her sexuality—no doubt it was this handicap that had thrown her into his arms during her vision. She couldn't separate the deeper aspects of magic and her sexual response. Her magic was sex magic, like Leanna's was.

The thought brought him up short. He considered Christine's magic with new interest. On the surface, her magic wasn't Leanna's brand of sex magic. Leanna's power lay in shock and intensity, like an explosion of fireworks. Christine's power was deep and abiding, silent as the inner currents of the sea. Leanna acted upon her lovers, sending sparks of artistic inspiration onto the tinder of their yearning souls. In contrast, Christine had drawn him into her complete embrace. Made him yearn to be the giver in their exchange.

He saw her again in his mind's eye, lying naked atop the rumpled silk coverlet, clothed with nothing but her hair. Abruptly, he sat up, kicking the same coverlet free of his legs. He rose, scooping his kilt from the carpet and belting it at his waist. He spied Christine's jeans lying in a heap. Absently, he wadded them into a ball and tossed them into the fireplace, lifting his hand to cause a smoldering coal to ignite the denim. He watched with satisfaction as the flames fed on the offensive garment. After a moment's thought, he found her ruined panties and added them to the blaze.

He doubted she was wandering his castle nude, however. The door to his wardrobe was ajar; she must have found something inside to wear. The thought of her small form swallowed up in his clothes brought a smile to his lips. He shaved quickly, scraping his night beard from this chin and neck with a straight razor. Pulling a clean shirt from the wardrobe, he donned it, belting it with his kilt.

As he tied the shirt's laces, his gaze lingered on the slight indentation on the bed left by Christine's small body. Moving to the mattress, he ran his hand down the length of it. Her essence lingered on the bedding like an expensive perfume. Kalen drew it into his lungs.

A strange sense of restlessness came over him. The feeling was similar to the artistic impulses that came to him after bedding Leanna. Christine's magic, he realized. His heartbeat accelerated. Excitement gripped him. His fingers itched for pencil and paper. He didn't keep drawing supplies in his bedroom—he did not, after all, entertain Leanna here. But the obsession that gripped him wouldn't permit him to make the long trek to the library. Striding to his writing desk, he snatched a sheet of vellum from a folio. Spreading it flat on the blotter, he uncapped the inkwell and took up a pen.

The urge to create, to form something of beauty from nothing more than pure imagination, worked its way through his veins until every cell in his body demanded he act. Still, for a moment, he hesitated. For the past ten years he'd had Leanna's magic to bolster him. He'd been convinced he needed her.

The artistic impulse wouldn't let him turn away. He might fail, as he invariably did after bedding Leanna, but he had to try. Hardly daring to hope, he held his breath as the tip of the pen touched the pristine vellum. His first line flowed.

It was a curving, sensuous stroke, wholly beautiful. But he'd created beautiful lines often enough in the past. Alone, it meant nothing. But merged with other, equally inspired lines, it could become so much more. His spark of inspiration flared. He reached for it, fully expecting it to flit away before he could capture it. It was always so hard to grasp Leanna's inspiration—her power was intense, but fleeting. Only the most talented—or most desperate—of artists could claim it.

Christine's magic, however, did not retreat. Like her, it wrapped him in soft, welcoming arms. The deeper he dove inside it, the more securely it flowed around him.

A drawing emerged under his hand. A woman's eyes. Slender nose, pouting lips. Dark hair cascading over bare skin. She lay atop silken, tousled bedclothes, her long hair a tantalizing curtain, concealing the tips of her breasts and brushing the soft curve of her stomach.

His pen passed over the delicate line of her shoulders, the curve of her hip. By the time he was done, he was breathing heavily and the bone handle of the pen had cracked under the pressure of his grip. His heart pounded, his stomach twisted. He stared at the scrap of vellum, the lines he'd rendered, committing the image to memory. Then he closed his eyes and steadied himself with a deep breath.

He couldn't be certain that when the magical inspiration passed, the reality of what he'd drawn would match his artistic revelation. When he created, he existed within a dream. Invariably, when he woke, he discovered his creation was a pale echo of his vision. He didn't dare hope this time would be different.

Drawing a deep breath, he opened his eyes. For a long moment, he did nothing but stare at what he had wrought.

Then his throat grew tight. His hand started to shake. He blinked, trying to clear the wash of moisture stinging his eyes. His drawing was simple, yes. Just a few lines rendered in black ink. And yet . . . it was . . . perfect.

The subject was Christine. Her reclining figure exuded sensuality, but at the same time, aching innocence. Her eyes held that hint of self-consciousness he found so enticing. The expression on her face was one of wonder, and of giving. The corners of her lips were turned up ever so slightly, as if she were contemplating some secret Kalen would never know.

He stood, his head bent for a long moment, unable to wrench his eyes from his creation. Finally he turned, cursed, and paced a few feet away. Raked a trembling hand through his hair. Turned abruptly, striding back to the desk to stare once more.

Kalen prided himself on his ability to recognize fine art. His extensive collection included not only known masters, but works by obscure geniuses who'd not had the good fortune to attract wealthy patrons. He respected true talent, abhorred mediocrity. He subjected his own work to the same unforgiving scrutiny. He was well aware that his work was passable, perhaps even good, but that wasn't enough. He longed to create a masterpiece worthy to hang between Buonarroti and da Vinci.

And now he had.

By all the gods in Annwyn. *Christine* had caused this. He had no doubt of it. In one night, she'd given him what ten years with Leanna had not.

He started for the door.

He had to find her.

The ancient Roman urn was almost tall as Christine, but it had survived the centuries with surprisingly few cracks. Elevated on an elegant marble pedestal, its rim hovered a good foot over her head. Which put the human figures on its surface directly at eye level.

Christine's cheeks flamed, but somehow, she couldn't tear her eyes away. Two-thousand-year-old pornography, that's what it was, pure and simple. A naked woman reclined on her back, her legs spread wide. One hand toyed with her own breast, the nipple erect and dark. Standing before her was a man with an erection as long as his forearm, the tip buried in the woman's vagina. The entire scene was rendered in extremely accurate detail.

The couple was only one of several pairs of lovers circling the urn's surface. Ten inches to the left, a woman was on her knees, suckling a man. Another step clockwise put Christine face-to-face with a man mounting a woman from behind. And in a fourth scene . . .

A step sounded behind her. She swung around in time to see Kalen's broad form emerge from the stairwell. He was dressed in his kilt from the night before, but he'd added an old-fashioned white shirt much like the one she'd pilfered from his wardrobe. The laces at the neck were undone, revealing a V of crisp dark hair. The ends of his unbound hair brushed his shoulders. His feet were bare.

Christine sucked in a breath. The sensual force of Kalen's presence was incredible. She resisted the urge to retreat, but it was difficult, especially while the memory of all the things he'd done to her—all the emotions he'd made her feel—was flashing in vivid neon through her brain.

She bit her lower lip. Kalen regarded her silently, his gaze raking her body, lingering a beat too long on her bustline. Christine didn't have to look down to find out why—she was well aware her nipples had drawn tight at the first sight of him, and that the fine linen shirt probably did nothing to hide them. She crossed her arms over her chest. He responded with a grin, and she knew he was remembering the many times she'd covered herself last night.

It was the first time she'd seen him smile—*really* smile—and the effect was breathtaking. His teeth were straight and white, and his left cheek sported a surprisingly boyish dimple. He was an incredibly handsome man—Uni certainly hadn't stinted on masculine beauty when she created her son. His smiling gaze flicked to the urn, then back to her face.

"Do you like it?" he asked softly.

She pretended she didn't understand. "Like what?"

He strode toward her. "It was one of the first pieces I acquired. It was crafted in the first century AD and excavated from the ruins of Pompeii in 1752. I bought it that same year." He paused before the urn, his finger hovering over one of the couples. "This scene is my favorite."

She didn't want to look, but couldn't seem to help herself. The pair he'd chosen showed a woman lying on a waist-high platform. A man standing between her spread legs, his cock fully buried inside her. His hands were on her breasts; the woman looked like she was on the verge of climax.

"Do you like it?" he asked again.

"No."

He chuckled. The sound was rich with promise, like a low rumble of thunder before a summer rain. He was somehow different today than he'd been the night before—he seemed more relaxed, less cynical. She found the transformation far too appealing.

"I think you're lying to me," he told her. "I think you're very much intrigued with the piece."

He was right. She blushed and he laughed again.

She turned her back and walked to the sole window in the room that was set at eye level. It had the added advantage of being the only aspect of the room that didn't have anything to do with sex. Each and every other item in the room was sensual, from the mosaic lovemaking scenes under her feet, to the erotic tapestries on the walls, to the painting of a Bacchanalia orgy on the ceiling. Even the low, circular couch in the center of the room, covered with fur and strewn with satin pillows, hadn't escaped erotic decoration. The couch's antique wooden frame was supported by four legs carved to resemble penises.

Had Kalen made love to Leanna there? For some reason, the thought made her ill.

"No." His whisper was soft in her ear.

She turned, startled to find him so close. How did a man so large move so silently? "What?"

"I've never taken a woman on that bed. In fact, I rarely allow anyone in this room."

She stared at him. "Is mind reading part of your Immortal magic?" Amber had told her each Immortal had unique powers. It occurred to her she didn't have the slightest idea what Kalen's special talents were. Translocation, certainly. And he seemed to have a grip on spellcraft. What else?

He laughed softly. "No, I can't claim to be a mind reader.

But when a woman looks at her lover's bed with an expression like that, it can mean only one thing."

Pointedly, she looked out at the sea. "I'm sorry I stumbled on this room. I didn't mean to invade your . . . um . . . private space."

He placed his hands on her shoulders. His magic flowed over her skin; just that small contact was enough to make her legs go weak. She locked her knees and gripped the window's wide sill. She would not give in to this mad feeling. She would *not*.

His head dipped, his lips touched the side of her neck, just beneath her ear. Her hold on the window tightened to a death grip. A heated rush of desire threatened to melt every bone in her body.

She jerked away, breaking contact. His magic was clouding her mind, making her forget what she came to Scotland for.

"Please. I think it would be better if you didn't touch me. Last night was nice, but it was a big mistake." She tried for a casual laugh, but the sound came out far too shaky. "I don't know what got into me. I'm not the type of woman who . . ." She coughed, trying to clear a sudden catch in her throat. "I don't usually fall into bed with strangers."

"Are we strangers, Christine?"

She wished he wouldn't say her name. She'd always thought it a plain, mundane sort of name. On his lips, it sounded exotic and forbidden. Like it belonged to someone she didn't know.

"Yes, we're strangers."

"Nonetheless, last night was not a casual experience for you."

"But it was for you, wasn't it? You've probably had sex with more women than you can count." The words bit into the space between them with a vehemence that surprised her. What right did she have to berate him?

His shoulders lifted and fell. "Sex is one of the more interesting things about the human race. Far more interesting than, say . . . politics."

A sudden distressing thought struck her. "We didn't use protection. I could be . . ." She couldn't complete the thought.

"No," he said. "You're not. An Immortal has control over such things, and I would never father a child without a woman's knowledge."

"Oh," she said, battling an unexpected surge of disappointment. Which only proved how messed up she was. There'd been a time when she'd very much wanted to conceive Shaun's child, blissfully unaware that he meant to use her blind love as an avenue for demon possession. But Kalen's child? Of course she didn't want that.

He reached for her. She took a quick step back, but not, apparently, quick enough. Once again, his big, warm hands descended on her shoulders, causing her traitorous body to thrum in response. For a trembling moment, she expected him to pull her into his arms, and she started gathering the strength to resist him. But the embrace never came. Instead, he kept her at arm's length, merely turning her to face a painting displayed on a nearby panel. Releasing her, he stepped back.

The painting was Peter Paul Rubens's *Abduction of Europa*. Zeus, depicted as an enormous bull, was carrying a frantic woman, Europa, into the sea. Rubens had captured Zeus's bestial power and Europa's feminine helplessness with brutal intensity. The painting was dark, brooding, disturbing in its sensuality. It was hard to tell whether Europa's expression was one of fear or of ecstasy. Heat crept up Christine's face. She knew how the poor woman felt.

"Does the scene arouse you?" Kalen asked softly, surprising her again with his nearness. He was standing way too close.

She struggled for air. "I don't think I want to answer that."

"Ah." A thread of knowing laughter laced his voice. "Too . . . vibrant for your taste, perhaps. What about that one?" He nodded toward another oil.

Titian's *Venus of Urbino*. A nude woman, reclining on a couch. Her nipples were erect and the fingers of her left hand curved over her sex as if she were about to pleasure herself while the artist watched. At least there was no man in the picture, but even this was too much with Kalen standing so close.

She looked around, desperate to find something less suggestive. Her gaze fell on a wholly unexpected painting of a fully clothed man and woman. She headed toward it. "I much prefer this one."

"One of my favorites as well."

She thought at first he was joking. But no, she couldn't detect even a hint of irony in his voice. She stepped closer to the painting. The scene took place in nondescript surroundings—an alley, or perhaps a servant's hallway, devoid of decoration. The man wore a simple brown traveling cloak, a hat with a single feather resting on his head. The dark-haired woman in his arms wore a rich blue gown with white lace at the sleeves.

The pair shared a kiss, the man's hands framing the woman's face, the woman clutching the man's neck. An air of desperation surrounded them, as if the meeting was fleeting. Forbidden. The fear of discovery was palpable.

"*Il Bacio*," Kalen said.

"Francesco Hayez," Christine murmured. "Nineteenth-century Italian Romanticist. *The Kiss* is his most renowned work."

Kalen looked pleased. "You know it."

"I saw this painting in Milan." She scowled. "Not more than two months ago, I'll have you know."

Kalen flashed her a clearly unapologetic grin. "And now you've seen it a second time."

She shook her head. "I can't believe this! Do you have the Sistine Chapel somewhere in this castle, too?"

A sudden bleakness appeared in his eyes. "No," he said. "I couldn't get to it in time. The Sistine Chapel is truly gone."

"Oh." The stab of pain was almost as great as it had been on the terrible day almost a year ago when a terrorist bomb had destroyed Michelangelo's crowning achievement. She saw her grief mirrored in Kalen's eyes. "I'm sorry."

"No more than I." He sighed. "The fate of the Sistine Chapel convinced me humans could no longer be trusted to guard their own heritage. A heritage for which the Etruscans laid the foundation. It was after the Sistine was destroyed that I started collecting masterpieces in earnest. These statues, these paintings . . . they're all I have left of my people."

Shame seeped through her. She'd thought Kalen selfish and arrogant, an unprincipled museum raider. In reality, he was a hero. "I'm sorry. I didn't realize."

He reached for her and she went to him, allowing herself to be wrapped in his powerful arms. He held her as though she were as precious as the artwork he revered. Framing her face between his palms, he dipped his head until his lips grazed hers.

"Let me make love to you again, Christine."

His touch worked on her like a drug. His thumbs flexed on her cheeks. His eyes grew dark. She was beginning to get used to the waves of aching weakness she experienced whenever he touched her. She wanted nothing more than to melt into his arms. And she would—just as soon as she gained his cooperation.

"I need to talk to you," she said seriously. "About the Calling."

He tensed, subtly. "I told you, I'm no longer bound by it."

"I don't understand."

"The other Immortals were created to guard all humanity. I was not. Uni created me to guard her chosen people, the Etruscans. More specifically, the line of Tyrrhenus."

She frowned. "Who was Tyrrhenus?"

Kalen's smile was tinged with sadness. "The first leader of the Etruscans, now long forgotten. The only trace left of him is the sea that bears his name. *Il Mare Tirreno*. The Mediterranean. Almost three thousand years ago, Tyrrhenus was cast out of his homeland in Asia Minor at the height of a brutal famine. His band of half-starved, ragged refugees sailed across the sea to the Italian peninsula. In the first months in their new home, roving packs of zombies led by a demon queen known as Culsu nearly wiped them out.

"My goddess mother, Uni, was furious. When Tyrrhenus appealed to her for aid, she sent me as the answer to his prayer. I had precious little time to prepare Tyrrhenus and his warriors for battle with Culsu's zombies. The imbalance of power was laughable . . . four dozen hungry, ill-equipped farmers and herdsmen, along with an equal number of starving women and children, against a zombie army that numbered in the thousands. I needed every ounce of cunning and strength I possessed during that war. In the end I prevailed, and Culsu withdrew. Afterward, Uni gave me a new role—teacher, guardian, and counselor to her chosen people."

"You were more than a warrior?"

"Yes. I transformed a ragtag band of desperate refugees into the most glorious civilization on earth. Art, culture, government, engineering—the Etruscans excelled at these things. Uni required me to answer the Calling spell only when it was cast by a direct descendant of Tyrrhenus. I guided his line well, and when the Etruscans merged with a neighboring tribe, I became guardian of the new city of Rome. Uni became Juno, queen of the Roman pantheon. As Romans, my people spread art, civics, and order throughout the world for nearly one thousand years."

"But it didn't last."

"No," he agreed. "It didn't. The government grew corrupt, the people became lazy and greedy. They valued Uni less than Jupiter and Mars, and she became angry and vengeful because of it. As for me—I allowed myself to become distracted by Adrian and his endless battles. Because I neglected my people's spiritual needs, Rome fell. Demons and vampires roamed freely. The line of Tyrrhenus survived the Fall, but the plagues of the Dark Ages took their toll. By the Middle Ages, the last of Tyrrhenus's progeny was gone." He let out a long breath. "So you see, the purpose for which I was created no longer exists."

"You're kidding me, right? Look, I'm sorry your original people are gone, but that doesn't mean your purpose in life has ended. There are people alive who need you. You have so much power—you can still use it for good."

"No. Everything has changed. My choices—and my life—they aren't what they once were."

"So you're just going to turn your back on us? Is that it?"

His expression darkened dangerously. She'd pushed him too far. Abruptly, he released her, sending her stumbling backward.

"I've told you my views on the matter. Accept them or not, that is your choice. It will make no difference. I will not fight." Pivoting, he started for the stair.

Christine stared after him for a moment, then ran and grabbed his arm. "Please. Just listen to what I have to say. That's all I'm asking."

He stopped and looked down at her hand, then up at her face. "Go ahead, then. Talk. Get it out of your system. But I warn you, it won't do any good."

"I . . ." She faltered. Faced with his anger, she nearly lost her nerve. But the danger was so monumental, so widespread, she had to try to convince him. "It's about your brother," she said finally.

He frowned. "Adrian?"

"No. Not Adrian. Your youngest brother. Tain."

His surprise was evident. "Your coven has called Tain to battle?"

"No. Just the opposite. Tain is the reason the Coven of Light is searching for the rest of the Immortals. I don't know how to tell you this, but Tain . . . he's out of control. If you and the other Immortals don't find a way to stop him, he's going to destroy the world."

CHAPTER NINE

"Tain? Destroy the world? That's preposterous."

Christine's small fingers tightened on Kalen's forearm. His lower body responded, despite the fact that sex was clearly not on the witch's immediate agenda.

"I only wish it were preposterous," she said. Her face was flushed. "But Adrian and Amber have proof. Tain's behind the alarming spread of death magic. Haven't you been reading the newspapers? Watching the BBC? Crime is epidemic—murder, rape, demon assaults, terrorism, war in any number of countries—you name it, it's out of hand. Vampires are prowling in packs, attacking humans in their homes. Resurrectionists are setting zombies loose on the human population in record numbers. Sorcerers are getting bolder—"

Kalen dismissed her harangue with a chopping motion of his hand. "Evil is nothing new. The world has always known it."

"Not like this it hasn't!"

"That's where you're wrong. Though I suppose that's only understandable for someone who's only lived—" He sent her a questioning glance. "What—twenty-two, twenty-three years?"

"Twenty-six."

He nearly laughed. She was so incredibly young, he almost couldn't fathom it. "Twenty-six years is a mere instant in human history. You think the world is falling apart now? You should have seen the Fall of Rome or the Crusades. The Vampire Wars of the Dark Ages. The Unseelie Menace. Those were terrible days, too, spurred on by demons and death sorcerers. But those times didn't last. Eventually life magic reasserted itself."

"With the help of you and the other Immortals. Humanity couldn't have survived without you."

Kalen found her faith touching, if naive. "The Immortals helped, yes, and we certainly saved some human lives that would have been lost otherwise. But the tide would have changed regardless. Balance is the nature of things."

"This time is different. Balance will be permanently lost, if we don't act now. The world will never be the same once Tain gets through with it. It might not even exist."

Kalen sighed. Over the course of his long life, he'd seen countless zealots and believers, many of whom hadn't hesitated to lay down their lives for the sake of dogmas that were patently ridiculous. Each one had had the same desperate, fanatical expression that was currently etched an Christine's face. She truly believed Kalen's youngest brother was going to destroy the world.

But that was absurd.

"Christine," he said, keeping his voice deliberately calm. "I've lived almost three millennia. I've lost count of how many times humans have predicted the end of the world. It's never happened. And it's not going to happen now."

Her hands went to her hips, elbows sharply pointed outward. The pose made the neckline of her too-large shirt gape. His gaze flicked involuntarily to her cleavage.

She glanced down, scowled, and yanked the lacings

closed. "Could you *please* stop ogling me long enough to have a meaningful discussion?"

"Since there's no such activity going on, I believe I'm entirely within my rights to take pleasure in looking at you."

She made a gesture of frustration. "Have you heard anything I've said? Your brother is out to destroy the world!"

"No. The Immortals were created to fight death magic. Tain loved humans more than any of us. He protected your race out of love, not duty. It's beyond belief he'd harm even one of you, let alone destroy the world."

"Maybe not if he were in his right mind," Christine persisted. "But don't you see? *That's* what I've been trying to tell you. Tain's not the same person you knew. He hasn't been for a long time. Kalen, your brother is insane."

"Impossible. Immortals can't get ill—physically or mentally. We can't go insane."

"I know it's hard to believe—Adrian didn't believe it at first, either. But he knew something had happened to Tain. He disappeared right here, in the Highlands. During the Immortals' defeat of the Unseelie Host."

"I was at that battle," Kalen said with a frown. "I wasn't aware of Tain encountering any difficulty."

"Adrian and Tain were separated from the other Immortals, and from each other. Adrian found a witness who'd seen Tain leaving the battleground with a demon. He searched for centuries, but Tain had just . . . vanished." She drew a breath and Kalen couldn't keep from dropping his gaze to her chest. "Didn't you think it was odd when Adrian and Tain didn't return to Ravenscroft after the Unseelies were banished?"

His stomach knotted. Christine had no idea what his life had been like in the century after that battle. Gods willing, she never would. "I didn't think it odd because I didn't return to Ravenscroft myself."

And he was sure as hell Adrian had never bothered looking for *him*. Kalen and his oldest brother mixed about as well as oil and water. But Adrian had loved Tain. He would have searched to the ends of the earth for their youngest brother.

"Just recently, Adrian and Amber discovered what had happened to Tain. The demon who lured him off the battlefield was an Old One known to Adrian as Kehksut. Kehksut imprisoned Tain for centuries, assuming a male form to completely flay the flesh from Tain's body, then shifting into female form and healing him with sex. Three days later, Kehksut would start the torture cycle all over again. After seven hundred years of that treatment, Tain's mind just snapped. Now Tain's Kehksut's most potent weapon."

"How so?" The tale was too fantastic. What demon could hold an Immortal captive for so many centuries?

"Tain's formed an intense emotional and physical attachment to his captor. He believes Kehksut loves him. Tain's so damaged he wants to die, and the demon has promised to help him. The only way that can happen is if all life magic in the human world is destroyed. That's Tain's goal. The horrors and atrocities going on all over the world, the rise in death magic and death animations—it's all Tain's doing." She paused, her face pale and deadly serious. "You have to believe me."

He didn't want to. The tale was too horrific. But if Adrian thought Tain mad . . . no matter what Kalen's feelings about his oldest brother, the fact remained that Adrian was fanatical about protecting the human race. If Adrian believed Tain was dealing in death magic, then it was probably true, fantastic as it seemed. But even so, there was nothing Kalen could do about it. Not while still serving the sentence he'd earned seven centuries ago.

"It hardly matters what I believe," he told her.

"Of course it does! The human world needs you desperately. It's not too late—Adrian has a plan."

"Yes," he said sardonically. "Adrian would."

She gave him a piercing look. "There's no love lost between you two, is there?"

"Is it that obvious?"

"But he's your brother! You were raised together in Ravenscroft."

"Yes. And believe me, there was no place in Ravenscroft where any of us could go to escape Adrian's arrogance. He appointed himself leader of the Immortals. Handed out assignments as he saw fit and demanded our obedience. If he wanted any of us at a battle, we had to be there or face his wrath."

"And you resented that?"

Resented it? Adrian's conceit had cost Kalen his honor. His people. He turned on her. "My duty was to the line of Tyrrhenus. Before all else. Adrian didn't respect that. He thought I should limit my involvement with Uni's chosen ones, guarding them only from physical threats. He saw no merit in art, in culture, in engineering and government. He insisted I answer his calls, even if it meant neglecting my people. He was an arrogant bastard then, and I'm sure he's still one now. A man never really changes."

"You have," Christine said quietly.

Her uncanny perception rattled him. The guilt and humiliation he'd endured during the last seven centuries had changed him so profoundly he hardly recognized himself as the young, brash warrior he'd once been. He glanced sharply at Christine. Could it be that she knew of his disgrace? She'd scried into his present—maybe she'd looked into his past as well. It was a rarer skill, but one some human witches possessed.

His stomach churned, until he realized how unlikely that was. If Christine knew his past, she never would have come so far seeking his help. The revelation did nothing at all to soothe him.

"What makes you so sure I've changed?" he asked. "You didn't know me—before."

The long blue lock of hair had escaped her braid. She shoved it behind her ear before answering. "I know what you were. And I can see what you've become. The two are very far apart."

Her criticism angered him. "How I live my life is none of your business. All you need to know is that Tyrrhenus's line is extinct, and I am no longer a warrior."

She was silent for a long moment. "You cared very much for your people, didn't you?"

He shut his eyes briefly. "Not enough, obviously, or they would still be alive."

"Help the people who are still alive, Kalen. They need you."

"No."

"Then help yourself. Because if life magic's completely destroyed, it won't be only Tain who dies. You and the rest of the Immortals will die, too."

Christine thought at first Kalen hadn't heard her. He didn't move, didn't give any acknowledgement of her words. If her statement had startled him, he gave no indication.

It was an incredible assertion, she knew. Immortals were just that—Immortal. Impossible to kill. Except that magical rules often had loopholes, and Amber had told her the Immortals weren't completely indestructible. Kalen and his brothers drew their essence from living magic. Once it was completely gone, their souls would shrivel and their bodies expire.

"Tain wants to die," she said simply. "And if his death leads to the death of his brothers, he's too insane to care. Please. At least talk to Adrian about it."

"I've no desire to talk to Adrian."

"Oh, that's very mature of you." *Goddess.* She hadn't counted on landing in the middle of a three-thousand-year-old sibling spat. "Look, will you just *call* him? Where's your phone? I can reach him on Amber's cell—"

"I dislike phones."

"*Fine.* We can e-mail—"

"I dislike computers even more."

It took a moment for his words to sink in. "You mean you don't have a phone or computer?" A sudden thought occurred to her. "Or even electricity?"

"Have you seen any modern conveniences in the castle?"

"No." She hadn't. Not a single lightbulb, outlet, switch, or anything at all attached to an electrical cord. "Well, that's no problem for you, is it? Just pop on over to the mainland and—"

"I said no."

"Kalen, don't be stubborn. Your life is in as much danger as mine."

He was silent for a long moment, studying her. She searched his eyes, looking for hope. But his expression had closed completely.

"Suppose," he said at last, "I *did* help your coven." He held up one hand as she sucked in a breath of surprise. "I'm not saying that I will, only that I want to know more of this plan of Adrian's. What is my hardheaded brother plotting?"

"Adrian and the Coven of Light are assembling an army. The Immortals and as many human witches and living magic creatures as we can recruit. We'll go to battle against Tain and the Old One. Once Kehksut is destroyed, Adrian will take Tain to Ravenscroft. He thinks Tain will heal there."

"And if he doesn't?"

"Then I guess . . . he'll have to be restrained somehow."

An ugly light appeared in Kalen's eyes. "Imprisoned, you mean. For all eternity."

"I . . . I suppose so. If he's still a danger, he'd have to be."

"He'd be better off dead."

Christine swallowed. An eternity in confinement was a grim sentence, but what choice would there be? "He'd be comfortable. And well cared for."

Kalen's voice was flat. "Shackled like a dog, forever." A dangerous note crept into his voice. "*This* is Adrian's plan? *This* is the cause he wants me to fight for?"

"But what else can we do?"

"Let Tain have his way. Let him die."

Christine stared. "And allow death magic to take over the world?"

"Will it really be so different than it is now? Look around you—humanity has been bent on destroying this world for over a century. Blasting each other to bits, pouring radioactivity into the air, dumping poison into water, earth, and air. Heating up the atmosphere. Forests have been raped, animals and the weaker living magic creatures turned out of their homes. You have no idea what a natural paradise this world was three thousand years ago. Humans hardly need Tain in order to destroy it. They're doing a fine job of it all on their own."

"All that is true," Christine said. "But there's still a lot of good in the world. It may not make the newspapers, but it exists. Truth, beauty, affection . . ." Her gaze fell on the painting of the furtive lovers. "Surely you must believe that, too, or you wouldn't have collected all these depictions of human love."

"Sex," he corrected. "Human sex. I collect scenes of physical fulfillment. There's no such thing as human love. Lust, greed, insecurity—that's what brings humans together. I'm not saying sex isn't pleasurable, even magical at times, but what humans call true love is an emotion that can't endure. In the end, the lust and greed that brings lovers together drives them apart."

"Not always. Sometimes love is endless."

Their gazes met. Held. He lifted a brow. "You know this from experience? You've experienced a great love, one with no lies, no deceptions?"

Shaun. She tried to breathe through the sudden tightness in her chest.

Kalen must have read the answer in her eyes, because his answering nod was grim. "I thought not."

"Just because I haven't experienced true love doesn't mean it doesn't exist."

"Perhaps not. But consider this—I've been alive for almost three millennia and have yet to encounter a human love worthy of the many masterpieces created in its honor."

"But what about your own life? Think of that, if nothing else."

"I assure you, I shall. I have no intention of dying. Now, my love, if you'll excuse me, I have some business to attend to."

Business? What *business* could be more important than saving the world?

Before she could ask, he gestured toward the open room. "Please. Feel free to linger over any artwork that interests you."

She stood motionless for several seconds after his footsteps faded. She toyed with the idea of running after him, but really, what good would that do? He'd only refuse her again.

With a sigh, she sank down on the fur-covered, penis-legged couch. So far, her quest was a disaster. Yes, she'd found Kalen, but had she convinced him to join the Coven's cause? No. Her arguments and talk of Adrian had only angered him.

But she wasn't giving up yet. She couldn't believe all was lost. Not when Kalen held human art in such high esteem. He'd gone to great lengths to safeguard Europe's artistic heritage. Surely his soul was not so hardened as he would have her believe.

She'd seen a hint of his vulnerability last night. His soul had been reaching for something he needed desperately. Exactly what that was, she didn't know. But Christine, who could never bear to see anyone in pain, had tried her best to fill that emptiness, to the point where she'd given up all control over her magic. And she knew she would do it again, if he asked.

Who was she kidding? How could she convince Kalen to fight his brother? She had no leverage, and no defense against her own overwhelming desire for him. As well as no way to contact anyone for help.

What in the name of the Goddess was she going to do?

CHAPTER TEN

"Miss?"

The clipped syllable, barked in a harsh female tone, nearly caused Christine to jump out of her skin. She spun around. A squat, plump, singularly ugly woman stood at the top of the tower room stairs. She was garbed in a simple gray gown topped by a snowy white apron. Her enormous bustline jutted forward like the prow of a ship. A fringe of dull, wispy hair protruded from the edges of her white mobcap, framing small black eyes, a bulbous red nose, and a pointed, warty chin. The features were set in an expression of intense disapproval.

She was too short to be human, too large to be a faerie, pixie, or brownie. Coarse hair curled in tufts on the backs of the woman's hands and fingers, and again on the tops of her bare feet and toes. Christine stared for a long blank moment before hazarding a guess as to what her unexpected companion was. A halfling? Maybe, but her skin was far too gray.

"Th' master sent me." Her tone made it clear there were better things she might have been doing. Her accent was such thick Scots that Christine had to run the words through her brain twice before deciding on their meaning.

"The master? Do you mean Kalen?"

"Aye, and what other master might ye be expecting? Of course Kalen, ye eejit. He said ye'd be hungry and thirsty and wantin' to break yer fast."

At the suggestion of food, Christine's stomach growled. "Oh!" she said, covering her midriff with her palm. "I guess he was right."

The woman didn't smile. "Come along, then." She turned and waddled off down the dark stair, moving far more quickly than Christine might have supposed she could.

She hurried to catch up. "Are you the one who takes care of things here?"

"Aye," the woman said, not stopping, or even glancing back. "I'm the master's housekeeper."

"What's your name?"

"Pearl."

"Mine's Christine."

No answer.

Okay. "Where are we going?"

Pearl did glance back then. "To the kitchens. Where else might I be takin' ye to eat?"

"Where else indeed," Christine murmured. She didn't attempt further conversation as she followed Pearl down the stairs to the great hall. Keeping to the edge of the room, the housekeeper disappeared through an arched opening.

The smell of fresh-baked bread and strong coffee drew Christine after her. The odors were punctuated with bangs and squeals and a good deal of high-pitched chatter in a language she couldn't guess at. It seemed as though Kalen had a good number of servants. She hurried down another steep staircase. It gave out into a long room with a low vaulted ceiling and whitewashed walls.

Windows marched down one side of the room, looking

into a green courtyard. Candles in sconces added to the illumination. A long plank ran the length of the space, which also included a black iron stove, brick and clay ovens, and shelves stacked with cookware and utensils. It took less than a second for Christine's eyes to absorb the scene—in that same second, the chatter and laughter she'd heard on the stair ceased.

Silence fell as a tribe of small, leathery-brown creatures turned startled eyes on Christine. Male and female, they were naked except for scraps of cloth tied about their hips and breasts. Some had been kneading dough; others had been chopping vegetables or beating eggs. One worked a butter churn.

The creatures froze for three long heartbeats, their eyes wide with shock. Then, with a collective squeak, they dropped whatever utensils they held and scattered, rushing for the edges of the room. An instant later they were gone, although what magic they'd used to evaporate so quickly and completely, Christine could only guess at.

"Brownies?" she asked.

Pearl grunted. "Aye, and a few imps and sprites. Troublesome little beasties. Skivers, the lot of them." But it seemed to Christine the housekeeper's tone was laced with grudging affection.

"They work here?"

"When the mood strikes them. When it doesn't, it's the devil's own work to collect them." She turned accusing eyes on Christine. "I hope ye're happy. Now that ye've gone and scared them it'll be a great stramash luring them back afore supper."

"I'm sorry. I didn't mean to—"

"Aye, but it's done now, innit?" Waddling to the stove, she snatched up an oven mitt and pulled a cast-iron pot off the fire. "Sit yerself down. Kalen said to feed ye, so feed ye I will. Though if 'twere up to me, I'd let ye starve."

Well. There wasn't much Christine could say to that. But

she *was* hungry, so she sat on one of the worktable stools, angling her knees sideways to avoid knocking them against the low tabletop. Pearl set an enormous bowl of porridge, cream, and berries in front of her, along with a generous mug of steaming coffee.

She cupped the mug in her hands, inhaling deeply. It smelled okay, but the first sip nearly choked her. Sludge would have tasted better. It wasn't likely to be drinkable without, say, six or seven spoons of sugar and a half pint of cream. Christine didn't bother pointing that out to her surly hostess.

"It's delicious," she lied, setting the mug discreetly aside and picking up her spoon.

Pearl grumbled. Moving to a sideboard, she hoisted a fat pitcher and poured a drink of her own—a mug of ale. She took a long swig, giving a sigh of satisfaction as she licked foam from her upper lip.

"So," she said, looking Christine up and down. "You're Kalen's latest whore."

Christine nearly spewed a spoonful of porridge across the table.

"Doan' be thinking ye'll last long," the housekeeper warned. "The human besoms never do."

"Does Kalen bring women here often?" she asked casually.

"Often enough."

Christine doggedly ate another spoonful of porridge. It was fine, but she really craved something salty. Potato chips. She would have cut her right arm off for a bag of salt and vinegar potato chips.

"Pushy creatures, Kalen's women be," Pearl continued. "Though to be fair, the human ones are a fair sight more tolerable than his Sidhe bitch."

Christine looked up. "You don't like Leanna?"

Pearl let out a sharp bark of disgust. "Like her? About as well as I like poison in my well, I'd say."

At last, a point upon which Christine and the odd little housekeeper could agree.

"When that *luid* first started sniffing about the master, I told him she was trouble. But did he listen to me?" Pearl took a swig of ale. "Nay."

"You've worked for Kalen a long time, then?"

"One hundred and seventy years," she replied proudly. "Since I was a wee lass." Another swig of ale. The drink must have been potent; Pearl's hard tone was quickly softening. "Found me on the cliffs, he did, not far from here. Barely alive, I was."

"Why? What happened to you?"

"I was cast out." Her thick lips twisted. She stared into her mug for a long moment, then tilted it to her lips and drained it.

Christine quickly lifted the ale jug for a refill. "Cast out by who?"

"My own clan. The halfling side. My blood had started to tell." She grunted. "I'm mixed race, ye see. My father was a gnome, if ye can believe that."

Christine had no difficulty at all believing it. "And your mother was halfling?"

Pearl's mug hit the table with a thud. "Aye. Never knew how it came to pass. Ma died when I was born. Eight years later, it became clear what I was. The clan turned me out."

"That's horrible!"

"It's the way of things in these parts. Halflings, faeries, Sidhe—they're clannish races. Mixed blood's a thing to be rooted out. I was lucky enough my kin didn't kill me outright."

"But it wasn't your fault! You didn't choose your parents!"

Pearl refilled her mug a third time, her hand none too steady. Ale splashed over the side. "The clans need pure blood. If they kept all the ones like me, what would they be? Not halfling."

"It's still barbaric. Are the brownies here mixed race, too?"

"Nay. 'Twas humans what drove them from their home down near Glasgow. Factories and pollution got to be too much. Kalen took 'em in, every last one. He's got a heart of gold, that one. That's why he needs me." She scowled. "To protect him from *beacharn* like you."

Taking a final swig from her mug, she rose and gave Christine a pointed look. "Are ye through stuffing your face, then?"

Christine looked down at her half-eaten bowl of porridge. "Er, yes. I suppose so."

"Then come along. The master bade me put you in the Rose Room. Fair startled me, that. He must be planning to keep ye."

Christine started. "Keep me?"

"For a while," Pearl amended. "Like I said, his human whores doan' last long. Most dinna make it farther than the library. He's put a few in the smaller bedrooms on the lower level. But the Rose Room?" She shook her head grimly. "He's never put one there, not in my day, at any rate." She waddled from the room.

Christine took a last gulp of porridge and followed. No use in taking offense with Pearl's prickly demeanor. After all, she *was* half gnome. Gnomes, even though they were life magic creatures, were not renowned for their good cheer.

Pearl led Christine back up the stairs to the hallway outside Kalen's bedroom. Opening the door of the room next to his, the housekeeper stood back and scowled as Christine preceded her into the room.

She could hardly believe her eyes. There was no sign of the brownies, but it was clear they'd been hard at work. The white sheets she'd seen when she'd looked into the room earlier were gone. The shutters and windows had been thrown open to the sea air. Every square inch of the room sparkled.

It was a small chamber, sumptuously decorated in various shades of pink and rose. Miniature roses decorated the flocked wall coverings; a rich oriental carpet woven with a pattern of rose vines covered the polished wood floor. The paintings gracing the walls were Impressionist—Monet, Renoir, Degas.

A graceful bed with a pink ruffled canopy, an ornate writing desk, a gilded settee, and a marble washstand all contributed to an air of cultured beauty. A mirrored wardrobe, a smaller, more feminine version of the one in Kalen's room, stood in one corner. A copper bathing tub filled with steaming water occupied the floor in front of the hearth. Christine's gaze fell on the painting above the mantel. It was Hayez's *The Kiss*, transferred from the tower room.

"Ye must turn a good trick on the mattress," Pearl said in a snide tone. "The master ordered that painting moved."

"But—it was still in the tower room when we left just an hour ago!"

"A brownie fetched it right after," Pearl replied. "Master's orders."

He must be planning to keep ye.

Oh, Goddess, what had she gotten herself into?

Pearl gave her a sharp look. "Ye know who he is, don't ye? *What* he is?"

"Yes, I know. It's why I came here."

"Ye want something from him. Your kind always does." The housekeeper's tone was laced with disgust.

"It's not what you think," Christine protested. "It's not just for me. It's important—"

"Aye, of course. It always is. Never, to my knowledge, has a female whored for Kalen without wanting something *important*."

"You don't understand—"

"And I dinna want to. Ye'll use him, like all the rest, plain and simple. The how and the why of it hardly matters."

Lumbering to the wardrobe, Pearl wrenched the doors wide. "Now then. The master says ye're to dress in something bright for dinner. No black, no gray."

Rummaging through the closet, she pulled out several dazzling dresses in silk, satin, and lace. They looked like something from a theater production or a long-ago ballroom.

"Ye're to wear one of these," Pearl said, tossing them on the bed.

Christine touched the lace sleeve of a gown fashioned from exquisite indigo silk. "But . . . where did they come from? Whose are they?"

"I dinna ken. They were here before I came."

Christine closed her eyes. Had the dresses belonged to one of Kalen's long-ago lovers? Or several long-ago lovers? How many women had there been, anyway, over the centuries? The question didn't bear consideration.

She opened her eyes to see a stiff, wickedly curved white lace corset dangling from Pearl's stubby gray fingers. The thing looked like some kind of primitive torture device.

"You'll need this underneath."

"Oh no," Christine said. "There's no way I'm going to wear a corset." The thing would push her breasts practically up to her chin.

Pearl's expression was distinctly unsympathetic. "The master ordered it, lass. I don't suggest ye disobey. After all, whatever ye want from him will come easier if ye work a bit to please him."

The contempt in the housekeeper's voice rankled, but what could Christine say? Pearl was right—Christine *was* here to get something from Kalen. How could she explain that *something* wasn't the reason Christine had made love to him? That the thought of trading her body for Kalen's cooperation was repugnant to her? She'd made love to Kalen because . . . because it had been impossible to turn him away. Especially when she'd seen the stark need in his eyes.

Pearl flung the corset on the bed with the dresses. "Strip

and get in the bath. I'll nay be sending the brownies to heat the water again if it cools too much for yer delicate skin." She grinned, showing a mouthful of crooked teeth. "Will ye be wantin' me to scrub yer back?"

"No," Christine said quickly. "I'll manage."

"I'll return to help ye dress."

"There's no need—"

"Aye, there is. Those gowns want help. Both going on and coming off. Now, 'tis already midafternoon, so ye'd better move quickly. The master'll return at six. He expects ye in the dining room then."

"Do you happen to know where he's gone?" Christine asked, feigning interest in the dresses on the bed.

Pearl's expression contorted, the gray tinge of her skin deepening. "To his Sidhe bitch," she muttered. "Perhaps ye didna please him as well as ye thought."

"That little American *beacharn* has to pay for what she did, Kalen. No human insults me and lives."

Kalen put his arm across the back of Leanna's butter-soft leather couch, his pose deceptively relaxed as he watched her pacing. Her black stilettos clicked restlessly on the marble floor.

Somehow—he suspected magic was involved—she'd compressed her voluptuous body into a dress that was little more than a section of synthetic rubber tubing. Her curves were now all but nonexistent and she carried the odor of petroleum. It was supremely annoying—she knew he hated that costume.

Her movements lacked her usual sensual grace. Her spine was rigid, her motions jerky. She had to be experiencing more than a little stiffness in the aftermath of Christine's spell. He also knew Leanna would damn herself to hell before she admitted such a thing.

"What do you care about one small witch?" he said dispassionately. "So she managed to get lucky and knocked you flat for a few hours. So what? Forget it. It's not worth your time looking for her."

"Satan's Gate, Kalen—how can you say that!" She halted in front of the sofa and leaned over him. Her faint industrial scent filled his nostrils. "The incident's all over town. Those cursed East Enders told everyone. It's humiliating."

"But good for business, I imagine."

She shot him a nasty look. "Not funny."

He shrugged. "The talk will die down soon enough."

"Not soon enough for me. I want that American witch's head on a platter. Preferably in time for tonight's show. It's the only thing that will save my reputation. I won't kill her until afterward, of course," she added as an afterthought.

"You will do no such thing."

She waved a hand. "Oh no, Kalen. You're not going to talk me out of this. I know how squeamish you are when it comes to killing humans, but in this case my mind's made up. Where is she?" When he didn't answer, her eyes narrowed. "I know you took her. Dougal told me."

He pulled his arm from the back of the couch. "Surely you don't expect me to lead you to her."

"Yes," she said. "I do." Her lower lip nudged forward. "Once I have her back, maybe I'll forgive you for taking her."

"The spell she cast was harmless. She doesn't deserve to die."

"Damn you, Kalen. It's not for you to interfere in Sidhe matters. Where did you put her?"

"I took her home. To the States."

She sent him a baleful look. "I do not believe that for an instant."

Kalen made an impatient gesture. "Forget the witch, Leanna. She's not worth your trouble. And besides, she's under my protection now. You'll never get at her." He unfolded his large frame from the couch. "Take out your anger on something else. A zombie, maybe. Or a vampire. Something that will get you on Mac's good side."

Leanna sent him a glance that could have withered an ancient oak. "The day I care about Mac's good side will be the day Annwyn turns to mist. And anyway," she added with a venom-tinged smile, "when was the last time I saw *you* acting the part of the fucking parapolice auxiliary?"

"Point taken." Aiding local law enforcement was, to Kalen's shame, another risk he couldn't afford.

Leanna turned with a huff, striding toward a black lacquered sideboard, where a Waterford decanter and six matching glasses were set out on a silver tray. Pouring three fingers of single malt into one of the glasses, she downed the amber liquid with one smooth flick of her wrist. Glass empty, she flung it at the floor. Crystal shattered on marble, punctuated by a blast of elfshot.

"A shame to break up the set," Kalen said mildly.

"You know, you're absolutely right." She picked up a second glass and launched it after the first. The rest of the glasses followed, one by one, exploding in bursts of green fire.

"Feel better?" Kalen asked when she was done.

"A little. You are a stubborn ass, you know."

Kalen inclined his head.

Grasping the neck of the decanter, Leanna brought it to her lips and took a long draught. "I need to make the little witch scream."

"There will be other amusements," Kalen said dryly.

She met his gaze. The tip of her tongue emerged to trace a circle on the decanter's rim. Then her lips parted, engulfing the neck of the bottle completely. She tilted it, sucking gently.

Kalen watched her.

She slid the bottle from her lips and placed it on the silver tray. "Other amusements," she said, her voice hitting a husky note. "I do like the sound of that."

She slid toward him, all grace and pure, sexual motion, her earlier stiffness gone. Entwining her arms around his neck, she rubbed her body against his. "We've got the whole afternoon and evening before tonight's tour," she purred. Her tongue flicked the shell of his ear. "Plenty of time to fuck. Plenty of time for you to paint, afterward. Then after we attend the tour, we can make our baby."

Kalen didn't respond. Leanna's hips cradled his cock, pulsing with seductive rhythm. But the mention of her sex tour killed any lingering attraction. Why did Leanna want his child? He no longer believed her story about being accepted by Niniane. Was Christine right? Had Leanna drawn death runes, been prepared to spill blood? To what purpose?

She rocked her pelvis against his crotch. Instead of inflaming him, as the bold maneuver usually did, it raised only revulsion. In a flash, he saw himself as if from a distance. The scene resembled nothing so much as the first frames of a particularly disgusting human porn flick.

He thought of the masterpiece he'd created after making love to Christine. It was the first artwork he'd ever created that he hadn't wanted to immediately destroy. Human though she was, Christine possessed a muse's magic. But none of Leanna's selfishness. The joy of what he'd shared with Christine made him giddy.

Leanna's rocking movements stilled as it dawned on her his body wasn't responding. She peered up at him. "What's so fucking funny?"

Kalen realized he was smiling. "Just thinking of . . . a book I was reading this morning."

Leanna made a sound of disgust. "One of your dry, ancient tomes, no doubt, in Latin, or Greek, or some other equally horrid language. Well, whatever it was, forget it. I want you in bed."

She tugged at the laces of his shirt, baring a patch of skin just below his throat. She graced the spot with a wet, open-mouthed kiss. She slid a palm down his stomach, cupping him through his kilt.

He grabbed her wrist and stopped her. "Leanna, no. There's not going to be any child."

She reared back. "*What?*"

He studied her stunned expression dispassionately. Ten years ago, he'd thought her the most beautiful creature he'd ever seen. Now the attraction had definitely grown thin. Yes, Leanna's body was every man's fantasy, and yes, she was an extremely inventive lover. But any feeling he might have had for her had evaporated. Because now that he'd experienced Christine's lovemaking, he realized the truth about Leanna. The Sidhe had never released the full energy of her muse magic to Kalen. She'd saved that for her human lovers, the artists who gave her their souls and their lives.

"Kalen." Leanna's tone had taken on a wheedling note. He still held one of her wrists—she sank into his body as if he were using the contact to draw her closer. "You *have* to give me a child. I need the baby to claim my rightful heritage with the Sidhe."

He released her. "I'm sorry, Leanna, but I can't help you. What's more, I think it's best we end our affair completely."

Her face drained of color. "You're *dumping* me?"

"Your words, not mine. Frankly, I can't imagine you'll miss me. How many other lovers do you currently have? Five? Six?"

"Seven," she muttered. "But they're *humans*!"

"They're artists. Brilliant ones. You enjoy them."

"For a few months. A year at the most. They're too fragile to last any longer than that."

"Then it's fortunate there's always new talent to discover."

"No. Don't do this, Kalen." She reached for the hem of his kilt. The movement was seductive, graceful, but he recognized it for what it was: the desperate grasp of a desperate woman. He stood motionless as her hand skimmed up his thigh.

"You're . . . you're just frustrated your art isn't improving as it should. We can fix that. Give me your child tonight. You'll see then how good it will be."

How had he ever thought her alluring? Why had he permitted himself to care, even a tiny bit? "There will be no child, Leanna."

"But—you can't just walk away! I'm *leannan-sidhe*! No man can resist me!"

He gave her a slight, mocking bow. "I just did."

CHAPTER ELEVEN

There was hardly need to worry. Nothing would go wrong during his dinner with Christine. She had a giving soul, and she couldn't control her response to him. Now that Kalen had found her, it was imperative he keep her happy in bed. Which shouldn't pose a problem. In three thousand years, he'd acquired quite a sensual repertoire. He knew he had pleased Christine last night.

And yet, he found he wasn't completely sure of her.

He chose conservative evening dress, hoping it would put Christine at ease. A late-eighteenth-century costume of waistcoat and cravat, breeches, and boots. He tied his cravat with a critical eye and cinched his hair at the nape. Satisfied, though none too comfortable—he much preferred a kilt—he considered collecting Christine from her room next door and escorting her to dinner. He decided against it. He found himself gripped with a desire to watch her come to him.

He didn't bother with the stairs. Here in the castle, there was no need to be wary of dropping his defenses in order to gather his magic and open a portal. He willed himself di-

rectly into the dining room and settled into his seat at the
head of the table.

The brownies, guided by Pearl's capable instruction, had
done an excellent job arranging the table. A spotless white
linen cloth, Meissen porcelain, Victorian silver. His gaze
lingered on the Etruscan vase filled with wildflowers. A
branch of candles laid sparkles on the Waterford stemware.
He nodded with satisfaction. Pearl might not approve of
Christine, but she was too loyal to disobey his orders.

He picked up a spoon. Put it down again. Longed for a
glass of wine, but he wouldn't open the bottle before Christine arrived. He pulled it from the ice bucket. Chateau Va-
landraud Saint-Emilion. His best.

He examined a fork. The silver shone. Pearl must have the
brownies firmly in hand today. He pressed a finger to the tip
of one prong, contemplating its blunt point. Guided by his
skill and magic, the utensil would be a deadly missile. Not as
useful as Uni's crystal spear perhaps, but lethal just the same.
But it had been more than seven hundred years since he'd
wielded his spear, or indeed, any weapon. And now Christine
had appeared, begging him to kill again. Did she consider
him weak for refusing her plea? If she ever discovered why he
couldn't fight for humanity, she'd despise him.

He frowned. Christine's tale of Tain and Kehksut was
highly disturbing. It would certainly explain the steep rise
in death magic the past year had seen. Would death truly
defeat life? If that happened, Kalen would be forced to
abandon the last remnants of his people and leave the human world.

The door opened, a blessed distraction from his dark
thoughts. Pearl's squat form appeared in the archway. She'd
changed from her usual gray homespun into polished black
satin. He bit back a smile. His housekeeper was following
his orders to the letter, the scowl on her gnomish face
notwithstanding.

"Miss Christine Lachlan," she intoned, and Kalen stood.

Pearl moved to one side as Christine entered the room. Kalen forgot to breathe. Christine was . . . perfection. Pearl sent him a baleful look as she backed out of the room, but he barely noticed. His attention was fixed on his muse, clothed in raw indigo silk. He couldn't even remember the woman for whom he'd ordered the dress some two hundred years earlier. The seamstress must have been prescient, because the gown had clearly been meant for Christine.

Christine studied the flower arrangement. Kalen's eyes drank their fill. Her hair was gathered atop her head and twisted into a soft, sensual style—he'd told Pearl no braids or any other adornment that would take too long to undo. The blue streak at her temple was the exact color of her gown. He found the effect enchanting. A smile sprang to his lips as his gaze traveled downward.

Her bodice was low and the thrust of the corset beneath it lifted her breasts delightfully. Their soft elegance quivered behind the narrow swath of silk in between. Kalen was sure the slightest tug would reveal her dusky rose nipples. His gaze skimmed Christine's flat stomach and lingered on the gentle flare of her hips. His head felt curiously light, his phallus most unsurprisingly heavy.

"Christine. Look at me."

She raised her chin with a tenuous smile. She didn't seem to know what to do with her hands. They kept moving, first twisting together in front of her, then hanging at her sides, her fingers flexing helplessly. Unwilling to have the length of the table between them, Kalen went to her. Catching her wandering hand, he raised it to his lips and brushed a kiss across her knuckles.

He guided her to the chair directly to the right of his. He caught a whiff of her scent as she sat—sea mist and roses, spiced with her sensual awareness of his presence. Fighting a sudden, exquisitely uncomfortable arousal, he took his seat, uncorked and poured the wine.

She glanced down the table. "This is lovely."

"Thank you."

She contemplated the candelabra. "You really don't have electricity? Or even a heating system other than the fireplaces?"

"I prefer it that way."

"But . . . what about your collections? The damp will damage the paintings."

"There's no danger," Kalen assured her. "Each piece is protected with an individual spell to control temperature, humidity, and light."

"Oh. That's good."

"I protect what is mine." He sent her a meaningful look. "And you are mine now. You need never fear anything, ever again."

"Kalen . . ."

He lifted his wineglass. *"Gun cuireadh do chupa thairis . . ."*

" . . . *le slainte agus sonas,*" Christine replied. *May your cup overflow with health and happiness.*

He raised his brows. "You have some Gaelic?"

She shook her head. "Not really. Just a few phrases my grandmother taught me. She raised me after my parents died." She lowered her lashes. "She's gone now."

"She was a witch as well." It wasn't a question.

She looked at him in surprise. "How did you know?"

"Your power. It's very ancient. You'd have to be a hereditary witch to be as strong as you are."

Christine opened her mouth, but her reply was lost when a darting movement at her elbow made her jump. A brownie, delivering the first course. The childlike creature was gone an instant later, disappearing through a crack in the woodwork. Christine stared at the crevice, which was barely a finger's width wide. Her gaze reverted to the table, where a large silver soup tureen had appeared. Kalen watched her struggle to make sense of it, then give up with a wry shrug.

"Your home takes some getting used to," she said.

"Magic. It shouldn't surprise you."

"I suppose not." She frowned as he lifted the tureen's cover. "I hope they didn't go to too much trouble. I didn't think to tell you or Pearl earlier, but I'm not sure I'll be able to eat much of this dinner. I'm a vegetarian."

He dipped the ladle into the tureen. "Then you're in luck, my love. So am I."

Her mouth fell open. "No way."

"Yes." He regarded her warily. He was well aware that some humans considered vegetarianism less than manly. His diet was only one of the many inconveniences and limitations he'd been forced to deal with over the last seven hundred years. "Does it surprise you?"

"Frankly? Yes. You're a warrior."

"And all warriors exist on raw, bloody meat," he observed with some sarcasm.

She blushed. "I didn't mean that."

"Strictly speaking, Immortals don't need to eat much at all. When we do, it's mostly for pleasure." He nodded to the tureen. "Lentil soup. Do you like it?"

Her smile made him suddenly glad there was no meat on the table. "It's one of my favorites."

"Good," he murmured as he served her. "I hope the rest of the meal appeals as well. I don't know what it is—I gave Pearl free rein."

"In that case, my share is probably laced with arsenic."

Kalen chuckled.

"Your housekeeper doesn't like me."

"She's half gnome. The race is supremely unpleasant. She doesn't like anyone."

"She adores *you*."

He shifted in his seat. "She's worked for me a long time."

"Yes," Christine said softly. "She told me how you rescued her."

"She did?" He was aware of his face heating. Suddenly his cravat seemed too tight. He didn't want Christine to cast him in the role of hero. He'd ceased to deserve that title a long time ago. "I needed a housekeeper. That's all."

She shot him a knowing glance before dipping her spoon in her bowl and tasting her soup. She swallowed, then paused, her gaze passing over the table.

"Do you need something?" he asked.

"Oh no," she said with an air of embarrassment. "I just thought there might be a saltshaker somewhere."

"I can ring for some." He chuckled. "Though I'm sure Pearl will have a few choice words about it. She's inordinately proud of her cooking."

Christine grimaced and returned to her soup. "Forget I mentioned it. The soup is delicious."

He ate some of his own soup, but eventually gave up in favor of watching Christine. Her movements were graceful. He especially liked watching the way her throat flexed as she swallowed. His gaze dipped lower, caressing the upper swell of her breasts, sweetly curved above her low neckline.

"Pearl did a fine job helping you find a gown," he commented.

Christine sent a self-conscious glance at her bust, then tried to tug the upper edge of the bodice higher. The fabric was too snug; it didn't give an inch. She abandoned the attempt.

"This getup is something from my worst nightmare. How did women ever stand wearing corsets every day? I can hardly breathe."

"You look lovely."

"I'll be lucky if I don't faint. I wouldn't have worn it at all, but not one of those dresses fit without it. I can hardly wait to take it off."

"Don't worry," he said smoothly. "I intend to do that for you very soon."

Christine averted her gaze and gulped some wine, her color rising. Kalen smiled. He enjoyed making her blush. He hadn't felt this lighthearted in centuries.

"I have to talk to you about that," Christine said as she set down her glass.

"About what?"

"You know very well about what. About this . . . *thing* between us. I told you before, it's not why I came here. I shouldn't have slept with you."

"You don't mean that." He reached across the table and took her hand. Instantly, her magic skittered over his skin. She really had trouble holding anything back. She was too young, too innocent, and her magic was too entwined with her sensuality. She simply didn't know another way. After a decade with Leanna, he found it very refreshing.

A sudden unwelcome thought occurred to him. "Do you belong to another man? A husband?"

She raised horrified eyes to his. "No! *Goddess*. Do you think that I'd have . . . with you . . . if I—" She swallowed. "Believe me, I'd never have slept with you if I was with someone. I'm not into casual sex." She twisted her napkin in her lap. "Not like you are with Leanna."

Hades. He wished Christine had never seen him with the Sidhe. "Leanna means nothing to me."

Her lips twisted. "But you went to see her today, didn't you?"

"Did Pearl tell you that?" He would strangle his housekeeper.

"Yes. Did you have sex with her?" Christine closed her eyes briefly. "No, look, forget I said that. I really don't want to know."

She was jealous, he realized. His heart expanded. He caught her hand across the table and felt a fierce rush of satisfaction when he felt her magic respond to his touch. "I told her you were under my protection."

"Oh."

He squeezed her hand. "There's no need for you to worry. I told you I'd keep you safe, and I will. You have nothing to fear from Leanna." He turned over her hand and traced a circle on her palm, smiling when he heard her breath catch. "Would you like to know what else I told Leanna?"

"I'm not sure."

"I ended our . . . relationship. Such as it was."

Her eyes widened. "But—a day ago you were planning to have a child with her."

"She wanted a baby, yes. I've decided I do not. At least," he added, "not hers."

The brownies arrived then, whisking away the soup dishes and delivering a fragrant saffron risotto. Kalen noted with pleasure that Christine seemed to enjoy the dish. A salad, then a selection of fruits and cheeses followed.

"Pearl told me the brownies fled pollution in Glasgow," Christine said between bites of pear. "I'm beginning to think you enjoy collecting outcasts."

Kalen didn't want to discuss the brownies. "Not particularly. I needed workers and they were available." He trailed a light finger up her bare arm, then let his hand drift to her breast.

"Stop," she whispered, her eyes fluttering closed.

"Why? You enjoy my touch."

"That's exactly why." Her color was high and her magic warmed his fingers, but her eyes were troubled. Thinking of Tain and Kehksut, no doubt. A feeling of utter helplessness stole over him, accompanied by a deep sense of shame. She wanted him to be her champion. How he wished he was free to fill that role.

He drew back, severing their connection. "I hope the food was to your liking."

"It was wonderful. I can't remember when I've had such a delicious meal."

"You don't eat well, do you?"

She shook her head. "Not like this. I can't afford it."

"You said you paint. Do you earn your living as an artist?"

"Barely. I'm an artist of the starving variety. I'm one of those awful sidewalk hawkers."

"You've been living in Rome."

"Yes. For almost a year."

"And before that?"

"Oh, lots of places. I've been a vagabond ever since—" She cut off abruptly and picked up her wineglass. "Well, for about two years now."

"What happened two years ago?" Something bad, he was certain.

She drained the wineglass and set it back on the table, her hand unsteady. "I . . . had a run-in with a demon. It nearly cost me my life."

"What happened to you?"

For a moment he thought she would refuse to confide in him. "Please," he said. She sent him a startled glance as if she hadn't thought the word was part of his vocabulary. "I want to know everything about you."

She sighed. "I was living with a man. Shaun. In south Boston. I'd met him while I was in art school. He was a powerful witch and a wonderful musician. Right after we got together, his music career took off. He attracted a huge local following." A bitter smile touched her lips. "He used to say his success was because of me. That I was his good luck charm."

Kalen's brows raised. That assessment was likely true, but she didn't seem to realize it. Christine didn't know she was a muse.

"Anyway, Shaun's music was hot, but he wasn't making much money playing the local pub scene. He wanted to break out, record a CD with a big international label. I believed it would happen eventually, but Shaun was impatient. He didn't want to wait years to become famous. So he started experimenting with death magic. He didn't tell me, of course. He knew I would've been horrified." She gripped the stem of her wineglass so tightly Kalen was afraid it would snap. "But I should have guessed what he was up to. The signs were all there. On a fluke, he landed a huge contract. One of his songs shot to number two on the charts. Money started pouring in. If I hadn't been so blind and stupid, I would have realized what it meant."

He extracted the wineglass from her rigid fingers. "You loved him. You believed in him."

"Yes, and what good did that do me? Life seemed so wonderful—Shaun started talking about having a baby. I'd set up a circle to do a fertility spell when it happened. He added a death rune to the spell and summoned a demon. The entity had been waiting—Shaun was already his whore. He'd been trading his body for success in his career for over a year, and the demon was growing restless. He told Shaun he'd continue to help him only if Shaun threw me into the bargain." A tear trickled from her eye. "I can only sense magic by touch. I didn't realize until I kissed Shaun that it was really the demon in disguise. I fought like a madwoman to get away. The only reason I wasn't taken was that I'd set the circle on the beach. Once I ran into the ocean, I was able to raise a strong magical shield. Eventually, the demon stopped battering it. In a fit of rage, the demon killed Shaun."

It was a good thing Christine's ex-lover was dead. If he hadn't been, Kalen would have been very tempted to hunt him down and kill him, and damn the consequences. "Your magic is strong. I'm not surprised the demon wanted it."

"I saw Leanna performing the same spell during the tour . . . I saw her add the same shadow runes at the end. And she had a vial of blood. She was summoning a demon."

Could Christine be right? He didn't like to think so. "That's . . . unlikely. Leanna can be cruel, but she's Sidhe. She wouldn't deal with demons." Privately, however, he wasn't so sure. He'd look into it later. "What did you do after your boyfriend died?" he asked.

"It took me a while to . . . adjust. First I gave away all his money—I couldn't stand the thought of benefiting from death magic. Then I left Boston. I'd graduated with an art degree and I'd always wanted to travel in Europe. I thought I could really concentrate on my art and offer some of my work for sale in galleries. So I sold everything I owned and took off. I went to London, Paris, Prague, Madrid, Milan, Florence—everywhere. Ten months ago, I arrived in Rome and decided to stay. I rented a tiny apartment near Santa Maria in Trastevere. A week later, a bomb went off in the Sistine Chapel and all hell broke loose. Death creatures everywhere. Murders and rapes daily. People in a panic. Museums all over Europe started reporting thefts, vandalism. Their most precious masterpieces were being destroyed." She sent him a pointed look. "I never guessed someone like you was behind *that*. All those paintings and sculptures were being saved, not lost."

"I only wish I could have saved more."

"It wasn't long after that I hooked up with the Coven of Light. I'd been haunting an Internet café, searching for spells to counter all the death magic. I met a Coven of Light witch in a Wiccan chat room."

Kalen had no desire to pursue another discussion about Christine's coven and their mission to save the world. There was nothing he could do to help them, and the shame of that, the knowledge that he was turning his back at a time when humanity was in sore need of his skills was something he wanted desperately to forget. He signaled to the brownies. There was a rustle of small feet, a flash of movement. Dessert appeared. Shortbread, raspberries, and cream.

Christine eyed the confection. "I'm not sure I have room for this." But she took up a forkful anyway.

"Tell me," Kalen said, steering the conversation to a safer subject. "Did you succeed in placing your work in a gallery?"

Christine gave a self-deprecating laugh. "Hardly. There was only one gallery I wanted to show in. I'd seen its show-rooms in every major European city I'd visited, including a very elite one in Rome. I beat my head against the wall trying to get an interview with the director, but the man's as insubstantial as a ghost."

Kalen lowered his fork. "You don't mean deLinea?"

"You've heard of it? Oh, I guess you must have, what with your love of art."

"That love doesn't apply to the art of the last hundred years. But yes, I've heard of deLinea, and believe me, it's no loss if you didn't get your work displayed there. The gallery specializes in modern art." He snorted. "Or I should say, modern garbage."

"Modern masterpieces," Christine retorted, her blue eyes flashing. "Artists on the cutting edge. Every bit as daring as Renaissance artists were in their day."

Kalen waved a dismissive hand. "Splatters on a canvas. Paintings a child or a monkey could have done. I hate to disillusion you, but deLinea's business is nothing but a game. The gallery supplies the rich and ignorant with mediocre art at obscene prices. One rock star or actor buys a painting at a deLinea show and the next thing you know, ten second-rate paintings just like it sell for five million Euros apiece. The whole setup is a scam."

"That's not true! There've been brilliant works exhibited in deLinea. I'd have given anything to see my watercolors in one of their showrooms. They wouldn't even look at my portfolio. I was stuck selling paintings of the Colosseum to tourists."

"You won't need to do that anymore," Kalen told her. "Your home is with me now."

She wouldn't look at him. "You know that's not possible."

He didn't answer. He knew she wouldn't accept it easily, but it hardly mattered. He wasn't about to let her go. Especially if she intended to go straight from his castle into battle with an insane Immortal and an ancient demon. There was absolutely no chance he'd allow that. Not when he could save her even if death magic won out.

"Leanna's still enraged," he reminded her. "Leaving the castle is not an option."

"That's a chance I'll just have to take. I'm leaving Scotland." She gave him a pointed look. "Whether or not you come with me."

"No," he said. "You will not."

She threw her napkin on the table. "Who are you to tell me what I can and can't do?"

He regarded her steadily. "I'm looking out for your safety."

"But why? Why am I so important to you? You barely know me."

"I know enough," he said. "We fit together. I feel it every time I touch you. You can't tell me you don't feel it, too." To emphasize his words, he touched her cheek. Her magic leapt to greet him.

She shut her eyes and took a long breath. "It won't be safe even here. Not if Adrian and the other Immortals fail. When all the life magic dies, you and all the enchantments on this island will die, too."

"We won't be in the human world if that happens. I'll take you to a place no demon or death creature may enter."

Her eyes were huge. "You mean Ravenscroft?"

"No. Not Ravenscroft. Another realm." He lifted her hand to his lips and traced a line from her palm to the tip of her index finger with his tongue. She shuddered and tried to take her hand back, but he wouldn't allow it.

"Where?"

"Trust me," he whispered. He kissed each of her fingertips in turn, then suckled the fleshy mound at the base of her thumb.

"Wherever . . ." Her voice hitched up a note. "Wherever this place is, I won't go. I won't leave my world, my people. I promised the Coven of Light—"

He cut her off her words with a kiss. She tasted of wine and raspberries, sweet and delicate. He cupped the side of her head, urging her lips to a more accepting angle, absorbing the shimmering splash of her magic with his mouth and tongue.

His hand wandered over her shoulder to her back. Her body tensed, then became pliant. "Don't fight this emotion between us, Christine. Please."

"It's not right."

"Ah, but it is." His claim on her mouth turned urgent. He let her feel his desire, parting her lips and licking into her mouth. His hand massaged her shoulder blade. Deftly, he softened her resistance, which was really very little resistance at all. Her lips might be protesting, but her body . . . that was another story. Where her magic led, she followed.

His Immortal essence flowed, drawing her to him. With a sigh, she responded, melting into his embrace. He lifted her free of her chair and pulled her into his lap. The silken cloud of her skirts settled around his legs. Her rounded bottom wriggled atop his arousal. Torture, to be sure, with so many layers of clothing between them. But that was all part of a pleasure too often disdained in this crude modern age. Today's women shed their flimsy garments in less time than it took for a man to draw a single breath. Didn't they realize how much more bliss lay in a leisurely unveiling?

He swept his thumbs along the lace edging of Christine's bodice, his touch featherlight on her skin. Barely an inch's width of fabric lay between his fingers and the pink tips of her breasts, but he didn't move to claim them. Not yet. He wanted her panting, begging, yearning for him as much as he yearned for her. She was his, and before the night was out, she would admit it. To herself and to him.

He buried his face in the valley between her breasts. Her scent intoxicated him—as did her fingers entwined in his hair and the sweet way her body arched into his touch. Her magic washed over him, clear and strong. Water magic, born of the sea, where life itself began.

Could a man be reborn? His soul awakened from the dark and dismal slumber of seven centuries? He'd heard of such faith, but even after seven hundred years of penance, he hadn't believed the stain on his soul could truly be washed clean. But now, with Christine warm and alive in his arms, he began to hope.

He tugged at the neckline of her gown. One breast spilled from its meager armor of silk. He covered the soft globe with his hand, flicked its taut peak with his finger.

He swallowed Christine's throaty moan with a hot, open-mouthed kiss. She wriggled against him, shifting in his arms like a summer rain. He took advantage of the movement to lift her skirts and arranged her legs on either side of his thighs. She wore no undergarments other than her corset and chemise—the only ones he'd provided. Spreading her wide, he pressed her naked, intimate flesh against the straining bulge in his breeches. Magic sparked at the point of contact; Christine's inhale came on a sob as she ground her mound against his phallus.

"Oh, Kalen . . ."

She was beyond any protest now. Masculine triumph put a razor's edge on his anticipation. He tangled his fingers in her hair, plucking out pins and clips and letting them drop to the table, the floor. Her beautiful hair, heavy and glossy black in the candlelight, tumbled over her shoulders. Even the glistening highlight excited him; the blue tint suited her. It was the color of the sea, the source of her magic. The thought made him smile.

He bared her other breast, then drew back and let himself gaze at her, enjoying the erotic picture she created. He nuzzled her ear. "Hold tight."

Obediently, she clung to his neck. He slid his hands under her bare bottom and rose, taking her with him. He carried her slight weight a few steps beyond the vase of flowers to an empty portion of the table. He eased her onto her back atop an open expanse of white linen, her skirts billowing around her. Fisting the filmy blue drifts, he eased the fabric past her ankles, her knees. Her thighs.

He bunched the silk at her hips, feasting on the erotic sight of her slender legs, encased in white silk stockings and secured by lace garters. And above . . . a treasure beyond price, veiled only by the fragile silk of her chemise.

His phallus reacted, straining at the buttons of his breeches. He wanted to fall on her, plunge hard flesh inside her, rush headlong into her magic, her pleasure, her inspiration. But not yet.

Not yet.

Her eyelids fluttered open. "Kalen, no. Not . . . here. Pearl . . . the brownies . . ."

"All know when to stay away." His hand smoothed up her calf, silk intoxicating his fingertips. He traced a path along the upper edge of her garter, where lace met bare skin.

He brushed the sheer veneer of silk that hid her intimate curls. Her breath quickened, her gaze lost its focus. Grasping the hem of her chemise in both hands, he rubbed the wispy fabric back and forth over the sweet bud hidden in her Venus mound. He watched her face the entire time. Pure emotion played over her features.

He was unprepared for the answering rush of feeling in his heart. Was this what humans called love? The sentiment depicted in the art he'd secreted in his tower room? Desire, delight, and need shone on Christine face. She was wonderfully responsive; she hid nothing from him. Each time his fingers touched her bare skin, she trembled. Each time he bent to place a kiss somewhere on her body, her magic shimmered like sunlight on water.

He needed to taste her. He bent and kissed her mouth deeply. Her flavor caressed his tongue, headier than any wine. His control fracturing, he slipped his hand under her chemise and allowed himself one quick caress of her feminine folds. She was slick and ready for him; her body arched sharply into his touch. Her fingers dug into his shoulders. Her throaty moan quickened his blood.

Drawing back, he realized his breathing was as erratic as hers. His heart was pounding, his palms were damp. He hadn't felt this way in centuries—no, he'd *never* felt this way. Not with any female, human or magical. Not in three millennia of lovemaking.

His erection strained painfully for freedom, and his stones ached badly. He eased Christine's legs open. She made some small move to resist, but he stopped her with a murmur and a kiss on the inside of her thigh.

She was magnificent, lying there, her skirts thrown up and her bodice crumpled at her waist. The corset thrust her breasts into his hands. She lay quiet as he touched her, her blue eyes huge, watching him.

He wanted her, always. The fact that he did not deserve her tried to invade his thoughts. He shoved it away.

"You're mine," he said softly. "Forever."

She didn't answer. But neither did she protest. The flutter of pulse at her neck and the way her blue eyes darkened told him she didn't deny his claim. She searched his gaze, and seemed to find something good there, something true, because she reached up and brushed a stay curl from his eyes.

"Kalen," she whispered. "Let me love you."

CHAPTER TWELVE

Christine gazed up into Kalen's beautiful eyes. They were dark with need—not just sexual need, but an emptiness that seemed to reach into a deep, painful part of his soul. She was powerless to turn away from such longing. Slowly, surely, it drew her to an emotional precipice higher than any physical cliff. She held her breath, waiting for the ground to give way.

And yet, she was curiously unafraid.

It must be the magic. Hers and Kalen's entwining, pulsing, flowing so freely between them. It was as if she'd found the mirror of her soul, the reflection that would make her whole.

His hands were hot on her skin, exerting a slight pressure on the inside of her thighs. Not a rough touch, but a force just enough to let her know that she couldn't hide. As if she could've done that! She didn't know how to hide from him, couldn't begin to guess. For Christine, lovemaking was a complete giving. There was no halfway, no secret places for her soul.

The heat between them grew. His eyes told her his

arousal was barely leashed. His hunger excited her. Her fingers curled, her nails sinking into his forearms. His eyes darkened.

Her inner muscles tightened unbearably. He moved closer, widening his stance, his legs relieving his hands of their task of keeping her thighs spread. His palms came to rest on the table on either side of her head. His powerful body blocked her vision. His scent wrapped around her. She was more turned on than she'd ever been in her life—more, even, than she'd been last night in Kalen's bed. Then, he'd taken her fiercely, and there had been little time to explore this deep agony of wanting. Tonight . . . tonight he was making her burn.

"Please . . ."

"Please what, Christine?"

"Please," she whispered. "Love me."

Satisfaction, hope, blessing . . . she saw all three emotions flicker through Kalen's eyes. Something darker rode with them—shame, perhaps, or regret. She didn't have time to wonder about it; his hands were on her. The next instant brought the sound of tearing silk. Her dress fell away. Her corset came next, his fingers delving behind the small of her back, finding and ripping the laces with one jerk of his wrists. She drew a sharp breath as the garment loosened, air filling her lungs in a heady rush.

He gathered her in his arms, lifting her as he swept her clothing from the table. Deftly slid her silk chemise over her head. When he eased her back again to the table, she was clad only in her stockings and shoes, while he was still fully dressed. The vulnerability of her position contracted a spasm of lust in her belly. She heard her own voice, begging him to hurry.

He gave a swift shake of his head and left her briefly, moving to the end of the table where the remnants of their dinner lay. When he returned, the wine bottle was in his hand. He tipped it, sending a thin red stream trickling onto her breast.

The liquid was cool on her heated skin; she sucked air. The drops struck her nipple and rolled between her breasts. A flick of Kalen's wrist sent a second spray over her skin. Wine cascaded to her belly, pooled in her navel. The wine's water magic sent a rush of pure, sensual pleasure through her body.

"*Goddess,*" she breathed.

"No goddess could be as lovely as you." He touched his tongue to her navel. "*Slainte,*" he murmured, lapping up the spilled wine.

Her belly clenched, her hands filled with fistfuls of tablecloth. A short, breathless laugh puffed from her lips. "That tickles."

"Ah. What of this?" His tongue drifted downward, licking her lower belly. He nuzzled her curls, parted her with his fingers until she felt the heat of his breath on her exposed clitoris. She gasped when she felt his tongue there.

"And this?" He draped her legs over his shoulders and reached again for the wine bottle. Her hips jerked as the cool wine splashed on her intimate folds. "Does this tickle?"

He bent his head and lapped at the wine he'd just poured. She cried out as he suckled her. Her legs quivered on his shoulders. She felt him so deeply she thought she would go mad with the sensation. He shocked her with hot, wet licks on the insides of her thighs. When his tongue entered her body, she couldn't hold back. A low moan vibrated in her throat and her hips lifted, silently pleading.

His hands slipped beneath her bottom and pulled her to the very edge of the table. She startled, grabbing at his shoulders.

"I'll fall!"

"I would never let you fall. Trust me, Christine."

Trust him. Did she dare? And yet . . . it felt as though the decision had been taken out of her hands. She *did* trust him. It was her magic, leading where her mind wouldn't have gone on its own. Her magic, entangling with the essence of Kalen's Immortal soul.

Her legs relaxed on his shoulders. His hands traveled to her breasts, toying with her nipples. The sensation was like a sweet fire burning to her core. His head dipped, his mouth and tongue once again on her slick, heated flesh. He entered her with his tongue and her inner muscles clenched, wanting more.

He slid one finger, then two, into her body. She moaned, head tossing from side to side, her hands urgent and seeking. Her fingers skimmed over his neck, tangled in his hair. She wanted to draw him up, to cover her. To plunge inside.

He followed her urging. She nearly sobbed in relief as he stood and unfastened his breeches. His erection, huge and beautiful, swung free. Fitting himself between her legs, he let her feel the fullness of his broad head against her soft folds.

"Yes." She tilted her hips in encouragement. With a growl, he executed a deep, satisfying stroke. Her climax began even before he withdrew. Her body clenched. Light converged on a single point, all awareness rushing to the place where their bodies were joined. She gave a sharp, desperate cry of release, lifting her hips as he filled her again and again. She shuddered and wrapped her legs around his waist, holding him tightly as the last fireworks exploded.

"Kalen . . . it feels . . . it feels like magic."

"It is magic," he whispered in reply. "*Our* magic."

And it was. Their powers, melded. Spread over them like a glittering blanket of stars. It felt like birth, like art, like the soaring sensation Christine experienced each time she took up a brush or a pencil and created *something* from *nothing*.

With a wrenching shudder, her body went limp as the magic drained away. It was hard to catch her breath. Or move. Kalen was still inside her, but she was spent, claimed, utterly used up. Gradually, her heartbeat slowed. When it did, she opened her eyes.

His smile was one of pure masculine pride. And mischief. Locking his gaze with hers, he moved again, inside her.

She wouldn't have believed it possible, but the movement awakened her sated body. Desire blossomed anew. *Goddess.* Her eyes fluttered closed as Kalen renewed his rhythm, pushing her, claiming her, devastating her.

"Come for me," he whispered. "One more time."

She gasped as he abruptly drove deep. She felt his seed spurt, felt his large body shudder. Her inner muscles spasmed. A hot, deep orgasm spread like lava through her veins.

Dimly, she felt him gather her in his arms. He cradled her body against his chest as he carried her up the stairs and down the hall leading to his bedroom.

He laid her down on his bed and pulled her into his arms.

Leanna returned to the circle after the show, alone.

The sex energy raised by the joining of Sidhe and human earlier in the night still vibrated in the standing stones. Leanna herself had enjoyed two particularly adventurous young men, art students on holiday from the university in Edinburgh. Intent on sating her anger over Kalen's rejection, she'd probably drained their souls a little more than she should have. They'd barely had the strength to climb back into Dougal's cart.

Now, standing alone on the stage, she called her power and pressed the tip of her iron blade into the fleshy base of her palm. Blood seeped from the wound and dripped onto the plank stage, hissing. Kalen might believe he had the power to refuse his role in her plan, but Leanna had an ally greater than he knew. Culsu would not fail her.

The top of Leanna's skull felt as though it had lifted into the air. She closed her eyes, waiting for the dizziness to stop. She couldn't go on spilling fresh blood—not if she wanted to remain conscious. Her fingers trembled as she unstoppered the precious crystal vial.

She tipped the vial. The death rune and the perverted Ouroborous formed. She spoke Culsu's name; the demon appeared a scant second later in a puff of oily smoke and brimstone.

Culsu looked around, frowning. "You are alone. Where is Kalen?"

"There's a problem," Leanna said. "He's been lured from my bed. By a human witch."

Culsu inspected her long, red fingernails. "And your Sidhe power is no match for that of a mere human?"

Leanna's face heated. "The witch's magic is less than nothing. But Kalen is protecting her. You know how powerful he is. But not as powerful as you are. You can fix this. I want the witch dead."

The demon's lips curved. "For death, I require payment in advance."

"As you wish."

"Strip."

Leanna's fingers were clumsy as she obeyed, unhooking her corset and stepping out of her thong. Her shoes and stockings followed.

"On your knees."

Instantly, Leanna obeyed.

Culsu's velvet dress disappeared. Naked, she sauntered forward. She stopped when her sex was a scant inch from Leanna's lips.

"Please me well, whore, and I will give you what you crave."

CHAPTER THIRTEEN

Christine slept, sprawled amid satin and silk.

Kalen did not.

He stood with his back to the window, watching her. She lay on her side, the inky shadow of her lashes a whispered silhouette on her cheeks. Her skin was rosy and damp from his lovemaking. Her magnificent hair lay tousled and tangled on his pillow. She'd been with him nearly a week now—plenty of time for Kalen to become used to her. But he had not. Each time he looked at Christine, it was as if he were seeing her for the first time.

She was so heartbreakingly young. So pure and untainted by death magic. And when he gazed upon her, he began to remember what it had felt like to be young. It was a sweet, aching sensation in his chest, and he knew he would do whatever was necessary to keep it.

The silken bedsheet rode low on her hips, leaving her upper body exposed. The slope of one breast and the pink of one nipple were bared to his view.

The scene seeped into his consciousness, distilled into its essence. Formed in his mind as a new creation. He saw every brushstroke, every drop of color. Every nuance, every tone, every wish. Pure emotion, rendered in light, spilled on canvas.

It was all there, mere child's play, for the taking.

He worked quickly, mixing colors with urgent intensity. He laid the lines in pencil, then rendered the background in a soft eddy of blue and violet. Christine's skin was soft peach and pink, with dusky rose nipples. Her hair was glossy dark, with a touch of pure cerulean at her left temple. The heavy locks cascaded in an elegant veil over her shoulders.

The oils dried quickly, aided by his magic. The work of days or weeks done in a mere hour. When it was done, he stepped back and viewed his creation. The air expelled slowly from his lungs.

Titian himself could not have done better.

The joy began as a small thing, a drop of forgotten gladness on his soul. As he gazed at the painting, inspecting it for flaws, finding none, his happiness expanded, flowing up and outward until his soul was bursting with it.

He walked softly to the bed and looked down at her. This was Christine's doing . . . if he was to be reborn, after being less than a man for so long, it was by her magic. Her generosity. Her love. He could not lose that. He would not. His heart clenched. She looked so vulnerable. So human. Her mortality was a fragile thing. It would be so until he brought her to Annwyn and claimed the boon Lir and Niniane, the King and Queen of the Otherworld, had promised him all those centuries ago.

Then Christine, like Kalen, would live forever.

Christine woke slowly, keeping her eyes tightly closed even though she knew she was no longer asleep. The mattress was so soft, like a cloud. The pleasant ache between her legs reminded her of Kalen and his lovemaking. It felt so good to give him everything, and if the small, strident voice in the back of her mind told her to beware, it was easy enough to ignore when Kalen smiled at her. She'd lost count of the days she'd spent in his arms, all but drowning in his sensuality. He kissed her awake every morning, moving atop her and entering her with the sunrise. The days had been filled with more lovemaking, interspersed with discussions of Kalen's art collection and meals serviced by Pearl's incredible cooking. The nights . . . Christine blushed. Apparently, three thousand years of lovemaking taught a man quite a lot about how to please a woman.

Even after having loved him so many times, she wanted to make love to him again. And never let him go.

Slowly, on that realization, her smile faded. Was she falling in love with him? That hadn't been part of the plan. This couldn't go on—what was she doing wasting time in Kalen's bed when she was supposed to be gaining his cooperation in the battle against Tain and Kehksut? Even if there wasn't a war to fight, a life with Kalen was out of the question. She was human and would age. He was Immortal and would not.

She cracked one eyelid, squinting against the sun streaming through the open window. Another clear dawn, in a country currently plagued with rain. Maybe it was a good omen. More likely, it was due to Kalen's magic.

A shaft of sunlight painted a bright path across the bed—a bed she had all to herself. Disappointment tightened her throat. Then she looked across the room and found that she wasn't alone after all. Kalen lounged in a deep armchair, a satin dressing robe carelessly thrown over his shoulders, the sash left untied. She could see his erection from where she lay.

"Good morning," he said, standing.

Christine blushed and pulled the sheet, which she'd kicked completely off, up over her breasts. *He* might be ready, but now that he stood before her completely aroused, suddenly she wasn't sure if *she* was.

"Good morning." She swung her legs over the side of the mattress and slid off the bed, winding the sheet around her body as she stood. There was a vague odor of turpentine in the air. Looking past Kalen, she saw an old-fashioned wooden easel. He said nothing as she approached it, circling so she could view the large canvas propped on it.

When she saw the painting, she gasped.

It was a masterpiece of light and shadow, brilliant colors glowing as if illuminated from within. It had all the sweetness of Raphael, all the drama of Caravaggio, all the sensuality of Titian. And *she* was the subject. Nude, heartbreakingly beautiful, she cast a spell of pure wanton sexuality. Christine was stunned. She hardly recognized herself. Was *this* how Kalen saw her?

"I . . . I didn't know you painted."

A faint red stain appeared high on Kalen's cheekbones. "Yes."

"You're . . . incredible. Why didn't you tell me?"

He busied himself with his brushes and pots. Christine regarded him curiously. It was the first time she'd ever seen him at a loss for words.

"Hardly a true artist," he said finally. "I'm an Immortal. I wasn't created for this."

"But you've done it just the same."

He picked up the canvas and tilted it into the light. "Do you really think it's good?"

She gave a disbelieving laugh. "Are you kidding? If I didn't know better, I'd think you'd snatched it from the Louvre or the Uffizzi."

She thought his hands trembled as he placed it back on the easel. "Perhaps. But . . . it's you, Christine."

She blushed. "I can see that."

"I wasn't talking about the subject. I mean . . . my inspiration. It's you."

"I . . . um . . . thank you."

For a moment, she thought he'd say more, but in the end, he just shook his head, as if clearing it, and opened his arms to her. She went to him at once.

His touch wasn't demanding. His arms around her were tender. For the first time, their joined magic wasn't incendiary. It was just . . . comforting. Christine buried her face in the lapel of his robe. Tears gathered behind her eyelids.

After all he'd done to her body—touching and licking and suckling, driving her to the edge of reason—it was this simple embrace that undid her. A chasm of need opened up inside her, a void left by Shaun's betrayal. She'd loved Shaun, and he'd tried to sell her to a demon. But Kalen . . . she sensed he'd never betray her.

His lips brushed her hair. With a deep sigh, she wrapped her arms around his waist. This couldn't last. Soon, she would have to broach the subject of Tain again. But not just yet.

He kissed her forehead and drew back to smile down at her. "You were wonderful last night."

"So were you."

She laid her cheek against his broad chest, atop the satin smoothness of his dressing gown. He smelled of salt and earth, and slightly of sweat. His erection prodded her stomach, but she sensed no urgency from him. No tightening of his arms, no searing kisses. Only peace, wrapping her in a cocoon of well-being. A part of her wished she could stay in his arms forever, just holding him and being held. But thoughts of her mission pricked her conscience. She had no right to feel such peace when the world was going to hell.

Somehow, though, it seemed obscene to interrupt this interlude with talk of Tain and Kehksut. She looked up to find Kalen's steady gaze upon her. "Could . . . I ask a favor?"

His expression turned wary. "If this has anything to do with Adrian—"

"No," she said quickly. "Not that. Not now. It's something a lot simpler. Could I borrow some of your art materials? Paper and charcoal? And maybe . . . do you have any watercolors?"

"Of course. You may use my studio."

"You have a studio?"

A smile tugged at his lips. "Yes, and it's yours to use whenever you want. In fact, I'm glad you asked—you can work there while I'm gone. Have Pearl show you where it is."

Gone? "You're leaving again?"

"I have business in Edinburgh. It won't take long. And much as I'd like to return you to that bed . . ." His eyes drifted to the piece of furniture in question. "I haven't the time." His arms fell away. Reluctantly, she stepped back.

Striding to his wardrobe, he dressed in a modern pair of crisply pressed charcoal trousers. A white dress shirt, shot through with gray pinstripes, came next. He pulled on socks and stepped into polished dress shoes.

Christine moved to the window. Sunlight streamed from the sky, and to the west the full moon was sinking toward the horizon. The North Sea was an intense blue studded with whitecaps. Death and destruction seemed very far away. There was a flash of pink and green on the water. Some kind of fish? She pressed her forehead against the windowpane, trying to catch a better view.

"Oh my *gods*!" she exclaimed. "A mermaid! No . . . more than one. And a merman, too."

Kalen joined her at the window, knotting a red silk tie. "Yes. There's quite a large school of them in these waters."

Another of the enchanting creatures surfaced. "I thought they preferred warmer seas."

Kalen slanted her a glance. "So do humans."

It took a moment for her to grasp his meaning. "Humans drove them from their home?"

He stepped away. "Merfolk are peaceful. Humans are not."

A deep sense of shame suffused her. Kalen was right—humans were as agile at perpetuating evil as death creatures were. She'd been laying the blame for the world's problems completely at Tain's door, but that was hardly fair. The human race shared the guilt for its troubles.

Not all humans were greedy and violent. Many followed the Light and practiced only life magic. But not enough, it seemed. Suddenly, she felt trapped in Kalen's castle. The sea was so close . . . she needed to touch it, renew herself with its magic. Think of what to do next. How to convince Kalen to join the fight.

"I need to get out," she told Kalen abruptly. "Now."

He turned back to her, frowning.

"To the cliffs," she clarified, turning back to peer out the window. She watched the merfolk frolicking, the green scales on their tails flashing like emeralds on the surf. "Or, even better, to a beach or dock, if you have one. Do you think the merfolk would talk to me, even though I'm human?"

"I'm sure they would, but the only beach on the island is treacherous. And I don't have time to take you now."

"I'll be careful."

The wardrobe door opened and closed. "Put it out of your mind. I'll be back this afternoon. I'll take you down to the water then."

His dismissive tone rankled. "So I'm just shut inside? Like a prisoner?"

His voice blistered with exasperation. "There are courtyards. You can walk in any one of them. Your safety is important to me."

She turned around. "I'm tired of hearing about my—" The words evaporated in her throat the instant she caught sight of Kalen, completely dressed. For a moment all she could do was stare. She'd never seen him in modern business clothes, and he looked . . . delicious.

The suit jacket encasing his powerful torso and broad shoulders must have been tailor-made; it fit him to perfection. The crisp collar of his white shirt contrasted sharply with his olive skin—there was a hint of gold cuff links at his wrists. His necktie's knot was a perfect Windsor and the hem of his smartly pressed trousers grazed his polished shoes. He held a slim briefcase. Only his long hair, brushed back but curling at his shoulders, looked familiar.

He exuded power . . . and money. More money than Christine could fathom, certainly more than she felt comfortable with. This was the man who had bought up the artistic heritage of Western civilization. He had to be a billionaire. Her head felt light. Next to that what was she? Nothing.

"Your business in Edinburgh," she said weakly. "What is it? What is it you do for a living?" She hadn't thought about it before, but it had to be something extremely lucrative.

He gave a self-deprecating smile. "I'm an art dealer."

She nodded. "That makes sense. What do you sell antiquities? The Renaissance and baroque pieces you don't want to keep?"

"No." His eyes sparkled with sudden amusement. "Actually, I buy and sell modern art."

If he'd said he mucked out stables, she couldn't have been more stunned. "*Modern* art? But you hate modern art! You called it modern garbage."

His shoulders lifted in a smooth shrug. "I won't have it in my home, no. But if some human whose ignorance is surpassed only by his wealth wants to throw millions at a painting that looks like a dog threw up on the carpet, who am I to deny him the pleasure?"

Christine felt a spurt of pure anger. "Just because you don't understand modern art doesn't mean it's garbage. Abstractions and transformations aren't child's play. Sometimes the simplest compositions are the hardest to create."

"A rationalization for the modern artist's lack of classical training," he scoffed.

"Picasso was classically trained. It was only after he'd rejected his training that he created his most magnificent masterpieces. Not one of which," she added hotly, "*you* saw fit to steal!"

Kalen chuckled and tapped her on the nose. "You're very sexy when you're angry, do you know that?"

She swatted his hand away. "Don't you dare patronize me."

He stepped back, still fighting a smile. "My apologies."

She eyed him. "So you deal in modern art. Do you have a gallery in Edinburgh?"

"Yes. It's my newest."

"But not the only one?"

"No. There are several others. In London, Paris, Prague, Madrid, Florence, and, of course, Rome. But then, I believe you've been to that one."

Christine's throat went suddenly dry. "You mean . . . deLinea?"

"Yes."

"You're *il direttore*," Christine breathed.

Kalen glanced at the Rolex on his wrist. "Yes. We'll talk about it later, if you'd like. Right now, I'm very late."

He inclined his head. For three long seconds, he stood motionless, head bowed. Then a door in space winked open.

He stepped through it and was gone.

CHAPTER FOURTEEN

Christine gaped. A moment before, Kalen had been standing in front of her, as handsome and frustrating as ever. The next instant he'd just been . . . gone. She stumbled to the closest chair and sat down heavily. It was one thing—a very nauseating thing—to experience zapping in and out of space herself. It was something else again—frightening and a bit like a slap in the face—to watch it happen.

Goddess. Kalen was *il direttore*. The man who single-handedly made or destroyed struggling artists. A year ago, she'd have given her right arm to grovel at his feet.

And now she knew he hated the art he sold for six and seven figures. The irony was deep enough to wade in.

Unsettled, she crossed the room to stand before Kalen's easel. He was an artist himself, a master. His painting showed not only technical excellence, but an incredible depth of emotion. There was truly something otherworldly about his style. By Kalen's talent, she'd been transformed from unexceptional human witch to shimmering, sensual goddess.

As an art student, she'd sketched plenty of nude models,

but she'd never been one herself. She wasn't comfortable baring her own body—she was too small up top, too round in the behind. And yet . . . the woman looking back at her from the canvas didn't seem inadequate at all. The passion in Kalen's brushstrokes made her seem . . . beautiful. Sensuous. The magic they'd created together shimmered in the image like a precious living thing.

There was a folio lying on the floor. Bemused, she picked it up and flipped through the loose pages. Each drawing she discovered was of her. Not all were nudes. One showed her sitting at Kalen's long dinner table, smiling. Another showed her half turned, her hair partially veiling her nude back. The Celtic knot tattoo on her right shoulder was intricately detailed and completely accurate. Kalen had certainly been paying attention! She turned the pages, one by one. More studies, all of her. He must have started this folio the day she'd arrived.

Where was his older work? She was sure she hadn't seen any displayed in the castle. Curious, she hunted around the room, opening desk and dresser drawers, peeking in his wardrobe, but found nothing. His paintings must be in his studio. Well, he'd invited her to use his work space; she'd just have to wheedle its location from his grumpy housekeeper. She was itching to paint—it had been over a week since she'd held a paintbrush and she missed it terribly. A smile touched her lips. Maybe she'd paint a nude of Kalen.

Back in the Rose Room, she hunted through the wardrobe. She managed to locate a plain white blouse and some comfortable shoes and stockings, but the long, frothy skirts were impossible. Returning to Kalen's room, she found an old, soft pair of breeches. The knee buckles fell to her ankles—good enough. The waistband was ridiculously large, of course, but she tamed it with a belt.

It was easy enough to find Pearl. The housekeeper was in the kitchen courtyard shouting orders to a crew of brownies. Apparently, it was laundry day. Two huge cauldrons were set over a blazing fire. Brownies perched on ladders, lifting and dropping clothing into the steaming water with wooden sticks.

"Off the west courtyard," Pearl snapped in response to Christine's question about the studio. Back into the kitchen, Christine hunted through the cupboards for something salty, but came up empty-handed. Pearl didn't seem to believe in salt. She ate a breakfast of crumpets, strawberries, and cream and washed it down with fresh milk. For the first time, she wondered where Kalen got his supplies. There was no food production on the island that she could see—did he simply beam his groceries over? Or did they travel in by other means, either magical or mundane?

The west courtyard was extensive, profusely green and sheltered by ivy-covered walls. The weather was warm, sunny, and extremely un-Scottish. She advanced farther into the oasis. The central tower rose behind her, with the wall of a lower wing on her left. The castle's perimeter wall enclosed the remaining two sides of the court. A profusion of flowering bushes were edged with daintier annuals and perennials. Here and there, a tree spread lacy green branches. Songbirds darted back and forth, their songs mingling with the gurgle of a hidden fountain.

The effect was charming. Further exploration revealed a door and several windows giving out onto the garden from the low building that intersected the main tower. The door was unlocked; she found Kalen's studio beyond it. The room was spacious, with whitewashed walls, a long worktable, and deep cabinets. These last were filled with art materials— everything from canvases and stiff papers to paints, pots, brushes, and palettes.

There was little, however, in the way of finished work— or even work in progress. Three easels were empty. A stack of mediocre landscapes and still life compositions lay discarded in a corner. Not Kalen's paintings, to be sure. She wondered whose they were and why he kept them.

She located a set of watercolors and the rest of the supplies she needed. There was no sink or other sign of running water, so she carried everything to the courtyard fountain. It was a beautiful sculptural piece, with water flowing from the mouth of a curling stone sea serpent.

She dipped her hand in the water, felt its magic move up her arm. It wasn't the sea, but it made her feel immeasurably calmer. There was a bench nearby, but she preferred sitting on the ground. Filling a ceramic pot with water, she spread her paints. Her brush dipped into water and blended color in a tin tray. She bent her head to her work, absorbed, as time passed unnoticed around her.

Some time later, she put down her brush. Judging from the angle of the sun, it was already past midafternoon. Her stomach was rumbling. She rose, gathering her supplies, collecting them on the bench. Then she paused, frowning.

A whisper of music hung in the air. She hadn't heard it while she'd been sitting so close to the fountain. The sound was faint, but definitely real. And very surprising, because it was Manannán. Her favorite.

The sweet, haunting strain faded. She shook her head. Had she imagined it? But no, there it came again, smooth as a glassy sea, but with a hint of wildness flowing in subtle currents beneath the surface. Keyboard and Celtic harp, the heart-piercing note of a bagpipe and the screaming voice of an electric guitar, all underscored with the natural sounds of surf pounding the shore. Mixed and transformed by synthesizer into a thoroughly original sound.

Exhilarating. Magnificent. *Modern*. The kind of music Kalen probably hated. It pulled her like a tide. Who could be listening to Manannán? Not Pearl or the brownies, she was sure.

Her steps led her to the corner of the garden, where two sides of the castle's outer wall met. The music flowed louder here, beckoning. The lilting strain led her around a thick clump of rhododendrons to a doorway behind. Not a normal door, but a panel of false stone set in the wall. If it hadn't been slightly open, she never would have known it was there.

She grabbed the edge and pulled. The panel swung noiselessly toward her. The music amplified. She peeked inside.

A narrow staircase led steeply downward, into the stygian gloom from which the melody flowed. A musty odor wafted on a cool updraft. Common sense told her to turn around. Walk away as fast as she could. She had no idea who—or what—was down there. But this was Kalen's home—no one entered without his permission. And surely Kalen would have warned her of any danger before he left.

Music surged toward her like water spray, the composition approaching its crescendo. The piece was one of her favorites. She ducked through the doorway and descended a step in its direction. Overwhelming curiosity sucked her down a second step, then a third. After that, she didn't kid herself; she was committed to discovering the source. She moved slowly, hands on the walls on either side of her, giving her eyes a chance to adjust to the dark.

Twenty-seven steps down; then the path turned and continued along a narrow hallway, toward an unmistakable slice of light bathing the floor some distance away. When she reached it, she found both music and light emanated from a crack beneath a closed door. A *steel* door. She ran her fingers over the cool, seamless metal, frowning. It was the first modern thing she'd seen since arriving in Kalen's castle.

No knob or lever was immediately apparent. Her fingers skated along the door's edge, searching for some kind of entry mechanism. She found it when a small square of metal yielded to her touch with a soft *snick*.

A bright line of light appeared at the door's edge. *Electric* light. Heart pounding, she eased the door open, blinking rapidly against the glare. She'd just take a quick look, then move away if the room's occupant looked dangerous.

She pushed the door open another inch. Then another.

Then she shoved it the whole way open and stared.

The room appeared to be deserted. It was a large space with smooth painted walls and wall-to-wall low-pile carpet. A gleaming black teakwood desk and side table ensemble, complete with matching leather swivel chair, stood facing the door. The desk's side table held a computer with an enormous flat-screen monitor and printer by its side. Piles of papers and neatly stacked CD cases were arranged on a wide blotter. Manila files stood upright in a sleek file holder. There was a phone, a pen holder, a stapler—even a tape dispenser.

A matching table with two chairs stood to one side; behind it, along one wall, were banks of black lateral files and shelving. The opposite wall was punctuated by closed sliding doors. The lights overhead were fluorescent rectangles, set in a grid of acoustical tile. Manannán blared from recessed speakers.

While the front of the room was pathologically neat, the extreme rear was a mess. Electronic equipment littered three battered cafeteria tables. Computers, scanners, printers, monitors were split open, their guts spilling like metallic intestines.

Well. This hidden office had to be Kalen's. Obviously, he *did* have electricity. Why had he been so evasive about it? To keep her from calling Amber? Most likely. Well, she could call now. Praying Amber was within reach of her cell, Christine started toward the phone.

"Bloody, bloody *hell!*"

She froze.

"No. No way. Take that, you sodding little bugger."

She peered in the direction of the voice. In the far corner of the room, half hidden behind a tall metal utility cabinet, a teenager sat at a computer monitor. She eased forward to get a better look.

His back was turned. Spiky blond hair protruded from the blue bandana tied around his head. He wore a baggy sea-green T-shirt and faded, ripped jeans. His heavy black boots were propped on the bottom rung of a swivel stool that was much too short for his lanky frame. His knees were bent at a ridiculous angle.

Figures and scenes flitted across his monitor. Rows and columns of incomprehensible symbols were aligned on one side of the screen. A headset with a microphone attachment protruded from his left ear, into which he directed a steady stream of conversation. After his initial outburst, his voice dropped. With the music so loud, Christine couldn't make out anything.

Cautiously, she crept closer. He kept his eyes trained on the screen as his fingers clicked madly on mouse and keypad. The screen responded with bursts of light. It looked like some kind of game. He fired an errant shot, slapped his palm on the table, and cursed.

She chanced another step and stumbled. He didn't turn. Looking down, she saw she'd nearly fallen over a messy heap consisting of a leather jacket, guitar, and backpack. That's when she realized the gamer was the kid from King's Cross Station. Mac. The one who'd shown her a glimpse of disturbing power, who'd been listening to Manannán, and who'd told her where to look for Kalen's castle. But he'd never said he *knew* Kalen.

Who was he? Or better yet, *what* was he? And why was he playing computer games in Kalen's basement?

There was another blast on the screen, brighter and bigger than the rest.

"Shit." Mac slapped the desk again; the table and computer shuddered. He returned to the keyboard and jabbed a frantic series of keys, all the while muttering a stream of rapid speech into his headset.

"Aw, man, throw a Fire spell, not that Arcane bullshit. It's a Dark Demon, not your bloody grandmother."

Christine blinked.

"Damn it, just wait until I . . . gods *damn* it. There's a pack of Brain Eaters! Don't rush them, they'll see the rest of us. . . ."

The explosions on the screen intensified. Mac leaned closer, his fingers working furiously on keyboard and mouse. "Okay, go for it. Now, now, *now—ballocks!*" A red flash filled the screen. A figure on the screen—it looked like a tall, blue-skinned Sidhe—exploded.

"Gods *damn* it." He ripped off the headset, threw it down on the table. "I've been bloody killed. *Again.*"

He shoved back from the table, the wheels on his stool screeching. He muttered another curse. Picking up the mouse, he bounced it once, twice, three times in his hand, then, spitting a final expletive, hurled it at the screen.

Metal and plastic exploded in a burst of green fire. Christine jumped back, gasping. Emerald sparks flew, some whizzing past her ear. When they faded, there was a twisted, melted, smoking mess where the monitor had been.

Mac leaned back on his stool, staring at the smoldering consequences of his tantrum. Then he let out a long breath and shook his head. Raising his right hand, he pointed a finger at the wreckage and spoke a single, vibrant syllable.

The sound rang pure and deep, vibrating like a bell in Christine's skull. The wreckage of the computer monitor responded instantly. Melted plastic turned liquid, collapsing into a shining puddle on the table. Mac flicked his wrist. The shining liquid flowed back upon itself, surging upward like a backward waterfall, molding itself into a quicksilver version of its original form. Another flick, and the monitor was back, as good as new. The screen flickered once, then sprang to life.

Christine stifled a gasp. By this time she was standing only a few steps behind Mac. Maybe she should have been halfway out the door, but some force she didn't understand had kept her inching forward.

The images on Mac's computer resolved into a computer-generated graveyard. Giving an exasperated half sigh, he pulled the bandana from his head and ran both hands through his hair. She must have made a sound, because suddenly he spun around on his stool. His eyes locked on hers, as green as she remembered. The blue half-moon tattoo below his left eye jumped.

"Bloody hell." He leaned back, tipping his stool so far it was a miracle he didn't fall over. A slow smile spread across his face. "So. The little witch found Kalen's place after all, eh?"

"Um . . . yes. But . . . who are . . . I mean . . ."

Strains of Manannán still flowed from the overhead speakers; the melody had shifted to something slower, underscored by a trickling stream.

Absently, Mac reached for his mouse and turned down the volume. "And you found Kalen, too, I'm guessing."

"Well, I could hardly miss him, could I?"

He snorted. "And I reckon he's taken full advantage of that." He cocked his head. "Christine, isn't it?"

"Yes. And you're Mac."

He stood. "I am indeed. At your service, love." He sketched an elaborate mock bow.

Cheeky bastard. "You're a friend of Kalen's?"

"Most of the time."

A tinny voice scratched its way through the discarded headset. "Mac? Mac. You okay, brother? What the hell happened back there? I thought you had that bastard Dark Demon handled."

Annoyance flitted through Mac's eyes. "Excuse me a minute, love." Reaching back, he snatched up the headset and hooked it over one ear.

"How was I supposed to know you were going to aggro a whole pack of Brain Eaters?" he said. "Bloody stupid move, if you ask me . . . Yeah, well, you too, man. Bugger the Nightbane Guild." He angled his head, eyeing Christine. "Listen, gotta go. Got a hot bird waiting."

What?

He flashed her a grin. "Yeah, she wants me. What lady doesn't? . . . Yes, *now*. I'm outta here."

He tore the headset off and tossed it on the desk. "Buggering git. Can't imagine why I joined his bloody Raid Group. Thinks he's a fucking god or something. And believe me, he's not."

Christine ventured closer and peered at the monitor. The medieval village was gone. The screen now showed an amorphous ball of light drifting down a country lane.

"This is a game?"

Mac shot her a look of pure disbelief. "You can't mean you don't know."

"No. I don't play computer games."

Mac groaned. "Gods. Just like *him*."

"You mean Kalen?"

"Yes, Kalen. Who else? The man's stuck in the nineteenth century."

Christine's lips twitched. "Um . . . yeah. I've noticed."

He gestured toward the screen. "That, my ignorant little American sweetheart, is World of Magic. It's only the most popular MMORPG on the planet."

"MMORPG?"

"Massively Multiple Online Role Playing Game," he enunciated. "W.O.M. is the biggest. Millions of players."

"And I take it you're not one of the better ones?"

A red flush illuminated his cheeks. "Hey, I hold my own. It's just that the Horde has been coming on bloody strong lately." Abruptly, his green eyes lost their humor. His expression turned downright grim.

"Horde? You mean zombies?"

"Sometimes. The game's the Horde against the Alliance. Death magic against life magic. There used to be a pretty even balance, but in the past year Horde players have been multiplying like nobody's business. And now there are these Dark Demons to contend with. Nasty buggers. A full hell's worth of them have flooded the game."

Christine went cold. "Demons?"

Mac shot her a glance. "Not real demons, love. Players who take on demon personas. They're wrecking the game's balance." He regarded the screen moodily. "Just like in the real world. Art imitates life and all that."

Christine rubbed her arms. "You play this often?"

His color deepened. "It can be habit forming."

She inched closer to the screen. "And now you're dead?"

"Only temporarily. But I won't come back at the same energy level. Those Dark Demon bastards suck some serious life out of a soul."

Just like in real life.

Christine shuddered. She looked away from the screen, eying the piles of computer guts. "Is all that yours, too?"

He clicked the game window closed. His screen saver was a wide expanse of open sea. "Yeah," he said, sounding slightly embarrassed. "Computers are a hobby of mine."

She eyed his guitar. "And music?"

"I play around some." Swiveling his stool around, he looked up at her. "Why do you ask?"

She was struck again by how young he was. Sixteen, barely. There was a zit on his chin. What was he doing here? A possible explanation occurred to her, one that would certainly explain the odd surge of power she'd felt from him back in London.

"Are you . . . Kalen's son?"

He blinked, clearly taken aback. "Gods, no." He sounded wistful, as if he wished he were. "Kalen doesn't have any offspring."

"Then who are you? What're you doing here? Why didn't you tell me you knew Kalen when I showed you my sketch back in London?"

He held up his hand in mock alarm. "One at a time, love. To answer your questions . . . nobody, nothing, and because I didn't feel like it."

"You're not *nobody*. That was quite a trick you did with the monitor."

He shrugged, fiddling with the mouse. "So I have a bit of magic. You do too, love."

"Nothing like yours."

He glanced up at her. "That's not entirely true, now, is it? You're a water witch."

"Are you?"

He hesitated. "Of a sort." He regarded her thoughtfully. "You came a long way, looking for Kalen. You know what he is, I'm guessing."

"Yes."

"You're not his usual type. I'm surprised he even let you in here."

"He didn't let me in. He brought me here."

"Even better. But I'm sure he didn't send you down *here* on your own." He gave her a cheeky grin. "Especially not dressed like that. He doesn't allow anyone in his office."

"You're here."

"Oh, me. Well, love, I hardly count, now, do I? Kalen needs someone to distract him, else he'd end up cramming every damn painting and statue in the world into this gods-forsaken castle. The man's bloody obsessed."

"Have you known him a long time?"

"Long enough." He placed his hands on his thighs and stood. "So now, tell me, my beautiful little witch, why are you here? Other than for the obvious, I mean."

Christine huffed. "Why does everyone assume I came here for *that?*"

"Ah, but you did get some, didn't you?"

She scowled.

He laughed and held up a hand. "Say no more, love. You don't have to explain. Kalen has a way with women." He paused. "Though I must say, it's been quite some time since he's brought one home."

"He brought Leanna here."

Mac's green gaze sharpened. "You know about her?"

"Do *you?*"

"More than I want to, believe me. I've been trying for

years to put Kalen off her, but does the almighty Immortal take my advice? No, he does not."

"I guess when you're three thousand years old, you don't tend to listen to teenagers."

Mac huffed. "As if you're the wizened elder. How old, love?"

"Twenty-six. And you're what, sixteen? Seventeen?" She was being generous.

He snorted. "Old enough to know my way around."

"And you're Kalen's what . . . friend?"

"Now, *that's* an interesting question. I suppose you might say I'm as close to a friend as Kalen's got."

She sighed. "That's a sad thought."

"What? You don't think I'm worthy?" He sounded put out.

"No! I didn't mean it that way." She ran her fingers along the edge of the table. "It's just that he seems so . . ."

"Alone," Mac supplied.

"Yes."

"You're right. He is." He peered at Christine as if seeing her for the first time. "You know, you're really very sweet. I can't fathom it. Kalen hates 'sweet.' Why didn't he send you off when the sun rose?" He waggled his brows. "Were you that good?"

"You're a little jerk, you know that?" But it was impossible to work up any real anger. Mac was cute, in a zitty, gangly, adolescent sort of way. She hesitated. "The reason I'm still here is that he's protecting me. I managed to piss off Leanna during one of her tours."

Mac whistled under his breath. "What did you do?"

She told him, and he threw back his head and laughed. "Let me get this straight. You, a human, attacked Leanna in front of a pack of tourists? Put a bind on her?"

"I didn't stop to think—"

He rubbed the sparse stubble on his chin. "Damn me, that's sweet. Wish I'd been there."

"You don't like her?"

"No one really likes—" The sound of Manannán's "Midsummer Bells" cut off his words. Mac pulled his cell from its clip, checked the display, scowled, and put it back.

"Aren't you going to answer that?"

"No. Let the bloody woman find someone else to bother for once. Now, as I was saying—no one likes Leanna unless they're in bed with her. You pissed her off? You're lucky you're not dead."

"Kalen saved me."

"And now he's keeping you here."

"Yes. For protection."

Mac gave her a quizzical look. "He might have just jumped you across the pond."

"What?"

"Taken you home to the States with that pop-in, pop-out thing he does. Leanna's not pure Sidhe—her power is limited. It fades the farther she gets from Celtic lands. She holds her own in Europe, but the New World?" He shook his head. "Her magic's dead there. Kalen could pop you out of her range in a heartbeat."

Christine felt like she'd been punched in the stomach. "Why, that arrogant . . . bastard! He never told me!"

Mac laughed. "Must like you pretty well then."

Christine harrumphed. Mac remained silent. The last strains of Manannán seeped from the speakers, fading gracefully into nothingness. The electric hum of the computers seemed to amplify in the new silence. Mac frowned and reached for his mouse. A few clicks and another track started up.

"You know," Christine said suddenly, "I don't think I've heard this one. It *is* Manannán, isn't it?"

He shot her a glance. "That's right. You said you were a fan, didn't you?"

"Rabid. The man's pure genius."

"He's passable good."

"Are you kidding? He's a god among men!"

"Not sure I'd go that far," Mac muttered. Reaching again for the mouse, he brought up another window.

Christine recognized the program. "Music Creator?"

"You know it? I thought you didn't own a computer."

"I don't. But my boyfriend . . ." She shook her head. "My *ex*-boyfriend was a musician. A composer. He used that program. Do you play—oh. Of course you do. You have a guitar."

"I fool around a bit."

"Do you compose?"

"A little."

"And Kalen lets you use his computers."

"*His* computers?" Mac snorted. "That pole-up-his-ass throwback barely knows what a computer is. All these are mine, even that sexy machine on his desk. I let *him* use them. Good thing, too, or he'd be running his gallery business by courier pigeon."

She laughed. "He *is* a bit stuck in the past, isn't he?"

Mac shot her a sardonic look. "Bloody mired in it. I can't blast him out. Believe me, I've tried."

"So the electricity in here . . ."

"I put it in. Furnace, air-conditioning, and modern plumbing as well." He nodded to the sliding doors on the adjoining wall. "Just open those and you'll find a real bathroom, with shower and Jacuzzi, and a small but fully stocked kitchen. Refrigerator, microwave, coffeemaker, and all the junk food you can eat."

Christine stared at the door. "Are there potato chips in there?"

"Crisps, you mean? Sure. There's a bag or two of Walker's, I think."

She was already there, shoving the door open and plunging into the kitchenette beyond.

"Try the cupboard on the left." He sounded bemused.

She found the package—salt and vinegar even!—and

tore it open. The chips were like heaven on her tongue. "Goddess, I needed that."

"Not into Pearl's cooking, I take it?"

"No, it's fine. It's just . . . I crave salt, and Pearl doesn't seem to keep any around."

He chuckled, turning back to the computer. "That's the sea magic in you." He moved the cursor over the screen, bringing up a playlist. He checked a selection and clicked. "Here, love. Tell me what you think of this."

Manannán again. Another piece she hadn't heard. "Where are you getting this stuff? That has to be so new it's still unreleased."

"You know Manannán's work that well?"

"I have everything he ever wrote. I'd love to see him in concert, but he never tours." She closed her eyes, letting the deep pulse of the melody wash over her. "He's got such powerful water magic."

"You know, most people don't realize that."

She opened one eye and looked at him. "Seems obvious enough to me."

Mac clicked off that track and started another. "How does this strike you?"

She listened to a few bars. It was similar to the first two, a techno backbeat combined with the drum of a rainstorm, but . . . in place of the usual electric guitar there was a series of acoustical riffs. She frowned. "Are you sure that's Manannán?"

"I'm sure, love."

"But he doesn't play acoustic. Only electric."

"It's something new he's trying." He gazed at her with an intent expression. "Do you like it?"

She let the melody drift over her. It was different, yes, but just as compelling as all Manannán's music. "Very much."

The tension went out of his shoulders. "Brilliant."

"Where did you get it?"

"Green Seas Studios. It was . . . um . . . just lying around."

Green Seas was Manannán's recording studio. Mac must work there, if he'd come away with a treasure like this. The melody soared, dipped, rose again. A rare harsh note rang, then faded. The minor key shifted to a soulful, soothing major—C-sharp, she thought. Christine body started to sway.

Mac held out his hand. "Dance with me, love!"

Christine smiled at his earnest expression. "Sure. Why not?"

Kalen's meeting with Fiona had been brisk and productive. His Edinburgh gallery manager—unlike some of his employees on the continent—was the epitome of efficiency. Kalen's last-minute addition to the upcoming show was no problem at all. Now there was only the matter of collecting the pieces. . . .

Christine's apartment in Rome was easy enough to locate. She'd mentioned the church it was near; all it took to locate her flat was a hundred Euros in the palm of a newsstand attendant. The building was decrepit. Christine's apartment was on the top floor, up five flights of dingy staircase. He swore. How could she live in such a place? The neighborhood was lousy with zombies and other diseased creatures. She was lucky she wasn't dead.

She'd set wards on her door, of course. The protections were strong enough, he allowed grudgingly, for most magical threats. They were nothing to Kalen, however. He dismantled them with a word and a touch and opened the door.

The apartment was a single room with a lone window that looked out not onto the street, but onto a narrow airshaft, which, being near the roof, at least let in a decent amount of light. Furniture was minimal but functional—a narrow bed, a decrepit table and chair, a shaky easel and stool. But it wasn't these elements that had Ķalen's jaw dropping.

The place was a wild riot of color. If there was a square inch of the place that had escaped Christine's brush, he couldn't see it. Blues and purples streamed up the walls, across the ceiling. Greens and gold pooled in bright puddles under his feet. The forms were liquid, sinuous, sensual. The walls were painted with horizontal strokes, gently wavering, giving the impression of an endless sea. His chest tightened. Christine had poured her very soul onto these walls. Did she never hold back? Did she *never* protect herself?

He moved to her easel. Her artist's materials lay in startling disarray on the floor all around. Nearby, clothing lay draped across her unmade bed. A tall bookshelf—painted in the same wild style as the walls—held a cluttered collection of books. Leaning against it was the item he sought—an oversized accordion portfolio. Retrieving it, he untied the ribbon and lifted the flap.

As chaotic as the rest of Christine apartment was, her portfolio was not. He felt the care with which she'd inserted each stiff sheet into its pocket and affixed labels to each tab. He pulled the watercolors out, one by one, and looked at them.

Abstractions all—the type of art Kalen generally hated. Christine's work, though, was somehow . . . different. Kalen had spent the last fifty years dealing in modern art. Despite the disdain he'd professed, he knew real talent when he saw it. And Christine *did* have it—in abundance. Her work was nothing short of magical. She poured her whole soul and being into her art. Her style was flowing, sensuous, yearning. It tightened his gut and caused his heart to ache.

He gazed at a work labeled, simply, *Hope*. *Hope* was vibrant gold and pink, gently rounded. The longer Kalen looked at it, the less abstract it seemed, the lines resolving into a human infant's face.

Extraordinary. He set the sheet on Christine's rumpled pillow. The next scene was *Peace*, a gentle series of strokes that melted into the face of an old man. *Joy* was next, a child playing on a sandy beach. *Peace, Hope, Joy* . . . where was *Love*? He thumbed through the labels, but didn't find it.

He replaced Christine's work in the portfolio. It was a short jump to Edinburgh, where he entrusted the paintings into Fiona's capable hands. Back at the castle, he materialized in the center of the west courtyard, hoping he'd find Christine in his studio. He'd enjoy making love to her amid canvases and pots of paint. He'd been away half the day and his hunger for her was already urgent. He wanted her beneath him again, wanted to lose himself in the welcoming cradle of her thighs. Needed to feel her magic flow into his soul, to emerge when his brush next touched canvas.

He cast out his senses. He caught the pulse of her life essence, cool and fluid, undulating like the sea. He started toward it, then paused, frowning. Christine wasn't in his studio—her essence vibrated in the stone below his feet. She must have found the old dungeons, where he kept his office. And she wasn't alone. He sensed another essence entwined with hers.

Damn it all to Hades. Mac was with her.

CHAPTER FIFTEEN

Kalen jumped to the dungeon level, materializing in the dank passageway near his office. He stood for several seconds staring at the light spilling from the open door. The music pouring from the room was loud enough to rupture a human eardrum.

He stepped forward. Stopped on the threshold. Peered inside.

Mac and Christine were dancing. *Dancing?* It looked more like sex with clothes on. Kalen stood in the doorway, temporarily robbed of his capacity for speech. Damn Mac. He'd make a move on anything human and female—he was obsessed with the species. But Christine? He hadn't thought her so easily swayed.

The two were facing each other, their bodies mere millimeters apart, moving in a sinuous, synchronized rhythm. Their combined magic flowed in an aura of emerald and blue. Mac looked young and human in his green shirt and baggy jeans; Christine looked incredibly sensual, despite her outlandish costume of white shirt and overlarge breeches. Mac's hands were on Christine's hips, guiding them in a thrusting movement that had Kalen contemplating murder, as if that were possible. Christine's head tipped back. She gazed into Mac's eyes, and laughed with pure delight.

She'd never laughed that way with Kalen.

Anger exploded in his skull; sparks of irrational, jealous rage ignited every nerve. Mac and Christine danced on, blissfully unaware of the explosion waiting to happen just a few yards away. Mac's hands glided around Christine's hip to the small of her back. He pressed her groin to his. Christine stretched her arms overhead, her body undulating to the liquid beat of the music.

Mac was playing Manannán, of course. What the hell else?

Damn Mac to Hades. He and Christine were good together. But then, Kalen might have guessed that they would be. They shared a talent for water magic. Even their bodies were similar, lean and rippling. But Mac's hands on Christine—*that* was intolerable.

Kalen's anger expanded, twisted . . .

Detonated. He surged into the room, white energy shooting from his fingers, taking out the ceiling speakers with a popping noise like gunfire. He sent a final, satisfying bolt whizzing past the back of Mac's head. It exploded on the wall directly above his computer.

Christine screamed as Mac shoved her to the floor and spun. His green eyes widened as they locked with Kalen's. For a second, all he did was stare.

Then he began to laugh. "*Shit*, Kalen. Can't you just say hello like a normal bloke?"

"There's nothing funny here, Mac. Get your hands off her."

"Feeling a mite possessive, are we?" Mac pulled Christine to her feet, wrapping one arm around her shoulder. His green eyes danced.

Christine's terrified expression caused Kalen a pang of remorse. He might have handled that better, but by the gods, Mac knew how to push his buttons.

"Take your hands off her."

Mac grinned and slid his palm down Christine's back.

Kalen raised a hand, took aim. "I'm warning you . . ."

Mac laughed. "You wouldn't—"

A white flash cut his words short. The bolt hit Mac's left shoulder, sending him spinning away from Christine. Stumbling, he grabbed for the computer desk, missed, and went sprawling on the floor with a crash.

Kalen grinned. Damn, that felt good.

His smile abruptly vanished as Christine rushed to Mac's side, dropping on her knees with a cry. Mac, who'd already been pushing to his feet, gave a theatrical moan and collapsed back to the floor.

"Oh, for the gods' sake," Kalen muttered.

Christine shot him a glare that might have killed a mortal man. "You brute! How could you? He's just a kid."

"A kid?" Kalen snorted. "Is *that* what he told you?"

"We were only dancing!"

"He had his hands on you."

"So what if he did? That's no reason to blast him!"

Mac rolled his head and moaned. Christine gasped and turned back to him, cradling his cheek in her palm.

"Mac, can you hear me? Can you move your arm at—" She cut off frowning, running her fingers over his shoulder. "Wait. There's nothing there. But I know you hit him."

Kalen propped his hip on his desk and crossed his arms. "Believe me, his hide is far too tough for that little blast to pierce it. Mac, get your ass off the floor. Now. I mean it."

Mac obligingly rolled to one side and rose, rolling his shoulder without so much as a wince. Kalen's blast had left a singed hole in the cotton, but the skin below was barely red.

"Damn, Kalen, nice shot. Good to see you, too."

"You've met Christine," Kalen said.

Mac glanced at Christine, whose expression had gone from enraged to gobsmacked. "Actually, we're just getting reacquainted. I ran into her in London, waving a sketch of your castle around the train station." He sent Kalen a probing look. "She told me Leanna's after her."

"I'm well aware of that."

"Then why haven't you popped the lovely Christine across the pond to America?"

Kalen made a dismissive gesture. "It's not necessary. She's safe here and Leanna will eventually lose interest. Although, come to think of it, now that you're back—"

"Oh no," Mac said. "If you're thinking I'm going to keep an eye on her, forget it. I've got more pressing concerns. As a matter of fact, that's why I'm here."

His sober tone gave Kalen pause. Mac was deadly serious—something he very rarely was. His habitual flippancy had vanished and his shoulders held a tenseness Kalen had rarely seen. His friend was truly worried. And for someone with Mac's powers, that was no trivial matter.

"What's wrong?" Kalen asked.

"I—"

A trilling cell phone melody interrupted. Mac pulled his mobile from his belt and grimaced. "Gods *damn* it. I have to take it this time. I can't put her off again." He scowled and turned his back, flipping the phone open and pitching his voice low. Rapid conversation ensued. Kalen snorted.

Christine regarded Mac curiously. "Girlfriend?" she asked Kalen.

"His mother," he replied. "You know," he said to Mac as the phone snapped closed, "you could turn the damn thing off."

"Wouldn't do a bit of good. She'd track me down some other way. The last thing I need is for her to show up in person."

"You have an overprotective mother?" Christine asked curiously.

Mac looked discomfited. "Niniane's a bloody maniac."

Christine started. "You can't mean the Sidhe Queen."

"None other," Kalen said.

"You're Sidhe? Leanna's *brother*? But—your ears—"

"So I didn't inherit the pointy ears," Mac said irritably. "So sue me. I'm only half Sidhe. Leanna's *half* brother. And believe me, love, it's not my better half."

"Why? What's your other half?"

Mac looked embarrassed.

"Divine," Kalen said.

Christine gaped at him. "Your father's a god? Really?"

"Really," Mac groused. "You needn't sound so doubtful."

"But . . . you look like a kid!"

"Yes, well, Niniane doesn't look a day over twenty-three, and she can't stand the thought of a son who looks older. She convinced Da to put a halt to my physical age. I'm lucky he capped me at sixteen. If Mum had her way, I'd still be in nappies."

"You're joking."

"If only," he muttered.

Christine dragged in a breath. Things were just getting too weird. "And just who is your father?"

"Lir," Mac said. At Christine's blank look, he added, "God of the Sea. Ever hear of him?"

She shook her head. "I thought Neptune was God of the Sea."

"Americans," Mac pronounced with some disgust. "You bloody Yanks never get past Greece and Rome. What do they teach you in those schools of yours? Lir is a Celtic god. Far more ancient and powerful than Neptune and Poseidon." He grimaced. "And far more *forgotten*. I'm his only son."

He spread his arms wide and offered a deep bow. "Manannán mac Lir, at your service."

"Manannán? You mean like the musician?"

He gave her a cheeky grin. "*Exactly* like him, love. Haven't you caught on yet? *I'm* Manannán."

Her gaze flew to the burnt speaker dangling from a single wire above his head. He followed her line of vision and swore softly. "Damn it, Kalen. Do you have to be so bloody hard on the furniture?"

Kalen shrugged. Mac shook his head and gave a flick of his wrist. Instantly, the speakers shimmered silver and reformed.

Christine's knees turned to rubber. She felt Kalen's arm encircle her waist, keeping her upright. She clutched his shoulder for added support. "You really *are* a god."

Mac gave a modest smile. "Only half. My musical talent is from my Sidhe side."

"Oh, Goddess! Your music is ethereal . . . incredible . . . magical . . ."

Kalen made an impatient sound. "It ought to be. He's been fiddling around with that noise for half a millennium."

"Five hundred years?" Christine said faintly. "How old *are* you?"

"Seven hundred twelve," Mac said. He frowned. "Or thirteen. I can never remember."

Kalen sent Mac a look a father might give to a particularly annoying offspring. "Look, Mac, you've quite worn out your welcome here. Leave."

Mac's demeanor abruptly sobered. "No. I need to talk to you, Kalen."

"Make it quick. Christine and I have plans for the evening."

"We do?" Christine murmured, suddenly aware Kalen's hand had drifted from her waist to her hips. He dipped a little lower and stroked her bottom, igniting an aching fire in her belly.

"Yes," he said softly. "We do."

"Well, the gods know I hate to wreck a party, but there's something you have to know. The Unseelie Host is back."

Kalen's hand dropped away, his body going suddenly tense. "That can't be true. My brothers and I banished the Unseelie Host after the Great Battle seven hundred years ago. We sealed them in Uffern permanently."

"Not permanently enough, as it happens. They've escaped through a fissure in the Channel Tunnel and are laying a path of carnage through the countryside. I've been to some of the massacre sights. They aren't pretty. And it's getting worse."

"Are you sure it's Unseelies?" Kalen asked. "Not vampires or demons?"

"Yes. I found a few witnesses—and an Unseelie corpse. Then, on the way here, I ran into a pack of the vermin." His eyes turned inward, and Christine thought she saw a shudder run through his body. "They're every bit as hideous as I remember."

"You're not a child anymore, Mac. Blast the miserable things back to Uffern."

"Believe me, I tried."

"And?"

Mac speared his fingers through his hair, leaving the blond strands in spikes. "I used every trick you've taught me, Kalen, but it wasn't enough. Sure, I killed a few, but then another pack would attack. They're bolder than they were back in the Middle Ages. More organized. Every brownie, halfling, and faerie is fleeing to the city."

"That's true," Christine murmured, remembering Gilraen.

"They've already begun attacking larger villages. Cities will be next. I can't stop them." He set to pacing. "I can't stop *any* of it. The human world is on a downslide, completely out of balance. At first I thought it was part of a natural cycle, but now? I think it's worse than that. These Unseelies are taking orders from someone. Someone with enough power to free them from Uffern. Someone with a plan."

"Tain," Christine breathed.

Mac stopped pacing and glanced sharply at Kalen. "Isn't Tain one of your brothers?"

"The youngest one," Kalen said tightly.

"Tain is why I came to Scotland looking for Kalen," Christine interjected. Quickly, she sketched the details of

Tain's imprisonment and his association with Kehksut. "Tain is insane. He wants to die. The only way he can do that is by draining every last drop of life magic from the human world."

"It certainly looks like that's happening," Mac said. "Buggering vamps and zombies are everywhere. And humans I've never pegged as being into dark arts are turning demonwhore."

"I think that's the case with Leanna," Christine said.

Mac started. "Not bloody likely. I know my sister's no saint, but she's Sidhe. We abhor demons."

"So Kalen has said," Christine replied. "But Leanna's half human, isn't she? I saw her draw death runes, and she had a vial of something that looked like blood."

Mac swore. "If I find out Leanna's been dealing with demons, I'll wring her neck. She'll get herself killed. Or worse."

"The world's gone insane," Christine said. "That's why I'm here. Kalen's oldest brother, Adrian, is assembling an army in Seattle, Washington. The Immortals and any practitioners of life magic we can find. We're preparing for a battle with Tain and the Old One who's manipulating him."

Mac's gaze cut to Kalen. "Please tell me you're not going to join them."

Kalen looked away. "No. I'm not."

The tension in Mac's shoulder's relaxed. "Thank the gods."

Christine glared at him. "I can't believe this. I thought you'd help me convince him!"

Mac eyed Kalen. "You haven't told her, then?"

Kalen didn't reply.

"Tell me what?" Christine demanded.

"Nothing," Kalen muttered.

"*Fine.*" She turned to Mac. "Look. Kalen's refused to help, but what about you? Will you come with me to Seattle? You'd be a huge asset."

"I'd like to, love, but it's complicated." He cleared his throat. "I'd need my father's permission first."

"Then ask for it! Once Lir realizes how bad things are, I'm sure he'll give you his blessing."

"It's not that simple. Da would have to put a motion for Divine Intervention before the Celtic Gods' Council. And as I'm sure you know, gods move in Their Own Time and in Mysterious Ways. The lot of them debate endlessly. Lugh and the Morrigan—that pair couldn't agree on what to have for tea, let alone when to start a war. And then there's Briga and Cerridwen. You don't ever want to get in the middle of one of their hissy fights. Bran? That bloke can filibuster for centuries."

Christine stared. "You can't be serious. Do you mean to tell me there's *bureaucracy* in the Otherworld?"

Mac scowled. "And why shouldn't there be? Humans like to think gods and goddesses just go about intervening willy-nilly in human affairs, but believe me, love, if that were the case, the human world would have been burnt to a crisp long ago. Gods have a mountain of rules and regs designed to keep apocalypse at bay. And in any case, much as I love humans, it's not like I could just drop everything and skive off to Seattle while Unseelies are slaughtering my charges. Lir's only given me one job to do here in the human world—protect the Celtic magical creatures living outside Annwyn. That would be Sidhe, faeries, brownies, halflings, leprechauns, and Selkies, as well as the wilder creatures like imps, boggarts, and phookas. They're all my responsibility. I can't just abandon them."

"The best way to protect them is by joining Amber and Adrian in the battle against Tain! Surely the Gods of Annwyn will be able to see that."

Mac scrubbed a hand over his face. "I wouldn't count on it, love. Much as it pains me to say it, it looks like death magic is at flash point. Celtic creatures have only one hope. Evacuation."

"Evacuation . . ." Christine stared at him blankly. "But—where would they go?"

Mac's features settled into a mask of resignation. "Why, to Annwyn, of course. That's why I'm here. I need Kalen's help to get my people home."

CHAPTER SIXTEEN

"How long before the end, do you think?"

"A couple weeks," Mac said. "A month, on the outside. I sense something in the air, Kalen. Dark excitement. Anticipation. The cities, especially, reek with it. I think something big's about to happen. Something that won't be able to be reversed. I don't want a single faerie or imp left outside Annwyn when it goes down. A good lot of them are already camped on the shore, but I'm afraid they'll be sitting ducks for the Unseelies while I round everyone else up. I know you can't fight, but if you could just provide a bit of added protection, it would be a big help."

Kalen nodded. "I'll set the wards immediately. When do you think you'll be ready to open the Gates?"

"With any luck, within a few days. Then the Opening spell will take a bit of time." He grimaced. "It's one of Niniane's. Designed to keep people out, not let them in. The reversal is a tricky bit of spellcraft." He paused. "You'll be coming with us, of course."

"Of course." Kalen had no choice, and now there was

Christine's safety to consider as well. He forced a light tone. "I wouldn't dream of leaving you to face Niniane alone."

Christine's color was high. "So that's it? The two of you are just going to run away and leave humanity to fend for itself?"

Mac's jaw tightened. Kalen knew how much he loved humans—this couldn't be easy for him. Unlike Kalen, Mac could help with Adrian's battle.

"My first duty is to my own," Mac told Christine. "I'll extend an offer of sanctuary to trustworthy humans—Niniane won't like it, but by the time she realizes what I've done it'll be too late. But that's about all I can do. You're welcome, of course. In fact, I insist you come."

"You want me to abandon the human world, too!" Christine was aghast.

Kalen caught her elbow. "You'll love Annwyn. It's a very beautiful place."

She regarded him as if he had two heads. "I'm sure it is, but that's not the point here, is it? I can't believe you two think I would just leave—"

"You will leave. You're under my protection now, Christine. You'll go where I say."

Her blue eyes widened like saucers. "Why, you arrogant, high-handed Immortal *jerk*! What do you think I am, some kind of *lapdog*? I'm not going with you anywh—oooh!"

Kalen hauled her against his body, hard.

"Let me go!"

Kalen nodded to Mac. "If you'll excuse us? Christine and I have a few things to discuss."

Mac raised a brow. "Far be it from me to intrude. After all, I've got work to do. A sister to visit. A hundred thousand or so magical creatures to evacuate."

Kalen nodded. Christine balled up her fist and hit him on the shoulder, hard enough for him to feel it. Scowling, he pinned her wrists at her waist. "Stop that."

"I am not going to Annwyn!"

"Quite the feisty wench you've got there, Kalen," Mac said dryly.

"Quite," Kalen agreed. He hoisted a struggling Christine into his arms. With a parting nod, he shut his eyes and let his power flow into the ground, preparing for translocation. Luckily, Christine was too busy pummeling him to realize she might have hit him with a spell while his defenses were down. One, two, three seconds . . .

He released his magic with a snap. A portal popped open. He stepped through it and willed himself and Christine to his bedchamber.

Thankfully, the shock of the trip shut her up.

Christine landed flat on her back on the bed, the room spinning around her. For a long moment, all she could do was moan as her stomach threatened to heave up her last three meals.

Kalen was beside her. He shifted on the mattress, drawing her into his arms. "Shh. Don't fight the nausea. It'll pass in a moment."

"Goddess, I hate portal travel." She clung to him while her stomach roiled. When she thought she could risk it, she struggled to an upright position and shoved a damp hank of hair from her forehead. Her hand was still shaking.

"What was wrong with the stairs?" she asked weakly.

A laugh rumbled in his chest. "Takes too long."

Goddess, his arms felt good around her. Solid and true. It was all too tempting to let herself get lost in them. But she couldn't. She turned her head slowly and caught his gaze.

"There is no way," she told him, "that I am going to Annwyn."

He sighed and pulled her onto his lap. For a moment she was distracted by the bulge of his arousal against her buttocks. The familiar melting sensation started up in her belly. The tips of her breasts tingled.

"Christine . . ." The weariness in his voice dove right to her heart. "Stop fighting me."

She shut her eyes. "Don't ask this of me, Kalen. I can't do it. I can't leave my people, even if it's a lost cause."

His arms tightened around her. She lost her breath when his lips caught hers in a devastatingly gentle kiss.

"I've waited so many years for you, Christine. I won't risk you now that I've finally found you." The tip of his tongue found her ear and swirled delicately around the shell. Delicious weakness flooded Chistine's body. Electric magic hummed in her veins.

"I love you, Christine."

Was it possible to soar and crash at the same time? "Oh, Goddess. Don't say that. Don't *do* this. I can't—"

He silenced her with another kiss, and she couldn't summon the will to turn away.

"You're mine now, Christine. *Mine*. And you're coming with me to Annwyn."

His hand found her breast. She gasped. He caught the sound with his mouth, consuming her with his lips, invading with his tongue. His magic flashed through her, hot and wild. Her own magic surged in reply. She was powerless to stop it.

Her arms tightened around his neck. When had she reached for him? She couldn't remember. She only knew she had to hold him, had to press every inch of her body to every inch of his. This was where she belonged, what she'd been created for. But how could she let Kalen carry her off to safety in Annwyn while the rest of her race was doomed to suffer?

How could she not?

He ran his hands over her body in blatant, possessive exploration. The buttons on her shirt slipped open. A second later, the garment disappeared over the side of the bed. Her pants, shoes, and stockings soon followed. Kalen slipped off his suit jacket and tie, and unbuttoned his shirt. The edges parted, revealing the dark swath of hair on his chest. He sat back on his heels and looked down at her.

There was no mistaking the expression in his eyes. He needed her. Desperately. She didn't know why, but she knew with a certainty it was true.

"Unbind your hair," he said hoarsely.

Wordlessly, she obeyed, unraveling her braid and shaking her head. Her hair tumbled about her shoulders.

Reverently, Kalen sifted his fingers through the heavy strands. Then he dipped his head and kissed the valley between her breasts. Trailed his tongue to one nipple and drew it into his mouth. She gasped as he suckled, scraping his teeth gently.

"You're mine," he murmured again, but there was fear in his voice, as if he didn't quite believe it. His unexpected vulnerability squeezed her heart.

"Why?" She threaded her fingers through his hair as his lips journeyed to her stomach. He pressed his open mouth over her navel, swirling his tongue in the indentation and causing her hips to arch off the bed. "*Why* do you need me so?"

He answered by kissing a path to her clitoris. Her womb clenched and her thighs went slick. All thought, all questions, fled. She was filled with an aching need to give and to love. He licked lower on her body, his lips sliding to the slick folds at the entrance to her body. He delved deep with his tongue. Their magic melded.

Pleasure—incredible, magical pleasure—consumed her. "Please . . ." She didn't know what she was asking. *Please love me? Please let me go?*

He shoved himself off the bed just long enough to rid himself of the rest of his clothes. When he mounted the mattress again, she pressed him down and crawled over him, dipping her head and lapping at his skin with her tongue. He tasted salty. She licked him again, her tongue traveling over his flesh in a long, erotic slide.

He groaned. Hands bracketing her hips, he lifted her and

positioned the entrance to her body at the tip of his erection. With a wrenching sigh, she impaled herself on his rigid shaft. Her inner muscles clenched, holding him safe as he moved inside her, her moans encouraging every upward thrust of his hips. His breathing was harsh, his skin slick. Their combined magic swirled, spiraling upward. Her head fell back; he sucked in a breath as her hair brushed his thighs.

She couldn't hold back. Didn't want to. He was so hard inside her, stroked her so deeply.

Her climax crashed like a tsunami. Kalen cried her name at the same time. She convulsed atop him, her head coming forward to press into the hollow of his shoulder. His breathing was ragged. She gave a final shudder and collapsed atop him. She could feel his heart pounding against her chest.

He soothed his hands over her shoulders, her back. When she lifted her head, he tucked her blue-streaked lock of hair behind her ear and smiled. Their gazes locked for long moments.

Finally, he looked away. "You'll come with me to Annwyn." There was an unmistakable note of finality in his tone. "Lir . . . he'll offer you a gift when you arrive."

She frowned. "What gift?"

"An Immortal soul."

Christine stared at him. "How is that possible?"

"Lir is an extremely powerful god. I once did him a very great service. In return, he offered me a home in Annwyn and immortality to any companion I wished to bring with me."

"Must have been some favor," Christine said shakily. Her? Immortal? *Impossible.*

"It was. I saved Mac's life."

She looked up, puzzled. "But Mac's a demigod. Isn't he immortal?"

"As an adult, he's like me. As long as he's in a realm containing life magic, he'll live forever. But as a child, his fate wasn't so secure. He's half Sidhe, and Sidhe children are very fragile. Most die in their first decade, especially if they venture outside Annwyn. Mac learned at a very young age how to open the Gates just enough to slip out. He was forever sneaking off—it's why Niniane is so protective of him now. The day I saw him for the first time, he was five years old. He'd wandered into the middle of an Unseelie battle. Three of the monsters had him cornered. If I'd arrived a few seconds later, he'd have been gutted."

"No wonder he loves you so," Christine said.

Kalen raised his brows. "Some way to show it. He was trying to seduce my woman." But he smiled as he said it, and she could see in his eyes how deeply he felt for his friend.

Christine rolled her eyes. "We were only dancing."

"Oh, is that what they call it these days?" He let his gaze drift down her body.

She didn't return the suggestive look. "Kalen, Mac said something odd . . . something about how you can't fight. Not that you *won't* fight, but that you *can't*. What did he mean?"

His smile abruptly faded. "Nothing."

He was motionless for a long time. He turned her in his arms so her back was to him, her spine cradled by his chest. A heavy arm draped over her waist anchored her to his body. When she tried to turn and look at him, he wouldn't let her.

"It's not nothing," she said softly. "Won't you tell me?"

He didn't reply immediately. She held herself silent. She sensed him searching for words. Painful words, she was sure.

"You deserve the truth," he said finally, more to himself than to her.

"You can trust me," she said, placing a kiss on his arm. "Nothing you could tell me would turn me against you."

"I pray that's true." He was silent a moment longer, then finally, he sighed. "I told you my goddess mother, Uni, charged me with the task of guarding the line of Tyrrhenus."

She murmured her assent.

"For centuries, I did just that. But not as well as I might have. Adrian was always pulling rank, summoning me to this battle or that. It only got worse in the Dark Ages. Death magic was rampant then. During the plague years, I wasn't always there to assist my people with sanitation, medicine, clean water and food. They suffered terribly. By the end of the thirteenth century, there was but a single descendant of Tyrrhenus alive. An infant. A male."

Christine sucked in a breath. "And he died, too?"

Kalen gave a bitter laugh. "No, I wouldn't allow that. Gerold lived. I was loath to entrust him to human foster parents, so I made a home in Tuscany and raised him myself. I ignored Adrian's frequent summons. I focused all my attention on the boy. Gerold was to become my new Tyrrhenus. The father of a new dynasty."

Christine waited for him to continue. When he did, his voice was steady, though the rise and fall of his breath was not.

"Gerold was a bookish sort, quiet, scholarly, and intense. I taught him everything—who he was, what was expected of him—but when he grew up, he turned his back on his duty. Rather than worship Uni, he found a new god. He wanted to take the vows of a monk. Poverty, obedience . . . and celibacy. I forbade it, ordering him to marry. He refused. He would not even take a woman to his bed. He vowed he would die chaste. Against my wishes, he entered a monastery.

"I couldn't accept that Tyrrhenus's line would die with Gerold. So in my arrogance, I conceived a plan. I found a young beauty who was experienced in the ways of pleasure. I told her I would shower her with riches if she put aside her other lovers and bore Gerold's child. She agreed. She seduced Gerold in the monastery fields, not once but many times, until her belly swelled. I was overjoyed. Gerold could dedicate the rest of his life to the church, and I had my new heir."

He fell silent for a moment. Christine could feel the tension gathering in his body. "The courtesan had just started her birth travails when Adrian summoned me. It had been two decades since I'd answered one of his calls, but this time the need was truly dire—the Unseelie Host had massed a hideous, brutal army and was laying a swath of destruction across Scotland. Humans and Celtic life magic creatures were being slaughtered. I couldn't turn my back on the conflict. So I went."

"That was when you saved Mac."

"Yes. And after the battle was over and Mac safely delivered into his parents' arms, I returned to Italy. I found both the courtesan and her midwife dead. The babe was gone. For a time, I couldn't move, couldn't think. And then I heard it. The Calling, like a whisper inside my brain, spoken by the only person alive with the right to utter the spell. Gerold.

"I went to him at once, materializing within the monastery walls. I found him presiding over a makeshift altar in a dank, dark crypt, his abbot hovering nearby. Gerold's newborn daughter, still bloody and trailing her birth cord, lay squalling on the cold stone. Just inches above her stomach, Gerold held a knife."

Christine gasped. Twisting in Kalen's arms, she searched his face. His eyes were hollow. "*Goddess*. He didn't . . . ?"

"He did. I tried to stop it, but I was too late. The infant I caused to be conceived ended her short life at the hands of her own father. Rage unlike any I'd ever known descended on me. My heart screamed for revenge. I lifted my spear and drove it straight through Gerold's chest."

"Oh, Goddess." Hot tears streamed down Christine's cheeks. Kalen wiped them away with his thumb. "The tale isn't yet finished. But perhaps you've heard enough."

She found his hand and gripped it tightly. "No. I want to hear everything."

"Gerold's lifeless corpse fell across the body of his infant daughter. The abbot gave a shout of laughter. I spun about and discovered not a monk, but a demon. Culsu, my nemesis of old. She'd masterminded the whole atrocity. And I hadn't even suspected."

"Oh, Kalen."

"As Culsu gloated, I became aware of another presence in the crypt. Uni, my mother goddess. She is not . . ." He grimaced. "Not known for her forgiving nature. Her wrath was profound. I'd killed the last of Tyrrhenus's descendants with the very spear she'd created to protect them. There was no defense I could offer for my actions—I'd acted in anger and arrogance, ignorant that Gerold had been Culsu's victim. I deserved death, but that was impossible. As it turned out, Uni's punishment was far more difficult."

If Kalen's eyes had been hollow before, they were completely dead now. "Uni transported me to a realm outside the human world, where I was suspended in a place where there was no vision, no sound, no scent or taste. No feeling at all. I couldn't move, couldn't speak. It was as if I'd ceased to exist, except in my own mind. She told me nothing—not how long I would be confined, or even if I'd been doomed to a living hell for all eternity. It was, you see, a taste of death. A taste of what I'd dealt to Gerold." He gave a harsh laugh. "It was an effective punishment. The hours, the minutes, the days—they bled together, taking my soul with them. I wished for true oblivion more times than I could count."

"Oh, Kalen! How long did Uni keep you there?"

"A hundred years. When I emerged, Uni told me my arrogant Immortal soul didn't yet understand the value of life. She forbade me to kill for nine hundred more years. And the edict extended not only to humans and living magic creatures, but to animals and death magic creatures as well. Nothing animated is to die by my hand. I am to eat no meat. If I violate Uni's decree, she will return me to that numb, lifeless hell—for eternity. It's been six hundred years since that day. Since then, I've learned to live without killing. Practicing only defensive magic. Learning to control my anger, swallow my pride." His eyes were bleak. "Do you want to know what the worst part of my life is, Christine? Watching innocents die because I cannot risk defending them."

"That's the reason you refused to help me?" Christine's emotions were in a jumble. "You can't fight for another three hundred years?"

"Two hundred ninety-three years. Yes, that's why I've refused you."

"You should have told me. If I'd known, I never would have pressed you."

"You know now. You also know I love you. I can't bear the thought of you putting yourself in danger for a cause that may very well be lost. Please say you'll come with me to Annwyn. We can live in love and peace there, forever."

It was too much for Christine to absorb. Especially coming on the heels of Kalen's heartbreaking story. She'd thought him heartless for not joining the Coven of Light's fight—now she understood why he'd refused. If he killed, he faced a fate worse than death. An eternity of numbed awareness. The thought sickened her. No, Kalen couldn't fight. Now that she knew what he faced, she wouldn't *allow* him to fight. But flee with him to Annwyn? How could she do that?

"Christine?"

She stirred in his arms. "Yes?"

"Does this . . . does what I told you . . . did it . . ." He paused, and her heart ached at the utter pain and self-loathing in his voice. "Did it cause you to hate me?"

It was hard to answer around the hot lump in her throat. "No," she said hoarsely. She pressed her forehead to his. "I could never hate you, Kalen. I love you."

She felt his tears on her cheek. "Thank you."

After a time, he spoke again. "It will be a few days before Mac's ready to open the Gates. There's something I'd like you to see before you leave your world for good."

Her heart twisted painfully. He thought her declaration of love meant she would go with him to Annwyn. "What is it?"

"DeLinea's Edinburgh gallery. I have a show scheduled for tomorrow night. It will be my last."

"But . . . what about the death magic? The Unseelies?"

"The gallery's defenses are extremely strong. You'll be completely safe, I promise."

Christine's mind raced. Attend a deLinea show in Edinburgh? A few short weeks ago she would've been thrilled at the prospect. Now it left her cold inside, because she knew what she had to do once she got off this island.

"I'd love to go to Edinburgh," she said.

But it was going to be so hard to leave him once she got there.

Once again, while Christine slept, Kalen painted.

This time he used watercolors, Christine's preferred medium. She was curled in a ball around a plump feather pillow, the intricate Celtic knot tattoo on her right shoulder riding just above the edge of the bedsheets, but he didn't paint her in that pose. No, the image emerging on paper was from his memory, a pose he was sure would bring a lovely blush to Christine's cheeks. She was nude, her legs spread wide, her breasts in full view. Dark hair tumbled about unblemished shoulders. One hand rested on her inner thigh, as if she were gathering the courage to pleasure herself for him. The other hand grazed the upper slope of her breast. Her expression was one he'd come to know deeply: love mingled with a soul-deep vulnerability.

Ah, she was so beautiful. And the painting? *Superb.*

His brush moved on the paper as his cock hardened—as much from the memory of Christine as from the sheer exhilaration of creating such a beautiful work of art.

He could not lose her. Would not.

In so short a time, she'd become vital to his existence.

When he buried himself inside her, stroked her into bliss as their combined magic swirled about them, he felt whole. After seven hundred years of feeling less than a man, he felt Christine had given him back his self. Her light invaded every part of his soul, casting forgiveness on guilt that had festered for centuries. He'd told her the worst, and she hadn't turned away.

Guided by her muse's magic, at last he understood what Uni had meant for him to learn. Love. It was life itself, the essence of creation. The inspiration of all art. In all the years he'd wielded his spear, he'd never understood the value of the human life he'd fought to protect. Until now.

He would honor Christine for all eternity for her gift. He would take her to Annwyn, present her as his wife to Niniane and Lir. Lir would gift her with an immortal soul. There would be children, many children. He and Christine would live unending lives free of death or evil.

And Christine would be happy.

He would see to it.

CHAPTER SEVENTEEN

"Kalen! Help me!"

The cry was Christine's. Gods! Kalen sprinted toward it, through a miasma so thick and putrid he nearly choked.

"Kalen!"

The call was behind him now. Impossible. He spun about, his warrior's senses taut. His grip tightened on the shaft of Uni's crystal spear. But that was impossible. He'd not held the weapon in seven hundred years.

His feet thudded on uneven ground. He was in some putrid hell. Shadows formed, sharpened. Suddenly, before him, Christine appeared. Her body was draped across a boulder, bound hand and foot. Looming over her, a glinting blade in her hand, was Culsu.

"No!" This would not happen. Not again.

"You love this woman." Culsu's cold, dead eyes brought him up short. "For that, I will kill her."

"No. I will not permit it."

Culsu's blade rose a fraction. "Kill me, then, Immortal."

At Kalen's hesitation, she laughed. "You can't do it, can you? You won't trade an eternity of nothingness for her life."

"I would," Kalen whispered, but the vow had come a heartbeat too late.

Culsu laughed. Her blade sliced in a downward arc. Kalen tried to move and found he could not. Darkness blotted his vision; the ground fell away.

Christine screamed. . . .

And the dream shattered. Kalen expelled a harsh breath. A nightmare. Just a nightmare. Except . . . slowly, he became aware of the disturbing fact that he was no longer in his bed, or even in his bedchamber.

He was in some dark, dank space, sprawled on slime-covered rock. A subtle odor of rotting fish struck his nostrils, along with the stench of stagnant sea water. The deep silence was punctuated by the muted roar of the sea. He knew where he was, though how he had gotten there was a mystery. Never before had he translocated in his sleep.

He hadn't set foot in this cell in over five hundred years, since the day he'd claimed this abandoned castle as his home. He'd not expected to return until another 293 years had passed.

He willed light into the darkness. A soft glow illuminated stone walls slick with slime and oozing with niter. He was in the lower level dungeons, directly beneath his office, close to sea level. The cell was little more than a cave hollowed from bedrock. Its ceiling was barely higher than Kalen's head, its width less than an arm's span. Remnants of iron shackles, now little more than lumps of rust, clung to the walls. The air was thick, rank, and not worth the trouble of breathing.

The original occupant of Kalen's home had been a tyrant—he could almost hear the sobs of the men who had rotted here. Kalen, however, had imprisoned something entirely different here.

Uni's crystal spear.

Once the magical weapon had been so familiar it had almost been a part of his body. Now, after so many centuries, looking at it was like gazing on the rotted remains of a severed limb. Except that Uni's spear hadn't decayed. It could not be destroyed.

Kalen would have shattered it into a thousand pieces if he could have. Even with it whole, he might have buried it or cast it into the sea. But the danger of the weapon being found was too great. In the wrong hands, the spear's magic crystal tip could cut a wide swath of destruction. So Kalen had done the only thing he could think of—hidden it in his own home, under his feet, protected by the strongest defensive magic he knew.

Gerold's blood still stained the spearhead. The sight of the rust-colored residue made Kalen's stomach churn. The spear was the instrument of his disgrace as a god and as a man. In three centuries, when his debt was paid, he might have again wielded it in defense of humanity. Now he had no faith there would be any life magic left in the human world to defend.

The spear lay discarded in a corner of the dungeon. He took a step toward it. As if sensing its master's nearness, the tip winked to life, white sparks tingling on the edges of the crystal. Ice-cold energy, awaiting Kalen's command.

He stared at it for a long while. Then he extended his right arm, his palm open. He didn't bend to retrieve it. He didn't have to. At this close range he had only to will it and the weapon appeared in his hand.

His fingers closed on the shaft. The spear's heft felt clumsy. Unnatural. He'd once felt naked without it. Now he could hardly remember how to use it. He rubbed his thumb over the shaft, revealing the Etruscan runes etched in the ancient petrified wood.

TARAN. It had been his people's name for him. They'd thought him a god. Built temples in his honor.

It was a name he'd not heard since Gerold's death. A name that no longer held any meaning.

He stared at the inscription for a long time, remembering. When he left the dungeon, his hands were empty.

CHAPTER EIGHTEEN

Unseelies.

Ugh.

The things were smelly, hideous, and vicious. Mac had killed three of them on the road between Nairn and Inverness. Now he felt like he needed twenty-four hours in a hot shower. The fetid odor of dung and rotting garbage was indelibly imprinted on his brain. Even worse, the ripe aroma had raised memories he thought long forgotten—the abject terror of a child surrounded by slavering monsters.

You're not a child anymore. Mac's jaw tightened. Kalen was right. He wasn't a child. He wasn't helpless. He was a bloody demigod.

It was well past midnight when he gunned his Norton through the outskirts of Inverness, slicing through a gloomy drizzle. His cell phone chimed, but he ignored it. If he talked to Niniane right now, he'd only piss her off. He gripped the Norton's handlebars until rubber and steel compressed under the force of his frustration. Pathetic, that's what he was. Seven hundred and twelve years old and still

tethered to his mother's apron strings. Not that he'd ever
seen Niniane wearing anything so mundane as an apron.

He sped into the center of town. Bank Street was deserted apart from a trio of vampires loitering on the sidewalk in front of the Free North Church. Smarmy creatures.
Not as bad as Unseelies, but Mac had never had much charity for the undead. He sent a bolt of elfshot whizzing over
their heads as he zoomed past. The vamps jumped and scattered, yelling curses. Mac grinned. An adolescent display of
power, but bugger it all, it felt *good*. There were far too many
death creatures around. He was sick of the lot of them.

Speeding over the Young Street Bridge, he rolled past
Leanna's tour office. According to the poster, a tour was in
progress at that very moment. Niall and Ronan had told
him as much when he'd called them earlier; he'd sent his
cousins to spy on the festivities. That would provide Mac
the opportunity to take a private look around Leanna's hotel suite.

He halted in front of the Palace and tossed his key to the
night valet. The hotel was the best Inverness had to offer,
but that didn't stop Leanna from complaining. She was used
to London's Connaught, Paris's Concorde, Vienna's Inter-
continental. Well, a fat lot of good those addresses had done
her. They were too far from the Gates of Annwyn, the
source of all Sidhe magic. Leanna had been forced to come
crawling back to Scotland to renew her powers. Which
she'd done in spades. Was some of that power due to death
magic? Gods, he hoped not.

He nodded to the doorman as he entered the hotel. A
human, one he'd seen before, though the bloke's name escaped him at the moment. At Mac's greeting, the man stiffened, fear flashing through his eyes. Mac scowled. He'd
never harmed a human, wouldn't dream of it. Leanna and
her half-breed friends weren't quite so particular.

The elevator whooshed to the top floor. Leanna's suite
was at the end of the hall. He grabbed the knob and all but

wrenched the door off its hinges. As he'd expected, her rooms were deserted. He rummaged about, opening doors, looking in closets and under beds, dreading what he might find. Damn it, if Leanna had gone to the dark side, he couldn't help but feel partly responsible. She was his kin, after all.

And their mother was a bloody nightmare. If only Mac had known about Leanna's birth, he would've raised his half sister himself. But he hadn't known, not until nearly a century later when Niniane had admitted the truth. In private. His mother had told him she'd deny it up and down and around the block if Mac ever told Lir about her indiscretion.

He strode into Leanna's dressing room and stopped abruptly. There was an unmistakable taint of death magic in the air—an aura of brimstone and sulfur. A close inspection revealed faint bloodstains in the grout between the marble tiles. Sniffing, he caught the unmistakable scent of dung and rotting garbage.

He closed his eyes. Damn it. Leanna wasn't stupid—she should know better than to fool with death magic. Calling his deepest power, he cast his senses into the subtle vibrations left by the events that had occurred in this space. When the vision formed, it sickened him. Leanna, piercing her own flesh . . . collecting the blood . . . spilling it out . . . forming the inverted Ouroborous.

In the haze of his mind's eye, he saw a portal open. A demon in female form, with wild black hair and glowing red eyes, stepped through the burning archway. Two vaguely human Unseelies emerged from the rift to hunker at her feet. One licked a viscous drop of drool from its red lips.

The demon placed her hands on the Unseelies' heads as if they were treasured pets. "These creatures owe me their freedom from Uffern. They and their brethren will be yours to command," she told Leanna. "If you prove yourself worthy."

Leanna inclined her head. "How can I serve you?"

The demon's crimson eyes flashed. "Strip."

Obediently, Leanna began to undress. Sickened, Mac let the vision dissolve. Christine had been right—Leanna had turned demonwhore. Why? What did she want that only a demon could give?

Emotions seething, he strode to Leanna's makeup table, where the scent of death was strongest. He yanked open the center drawer, breaking both the mundane lock and the spell that enhanced it. The vial he'd seen in Leanna's hand, filled with dark red liquid, lay in a padded velvet case. He picked it up.

The glass warmed his palm, then began to burn. The blood it contained was potent. He felt its essence: half human, half Sidhe. Powerful enough to summon an Old One. He'd destroy it, but not here, where its power would mingle with the darkness she'd already unleashed. He dropped it into his pocket and contemplated his next move. Wait here for Leanna? Or leave and plan a meeting on his own turf?

He opted for the latter. There was no telling how much dark power a half-Sidhe demonwhore could command. He'd listen to Niall's and Ronan's report before he made any decisions. Retracing his steps, he left the hotel, laying a patch of rubber as he roared up the hill to his tiny, unexceptional graystone house. He frowned as he noted lights blazing from the first-floor windows.

He opened the door and saw red. Ronan and Niall weren't on Leanna's tour at all. They were kicking back on Mac's sofa, swilling Mac's Guinness and streaming MTV over Mac's broadband. Half-empty Chinese take-away containers were strewn about the table and floor.

To make matters worse, the pair didn't even notice his arrival. The were too intent on Mac's sixty-inch plasma screen.

"*The Real World?*" Ronan scoffed, gesturing with his bottle. "What's so real about three virgin werewolves sharing a two-room London flat with three newly made vampires? There's no bloody chance that would ever happen."

"Who gives a shit about real?" Niall answered. "They've got cameras in the bedrooms."

"What's the matter, mates? Can't find your own action?" Mac entered the room, slamming the door behind him.

Ronan leapt off the couch, spilling his stout on the carpet. "Bugger it all, Mac. You scared the shit out of me."

Niall hastily kicked a take-away carton under the coffee table. "Didn't expect you home so early, Mac. How'd your visit to the Palace go?" As an afterthought, he snagged an unopened bottle off the floor and tossed it in Mac's direction. "Here. Have one."

Mac caught the bottle in one hand but didn't open it. "Turn that damn telly down," he barked. His ire didn't abate as Niall scooped up the remote and complied. "Why are you two here? You're supposed to be on Leanna's tour."

"We joined it for a time, Mac, but then she spotted us and started peppering us with elfshot. Now, we could've fought back, but there were too damn many humans underfoot. So we backed off." Ronan took a swig of ale and shook his head. "Your sister's in a rare temper."

Mac sank into a leather lounger. "She's turned demon-whore."

"She couldn't," Ronan protested, aghast. "She's Sidhe. We despise the sodding things."

"Apparently, Leanna's human side isn't so particular." He extracted the crystal vial from his pocket and held it up to the light. "I found this in her dressing room. Her own blood."

"She's collecting it? That's sick." Niall looked slightly nauseated.

Mac could sympathize. Holding the vial was making his own stomach more than a little queasy. "Leanna's demon mistress has given her dominion over the Unseelies. She was probably the one who helped them escape in the first place."

"Damn, Mac. What are you going to do?"

A female laugh sounded in the doorway. "Yes, Mac. What *are* you going to do? I'd *love* to know."

Mac leaped from the lounger and spun to face the door. "Leanna."

She stood on his threshold, her lush body adorned in nothing more than two horizontal strips of leather. One encircled her chest, barely covering her nipples. The other did a piss-poor job of hiding her shaved mons.

Mac stared at his half-sister. She was younger than Mac by a few hundred years, but looked a few years older. How many men had she driven to death with that perfectly formed body?

Niall reached again for the remote. The TV sputtered into silence. Leanna arranged her body in a seductive pose against the doorframe, regarding Mac with hooded eyes. Dougal, her ever-present watchdog, lurked behind her on the stoop, a snarl twisting his ogrelike features. Mac's fingers curled around the crystal vial. He ignored the pain the contact brought.

Leanna's eyes made a long sweep of Mac's body, lingering on his crotch. When at last she raised her gaze and licked her lips, his stomach turned. She'd never hidden the fact she wanted to fuck him. Her own brother. The thought disgusted him. And made him hate the circumstances that had given Leanna such a twisted view of the world. Damn Niniane for her part in this.

He pitched his voice low. "You know better than to fool with death magic."

Leanna pushed off the doorjamb and sauntered into the room, her bare feet silent on the wool carpet. Ronan and Niall—bloody cowards that they were—retreated to the far corner of the room.

Leanna trailed her hand along the back of the sofa as she approached him. "When was the last time you had a woman, big brother?" A surge of magic accompanied her words.

He regarded her dispassionately. "Give it up, Leanna. Your magic doesn't work on me." He opened his palm, revealing the vial of her blood. "Dealing with demons,

Leanna? Unseelies? Are you bloody nuts? You're going to get yourself killed."

"Killed? I daresay not. Just the opposite." She looked all too smug.

"What are you talking about?"

"You'll find out soon enough." She glided around the couch and came to stand before him. "Now give me that. It's mine."

"You're kidding, right?" He crushed the vial in his grip, incinerating it with a blast of elfshot. His hand stung with the force of the implosion, but he didn't so much as wince.

Leanna's eyes blazed. "You little shit! You have no right."

"Oh, I have every right. You'll stop the death magic, Leanna. Now."

Her leather-bound breasts brushed his chest. "And if I disobey, will you punish me?" Her bottom lip nudged forward and her lashes lowered in a mockery of submission. "Just the thought of it makes me wet, Mac. It's been my secret fantasy for years."

A starburst of magic accompanied her breathless whisper. Her lashes swept up, her ice-pale eyes glinting. She arched against him like a cat in heat, wrapping one leg around his thigh and riding it.

Mac shoved her away with an oath. "You're disgusting."

He turned his back, knowing the dismissive gesture would infuriate her. "I'll give you one last warning. Whatever demon you've been fooling with, don't perform the summoning again. Because if I find out you've done so, you won't have to worry about death magic hurting you. I'll be a much greater threat."

There was a profound moment of silence in which Mac felt Leanna's hatred radiating in waves. His door slammed a second later, but he felt no satisfaction.

Leanna pressed the blade to her wrist. Closing her eyes, she drew a breath and cut. The hot streak of pain was so intense she couldn't stifle a gasp. Damn Mac, for making her do this. Cold sweat beaded at her temples and trickled in a thin line down the side of her face. She felt nauseated, and light-headed, and for several long seconds her vision faded to red. When it cleared, she was panting.

She forced herself to watch the blood drip from the wound into the shallow bowl on her dressing table. She was oddly detached from the scene, as if she were about to float away. It didn't matter. This was necessary. Fresh-spilled blood was more potent than stale blood. It would afford her a deeper measure of Culsu's power.

The dizziness got the better of her. Reaching for a gauze square, she stanched the flow. The room didn't stop spinning until she'd wrapped her wrist in a tight bandage. Only then did her heart slow.

Once she'd regained her equilibrium, she looked into the bowl and breathed a sigh of relief. It contained more than enough blood, at least for the moment. Dipping her finger in the thick liquid, she smeared a circle on the marble tiles. Then, taking the bowl with her into the center of the circle, she traced the sigils. When the shadow aspect of the Ouroborous sprang to life, she said the words.

"Culsu. Come to me."

The demon appeared immediately, in a curling, hissing cloud of smoke that mimicked the dark, writhing locks of her hair. Her intense frown clearly indicated her displeasure at being summoned. The answering thrill that shot through Leanna's body was a visceral thing. Already, her sex was tingling and softening. Remembering. The leather strips at her breasts reminded her of the bonds Culsu had used to restrain her during sex. The experience had been humiliating—and mind-blowing. Finally, she understood the dark desire that led her human lovers to sacrifice their souls to their muse. She craved more.

She forced a casual tone. "Bad timing?"

"What do you want?" Culsu snapped.

Leanna met the demon's gaze. "My brother knows about the Unseelies."

Culsu gave a smooth shrug. "He can do nothing."

"Then tomorrow night . . ."

"Will proceed as planned."

Leanna let out a sigh. "Good."

Culsu's gaze sharpened. Her eyes glowed red as she scrutinized Leanna's body, lingering on her breasts and sex. Wetness streaked down Leanna's thighs.

"But first," Culsu said, "there is the small matter of payment."

"Yes, Mistress."

"Strip."

"We could take the train. Or rent a car."

Kalen snorted. "You'd prefer five hours in a rattling mundane death trap to a twenty-second translocation?"

Christine wanted to wipe the smirk right off his handsome face. "Yes, I would. I know it's hard to believe, but I have this illogical aversion to having my body exploded and put back together again."

"I won't ride in a human-made vehicle." He touched his finger to her chin, urging her to meet his gaze. "Go and dress. It'll be fine, you'll see."

Christine sighed. "I don't have any choice, do I?"

"Not if you want to attend the opening. It starts in two hours."

She shut her eyes briefly, gathering her courage—both for the translocation and what she had to do afterward. Find a way to leave Kalen. She knew it wouldn't be easy. Kalen was sure to have the gallery warded. And then there was the matter of her heart, and her guilt at deceiving him. How was she going to find the strength to walk away?

"All right," she told him. "I'll be ready in half an hour."

She fought back tears as she dressed. Pearl had laid out a simple, strapless gown of indigo satin, tight at the bust, snug at the hip and thigh. The skirt flared just below the knee into a swirling blue cloud. The matching stiletto sandals made her appear almost tall and willowy. She grimaced. Not exactly the most practical attire for running away, but it would have to do.

She sat at the dressing table in the Rose Room and swept her hair into a loose bun. Behind her, reflected in the mirror, the door opened. Kalen entered, attired in formal Scottish evening wear of white shirt, short jacket, and tartan kilt. A furred sporran hung at his waist. The gold buckles on his shoes shone.

The costume only served to accentuate the primitive power of his body. His hair, severely tied at his nape, drew attention to his harsh cheekbones, slanting brows, and dark eyes. Christine drank in every line of him, committing the image to painful memory. It would be all she would take of him when she left.

Their eyes met in the mirror.

"You look lovely," he said softly, advancing.

He halted behind her, his fingers dipping into the pocket of his jacket. A glittering necklace appeared—a collection of thin, silken cords strung with translucent stones. Christine watched as Kalen draped it about her neck. Each gem was a teardrop reflecting a dazzling rainbow. As soon as it touched her skin, she knew that it was more than a simple necklace.

She touched it, awed. "Why, these aren't stones at all, are they?"

"No. Each one is a drop of sea spray, spelled to hold its shape. Do you like it?"

"How could I not? It's the most astonishing thing I've ever seen! Where did you get it?"

"It's a gift from the mermaids. They saw you in the window, it seems, and recognized your power as akin to theirs." He bent and kissed her bare shoulder, sending a delicious thrill over her skin. "When we return, you can thank them in person. The merfolk will be accompanying us to Annwyn."

"I'd like that," Christine said, swallowing around the lump in her throat. She would never travel to Annwyn.

Kalen took her hand and helped her rise. "Ready?"

For the jump to Edinburgh. "As ready as I'm ever going to be."

He drew her in close, hip against hip, his strong arm encircling her shoulders. "Don't worry," he said, his lips at her temple. "Just relax. It's easier that way."

"They say that about plane crashes, too."

Kalen chuckled. Her body went rigid as she braced herself for a terrifying, nauseating trip. Twenty seconds, Kalen had said. Longer than either of the other jumps she'd made. She could survive twenty seconds. She hoped.

It was the longest twenty seconds of her life.

A loud *whoosh* . . . a sensation like her body exploding, each cell spinning into nothing . . . the sick, helpless feeling of being totally without anchor. And it went on and on . . .

When her feet touched solid ground she kept her eyes squeezed shut. Clutching Kalen's shoulder, she waited for the twisting world to right itself.

His low voice held a note of concern. "Are you all right?"

No, she was *not*. She took a deep breath and cracked open her eyes. "I'll live."

"Forever," he said gently. "I'm counting on it."

She looked away quickly, not wanting him to read the truth in her eyes. Forever. With Kalen. It was a dream she yearned to grasp. If Tain and Kehksut were defeated, and if Christine survived the battle, maybe Kalen would come back from Annwyn for her. Or maybe he'd remember how she'd lied to him and decide she wasn't worth the trouble.

The room they'd landed in was beautifully furnished— soft, thick carpet, antique furnishings, exquisite paintings. The heavy, brocaded drapes were open. A multipaned window faced the buttressed steeple of a stern graystone church. Beyond its spire, the road rose to meet a castle on a high hill.

"Edinburgh," Kalen told her.

The scene might have been charming, had it not been obscured by a dirty veil of rain. Usually rain cheered her. Not now—*this* rain left bloodred streaks on the window.

The street below was nearly devoid of activity. The few souls who did brave the storm walked swiftly, heads down and shoulders hunched. Christine turned away, her heart heavy. She'd spent the last week sheltered by Kalen's magic, on an island untouched by death magic. Now, back in the real world, she was shocked by how much the human world had degenerated in the short time she'd been hidden away.

She glanced up at Kalen. His expression was grim as he moved to draw the curtains. With a sigh, she turned back to the room. It was part of a large suite. Several doors led to other rooms—she caught glimpses of a dining room, kitchen, and bedroom. She could see nothing amiss. No doubt the building was under heavy magical protection.

"Where are we?" she asked. "A hotel? Is the gallery nearby?"

"Right under our feet, as it happens. These are my private rooms on the upper floor." He guided her to a brocaded sofa. "Sit for a moment and catch your breath. I need to check with Fiona, my gallery manager. She's Sidhe—all my employees here in Scotland are. She'll need to know tonight will be deLinea's last show. Mac asked me to brief her on the evacuation."

He moved to an intercom panel on the wall. Lifting the receiver, he spoke in low tones while Christine reviewed her options. Her plan—such as it was—involved slipping out of the building while Kalen was greeting his guests. The wards would have to be lowered at the gallery entrance to allow Kalen's human patrons to enter. If she was going to leave, that was her best bet.

Her first move when free would be to contact Amber. With Christine's passport and money tucked away at the Faerie Lights in Inverness, she was going to need some help getting out of the country. Amber and Adrian had the resources to help her get on a plane to Seattle as soon as possible. They would be disappointed about Kalen, of course, but that couldn't be helped. Every time Christine thought about what would certainly happen if Kalen joined the battle against Tain, she felt ill. She wouldn't risk him.

His instructions to his manager complete, Kalen moved to her side and helped her up from the couch. "Come. The guests will be arriving soon. I want to give you a preview of the show."

He led her to a small elevator set discreetly in an alcove. Inside, there was barely enough room for two people—especially when one person was as large as Kalen. Anchoring Christine snugly in his arms, he bent his head and kissed her deeply as the elevator cab dropped.

"I love you," he said. "You are my life. I will never forsake you. Remember that."

"Always," Christine whispered. Her heart squeezed so painfully she was sure it was bleeding.

The elevator door swooshed open. With his hand placed protectively on her lower back, Kalen guided her onto the main gallery floor.

The building must have been several hundred years old, but the space Christine stepped into was modern and dramatic. At least three levels had been gutted to produce one soaring space. The floor seemed to float; a sleek black staircase led down to a foyer at street level. Polished chrome railings gleamed and unobtrusive lighting cast a dazzling glow. Colors were neutral—stark white, shining black, muted beige. A perfect foil for the art displayed on curved stands and freestanding easels.

Music played, drifting from hidden speakers—Manannán, of course. Tables spread with white linen and set with crystal and china graced the perimeter of the space. A dozen or so tuxedoed Sidhe waiters stood nearby, waiting for the guests to arrive.

"They function more as guards than servants," Kalen told

her. "They're Mac's clan. Nothing gets by them. You'll be entirely safe here. I've got magical protections everywhere."

"What about the entrance? Won't the guests have to pass through the wards?"

"We'll bring the spells down, but only for as long as it takes the guests to enter. Stragglers will be turned away. We'll go downstairs just before the doors open. But right now, I want you to tell me what you think of the artist I've chosen to spotlight the show."

They traversed the gallery floor to the dais upon which the central exhibit was displayed. It took a full thirty seconds for Christine's dazed brain to register what her eyes were seeing. Floating as if in a dream, she allowed Kalen to guide her up the steps onto the stage.

"Why . . . they're mine."

He smiled down at her. "Yes."

And they were. *Her* paintings, *her* creations, framed and presented as masterpieces. *Faith* hung on a glittering background of gold, *Hope* on a shining sheet of silver. *Modesty*, *Generosity*, *Joy*, *Vision* . . . and all the rest. They were all there.

Only one virtue was missing—the one she hadn't known intimately enough to portray. *Love*. The sudden constriction in her throat told her she'd have no trouble painting it now.

She turned wondering eyes on Kalen. "What have you done?"

"Given your talent the recognition it deserves. I only regret that it comes now, at deLinea's final show."

"But how did you find them? These paintings were in Rome. You don't even know my address."

He shook his head and smiled. "Small obstacles."

"But . . ." She turned back to the exhibit, suddenly frozen with panic. In just a few minutes, the gallery doors would open. People would enter. Strangers. They would view her paintings not as beloved children, but as commodities. And they would pass judgment. Would they smile and nod?

Grow thoughtful? Laugh and make disparaging comments? Or worse . . . would they be *unmoved*?

A windstorm of butterflies beat their wings in her stomach. How had she ever thought she wanted her soul displayed before strangers? For a moment, she couldn't think. Couldn't breathe.

"Christine?" Kalen's whisper carried a touch of selfdoubt. "Are you angry? I thought you'd be pleased."

She struggled to find her voice. "I . . . I *am* pleased." Her smile was forced, she knew, but it was all she could manage. "I'm just overwhelmed. My work—my *true* work, not the tourist scenes—hasn't ever been shown." She swallowed. "It's humbling."

It was made even more humbling by the knowledge Kalen had done this for her. Because he loved her. And all the while she'd been plotting to leave him. Tears of guilt burned her eyelids.

"Come with me," he murmured, glancing across the room. He took her elbow. "There's someone I'd like you to meet."

Christine blinked as he guided her to a stunning older woman. She was tall and willowy, her upswept blond hair gone to silver. The black sheath dress she wore was as elegant as it was understated. Pointed ears declared her Sidhe ancestry.

"Christine, this is Fiona, my gallery manager."

Fiona inclined her head. "Miss Lachlan. An honor. Though it hardly matters under the circumstances, I should tell you that the advance viewing of your show netted several offers between six and seven hundred thousand."

Christine's jaw dropped. "Dollars?"

"Pounds sterling, actually." With a nod, Fiona excused herself to check on last-minute arrangements with the caterer.

Christine stared after her. Seven hundred thousand pounds? That was more than a million dollars! Someone was willing to pay *that* much for one of her watercolors? It wasn't possible.

"You shouldn't be surprised," Kalen told her as he escorted her down the stairs to the foyer. "Your work is . . . magical."

Christine looked at him in surprise. "You can't really mean that. You only displayed my work as a favor to me. You think contemporary art is garbage."

He grimaced. "I've reconsidered. Your paintings . . ." He shook his head. "The moment I saw them, I knew they were unique. Unlike anything I've ever seen, in this or any other century. They're . . . timeless. Ethereal. Created from a dream of another world." He cleared his throat. "A better world."

His praise warmed her. Impulsively, she went up on tiptoe, unfurling her magic and sending it to him in a searing, openmouthed kiss. After a brief reflex of surprise, he absorbed her power. Christine pressed close, love and lust rippling through her body. The gallery, her paintings, the escape she'd soon make—all of it faded from her consciousness. For one brief, shining moment, there were only two lovers joined by magic. If only it could last. But she knew that was a foolish dream. The world was on a collision course with hell. People were dying. She had no right to be here, safe in the arms of the man she loved.

A chill ran through her. She ended the kiss, unlinking her arms from Kalen's neck and stepping away. She rubbed her bare arms, shivering. Kalen's gave her a concerned glance. He might have spoken, but at that moment Fiona reappeared.

"Kalen, it's time. Quite a crowd's gathered outside in that foul rain. Shall I bring down the wards?"

"Is everyone in place?"

"Of course."

"Then, by all means, admit our guests."

Christine stared at the door. It was time. Her chance at escape had come. All that was left was for her to take it.

CHAPTER NINETEEN

The next fifteen minutes were a blur of unfamiliar faces and murmured greetings. Christine stood at Kalen's side in the receiving line, a false smile nearly cracking her face as the appropriate banalities sprang to her lips. All Kalen's guests were clearly wealthy. The human women were beautiful and slender, draped in silks and dripping with jewels. The human men, arrayed in tuxedoes or traditional Scottish attire, all but reeked of power and money.

There were a few magical creatures in attendance as well—a group of tiny fluttering faeries and a trio of sultry Selkie men with long sable hair and smoldering dark eyes. The Sidhe guards stood silently, but she sensed their watchfulness. Their presence at the door was a problem, but not an insurmountable one. Kalen had, after all, unwittingly handed her a powerful tool that would ensure her escape.

She waited until about half the guests had filed through the Sidhes' security checkpoint. The wards wouldn't remain down much longer. She touched Kalen's arm. "I'm going to visit the ladies' room."

"All right. Hurry back."

In answer, Christine laid her palm against his cheek. He took her hand, kissed it, then searched her eyes before letting it go. Christine fought to keep her expression neutral. If he saw any reason to doubt she would return, he didn't show it.

"I'll be waiting," he said.

She left without looking back, though she wanted to in the worst way. Blinking back tears, she slipped into the ladies' room. As she'd hoped, it was empty. Quickly, she crossed to the nearest sink and cranked open the faucet.

The sound and sensation of running water calmed her. She held her hand under the thin, clear stream, seeking her magic. At once, the sea-foam necklace Kalen had given her combined with the trickling flow to send sparkling waves of magic over her skin. Working quickly, she raised a glamour. Wrapping it around her, she summoned the image she wanted. Male, middle-aged, with a thick waist and a bald spot that was badly concealed by an oily comb-over. He wore a long raincoat over a hand-tailored tuxedo jacket and kilt. An umbrella was tucked under one arm.

When she was sure the illusion was firmly in place, she stepped out of the ladies' room. The men's room door was nearby; both doors were out of sight of Kalen's position. If he spotted her once she emerged from the hallway, she hoped he wouldn't see through her disguise. She traversed the foyer to the entry, acutely aware of his presence just yards away.

"So sorry," she said to Fiona, who stood greeting the last of the guests at the door. "I've just had a message, most urgent, I'm afraid I can't stay."

"A shame," Fiona murmured. She looked closer and frowned. "Mr. . . ."

"Weatherby," Christine offered. "Timothy Weatherby." She wasted no time in hurrying out the door to the street. "Pleasant evening to you."

She was out. The breath left her lungs in a rush as she

hurried down the street. It was still raining like a fiend. Her umbrella, though hoisted overhead, was useless—it was an illusion, after all. As was her raincoat. Within moments, she was drenched and chilled to the bones.

She wouldn't have minded if it had been a normal rain. It wasn't. It was something sinister and deadly. The oily deluge falling from the leaden sky left smears on her skin that looked like blood and smelled like death. She ignored the crawling sensation as she hurried up the street, her high heels skidding on the scum coating the sidewalk. She was forced to slow her steps and keep to the shelter of the buildings.

She crossed one intersecting street and hurried on. There was a pub on the next corner—it looked like it was open. She'd stop there and call Amber. Then she'd ask directions to the train station and head for the closest airport. Intent on her plans, she didn't notice the hissing sound until she was almost upon the alley from which it emanated. A cloud of acid smoke billowed from the narrow archway, tendrils reaching out to swirl around her ankles like snakes. She shrank back into a doorway, heart pounding.

Scraping footsteps approached, claws screeching on cobbles like fingernails on a blackboard. A dozen shadowy figures darted from the alley, accompanied by a miasma of filth. *Unseelies.* The foul monsters could be nothing else. They were even more hideous than she'd imagined. Roughly human, with corpse-blue skin and twisted, emaciated limbs, they looked like a nightmare sprung to life. Bulbous heads perched on lumpy torsos, translucent bat wings unfurled from hunched shoulders.

Communicating with a series of grunts and whistles and body motions, the largest creature, clearly the leader, herded his pack in the direction from which Christine had just come.

They halted directly in front of deLinea. They seemed to be waiting, craning their necks as they peered upward.

Christine eased away from her sheltering doorway and looked up.

The sky was angry—at first she saw nothing but an amorphous dark blotch against a grimy background of low-hanging clouds. The wind howled. As she watched, the stain on the sky grew larger, resolving into a writhing mass of bodies and wings. Christine's stomach turned. More Unseelies. Hundreds of them.

They dropped out of the sky like a rain of brimstone, trailing fire in their wake. Several landed on the roof of the gallery; others crowded the street or hung from the window casings and eaves, banging eagerly on the glass.

The Unseelies in the street shrieked and rushed deLinea's front door. White energy flashed, then dimmed. Kalen's wards held—one monster dropped to the pavement, shrieking. His companions were undaunted; they rushed the doorway in a second assault. A barrage of elfshot met them; Kalen's Sidhe had joined the fight. A brief exchange of fire and light ensued. One vivid blast left several Unseelies writhing on the pavement. The rest drew back, communicating with whistles and grunts. Regrouping, they fell into a wedge formation and charged the door.

It gave way with a crash. On an upper level, a window shattered. The creatures screeched, clawing each other as they fought to get inside. Christine stood frozen, her fist pressed against her mouth. *Kalen.* Would he stand by while the Sidhe fought? Or would he join the fight? If he killed even one of these monsters . . .

She darted back down the street, all thoughts of her own escape forgotten. She had to get to Kalen. Protect him . . . A hysterical laugh rose in her throat as she realized how ludicrous that thought was. Still, she had to try. She had to be with him.

Three steps and she stumbled on her heels, wrenching her ankle. Cursing, she tried to kick the shoes off. Before she could loosen the straps, a claw caught her arm.

Sharp talons dragged across her skin, scraping like blades of fire. Christine cried out, trying to pull free, choking on a foul stench. An Unseelie loomed over her, yellow eyes aglow. A line of slobber dribbled from the corner of its mouth.

She didn't have time to think. Gathering her magic, she drew what power she could from both the sea spray necklace and the water hidden in the Unseelie's own body. With a cry, she focused the magic and sent it blasting toward her attacker.

The Unseelie recoiled with a shriek. Christine wrenched herself from its grasp and lunged in the direction of the gallery. Before she'd taken two steps, three more of the monsters dropped into her path. She spun about, only to find that her first assailant had recovered and was closing in from behind.

She was trapped.

CHAPTER TWENTY

Unseelies were storming his gallery.

Inconceivable.

And yet, it was happening. The creatures had crashed through his perimeter wards and attacked his Sidhe guards. Mac's clan was meeting the challenge. Fiona had reacted with her usual efficiency, herding the guests onto the gallery's center dais and deploying a defensive circle around them. The rest of the clan were battling the Unseelies at the doorways and windows and Kalen was confident they'd soon deal with the invasion. Unseelies were essentially undisciplined, while Mac's clan battled with deliberate, exacting strategy. They were the best fighters in the city. Kalen should know, he'd trained them himself.

He had no doubt his guards would repulse the monsters. More troubling was the fact that Christine hadn't yet emerged from the ladies' room. Kalen ducked across the foyer, aiming a burst of cold, white energy at a knot of Unseelies just inside the door. He was careful not to actually hit any of the creatures. He couldn't risk causing a wound that might prove fatal.

He slammed open the ladies' room door. "Christine?"

No answer. Damn it all to Hades. The room was empty.

Water sprayed from one of the sinks, and there was a lingering aura of glamour magic. Cold dread seeped through Kalen's senses. Christine had asked questions about the building and its magical security system. He'd thought she was frightened—what an idiot he was! While he'd been mooning over her like a lovesick puppy, she'd been planning her escape.

With his wards in place, the only way she could have left the building was through the front entrance—and to do that, she had to have passed him in the foyer and slipped out the front door. There'd been a man who'd hurried past, a human he didn't recognize. At the time, Kalen hadn't paid much attention. Now he knew he should have.

A fear unlike any he'd ever known caught hold of his throat and squeezed. Christine was in the street with the Unseelies, alone and unprotected. Cursing, he flung himself through the shattered entranceway.

The scene that greeted him was like a kick in the gut. Four of the slavering monsters had cornered Christine. She fought them off with blue waves of energy—drawn from the sea spray necklace, Kalen realized. He sent silent thanks to the merfolk.

One Unseelie took a swipe at Christine, opening a gash on her shoulder. Pure, primitive anger, raw and fierce, erupted in Kalen's gut. *Bloodlust.* An emotion he'd thought he'd banished. An emotion that could doom him for all eternity.

He found he didn't care.

He flung a burst of white energy at the monster. He'd aimed to kill, but at Christine's scream the thing twisted, catching the bolt on its arm instead of square in the gut. It yelped in outrage, swinging toward Kalen with murder in its yellow eyes.

"Bring it on, scum." He aimed his second shot.

"No, Kalen—don't kill it! You can't!"

Christine's cry pierced his concentration—his blast went wide. The Unseelie rushed him. With an oath, he grabbed it with his bare hands and tossed it aside—but not with enough force to kill it. The bloodlust was fading. A measure of sanity had returned.

Christine swept her arm in a horizontal arc, sending a wave of blue energy toward the remaining three monsters. The Unseelies recoiled only momentarily. A heartbeat later, they resumed their slow advance.

Kalen swore, eaten alive by his helplessness. Christine's magic, focused by the sea spray necklace, was strong, but three Unseelies were more than any human witch could hope to defeat.

One of the creatures shifted on its feet, preparing to lunge. Kalen flung himself in front of Christine as the Unseelie leapt, taking the brunt of the monster's attack on his upper back. He snatched Christine into his arms and spun about, shaking the beast off and giving it a vicious kick. No sooner had its body collided with the pavement than one of its comrades sprang up in its place. Worse, a second pack of the creatures had caught wind of the fight and were racing to join the sport. Now he had seven of the things to contend with. Kalen couldn't hold them all back, not without killing some of them.

He could translocate and take Christine with him. But the preparation would leave him vulnerable for three long seconds. He could keep the Unseelies at bay, hoping they'd eventually tire. But the chances of doing that without casualty were slim.

His third option? Blast the fucking things to bits and be done with it.

Christine shot a bolt of blue energy at one of the creatures. Abruptly, Kalen realized she was trying to protect *him*. Gods. As if he weren't emasculated enough.

"Get behind me," he said tersely, setting her on her feet. "I'm going to blast through them."

"No!" Christine clung to his arm. "You can't!"

"I can and I—" Air abruptly vacated his lungs as an Unseelie leapt onto Kalen and sunk its foul claws into his shoulder. He ripped the creature from his back and flung it into the street.

"Disgusting slime." He eyed the others, noting a subtle flick of a webbed hand, an answering whistle and nod. The things were communicating. Working out a plan of attack. Unbelievable. The Unseelies he'd faced seven centuries earlier had been mindless brutes. Mac was right—someone was guiding them, training them as an army. Tain? The notion sickened him.

He felt Christine gathering her magic. "I'll take the three on the right," she whispered urgently. "You hold back the four on the left, but for the gods' sake, don't kill any of them."

"I will if I have to," he muttered.

"No." Her beautiful eyes were stricken. "I couldn't bear it. Promise me you won't."

"You'll stay back. Behind me."

"I won't! You need me—"

Her protest evaporated in the deafening roar of a motor. The blinding glare of a headlight arced over the scene as a motorcycle sped around the corner, tires squealing. The machine's front wheel burned as it skidded in a tight half circle, spewing green sparks. The Unseelies scattered, screeching. The driver lost control of the vehicle; he leapt free as four hundred pounds of metal and chrome shot across the pavement and slammed into a streetlamp. Sparks showered all around the driver's tall, leather-clad form.

"Mac!" Christine's eyes were huge. "How—"

"No time to chat, love." The demigod sent a blast of elfshot at the last lingering Unseelie. The emerald stream left a gaping hole in the center of the creature's stomach. The monster looked down, whimpered, and collapsed in a smoking heap.

Christine let out a shuddering breath. Kalen felt her knees go; his arm tightened around her, holding her upright. "Are you hurt?" he demanded, running his free hand over her limbs.

"No," she gasped. "I'm fine." She leaned heavily on Kalen as her gaze found Mac. "How did you know—?"

"I was following them," Mac replied grimly. "They've been wreaking bloody havoc." He scrubbed a hand over his face. "I tried to talk some sense into her, but . . ." He shook his head. "She's in deep. Deeper than I'd guessed."

"Who?" Kalen asked, frowning.

"Leanna. She's turned demonwhore. The demon she's servicing is the one who freed the Unseelies from Uffern. The entity has given Leanna dominion over the Unseelies." Screams spilled from the gallery. Mac's eyes cut toward the building. "They're inside?"

"Yes. Your clan's dealing with them."

"Bloody hell." Mac was already stalking toward the door. He paused to send a glance toward Kalen, then Christine. "You'd better take her out of here."

Kalen knew it was Mac's way of helping him save face, but the dismissal still stung. "I'll be back once Christine's safe," he told his friend.

Mac's eyes were grave. "Don't risk yourself, Kalen."

"It's my gallery. My people."

"Mine as well, mate. Don't worry. I'll take care of things. I had a good teacher." With a parting wave, he turned and darted for the gallery entrance.

"Wait!" Christine twisted out of Kalen's arms and started after Mac. "I'm coming with you."

"*Hades.*" Kalen surged after her and caught her by the wrist. "Forget it, Christine. You're coming with me."

Mac disappeared through the door, ducking past a barrage of elfshot. A second later, an Unseelie climbed out of a third-floor window, dragging a screaming woman. The creature bashed its burden against the sill. The women went limp, her screams silenced. Kalen swore silently. What was going wrong in there? The Sidhe should have had the Unseelies routed by now.

"Oh, Goddess," Christine breathed. "Let me go! People are being *killed*."

"Let Mac handle it."

"He'll need help. I've got to go back in!"

"Why?" asked Kalen tersely. "You were eager enough to get away. So eager you skulked past me disguised as a man."

Guilt flashed through her eyes. "You didn't give me much choice."

"I offered you eternity in Annwyn. With me. I thought . . ." A wave of profound hurt washed over him, making it hard to keep his voice steady. Where was the fearless warrior now? His tone hardened. "Never mind what I thought. You're coming home with me. Now." He let his magic drop in preparation for the jump to his castle.

Christine's eyes widened. "No. I won't go back there."

She sent a blast of water magic straight into his chest just as his power reached its lowest point. Caught unaware by the sheer force of her blow, he staggered backward with a grunt.

Christine twisted out of his arms. "You go back to the castle. I have to stay here."

"You don't honestly think I would allow that."

"It's not your choice to make!"

"It certainly is," Kalen said through clenched teeth.

"I won't run while people are in danger."

But you would. The unspoken words hung in the air between them. Centuries of shame and impotence hit Kalen like a kick to the solar plexus. And in that instant, he knew what he had to do, consequences be damned.

Understanding flared in Christine's eyes, then turned to panic. "No, Kalen. You can't. I didn't mean—"

He cut off her words, clamping a hand on her wrist and jerking her across the street to where a small crowd of human onlookers had gathered. The Edinburgh parapolice had just arrived and were in the process of erecting both physical and magical caution barriers. Kalen thrust Christine roughly toward the largest policeman.

"Look after this witch," he told the man. "Don't let her in the building. If I see her enter, I'll come back out here and kill you. Do you understand?"

The policeman's eyes bulged. He swallowed visibly. "Yes, sir."

Christine didn't take her eyes off Kalen for a second. "Don't do this," she pleaded. "Don't risk yourself."

"What do you care?" he asked her. "You were leaving me."

"I had to! Don't you understand? What you wanted for me wasn't right!"

"What you want for me isn't right, either, Christine." He looked toward the building. "I have to go back. It's my gallery. My responsibility."

"But—"

He turned and faced the battle, Christine's pleas fading to nothingness in his mind. His spine straightened as his emotions fell away. His mental turmoil faded. In its place rose a warrior's instinct, as ancient and as sure as the earth beneath his feet. An instinct he'd never quite been able to repress.

His senses sifted through the sounds and vibrations of the battle going on inside the darkened building. War-energy pulsed, shifting and moving like a living thing. Like a creature of death. And Kalen understood it as if it were a part of him.

His world narrowed, his vision sharpened. Mac and his Sidhe were making progress, but the threat was still vivid. Humans were at risk. The Unseelies were unbelievably strong, drawing power and intelligence from some dark force outside themselves.

A man shouted a curse. It was followed by a female sob. The sounds propelled Kalen to action. Bloodlust rose, but this time Kalen didn't let the emotion overshadow his rational mind. A balance of logic and passion was needed to win a battle. He'd often faced a battle with both those weapons in his arsenal. Tonight, however, a third, all-too-human emotion threatened to disarm him.

Fear. It was as palpable as his own heartbeat. For the first two millennia of his life, he'd never known it. Then came Gerold's betrayal. The moment Kalen had arrived in the monastery crypt to find the monk with his knife poised over his own child's heart, Kalen had learned the meaning of true terror. Imprisoned by Uni, not knowing if his confinement would ever end, he knew the emotion as his constant companion. And since his release, he'd lived with the fear that one act of irreversible violence could put him back in that cell for all eternity.

An acid tide of panic burned Kalen's veins. Fear for Christine, for Fiona and the other Sidhe, and even for Mac, the son of his heart who had given Kalen the loyalty that Gerold hadn't. Under it all, a swift current running, was fear for himself. Fear of an eternity passed in deadening numbness.

And yet, he could not turn from this fight. Would not. Not with people dying. The instinct to protect was deeper even than his terror.

He drew a deep breath and plunged into the battle.

There was no way Christine was going to stand by and let Kalen doom himself for eternity.

With a silent apology to the parapoliceman, who thought he could keep her on the safe side of the barriers, Christine touched the sea spray necklace. It was easy enough to cloak herself with a look-away glamour. Easier still to bypass the Edinburgh parapolice's wards and protections. She darted across the street and burst through deLinea's doors at a full run.

The scene inside was straight from hell. She paused, chest spasming against a lungful of oily fumes. Demon smoke clogged the foyer; she could see almost nothing. She bent double, coughing, desperate to expel the poison from her lungs. Overhead, fetid blasts of fire spattered, falling in an odorous spray on her head. She clutched the sea spray necklace. It enabled her to fight at a distance—an advantage she was sure to need in this battle.

Sounds of fighting erupted from the upper level. An errant dart of elfshot sizzled out of the screen of smoke and hit the wall above her head. She bent her head and ran in the direction of the stair. Finding it, she sprinted to the upper level.

Here, the smoke was less opaque. She could make out the forms of Sidhe and Unseelies at battle. A yellowish, one-eyed beast emerged from the cloud, its veined wings beating a cloud of smoke. Turning abruptly, it spied her.

With a single beat of its wings, it was on her. Christine screamed as its claws dug into her shoulder. She managed a blast of power, momentarily stunning it. Scrambling backward out of its reach, she came up hard against the railing that overlooked the lower level. The Unseelie lurched upright with an enraged hiss. It shook its hand wildly, hopping about and screeching as if the appendage were on fire.

With a spurt of horror, Christine realized her necklace was tangled in its claws.

The Unseelie succeeded in dislodging the strands of sea spray with a vicious shake. The necklace sailed through the air. Christine made a jump for it and missed. It arced over her fingers and disappeared into the smoke on the lower level.

A low snarl snapped her attention back to the Unseelie. The thing had gone still, watching her with an unnerving intelligence in its red eyes. Christine gripped the railing at her back. She could jump, but the drop was at least twenty feet.

The Unseelie hissed and started slowly forward, its wings rising malevolently. Christine held her ground, intent on the creature's every movement. Without the necklace, she'd have to touch it to use her magic. If she could only lay hands on it before it killed her . . .

The creature lunged. She dove at the same instant, grabbing hold of its clawed foot. Sharp, wiry hairs bit into her palm, sending sparks of pain up her arm. She ignored it and held tight. Unseelies, unlike demons, were flesh and blood. She drew on the water in the creature's body, centering her power on it.

Life magic burst through her fingers. The Unseelie reared with a hideous screech, twisting and flailing. It was young, she realized, recently spawned and not yet secure in its power. She'd wounded it gravely. Twisting out of her grip, it launched itself with a bone-chilling screech over the railing, plummeting into the thick smoke below. There was a dull thud, then silence.

She leaned over the rail, searching for movement. Nothing. Had she killed it? A sharp pang of regret twisted in her chest. The thing had been hideous, a creature of darkness, but it had been *alive*. And now it wasn't.

She had no time to dwell on the thought. A soul-curdling scream—human—split the air. She spun around. Not ten feet in front of her, another Unseelie had staggered out of the smoke, dragging a hysterical human male behind it. Before Christine could react, the snarling monster scooped the man up and wrenched his head from his shoulders.

Blood spewed. With an eager hiss, the Unseelie fitted its gaping maw over the corpse's mutilated neck. Its distended throat worked as the monster swallowed greedy gulps of its victim's blood.

"Holy Goddess," Christine breathed. The Unseelie must have heard—it looked up, grunted, and dropped its prize. Its filmy gaze fixed on Christine as a long, slimy tongue snaked between its thick lips to swipe a trickle of blood from the corner of its mouth.

With a hiss, it loped toward Christine. Horror rose, choking her. No time for tender feelings—she wanted the thing dead. *Now*. She dove, sliding through slick gore to catch hold of the Unseelie's lumpy leg. Calling the deepest wave of power she could muster, she blasted the full force of it through her hands. The thing shrieked as the living magic hit. It crashed to the floor, writhing in pain and fury.

"Gods in Annwyn, what the holy *fuck* do you think you're doing?"

A blast of elfshot whizzed past Christine's ear. It struck the Unseelie in the chest, burning a hole through its tough blue-black hide. The thing convulsed, then lay still. Rough hands grabbed Christine from behind and hauled her to her feet.

"Mac," she panted. "Thank the Goddess."

"What the hell are you doing in here?"

"Helping you and Kalen."

He gave a short, disbelieving laugh. "Help? Is that what you call this? Believe me, love, Kalen and I don't need this kind of help. Everything's under control"

"Yeah, I can see that," Christine said dryly. She gripped Mac's shoulder as a wave of vertigo spun the room.

"Whoa, love." Mac's arm tightened around her. "You okay?"

"I'm fine. But where's Kalen?" The fear she'd been holding back erupted. "Oh, gods, has he—?"

"Killed anything? No. He's there, see?"

Mac jerked his chin to the left. Christine followed the motion. The smoke had dissipated enough for her to make out what was going on. With sharp relief she spied Kalen on the gallery's center dais, holding a protective shield around the humans who'd taken refuge there. The Sidhe were scattered about the room, blasting the Unseelies. Many had fallen—others were diving out the windows. The tide of the battle had indeed turned.

"See?" Mac said. "No worries. We're just about through here."

"No worries? I just saw a man decapitated!"

"Yes, well, that bloke wouldn't stay behind Kalen's shield, now, would he? Humans." He gave a disgusted shake of his head. "The lot of you have the hardest time taking orders."

The last of the Unseelies leaped into the night. Mac shouted orders for the Sidhe to give chase. Christine breathed a sigh of relief, only to suck in her breath again when Kalen appeared, his handsome face twisted with rage. He grabbed her by both shoulders and shook, hard.

"You! I told you to stay outside."

She stiffened her spine. "Yes, well, I was hardly going to sit quietly by while you were in danger."

Kalen swore. "You little idiot! You could have been killed."

Their eyes met. Clung.

"You risked far more than I did," she said quietly.

"Christine." Kalen's voice was raw.

A noise in the foyer drew Christine's attention. "Bloody hell, look who's here," Mac said, looking over the railing to the level below. "I am going to kill that fucking bitch."

Christine peered around Kalen to see Leanna gliding up the stair, a translucent white mantle wrapped seductively around her voluptuous body. She looked like a Greek goddess. Four Sidhe half-breeds, including the phooka driver, climbed the steps behind her. Leanna stepped daintily over an Unseelie corpse, advancing until she stood face-to-face with Kalen.

"Why, my dear Immortal Warrior. You really should have invited me to your little party. After all, I went to so much trouble to liven it up for you."

CHAPTER TWENTY-ONE

"You," Kalen spat. "You did this." *Gods*. How had he ever thought Leanna desirable? Now, with very little provocation, he could kill her. If Mac didn't wring her neck first.

Leanna surveyed the gallery with an air of satisfaction. Kalen followed her gaze, focusing for the first time on the damage the battle had wrought. The paintings, including most of Christine's, were damaged beyond repair—drenched in slime, slashed, or covered with blood. Furniture was no more than charred leather and chrome, silver serving trays littered the floor. The surviving humans huddled on the dais, too frightened to move.

But by far the worst was the sight of the dead bodies sprawled across the gallery floor. Most were Unseelies, but some—some were not. Humans lay in puddles of their own blood. He caught sight of a ripped faerie wing and the bloodless face of a Selkie, half hidden by an overturned table. Bile rose in Kalen's throat. These were his guests, his responsibility. And he hadn't protected them.

A smile tugged at Leanna's red lips. "I say, quite a show. I'm so sorry to have missed it."

Mac looked as though he were about to explode. "You're dealing with forces you don't understand, Leanna."

"Ah, but that's where you're wrong, big brother. *You* may not understand—how could you, being so far removed from death magic? But I? With my Sidhe heritage and tainted human blood? I draw power from depths you could only dream of."

"Demonwhore," Mac ground out. "Where's your mistress? Here? Lurking outside? Let's have her come in and face me rather than sending her slave to do her bidding."

Leanna's laughter drifted like an obscenity over the carnage. "Ah, so passionate." She licked her lips. "Too bad you never put your wilder emotions to good use, *brother*. I certainly have. The Unseelies are just the beginning. Just a little display, Kalen, to show you how displeased I am with you." Her gaze flicked to Christine for the first time. "You chose this mousy little witch over me? You'll toss her aside. Because if you don't, the future will be far, far worse than what happened here tonight."

"Don't try it, Leanna," Kalen warned.

Mac started for her. "You've gone too far this time."

"Not nearly far enough." Leanna swung about, facing Mac, and raised a hand. A subtle red aura sprang to life before her, curving like a shield.

Mac struck it and recoiled, cursing. "Demon magic."

Leanna dismissed her brother with a sneer. "Stay in your place, *Mackie*." She turned back to Kalen, her pale eyes taking on a sultry glitter. Her power gathered, potent and alluring.

The erotic magic was stronger than it ever had been. Stronger and more compelling. Leanna was a dream, a goddess, impossible for any human man to resist. Kalen couldn't tear his gaze from her as she shrugged the loose mantle from her shoulders. The fine fabric sifted over her ivory skin. It slid down her arms, whispered over her breasts, and crested her taut nipples. Grazed her hips and pooled in a shining puddle at her feet. His human blood boiled. His lower body clenched, his phallus thickening and lengthening.

Magic poured from her, sexual magic, muse magic, impossible for Kalen's human half to resist. She was naked before him, her body a magnificent work of art, finer than any nude displayed in oil on canvas. She ran her hands up her body and cupped her breasts, offering them to his touch.

He fought the urge to accept her invitation. Against his will, he lifted one hand. His palm hovered above her breast.

"Kalen." Mac's voice was low and urgent.

Dimly he became aware of Mac and Christine standing on either side of him. Mac, who had no human blood, was unaffected by his sister's magic. Christine's reaction was one of unadulterated disgust. The emotion poured from her in waves. It snapped him back to himself.

His hand fell to his side. "No."

"No?" Leanna's denial was a shrill screech. "You cannot deny me! I have what you need. What you crave."

"You have nothing."

"Have you given up your dream of creating a masterpiece? You know you need my magic for that."

Christine drew in a sharp breath. "What do you mean?"

Leanna's attention grazed her. "I'm *leannan-sidhe*. A love muse. Men sacrifice their lives and their souls in return for my inspiration. Kalen, Immortal though he is, is no exception. His talent is mediocre at best. He craves my touch. My magic."

"Is that true?" Christine's whisper was raw. Kalen felt her horror, her shame. "Oh, Goddess. You said I was your inspiration. Did you mean that your talent wasn't your own? That it came from me?"

"Christine—"

"You used me. You made love to me for my magic. And I never even realized it. . . ."

Leanna's pale eyes sparked. "Ah, now I begin to understand how you were able to reject me so easily. You thought to replace my muse magic with hers. That's why you took her."

"I took her to save her from you."

"But that's not why you kept her, is it?"

Christine's eyes were on him. He couldn't lie to her. "No. That's not why I kept her."

"You don't need her anymore," Leanna breathed. "You have *me*. Give me your Immortal child and create a masterpiece beyond anything you've imagined." She approached him, running her hand down his chest. "Fuck me. Here. Now. In front of your human whore."

He drew back, startled beyond disgust. "You're insane."

"No. I'm a force to be reckoned with. Give me what I want, Kalen, or my Old One will punish you."

"Bring the demon in," Mac growled. "I'll fight her."

"Oh no, I think not. We have another plan. One that concerns all those little faeries and halflings camped by the ocean waiting for the Gates of Annwyn to open. Just think of them, trapped there in that cove. When the wards break, as they did on this building, there will be quite a lot of lovely blood."

Mac made a sound of absolute fury. "You won't harm a single one of them. I'll see you dead first."

Leanna laughed. "My death won't stop the carnage. Kill me, and my master will only attack all the more quickly."

"No," Kalen cut in. "There's been enough killing. I won't allow any more. I'll give you what you want, Leanna. But not here, in the midst of all this death. Meet me at your hotel, at sunset."

She eyed him. "And you'll give me an Immortal child."

"Yes," he said through clenched teeth.

"How do I know you'll be there?"

"You have my word."

"Your word," Leanna sneered. "How quaint. I'm sorry, but that's not good enough."

Kalen crossed his arms. "It will have to be, Leanna. Sunset tonight or never. You choose."

She searched his gaze for a long moment; then her lips

thinned. "Sunset. Not a minute after." She cast a derisive glance at Mac. "I know my brother can't open the Gates that quickly. But if I don't get what I want tonight, there will be carnage before dawn. You may take that as *my* word."

"Understood." Kalen stepped back. "Now go. We have work here."

Her gaze swept the ruined gallery, lingering on the huddle of terrified humans on the dais. She smiled. "But of course you do. Until sunset, then."

Turning, she swept down the stair, still regally, brazenly naked. Dougal and the other half-breeds closed rank behind her. A moment later, she disappeared through the shattered doors.

Mac let out a long breath. "You can't mean to go to her."

"I can't let her unleash an Old One on a refugee camp." Kalen glanced at Christine, then sent Mac a long, hard look, willing him to hear what he didn't want to say out loud. That he didn't intend to impregnate Leanna. He intended to kill her and the Old One she served.

Mac's brows rose. The lad was quick; he shut up directly, though his expression promised an argument later.

Kalen turned to Christine. "I'll take you back to the castle now."

Her eyes widened. "Oh no. You're not getting rid of me that—"

His tone could have cut steel. "You'll return to the castle. Mac will take you to Annwyn tomorrow."

"How thick is your Immortal skull? I'm not going back to your castle, and I'm not going to Annwyn. If I'm going anywhere, it's to Seattle."

The thought of Christine preparing for a battle with his youngest brother and gods knew what other fetid followers of darkness made Kalen's blood run cold. He took in her determined expression and made a decision. He only hoped she wouldn't curse him for it.

"All right, then. I'll take you to Adrian. Get ready for the jump."

She blinked. "Right now?"

"Yes."

All the color drained from her face. "No. I don't want to travel by portal. I—"

"No arguments, Christine. The only way you're going to go to the States is if I take you there, my way."

She swallowed hard. "Okay."

Kalen's arms came around her in a bruising hold. Christine closed her eyes and braced for the nauseating rush of his magic. Portal travel seemed to take longer the farther the distance involved was. How long would it take to get all the way to Seattle? She felt his power fade—one, two, three long seconds. Then came that brief instant—the one she'd taken shameless advantage of outside the gallery—when Kalen was no more powerful than a mundane man.

When his magic surged back, it was with a vivid blast far too strong for any mortal flesh to contain. A portal opened. The floor fell away, her stomach heaved, and a screeching roar sounded in her ears. Her body detonated. For a terrifying stretch of time, only Kalen existed, her anchor in a maelstrom.

Much more quickly than she expected, she felt a solid surface under her feet. She sagged against Kalen. Now that she was finally here, in Seattle, she didn't want to let him go. She didn't want to admit her time with him was really over.

"Steady," he whispered, guiding her a few feet ahead to a cushioned seat. Her fingers spread on brocaded silk and intricately carved wood.

Her eyes flew open. Kalen was kneeling before her, an expression of deep concern on his face. She looked past him to the image of the *Mona Lisa*, casting her secret smile over Kalen's bedroom.

A deadweight pressed her chest. "You lied to me."

Guilt flashed through his eyes. "For your own good. I won't let you sacrifice yourself. I need you safe."

She resisted a surge of nausea. "You need *me* safe? Or my magic?"

When he didn't immediately answer, she drew a harsh breath and continued. "You used me. Like you used Leanna." She was an idiot not to realize she had muse magic. After all, she'd had the same effect on Shaun as on Kalen. "You never loved me for myself, did you?"

He wouldn't look at her. "That's not true."

"Are you saying you didn't keep me here for my magic?"

He rose. "I did at first, I admit." He seemed to want to say more, but in the end he set his jaw and crossed the room to the bellpull. A few moments later, Pearl appeared in the doorway. Her sharp eyes widened as she took in Kalen and Christine's gory clothes and bedraggled appearance.

"Prepare a bath. Immediately."

The housekeeper nodded. "At once."

The brownies appeared almost instantly, dragging the copper tub to its place by the fire, scampering back and forth with buckets of water. Christine watched them dispassionately, too tired to move. Her heart was aching, both with the revelation that Kalen had used her and the knowledge that he'd soon return to Leanna's bed.

"Are you really going back to her?"

He still didn't look at her. "I have no choice. I can't risk her loosing an Old One on Mac's refugees. But I don't mean to give her a child. I only mean to keep her occupied until Mac can get the Gates open."

Keep her occupied. *With lovemaking.*

She wanted to beg him not to go. But she didn't, because she sensed it would do no good. There was a new severity about him, a harsh look about his eyes and mouth that told her his decision was made. He couldn't fight and kill to save innocent souls, so he would do this.

And she couldn't hate him for it.

"I love you," she said simply.

He didn't answer. Instead, he knelt before her, taking her hands in his and massaging gently. "Promise me that if . . . for some reason I don't return to the castle . . . that you'll let Mac take you to Annwyn."

"I . . . can't promise you that."

She thought he would argue. Instead, he merely searched her eyes and nodded. After a brief hesitation, he eased the tattered remains of her evening gown from her bruised body, frowning at the gouges and scratches the Unseelies had left. She didn't have the energy to help him. She lay limp as the tingling magic that accompanied his touch skittered over her skin, soothing her wounds.

When she was naked, he lifted her from the sofa and lowered her gently into the tub. The heated water enveloped her tired body like a mother's arms. She pulled her knees to her chest as he stripped off his clothes. Even in her exhausted state, she couldn't help but respond to the sight of his naked body, broad and hard and already recovered from battle. He stood by the side of the tub, gazing down her.

Tears stung her eyes. "Uni should never have given you such a ruthless sentence. She must be a monster to have done it."

"No. She's my mother. Hard, but fair. It's her right to discipline me as she sees fit."

"No loving mother would force a punishment like that on her son."

"Goddesses aren't like human women. Uni gave me a task. My own arrogance brought about my failure. She passed sentence, and she will not be disobeyed."

"If you asked her—"

A painful emotion passed through his eyes. "I would never insult her that way. Let us speak of it no further."

He joined her in the tub, settling behind her and pulling her between his open legs. He found a bar of soap and, working silently, lathered her back, her arms, her breasts.

She winced when he grazed her bruised shoulder. He responded with a scowl, but in reality her wounds were already healing under his touch.

Urging her to lean forward, he soaped and rinsed her hair. Then he turned his attention to her belly and legs, his fingers gliding and massaging her intimately. Christine shuddered as the familiar weakness overtook her, spreading through her veins like liquid fire.

His erection prodded her buttocks, but he made no move to take care of his own needs. He didn't speak, but she didn't need words to understand his restraint. It was regret. For his lies, for his omissions, for what he couldn't give her. For this bittersweet ending.

She took the soap and turned to lather his chest and arms. When she finished, he rose and lifted her from the tub. He laid her, wet and dripping, on the bed. She lifted her arms in wordless invitation. He accepted. Lowering himself atop her, he eased slowly inside. She tilted her hips and took him in deeply.

He loved her with a raw, silent need that touched the deepest part of her soul. She wrapped her legs around his body, holding him to her with all her strength. The only sound was their breath and the movement of flesh on flesh. Their magic and their souls circled, touched. As always, she held nothing back, but even still, there was an incompleteness about the union that hadn't been present in their previous joinings. A loss of joy, of freedom.

He groaned his release at the same time the bittersweet pleasure speared her. The denouement of their love was a slow, shuddering slide. When it ended, Christine lay spent in both mind and body.

"Christine," Kalen murmured.

She opened her eyes. "Yes?"

"Promise . . . if you never see me again . . . that you'll remember me."

"Oh, Kalen." She turned, buried her face against his chest, and let the tears come.

* * *

Mac supposed he could ignore the call.

The phone chimed a second time. A third. With a curse he snatched it from his belt before it switched over to voice mail. Niniane hated voice mail. And his mother had the power to make life very, very difficult for him.

Especially if he had to live in Annwyn for eternity. There'd be no way to avoid her then. She'd hound him night and day, century in, century out. He broke out in a cold sweat just thinking about it.

He flipped open the phone and grunted into it.

"Mackie?"

He winced. "Yes, Mum. It's me."

"What took you so long? I thought you'd never answer."

Mac sent a glance skimming over what had once been de-Linea's gallery showroom. The place was crawling with medics and parapolice. "It's rather busy around here right now."

"I don't know why you're getting so involved in human affairs, Mackie. It's none of your business, and it's not safe. Why, the things I've heard! Death magic, demons, Unseelie attacks. The human world is sliding straight into hell. If you get yourself trapped out there when the life magic's gone . . ." She stifled a sob. "You could die, Mac. *Die*, do you hear me? If anything should happen to you . . . well, I'd just die along with you, Mackie."

He rather doubted that. "Look, Mum, no one's going to die."

She gave an audible sniff. "I love you, Manannán."

Gods. "I love you too, Mum, but—"

"Come home, Mac. Now. Lir . . . he agrees with me. He doesn't need his only son getting himself killed."

Mac sighed. "Tell Da I'll be home as soon as I can. I need to settle some things here first."

"You're talking about that evacuation of yours, aren't you? Well, if you ask me, it's not worth risking your life over.

Just give it up. All those Celtic creatures *chose* to live in the human world—why should *you* be the one to help them escape it?"

"Mum—"

"I swear, Mackie, you're going to age me a millennium. Come home. Now."

"Not until everyone gets through."

"Everyone." There was a suspicious silence on the other end of the line. "Mac, just who is *everyone?*"

There was nothing for it. She'd find out soon enough—might as well prepare her for the worst. He tried to keep his tone casual. "Oh, you know—Sidhe, faeries, halflings, imps, sprites, brownies, and the like. Oh, and a few humans."

There was a period of dead silence on the other end of the line. A bad sign, in Mac's experience. Niniane was rarely silent.

"Humans?" she said at last. "Did you say *humans?*"

He sighed. "Yes, Mum."

"Humans." Disgust was thick in her voice. "Magical or mundane?"

"Some of each, actually." So sue him. Some of his best friends were human. His backup musicians, for one. His producer, for another. His agent . . . well, he hadn't worked out whether his agent was entirely human, but he'd invited the bloke along anyway. And then there was his fan club . . .

"How many?" Niniane asked at last.

"About ten thousand," he mumbled. "Give or take."

"What?"

He hardened his tone. "You heard me."

"Ten thousand? Ten *thousand* humans! We've never had more than *ten* humans at one time in Annwyn, and believe me, that was ten too many!" A pause. "Does your father know about this?"

"Yes," Mac said tightly. "He's agreed to accept whomever I bring to the Gates."

"Humph." Niniane was silent as she digested this bit of information. "He didn't say anything about it to me."

No shit. "Then you'll just have to ask him about it, won't you?" *Preferably right now.*

"You can be certain I will. It's one thing to have Lir grant Kalen's little human witch an immortal soul. It's quite another to have to have Annwyn overrun with mundanes. It's obscene!"

She rang off without saying good-bye. Mac stared at the phone. That had to be the first time Niniane had *ever* done that. His mother was bloody livid, and she hadn't even heard the worst of it. If she found out he and Kalen were planning to confront Leanna and her Old One, Niniane would bolt through the Gates and drag Mac home herself. Come to think of it, if Christine knew, she'd probably do the same to Kalen.

He shoved his cell back on its clip just as Kalen winked into the far corner of the gallery. His friend looked grim.

He started toward him. "How's Christine?"

Kalen grimaced. "Better. But none too pleased about me leaving her at the castle."

"She'd be even angrier if you'd told her what we were planning to do. You didn't, did you?"

"Of course not. She'd want to come with us."

Mac considered this. "Her magic is strong. She could help, I think. If she learned to take orders."

"No." Kalen's reply was swift and angry. "Absolutely not. I will not risk her. I need you to promise me, Mac, that you'll take Christine to Annwyn with you . . . after . . . if I don't make it."

"Hell, Kalen, you'll take her yourself. I don't intend to lose you. There's no reason we can't end this without you killing anyone. Just like we did here in the gallery."

Kalen shook his head. "Possible, but doubtful. Unseelies are one thing, a demon Old One is another entirely. You know that as well as I do." His gaze passed over the wreckage of his gallery. Pools of blood marked where bodies had fallen. The human ones were gone, but unfortunately, the Unseelie corpses remained, stinking up the place. A tight knot of paradetectives, gas masks firmly in place, were examining the bodies.

"So much destruction," Kalen said tightly. "So many dead. And this is only a small part of what the human world has become. Death is taking over, Mac. Soon everything good will be gone." He slammed his fist into the wall. "And what have I done to stop it? *Nothing*. I can't sit on the sidelines any longer."

One of the human investigators, a tall, thin male with a face as pale as a vampire, detached himself from his colleagues and strode toward Kalen.

"Excuse me, sir, are you the owner of this gallery?"

"I am."

"I'd like to ask you a few questions."

Kalen nodded.

Mac cleared his throat. Fear for Kalen churned in his gut, but one look at the Immortal's face told him arguments would be useless. "I'll leave you to it, then. I want to check on the evacuation and set the spell to open the Gates before we get together for our little party at Leanna's. That way, even if we run into trouble, the Gates will still open tomorrow at dawn."

Pain. *Glorious* pain. Leanna had to admit, it took sex to a whole new level.

She let out a moan as the hot wax dribbled onto her areola, her back arching as the exquisite agony pierced her senses. Culsu loomed over her, her long fingers stroking a thick, black candle. The demon's eyes were so flat and dead that Leanna's stomach spasmed. In the past, Leanna had always been the dominant one—and had scorned her human lovers because of it. She'd never fully understood the pleasure she'd given them as she milked the souls from their bodies. Now she did.

The candle withdrew. She tested the bonds at her ankles and wrists and found them secure. She couldn't move, couldn't defend herself. Culsu had laid a thick blanket of death magic over the circle, rendering even Leanna's most potent spells null. She waited, trembling, for her mistress's pleasure. And her own.

Culsu's regal form blurred. She was changing again. Leanna had discovered the demon could take on the shape of many, many creatures. Some shapes were better for fucking than others. The thrill of not knowing—and the certainty that whatever Culsu demanded, Leanna would have to give her—made Leanna tremble. Brimstone scalded her nostrils as the dark ash that was Culsu's essence solidified before her eyes.

A male ogre this time. Leanna's hips arched upward. Squat and ugly, with flat features that seemed to have been pounded into its green face, an ogre's visage would turn the stomach of any female—even his own kind. But an ogre's cock—that was another matter altogether. Dougal's cock, after all, was long and thick and lovely. And Dougal was only half ogre.

Culsu thrust into Leanna's body without preliminaries, and pounded her until she'd gone limp with the mingled pain and pleasure of the invasion. Afterward, Leanna's bonds dissolved, but she didn't move for a long time.

"Rise," Culsu commanded.

Leanna's eyes slit open. The demon had reverted to her usual form. Her black velvet gown clung to her shapely body like a second skin. Her hair writhed about her pale face.

Leanna struggled to her feet. "Tonight . . ." she whispered.

Culsu smiled. "Yes, tonight. The witch and the Immortal will be mine."

"And . . . my prize? The child?"

"Immortality will be yours."

Leanna splayed her fingers on her stomach, smiling, imagining Kalen's immortal seed growing inside her. Rounding her belly with the essence of a timeless soul. A soul from which she would suck immortal juices. She'd absorb its essence, as she'd soaked up Kalen's for the last decade. But with one vital difference—the dark spell Culsu had taught her would allow Leanna to claim the child's soul as her own. The babe would die, but that detail didn't disturb her. The prize was too great.

She would be Mac's equal. No. Her power would be greater, because she would command the magic of both life and death. And once life magic was gone, Mac would be powerless. He'd flee to Annwyn, or die. Leanna would take her rightful place in a new world. One in which mortals would bow before her.

And Leanna would live forever.

CHAPTER TWENTY-TWO

Damn it, she had to get off this island!

Christine paced back and forth in front of her window, fuming. She had to stay focused on her anger—it was the only way to avoid facing the aching dread in her chest. Kalen's eyes had been flat and emotionless when he'd kissed her good-bye, but his body had trembled with deep emotion.

She was a fool. Up to the very moment he'd left her, she'd thought he was going to Leanna in order to make love to her. Stall her until Mac's refugees had gone through the Gates. But once he'd disappeared, and Christine had had a chance to think things through without the distraction of his presence, she realized that wasn't what Kalen intended at all. Because if that was the case, he wouldn't have loved her as though it was the last time. He wouldn't have asked her to remember him.

He was going to battle. With Leanna, and maybe her Old One as well. He would fight to kill, and there was every chance he wouldn't be coming back. Even if he won, he'd be banished to nothingness forever.

And here she was, stuck on this island.

She'd spent the last hours trying to find a way to the sea. If she could just reach the water, she could use her magic to find a way across. Her quest had been hopeless. There was just no way through the castle walls—no doors, no low windows, no breaches in the outer walls at all. She looked out over the waves. The mainland shore, about a half mile away, was teeming with activity. It seemed Kalen's castle stood directly across the strait from the Gates of Annwyn. The portal would open fully at dawn, Kalen had told her. He expected her to cross, with or without him.

Like hell she would.

"We got a lovely basket of peaches in today, miss. And fresh cream."

She spun around, startled by the squeaky voice. It was the first time a brownie had dared speak to her—the creatures were incredibly shy. The female seemed dazed at her own boldness; she lowered her eyes and scuttled to the table with her tea tray.

The import of the brownie's words struck her. "The peaches just arrived?"

The brownie looked up, startled. "Oh! Aye, miss. Just this morning. I was sore surprised. We're all getting ready to leave, ye see."

"How did the supplies get here?"

"Why, on one of the boats, of course. The mermen pulled them in."

"Boats?" Christine's heart started pounding. "You mean there's a dock somewhere?"

"At the sea gate under the castle." The brownie backed away, clearly unnerved by the length of her interaction with a human. The next instant, she disappeared through a crack in the paneling.

Christine dressed quickly, in a simple sky-blue gown and low boots. A moment later, her tea tray untouched, she gathered her skirts and hurried down the corridor. Her mind skimmed through what she knew of the castle. The docks were under the castle. Where hadn't she looked for an outlet to the sea? The dungeons. Presumably, prisoners would once have been brought to the castle by sea—maybe there was an entrance near Kalen's office.

She all but flew down the stairs to the great hall. Crossing in front of *David* and the other masterpieces with barely a glance, she let herself out the door to the main courtyard. The hidden door behind the rhododendrons was closed tightly. Opening it was a little tricky. Grabbing a cup from Kalen's studio, she filled it with water from the fountain and placed it in front of the door. She dipped her fingers in the water and drew a rune on the door.

Isa. Challenge.

The lines of the portal glowed with soft blue light. In a sharp voice, she commanded the door to open. After a brief moment in which she thought the spell had failed, the false stone panel swung forward just enough for her to get her fingers behind it.

She pulled it the rest of the way open and left it ajar to throw light on the stair beyond. Carefully, she made her way down the steep stair and through the passage. She reached the door to Kalen's office—no light shone from under the door, but the muted whir of computers and air-conditioning gave her pause.

She eased the door open and searched for a light switch, blinking into the sudden glare when she found it. Once her vision cleared, she made a beeline for the phone of Kalen's desk and punched in Amber's cell phone number.

"We're sorry, the mobile customer you are calling has gone beyond the calling area. Please try again another—"

"Damn." She pressed the flash button and tried Amber's home phone.

"This is Amber Silverthorne. Blessed be to all who walk in the Light. I can't come to the phone right now, but if you'll leave a message—"

She waited impatiently for the beep. "Amber, this is

Christine. Sorry I've been out of touch, I've had some . . .
problems. Something big's going down tonight. I think
Kalen's going after an Old One, and—" She closed her eyes
briefly. "I'm not sure what's going to happen. I'll . . . call you
tomorrow, if I can."

Exhaling, she laid down the receiver. When Amber got
that message, she'd be frantic. Christine couldn't think of
that now, though. She had to get to Inverness. And to do
that, she had to get off the island.

She left the office, leaving the door open and the light on
to illuminate her path. She continued to the far end of the
corridor, where she almost missed the hidden door concealing a winding stair that led downward into a murky light.
The scent of the sea rose to greet her, along with the blessed
sound of surf slapping against rock.

The stair gave out onto a flat slab sheltered by a domed
cavern. The arched opening beyond looked out to the sea
and a crude dock. Two longboats with dragon prows were
tied to posts.

A short distance away, a wooden platform was suspended
over her head by a creaking network of ropes and pulleys.
The primitive elevator was lowering slowly, revealing an
opening in the cavern ceiling. It hit the ground with a
thud. A dozen brownies scampered off, followed by Pearl.
Christine watched as Kalen's housekeeper herded the
brownies onto one of the boats, bullying and scolding and
generally making sure all her charges boarded safely.

When the last brownie had stepped off the dock, Pearl
put her fingers in her mouth and summoned a shrill whistle.
Immediately, two brawny mermen surfaced and donned the
harnesses attached to the vessel.

"All ready," Pearl told him. "There's only the human
witch left. Kalen will come for her himself."

The mermen nodded. Pearl surveyed the dock with an air
of finality. Christine shrank into the shadows, but not before the housekeeper's gaze narrowed dangerously.

"You. What are you doing here?"

Christine stepped into the light. "I'm leaving," she said. "I have to get to Kalen."

"The master bade ye stay."

"The *master* needs my help. He's going to battle a demon, for the gods' sake!"

Pearl regarded her impassively. "He's an Immortal. 'Tis what he was born to do. Ye came here wanting to bring him into the war, did ye not? Ah, but ye wanted him to fight in America, for humans, is that it? Ye canna stand the thought of him battling for magical creatures and half-breeds."

"No! That's not true. It's Kalen—he's doomed, even if he wins the fight. Because of Uni's sentence." Pearl's blank expression said clearly she didn't know what Christine was talking about. Quickly, she explained the restriction Kalen's mother goddess had put on him, and the consequences should he disobey. Pearl's expression turned horrified.

"He never told me," the housekeeper said. "I thought he was just weary of the world. Disgusted with modern humans." Her sharp eyes cut to Christine. "He has every right to be, ye know."

"I know. But that hardly matters now. I need to find him." She climbed aboard the last boat. "May the Goddess speed your trip to Annwyn."

Pearl snorted. "What would a half-breed like me do in that realm? I'll nae be running through the Gates with all those cowards. I'm headed elsewhere."

Christine looked at her in surprise. "Where?"

"Ah, an' I've not worked out that bit yet. But if the death magic is advancing, the followers of life will have to take a stand sometime. If there's a battle to come, I want a part in it. Goddess knows my magic's not much good in a fight, but warriors have to eat, don't they? I can cook up a meal to keep their bellies full and their arms strong."

"Do you think you could get all the way to Seattle?" Christine asked.

"The United States?" Pearl replied with a good bit of suspicion. "Why? What's goin' on there?"

"Kalen's older brother, Adrian, is forming an army. I'm sure they could use a good cook."

Pearl's substantial chest puffed out even more. "I can do right by them."

Christine nodded. "Good. Tell Adrian and Amber I sent you."

"Aye, that I will." Pearl smiled then, her gray teeth huge in her wide mouth. "Ye know, I might have to revise my opinion of ye, lass. Ye're not half bad." She paused, growing sober again. "Take care of Kalen, will ye?"

"I'll try."

Pearl gave a signal to the mermen. They dove. A moment later, the boat pulled from the dock. Christine watched it go; then, trailing her finger in the cold sea water, she drew a series of gentle circles. Her water magic swirled around the boat. A moment later, the vessel left the dock, cutting a sleek line through the water.

The sky was dark and the waves huge. A storm was brewing. The boat pitched up over a swell, then down, into the valley between two waves. Christine grasped the edge of the craft, hoping it wouldn't tip over. But she wasn't unduly frightened—not by the sea. It was a part of her. She closed her eyes, absorbing the power of the ocean.

The current was swift. It left her boat on the shore a short distance from the refugee camp, in a smooth cove sheltered by rocky hills on either side. She stepped out onto the shore about fifty yards from a large contingent of faeries. She'd covered her approach with a look-away spell; not one looked in her direction.

Turning west, she made her way along the shore until she reached the hard edge of Kalen's circle of protection. Since it had been spelled mainly against death magic, to allow the refugees to enter, it didn't prove much of a challenge to Christine. Scooping up a handful of seawater, she murmured a spell and stepped through it. All she felt was a gentle tingle flowing over her body.

She was free.

She headed up the cliffs and found the road. Her quickest route to Inverness would be to hitch a ride. Easier said than done—the road was deserted. She trudged for over a mile before she heard the drone of a car engine.

She turned eagerly, thumb out. The car was a battered Land Rover, one that looked like it had actually spent some time off-road. The driver was an elderly man, certainly harmless looking. The gent rattled to a stop, leaned over, and popped open the passenger-side door.

His accent was thick Scots. "Where ye be goon, lass?"

"Inverness."

"Weel, I'm heided tha' way meself."

Christine climbed in with a grateful smile. "Thank you," she said, fastening her seat belt. She turned back to the driver. "I —" The words died on her lips. The elderly Scot was gone.

In his place was a redheaded Sidhe female.

Leanna's red lips thinned into a mirthless smile. "Why, if it isn't Kalen's little witch. You really should be more careful. I've heard hitchhiking can be very dangerous."

CHAPTER TWENTY-THREE

The enchantment to reveal the Gates of Annwyn was a long and complicated bit of spellcraft, courtesy of the Sidhe queen herself. Mac's mother abhorred intruders, and she'd taken every precaution to avoid any nasty surprises in Annwyn. Those magical creatures who chose to live in the human world understood they had limited access to their homeworld—apart from Niniane and Lir, only Mac and a handful of his high-placed aunts and uncles were entrusted with the opening spell to the Gates.

Mac's concentration stretched to its limits as he delineated each successive element of the spell. First protections had to be drawn, then the elements called: earth, air, fire, and water. After that, Mac invoked the spirits of the Sidhe ancestors who had traveled permanently to the West. Once all these preliminaries were in place, he spoke the Invocation, ending in the Word of Revelation.

Green mist swirled from the place where the ocean met the shore. Mac lifted his hand, chanting Niniane's complex spellforms under his breath. The mist rose slowly from beach to sky, scattering a trail of sparks. The sparkling points of light coalesced, shifting and gathering into glittering lines, swirls, highlights and shadows. The foundations of two giant piers took shape.

The slow process of forming the great gateway had begun.

Mac stepped back, rolling the kinks out of his neck. The Gate wouldn't be completely solid and able to be used by the throng of refugees until dawn. And since the spell was a self-limiting one, the passage would remain open only for a few hours. The refugees would have to pass under the archway quickly before it collapsed.

He let out a long, slow breath, his gaze traveling over the host of magical creatures on the shore. Their faces were full of trust; Mac sorely hoped that sentiment wasn't misplaced. A lot could happen in one night.

He rejoined Ronan and Niall. The pair exchanged a look, and then, with a sigh, Ronan faced Mac.

Mac felt a tingle of alarm. "What is it now?"

Ronan cleared his throat. "We didn't want to bother you with this before you set the gate spell, but . . ."

"But what?"

"It's probably nothing," Niall cut in. "But we thought you should know."

"What *is* it?"

Niall's frown deepened. "I'm not sure, Mac. Like I said, probably nothing. Things have been mostly quiet, no sign of any death magic."

Mac expelled a sharp breath. He didn't have time for his cousins' meandering. He was worried that Kalen would try to take on the Old One alone. There was no way Mac was going to allow that. He couldn't linger here. "Just spit it out, mate."

Ronan cut in. "Niall was looking out over the sea, just about there. . . ."

He pointed in the direction of Kalen's castle, looming on the horizon across a blue swath of ocean. Nothing looked amiss.

Mac crossed his arms. "And?"

Niall scratched his head. "And there was this crinkly spot, you know? Like what happens sometimes when someone's casting a glamour or a look-away?"

"Did you check it out?"

"Of course," replied Ronan testily. "What do you take us for?"

Mac let that one pass. "Did you find anything?"

"A boat. One of Kalen's. Beached on a cove about a half mile west. Not that that's a problem in itself—we've been evacuating the castle most of the day, brought off nearly fifty brownies in about a dozen boats. But this one? It was shielded with glamour, and only one set of footprints led from it. And not to the gathering place, either. The tracks went in the opposite direction, right through Kalen's protection and onto the road."

Mac's attention abruptly focused. "Male or female tracks?"

"Female. Too big to be a brownie. Human, most likely. Though she'd have to be pretty powerful to get through Kalen's wards."

A very unwelcome thought formed in Mac's brain. "But you didn't see anyone? Anyone at all?"

Ronan shook his head. "No. Niall and I, we scouted about. There was nothing. It's like the intruder just vanished." He shifted. "You want me to do anything else?"

"No. I'll take care of it."

With a growing sense of dread, Mac jogged up the beach to the abandoned boat. Definitely one of Kalen's. An aura of water magic clung to it.

Christine.

He traced her footsteps to the road. A subtle trail of magic continued along the pavement for about a mile, then abruptly disappeared. Mac spent one precious hour circling ahead, trying to reconnect with the trail. It was no use.

Kalen's witch had vanished without a trace.

* * *

Leanna sat with one hand on the steering wheel as she sped down the road at a reckless speed, barely looking where she was going. She exuded an air of triumph. And of anticipation.

She was dressed much the same way she'd been on the sex magic tour—black corset and gartered stockings, with matching stilettos. Her bright hair was gelled and slicked back around her pointed ears. Her wrists were wrapped in white gauze bandages. A faint odor of brimstone seemed to seep from her skin.

She looked at Christine and laughed. The next instant her pale eyes went as red as her hair.

Christine's heart pounded into her throat. As a demon's whore, Leanna served as a conduit for dark powers beyond her own magic. Christine scrabbled to open the car door, but the handle wouldn't lift. Of course it didn't. Leanna had planned this. She was trapped.

The Sidhe made a subtle gesture with her forefinger. Christine shrank back in her seat, but there was nothing she could do to avoid the spell. She felt it hit. At first there was no effect beyond a curious numbness. No pain, no fatigue, no urge to cry out. Then a low buzz filled her ears and her senses seemed to amplify. She became hyperaware—of the vibration of the car, the abrasion of the upholstery under her fingertips, the soft, threatening rumble of Leanna's laughter. Even the faraway churning of the sea as the Rover rushed along the shore road. The sensations were unnerving. Cold sweat broke out on her brow. Her breath grew shallow.

She tried to speak and found the slightest sound took incredible effort. Tried to lift her arms, but her hands were as heavy as boulders. Panic clawed at her throat. Without use of her hands and voice, she couldn't perform magic.

Leanna broke into a hearty laugh. "A taste of your own medicine, my sweet. A binding spell. But this time, *you're* the prisoner."

She drove on for a short stretch of road, then left the pavement to drive a considerable distance over a rocky field. Christine glimpsed Leanna's burly ogre half-breed standing between two large, lichen-covered boulders. He advanced before the Rover reached a full halt and flung the passenger door open.

He was carrying a heavy blanket. Even before he threw it over Christine's head, nausea threatened to raise the contents of her stomach. The blanket was a lead shield, the kind X-ray technicians used. The weight settled atop her, its burn seeping through her skin and into her bones and muscles. Pain screamed in every nerve ending. The little magic Christine still clung to drained right out of her body.

And Leanna laughed.

Leanna's suite at the Palace was dark and empty.

Kalen swore. He'd arrived in Inverness early, Uni's crystal spear in hand, hoping to force the issue. He found the city in a panic. A series of explosions, both mundane and magical, had ripped through town a scant hour earlier. Water, electricity, and telephone service had utterly failed. Zombies and minor demons roamed the streets, looking for victims. No doubt the vamps would join them once the sun went down. Humans and life magic creatures had either fled or gone to ground. Leanna's demon master had to have had a hand in this.

A quick search of the suite revealed a faded stench of death in Leanna's dressing room, but no sign of any active death magic spells. Kalen propped Uni's crystal spear against the wall and sank down on one of the twin zebra-striped leather sofas. The sun would set in one hour. Mac would be here before then.

Fifteen seconds later, he was on his feet again, spear in hand, prowling the edges of the room like a caged panther. He scowled at the dead phone. Waiting was hell. Had the whole arrangement been a scam, designed to distract him?

He thought not. Leanna wanted his child with a rare desperation. For the first time, he allowed himself to think more deeply on why that might be. Her earlier explanation of presenting the child to Niniane had certainly been a lie. He was equally sure her true purpose had something to do with death magic. A babe with an immortal soul—could it be that Leanna had found a way to take that soul for herself?

The horror of that prospect was overwhelming. Soul stealing. From an innocent babe. The child would die an empty husk.

Kalen shifted on his feet, his anger rising by slow degrees with every passing second. Would Leanna ever appear? Or would he have to hunt her down?

She would be here. She wanted his child. Wanted an immortal soul. To gain it, she'd have to seek him out. He took up a position by the window, in sight of the door, and waited.

Leanna's half-breed goon tossed Christine over his shoulder like a sack of dog food. Half suffocated by the lead blanket, feeling as though her soul was being consumed by slow, unforgiving fire, Christine could only squeeze her eyes shut and endure.

Her captor descended an uneven slope, jostling her against his shoulder. He passed through some kind of portal and a flash of green elflight filtered through a gap in the lead blanket. She heard a door thud, then silence as the outside world faded. The faint smell of rich loam reached her nostrils.

The half-breed's heavy footsteps, and Leanna's lighter ones, paced for what seemed to be a long time. Finally, they came to a halt. Another door opened, then shut behind them.

"Dougal," Leanna ordered. "Release her."

Dougal obeyed, dumping Christine unceremoniously on hard ground. She bit back a cry of pain. Rough hands tugged at the blanket, liberating her head and shoulders but keeping her arms tightly bound. Christine gulped in a lungful of cool air. Leanna's face appeared in her line of vision, a cruel smile on her lips.

Christine turned her head, her cheek pressed to the ground. Slowly, her gaze focused on her surroundings. She lay on the ground near a tall standing stone. Before her, bathed in the last rays of the setting sun, rose the cairn stage where Leanna had conducted her sex magic tour. But that site was near Inverness, a full twenty miles from Kalen's castle.

"We traveled by faerie barrow," Leanna said in reply to Christine's unspoken question. "Much more efficient than the Land Rover. It would have been even quicker if my do-good brother didn't have hordes of creatures streaming through the barrow nearest the Gates. But no worries. We're here now."

Leanna watched with an amused expression as Christine tried to struggle into a sitting position. With her arms and legs bound by the noxious blanket, the attempt was futile. After a few minutes, she was forced to concede defeat and lower herself back to the earth.

Leanna chuckled. "Uncomfortable? Enjoy it while you can. By the time we're done here, your present distress will be only a fond memory."

Christine couldn't suppress an overwhelming spurt of terror. "You're practicing death magic," she gasped. "Dealing with demons."

"Power, my dear, is wherever the strong find it."

"Death magic will destroy you. Suck every bit of youth and beauty from your—"

"Silence!"

Christine grunted as Leanna's heel came down, grinding the lead blanket into her ribs. A hot blade of fire pierced her chest.

"My power will be unending."

"No . . . such . . . thing," Christine gasped.

Leanna laughed. "Your naiveté is charming, my sweet."

"Yours isn't," Christine ground out. "No demon powerful enough to give you that kind of power will let you keep your soul."

"Ah yes. You know something about demons, don't you? That will make your . . . seduction . . . all the more pleasurable for my mistress. Yes, I believe Culsu is going to enjoy you, my little witch."

"Culsu? The demon who destroyed Kalen's people?"

"Yes. Which is exactly why Kalen has been invited to our little party."

CHAPTER TWENTY-FOUR

The lead blanket closed over Christine's head once again.

She managed to gulp some air before the heavy fabric cut off her vision. A moment later she felt herself being lifted and carried by Dougal. His steps rose. The edges of the blanket parted and she saw she was atop the cairn stage. The ogre gave her a nasty, pointed-tooth smile as he jerked the blanket. She rolled out of its heavy embrace and fell hard. It was only after she hit the wooden planks that she realized they'd been painted with blood.

The blood was hot and spelled with death. She lay on her back atop it, nearly suffocated by its stench. She couldn't rise, couldn't move, not even an inch.

Dougal's green faced loomed over her. Leanna joined him. Her bare, erect nipples crested the top rim of her corset. Her complexion was flushed pink, her eyes gleaming with triumph.

Tears sprang into her eyes. Leanna took note of them before she could blink them away.

"Go ahead and cry, witch. It won't help you, but at least

it's entertaining for the rest of us." Dougal guffawed in agreement.

"What . . ." Christine's lips felt numb. She struggled to form words. "What are you going to do with me?"

"Wouldn't you like to know?" Leanna tapped a finger on her cheek. "Hmmm . . . Should I tell you what I have planned? The thought of watching your dread blossom as your fate draws nearer holds a certain appeal. But then again, so does the prospect of seeing the shock hit you all at once." She paused, considering. "Maybe I'll treat myself to the best of both worlds. Let's give you a small taste of your fate now."

She traced a rune in the air. The lines glowed with crimson fire. *Wunjo*. Normally, the symbol meant *fellowship*. But Leanna had traced the lines in mirror image, invoking its shadow meaning. *Enslavement*.

It could mean only one thing. Christine was to be given to Culsu.

"No!" She struggled, trying to crawl from the stage, but succeeded only in scraping her knuckles on the blood-stained wood. "No. Not that. I'd rather die."

"I have no doubt of it." Leanna lifted her slender shoulders. "But alas, I made a promise. And I can't go back on my word."

"It won't work. Kalen will stop you. And Mac—when your *brother* finds out—"

"Mac," Leanna spat. "He is nothing. *Nothing*, do you hear me? He will bow at my feet when all is done. *If* he survives at all. Now, my sweet, my advice is to relax and try to enjoy what's to come. It's really the best you can hope for."

She made a slashing motion, erasing the lines of the blasphemous rune. Unsheathing a small knife, she pricked the tip of her finger, drawing a drop of blood. It dripped onto the stage with a hiss. The air cracked, revealing a slice of fathomless void. Black smoke emerged from the fissure, dipping and curling. The menacing tendrils reached for Christine.

She jerked when it touched her right foot. The unholy sensation burned worse than the lead had, but in a completely different way. This touch was hot and oily. Unclean. Painful, yes, but it was pain with an unmistakable undercurrent of pleasure.

A dart of unwanted awareness jolted through her. She groaned, twisted, but could not escape it. The smoke resolved into long, thin fingers. They touched her ankle; then suddenly, the shoes, stockings, and long skirt she was wearing turned to ash, leaving her legs naked from the thigh-length hem of her long shirt to her bare feet. Smoky fingers drifted up the inside of her calf. Circled to the hollow behind her bent knee.

Christine fought her body's response. Pain and arousal—and the arousal was definitely the worse of the two. Perspiration dripped into her eyes; her breath grew short. Tiny bursts of pleasure/pain exploded on her skin. She writhed.

"Please," she begged. "Make it stop."

Leanna was watching with avid interest. "Not so proud now," she murmured. "Not so proud at all. A demon's touch is sublime, isn't it, my sweet?"

"No." Christine gasped as the smoky hand skated up the inside of her leg. "It's hideous." It teased the inside of her thigh, just above her knee. "Obscene. You don't have to do this. You have nothing to fear from me. Please . . ."

Leanna clapped once. The sharp sound reverberated against the standing stones. Abruptly, the smoke snapped back into the void, as if sucked away by a sudden vacuum. The fissure snapped shut.

Christine sagged on the altar, gasping. The demon's fingers left a fetid, oily residue on her skin. She felt unclean. Used. A surge of bile rose in her throat.

This was only a small taste of what was to come if she couldn't escape.

"Why are you doing this? Why me?"

Leanna's eyes took on the gleam of a madwoman's. "You

took Kalen from me. Became his muse in my place. You separated me from his Immortal essence. He was going to give
me his child, his immortal soul. And then *you* arrived and
ruined it all."

She stepped away and turned to Dougal. "Prepare her."

The half-breed approached. Working quickly, he tied
Christine's wrists and ankles with ropes entwined with lead,
fastening her limbs to iron rings set at the corners of the
stage.

When they were finished, Leanna gave an approving
nod. "Yes. That will do nicely."

"No," a voice said. "It won't. Release her. *Now.*"

The sun dipped below the horizon, the blue of the sky taking
on a leaden cast. The city lay beneath it, illuminated by angry
fire in several locations. One blaze was very close—it would
certainly reach the hotel before the hour was out. Kalen
turned away from the window, scowling. Leanna wasn't going
to show. And what in Hades had happened to Mac?

A prickle of apprehension lifted the hairs on his nape.
Only the gravest of circumstances would have kept Mac
away from this encounter. Had Leanna and Kehksut attacked the Gates? There was only one way to find out.

Grimly, Kalen picked up his spear.

Mac had come.

Thank the Goddess.

His voice came from behind Christine's head. She
twisted her neck, trying to see him. Leanna, standing at the
foot of the altar, sent her brother a baleful look. The next
instant Dougal sprang into action, putting his considerable
bulk between Mac and Christine.

"You're not welcome here, Mac Lir," the half-breed muttered.

Mac ignored him. "Release her, Leanna. Now. I'm not going to ask a third time."

"I don't take orders from you."

"No," he said grimly. "You take them from your *mistress*."

He made a move toward Christine. Leanna snarled and sent a blast of elfshot whizzing. Mac threw up an arm, deflecting it. The missile exploded harmlessly in the dirt.

"Get him!" Leanna screamed.

Elfshot screeched across the cairn. Dougal rushed him, throwing his considerable weight into the attack. He slammed into Mac at a full run, pitching them both off the cairn. They hit the dirt hard, thrashing.

Leanna shut her eyes and went very still. When she opened them again, the pale orbs shone with crimson light.

"You will not defeat me." The voice that emerged from her throat was low and guttural. She lifted an arm and took aim. A bolt of red demonfire burst from her fingers, engulfing both Mac and Dougal. Christine twisted in her bonds, a cry scraping her throat. Mac had to win this fight. He *had* to. She wouldn't consider the alternative.

Her heart leapt when she saw Mac, battered and burned, push to his feet. Dougal remained motionless, sprawled on the ground.

Mac advanced toward the cairn. "You *will* release her, Leanna."

"No. This witch is mine." A brazen smile played on her lips. "But you're welcome to try and take her."

Mac hoisted himself onto the edge of the cairn stage. Leanna, facing him, traced a shadow rune in the air.

Berkana. Renewal. Its inverted form meant death.

A ring of fire sprang up out of the stones, encircling Christine and Leanna. Mac was left outside the barrier. He paused, frowning, then traced a rune of his own.

Sowulo. Success. The fire died.

Leanna countered with the same rune, reversed. Failure. The fire jumped to life, higher and hotter than before.

"Give it up, *Mackie*. Go hide in Annwyn. You're no match for my power."

"Don't be so sure of that," he said quietly. "Death has its own weaknesses."

"Big words from a little man. I'm getting tired of this, Mac. Let's end it now."

A knife appeared in her right hand. Christine gasped. In the next instant, before Mac could react, Leanna turned the blade on herself. A wide gash appeared on her upper arm, blood blossoming from the wound. It dripped onto the stage, sizzling, raising a sick odor.

A horrendous squeal sounded. The air tore in two, the portal widening and lengthening until it was as tall and wide as a human body. Fire burned at its edges. Beyond was the dark, dull void of death.

Mac's expression was one of pure revulsion. "You are Sidhe, Leanna. How could you sink so low?"

"Quite easily, I assure you." She half turned to the portal. "Culsu," she cried. "Come to me."

Mac's eyes darted to the portal. Christine sucked in a breath as a rush of billowing smoke ushered a female figure onto the stage. She was tall and shapely, garbed in flowing black velvet. Her features were pale and flawless. Her dark hair glowed black against the backdrop of orange flame, the thick locks writhing about her head like snakes. Kalen's ancient enemy was as beautiful as she was terrifying.

Culsu's gaze swept over Mac. She raised her brows and turned to Leanna. "*This* is the one you cannot handle? This . . . *boy?*"

Leanna scowled. "Hardly a boy. He's centuries old and his father's a god."

Mac flicked a wrist, directing a blast of elfshot at the demon. The blow disappeared harmlessly into Culsu's body. She hardly seemed to notice.

Uncertainty flashed in Mac's eyes.

"I want you to get rid of him." Leanna's voice had taken on a petulant tone. "He's wrecking our party."

"As you wish." Culsu lifted her hand. Christine strained

to see Mac through the screen of the fire. The flames cast Mac in sharp relief as he brought his arms up in a shielding motion. The next instant demonfire flashed from Culsu's fingers, sailing though the circle of flames with a sizzle. Mac couldn't dodge it quickly enough. The bolt hit his arm, spinning him around. He staggered, lost his footing, and toppled off the cairn.

It took him only an instant to shake off the blow and stagger to his feet. A second fireball zinged from Culsu's hand. Mac met it with a blast of elfshot. The green missile disintegrated, but not before it blasted the demonfire off course.

Mac leaped onto the cairn, prowling around the fire, tracing runes. The flame faltered. He batted away a shot of demonfire. Leanna, cursing, added elfshot to the barrage. One deflected dart glanced off Christine's arm, sending a sickening shock of pain through her nerves. She cried out before she could stop herself.

At the sound, Mac jerked back. The distraction lasted only a second, but it was enough to gain Culsu a direct hit. Mac took a savage blast of demonfire squarely in the stomach.

The blow sent his body hurtling through the air. He struck a standing stone, his skull impacting with a nauseating crack. His body slid down the stone, slumped to one side and lay still.

No! Christine shut her eyes, helplessness cascading over her. If Culsu could defeat Mac, a demigod, her power was tremendous. Far beyond any resistance Christine might raise. There was no hope she could escape.

"Look at me, human."

Christine's eyes snapped open. Culsu was standing over her. A dark glow enveloped her figure. The movement of her hair was mesmerizing. Christine couldn't move, couldn't even cry out. Her panic reached flash point, igniting every cell in her body. Culsu leaned closer. Christine's mind shrank away, but her body had frozen, as if turned to stone as the ancient legends of the gorgon described. Those legends had surely sprung from humanity's terror of the creature looming over her now.

Culsu smiled, absorbing her victim's terror. One long finger reached toward Christine's face. Christine turned her head and screwed her eyes shut. The touch came, a soft line of fire across her cheekbone and along her jaw.

"So sweet," Culsu breathed. "So much power."

Her fingers slithered down her neck and lower, inside her blouse, her hot palm cupping her breast. "Your soul will feed me for a millennium." She squeezed gently. "It will be a fine feast."

Bile burned in Christine's throat. Her stomach heaved. Her nipple had gone erect, her spine arching slightly into Culsu's touch. The demon rolled Christine's nipple between her thumb and forefinger. Christine moaned; Culsu chuckled.

"I will enjoy you immensely, my little witch."

Christine stifled a sob. There would be no escape this time. Culsu was far more powerful than the demon that had enslaved Shaun. This entity would drag Christine to hell. Feed on her soul while she begged for oblivion. Her magic would be twisted into something dark, used to snare others as she'd been snared. And there was nothing, absolutely nothing, she could do to stop it.

"Goddess," she whispered. "Uni. Help me."

Leanna laughed. "That bitch? She won't help you. But someone else might attempt it. . . ." Her eyes slitted, gazing past the fire into the forest. "Ah yes. I believe he's here now."

CHAPTER TWENTY-FIVE

Christine whipped her head around. Kalen stood at the edge of the stone circle, a long and deadly spear in his hand. The tip of the weapon glowed an unearthly white. The Immortal's gaze took in Mac's inert form, but whatever Kalen's inner reaction was, his expression betrayed nothing.

Culsu glided toward him, passing through the ring of fire to the edge of the cairn.

"It's been a long time, Immortal."

Kalen's voice was entirely devoid of emotion. "Culsu. This time, I *will* destroy you."

"And risk an eternity of nothingness?" She gave a shake of her head, setting the wild strands writhing and sliding. "A hard bitch, your mother is. She should have been a demon rather than a goddess."

"Release the woman."

"I may be persuaded to do just that." She smiled. "A duel, perhaps? This witch can be the prize."

Kalen nodded. "If you wish."

"Ah, but you are eager. And even before you hear your penalty should you lose."

"Name any price."

"Your body and soul, in exchange for hers. Forever."

"Kalen, no!" Christine barely choked out the words. There was no way for Kalen to survive this contest. If he lost, he would belong to Culsu. If he destroyed the demon, he'd doom himself to an eternity of imprisonment. "I'm not worth this," Christine finished in a broken whisper.

Kalen's eyes flickered, catching her gaze for the briefest of seconds before returning to his enemy.

"You will fight," Culsu stated.

"Yes. And I will kill you."

"We shall see."

Culsu descended from the cairn to stand on the bare earth within the stone circle. Christine held her breath as Kalen and his ancient nemesis squared off. Kalen raised his spear, white fire crackling at it tip. Culsu gave a mild, disarming smile as she palmed a ball of demonfire. Leanna lowered the fire encircling her and Christine and peered avidly at the dueling field. Leanna looked inordinately pleased. Clearly, she had faith in her mistress's powers.

Culsu cast a ball of demonfire. Kalen parried it with the tip of his spear. He swung the weapon around, releasing a stream of white energy. Culsu absorbed it easily in a flash of red.

The battle quickened, red and white bolts colliding in fury. A blast of demonfire caught Kalen in the stomach. He staggered backward and lost his footing. Culsu rose, triumphant, but her glory was short-lived. Kalen rolled and sprang to his feet, swinging his spear and slicing the demon's legs out from under her, severing them from her body.

Leanna cried out in shock as Culsu collapsed. But where Kalen's attack would have destroyed a human opponent, the demon was only briefly incapacitated. Culsu's severed legs evaporated, forming a cloud of thickening black smoke that obscured her torso. An instant later the mist seeped away to reveal the demon whole and standing.

The attack had taken its toll, though. Christine could see

the strain in Culsu's posture, the slight hunch in her shoulders. Kalen was ready. He lunged, his arm snapping forward, his spear spitting sparks as it shot toward his enemy. The weapon flew directly at Culsu's chest.

"No!" Leanna cried.

No, Christine echoed silently. If the force of the blow destroyed the demon, Kalen would be lost.

The spear never struck its target.

A medieval warrior lunged from the portal atop the cairn. Clad in chain mail, a sword sheathed at his side, the improbable specter flung himself between Culsu and Kalen, his wide body spread in defense of the demon. Kalen's spear came to a stop in midair, its tip barely touching the warrior's armor. It quivered for several seconds before dropping to the dirt with a thud. The warrior nodded and stiffened his spine. Lifting a gauntleted hand, he raised the visor on his helmet.

"This I will not permit. You will not harm her."

"Tain." Kalen stood stunned. "What are you doing here?"

The warrior's reply was incredulous. "Why, brother, don't you know? I am here to destroy you."

A ball of demonfire sprang to life in the Immortal's hand. A white nimbus pulsed around it. With an abrupt motion, Tain fired the unholy combination of life and death magic at Kalen.

It exploded in Kalen's face. He fell to his knees, clawing at his eyes. With a hoarse cry, he crumpled sideways onto the ground and lay still.

CHAPTER TWENTY-SIX

The impact of flesh and bone with hard, unforgiving earth sent a sharp jolt of pain through Kalen's body. He tried to move; he found he could not. A great weight crushed his chest, making it difficult to breathe. He called his crystal spear to hand, but the weapon didn't obey. Above him, Tain stood with hand outstretched, holding Kalen in place as if he were a doll. Immortal magic and death magic snapped like lightning around him.

Kalen's mind was still reeling with the revelation that Culsu and Kehksut, the Old One who'd led Tain off the battlefield all those years ago, were one and the same. That the demon had imprisoned and tortured Kalen's brother, and held him in thrall now. Under Culsu/Kehksut's influence, Tain's strength had grown incredibly.

Tain remained motionless, but his eyes didn't stop moving. The gaze that flicked over Culsu was at once adoring and anguished. "Did he hurt you?"

Culsu's answer was calm. "No, Tain. I am unharmed."

"You should have let me come to you sooner."

Kalen tried to rise. A subtle motion from Tain's finger kept him firmly in place.

Tain's agitation grew. His eyes darted from Culsu to Kalen, then to the cairn stage where Christine lay bound and Leanna stood triumphant. "May we finish this now? I . . . I do not feel well."

"Of course, my love," Culsu purred. She went to him and stroked a soothing hand down his back. Some of the tension seeped from Tain's body. When Culsu pressed her lips to his nape, he shuddered.

She stepped away. "Bind him."

Shackles appeared in Tain's hand. Kneeling, Tain fitted the cold steel around Kalen's wrists and ankles. Tain kept his head down, refusing to meet his brother's gaze, murmuring all the while. "They hurt . . . they burn . . . but you'll soon grow to love them. And love what she does to you. The pain—it will keep you safe. It kept *me* safe."

"You are her whore."

Culsu laughed. "Yes. I've claimed him. Tortured him. Loved him. Pleasured him. In many, many guises." Her features began to morph, the bone structure of her skull shifting and sliding to accommodate the change. Her long, twisting tresses were absorbed into her scalp. Her chest expanded, her shoulders grew wider, her height increased. The black velvet dress transformed into a human man's dark business suit. A red necktie was held in place by a gold and diamond stickpin.

"Yes." Culsu's male body was as beautiful as her female one had been. "I am known by many names. Culsu. Kehksut. Amadja. And many, many others."

Advancing, the demon stroked Tain's bent head. Tain looked up at his master with eyes as adoring as any dog's. He made a low sound in his throat and pressed his cheek into the palm of Culsu's hand.

Kalen's voice was flat. Was his brother truly as mad as Christine had claimed? "Tain. How could you have given your body and soul to death's purpose? You are an Immortal. Created to guard life."

Tain's expression softened. "But death is so sweet, Kalen. It's the ultimate release, the ultimate bliss. Why should so many mundanes know its pleasure while we Immortals are denied it? I want to die, Kalen, and Culsu has promised to help me. Because she loves me. But . . . I don't want to be alone. Come with me, Kalen. Die with me. We'll be together, like the old days in Ravenscroft."

Kalen swallowed the thick lump in his throat. It was true—Tain's mind was gone. Insanity shone in his eyes. *Gods.* Kalen hadn't truly believed it possible until that very moment.

"Culsu." Christine's voice was a thready gasp. "Destroying Kalen will make no difference. There are others. United by light and life magic. They will not let you win."

Culsu smiled. Christine's bravado faltered. Her body seemed to shrink into the stage as Culsu's male incarnation— Kehksut? Amadja?—paced toward her, climbing the cairn with deliberate steps.

"So brave," the demon murmured, bending. His open hand hovered above Christine's stomach. When he made contact, Christine inhaled sharply and tried to shrink into the stage. But she couldn't escape the demon's touch.

With an oath, Kalen wrenched at his manacles.

"Hush, Kalen," Tain whispered in his ear. "Everything will be fine. Culsu is supreme. A goddess. A god. Christine will be safe forever."

Kalen strained against his bonds, then cursed and lay still. "Tain. Brother. Release me. I'm begging you."

Tain gave him a sad smile. "I can't do that. Culsu needs you, Kalen."

"So beautiful." Culsu's masculine hands drifted over Christine's body. "As beautiful as you were that night, naked in the sand, ready to fuck that worthless musician of yours. You gave him everything. All your magic. Didn't you realize how worthless he was? How he'd bargained your soul for riches?"

"You . . . you know about that?"

"It was I you kissed that night. I you evaded." The demon's white teeth flashed. "I admit, I'd underestimated you badly. Until that night, I'd no idea of the depth of power you possessed. Ah, I shall enjoy drinking that power. We'll have centuries together in hell before your body and soul turn to ash. And your Immortal lover . . ." Culsu turned to Kalen. "He may watch."

Kalen's jaw clenched. Christine's terror was palpable—and he could do nothing. He experienced a wave of overwhelming helplessness.

"Should I fuck you with a man's body," Culsu mused, "or a woman's?" His body wavered, then morphed into the female form Kalen knew all too well. Tendrils of wild hair snaked about the demon's head. She raised her hand. The portal to hell, still wavering on the cairn between Leanna and Christine, widened. Smoke hissed anew from the void.

Culsu met Kalen's gaze. "Your new home, Immortal."

Leanna's pale eyes blazed with sudden anger. "Wait a minute! What about me? What about the reward you promised me?"

Culsu raised her brows. "What of it?"

Leanna traced a rune. Demonsmoke rasped backward into the portal. The rift vanished with a loud crack. "Have you forgotten? *I* opened that portal with my blood. *I* delivered the witch into your hands. *I* called you to this circle. I *will* have what you promised me!"

"You presume to command me?"

"I do. Here in the circle, on the graves of the ancient ones, living and death magic intertwine. You are bound by my blood. You promised me immortality and *you will give it to me!*"

Culsu's eyes flashed red, but in the end she inclined her head. "Let it be done."

Leanna gave a smug nod. Descending the cairn, she approached Kalen. "You'll give me your child now. Your *immortal* child."

"You mean to steal the babe's soul for yourself."

"Yes."

He jerked his head toward Tain. "Why not have his?"

"He's insane. You're not."

Kalen's eyes didn't leave Leanna's face. When he spoke, his tone was derisive. "You can't conceive my child unless I will it. What will you trade for such an honor?"

Leanna didn't blink. "Your witch. She'll go free when you give me what I want."

Kalen's gaze cut to Culsu. "You agree to this?"

Culsu looked none too pleased, but waved a regal hand in acquiescence. "It will be as my slave says. Once you're in hell with me, and your immortal child in the Sidhe's belly, the witch may go free."

Christine's life in trade for the soul of Kalen's unborn child. It was an ugly bargain. And yet . . . he might still turn the circumstances . . .

"No," he said. "Christine must be freed first. And I need assurance Leanna won't harm her once I'm gone."

"You ask too much, Kalen," Leanna said dangerously.

"It's not a request," he said tightly. "You *will* do this, or I'll go to hell now and your soul will remain mortal."

There was an angry moment of silence as Leanna considered his words. "Very well. I'll take an oath of no harm against the witch. But it won't be binding until I conceive your immortal child. If I don't, the witch accompanies you to hell."

Kalen nodded. "As you say."

Christine's bonds dissolved. "Get up," Leanna spat.

She did, slowly, resisting the urge to massage her wrists.

"Come down here."

The circle of fire evaporated. Christine descended the stage, her knees shaking so badly she almost fell. If she could get close enough to Leanna to touch her, she might be able to knock her unconscious. But what good would that do? She couldn't fight Culsu. The demon was as dry and ancient as hell itself. Nor could she fight Tain, an Immortal. But maybe, if she could reach Kalen, merge her power with his, they could fight together. . . .

"Say the oath, Leanna." Kalen's tone threatened violence.

Leanna scowled, but lifted her hands. Her fingers moved swiftly, tracing a rune. The lines glowed with a soft green light. *Ansuz*. Harmony.

"I vow before the stones and sky, I will not harm this witch once the Immortal's vow to me is fulfilled." She closed the spell with a symbol Christine didn't recognize.

Christine felt the power of the oath descend in a spiral all around her. She felt a brief wave of vertigo, but the dizziness passed quickly. Culsu was watching her closely, her brows slightly lifted. Christine's gaze slid past the demon to Tain, who stood nearby but didn't seem to be entirely aware of what was happening. His eyes had taken on a faraway look. He removed his helmet, revealing a bright shock of red hair and a pale complexion accented by a pentacle tattoo on his left cheek. Moving to one of the standing stones, he bent close, scrutinizing the markings carved on its surface.

Her gaze shifted to Kalen. Should she make a dash for him? Could she reach him before Leanna or Culsu intervened?

Anticipating her action, Leanna moved to block her. "Get back. Now. Or have you forgotten the oath is not yet binding?"

She looked helplessly at Kalen. His eyes met hers, then slid away, darting to a point beyond the circle. Christine's eyes widened, but she didn't follow his gaze with her own. She knew what he was trying to tell her.

She backed away, to the edge of the circle, into the shadow of a broad, flat standing stone. Mac's body lay supine in the dirt—Leanna and Culsu had forgotten him. Dropping into a crouch, Christine inched toward the Sidhe.

"I need Kalen naked," she heard Leanna tell Culsu.

With a smirk, the demon lifted a hand. Kalen's clothing dissolved in a flash of fire and smoke.

Leanna eased her thong over her hips and down her long legs. Straddling Kalen's hips, she paused expectantly. A moment later, she frowned. Lips thinning, she took Kalen's soft penis in her hand and began stroking. Christine dragged her gaze away. She knew Kalen was giving her time to act. If she failed, would he truly sacrifice his own child in order to save Christine's life? Christine couldn't let that happen—she had to rouse Mac and hope his magic could swing the advantage.

She laid a hand on the Sidhe's shoulder. He gave a soft groan, his head rolling toward her.

"Shhh."

His eyes opened a fraction. He tried to prop himself up on his elbows, but didn't get far before collapsing back to the ground. "Fucking demon," he muttered. "Got me good."

Christine dared a glance into the circle. Leanna was still trying to arouse Kalen, with no success. Culsu looked distinctly amused. Tain merely stared blankly at a standing stone, frowning.

Mac followed her glance. He swore under his breath. "What the hell is going on?"

Christine explained in a few words. Mac gritted his teeth and pushed himself to a sitting position, his spine against the stone. His face went white. Beads of sweat appeared on his forehead. Christine ran her hands over his stomach, inspecting his wound. It was as big as her hand, gory in the center and charred at the edges. No human, and few magical creatures, could have withstood such a blast. Even Mac, half god, was clearly suffering.

She put her hand directly over the wound. He hissed in a breath. Closing her eyes, she sought his magic, water magic like her own, and whispered a spell. Reaching for the power hidden in the blood coursing in his veins—the hidden streams and rivers flowing through his body—she called a spell of healing, washing his pain out of his body and into the earth.

"Feels like a cool stream, love." Mac sounded more like his old self. His breath came easier. "Thanks."

She took away her hand. The burn looked much better, though not fully healed. It was enough for Mac, though. He rolled easily into a crouch, his eyes intent on the scene inside the circle.

"Culsu won't be able to leave the circle," he mused. "Not if Leanna bound her with blood. I wonder about Tain, though . . ." He rubbed his chin. "Do you think you could distract him while I break Kalen out of those shackles?"

Christine swallowed. "I can try. But what about Leanna?"

A muscle in Mac's jaw ticked. "I'll take care of my sister."

Leanna bent over Kalen, magic swirling in a maelstrom of green sparks, trying desperately to arouse him. Culsu was chuckling, her dark hair whipping about her face. Incredibly, Tain had taken to wandering the perimeter of the circle. Stopping before each stone, he inspected its spiral markings. After a moment, he shook his head and moved on to its neighbor.

The next stone in line for Tain's scrutiny was the one behind which Christine was crouching. She met Mac's gaze.

"Go," she said urgently. "I'll take care of Tain."

CHAPTER TWENTY-SEVEN

"Stay outside the stones," Mac said in a tight voice. "Keep Tain from coming to Culsu's aid. Can you do that?"

Christine hesitated. "I think I could if I had water."

"There's a stream down the hill."

"Too far away." She eyed Tain, who'd left the neighboring stone and was plodding toward them. "There's no time."

"How about rain?" Mac asked.

Had he lost his mind? "What rain?" she whispered urgently. "There isn't a cloud in the sky."

"This is Scotland," Mac muttered. "I can bring the clouds."

She stared. "You can?"

"Normally I'm not allowed to mess with the weather, but I'm not overly concerned with the regs right now." He grimaced. "Of course, it'll take a spot of time."

Christine eyed Tain's progress nervously. "How long?"

"Depends on where the clouds are. Five, ten minutes, tops."

She drew a breath. "All right. I can work with that."

He nodded. "Be careful."

"You too."

A triumphant laugh drew her attention back to the circle. Leanna's magic had deepened into a pulsing green light, and Kalen's rod had begun to stiffen in her hand.

"Go now, love," whispered Mac.

Christine nodded and rose. Tain was just approaching the stone she'd been crouching beside. The Immortal didn't seem to notice her—he was too engrossed with the stone's spiral markings. The enormity of her task struck her. Her courage wavered. This was Tain, Immortal Warrior, a demigod bent on destroying himself and the world. How many humans and life magic creatures had he killed? How many others had succumbed to demon slavery because of the death magic he'd unleashed? He was vicious and terrible, and insane to boot. A scourge on the earth.

But at the moment, he looked like a lost little boy.

She glanced at Culsu. The demon's back was turned. Mac had crept around the edge of the circle, gaining some distance from Christine while he readied for his attack.

Christine took a deep breath and slipped around the stone to stand at Tain's side.

"Hello," she said softly.

The Immortal's head snapped up. His eyes darkened. He towered over her, his broad form made even more threatening by his armor and sword. His arms, thick with muscle and sinew, bore an angry tracework of scars. Panic clawed its way up her throat. This man could crush her in a heartbeat.

"What are you looking at?" she asked, trying desperately to keep her tone conversational.

Tain frowned. He walked his fingers over the lichen-covered stone, pausing when he reached a spiral marking. "This . . ."

"The symbol of the Mother Goddess."

"Cerridwen is my mother. She's a goddess. I think she loved me once." His brow furrowed more deeply. "But . . . I can't feel her anymore."

"That must hurt you."

"Hurt?" His voice was suddenly sharp. Anger flashed in his eyes and his stance shifted threateningly. "Who are you?"

"No . . . no one," Christine stammered, shrinking back.

"Ah." He seemed to relax. He returned his attention to the stone, tracing the spiral over and over with his forefinger, from outer edge to center.

Christine caught sight of Mac moving farther into the circle, easing into place behind Culsu. Leanna struggled with Kalen. Kalen's gaze darted toward Christine for the briefest instant and his expression turned thunderous. Resolutely, she looked away. Kalen might prefer that she flee, but that was one thing she'd never do. Not when his life was at stake.

"I cannot feel her," Tain said mournfully. He left off tracing the spiral to spread his palm flat upon it. "She's gone."

"Your mother?"

He nodded, a tear slipping from one eye to track down his rough cheek. Christine's heart twisted. Without thinking, she laid her hand over his and cast her senses into his body.

The surge of death nearly choked her. Tain's Immortal magic was nothing like Kalen's. Whatever light he'd once known was all but gone. His power was sinister and twisted, perverted by pain and dark, anguished eroticism. Little wonder he couldn't feel the living magic of the Mother Goddess. His psyche was a cesspool, a writhing pit of evil. It was all Christine could do to keep herself from snatching her hand away.

But she didn't. She steadied her breathing and sent a tentative spiral of light into his darkness. Tain reacted with confusion, then a suspicious anger. *Oh, Goddess.* But she couldn't pull away, not now. Not when Mac was about to strike.

Don't think of that. Focus. Tain hadn't turned completely evil—she could sense a thin thread of goodness, a tiny trickle amidst a torrent of death magic. Could she strengthen it?

Calling her deepest power, she sent a river of living magic flowing through her hand and into the Immortal.

Tain's eyes widened. Some deeply buried emotion flickered in his soul.

"I . . . I think I feel her." His tone was one of awe and reverence. And . . . hope.

In that instant, Mac attacked, elfshot erupting from his hands. The first bolt hit Culsu between the shoulder blades.

The demon let out a roar. Mac launched himself at the entity. Tain's head snapped around. Christine clung to the Immortal, summoning every drop of magic she possessed and pouring it into him. She had to keep him from entering the fight.

She succeeded for scant seconds, before Tain's features twisted horribly. His eyes went red; an inhuman growl sounded in his throat. Death magic zinged through his body, surged through his point of contact with Christine. A jolt like a lightning strike shook her body. She flew backward. The painful impact of her body on hard ground raised stars in her vision.

"Mac! Behind you!" she managed to gasp out.

Mac spun around too late to avoid Tain's enraged stampede. Tain slammed into the Sidhe; Mac collided with Culsu. The three fell in a grappling heap on the ground, elfshot and demonfire zinging. Christine dodged the bolts, launching herself at Leanna.

She crashed into the Sidhe, knocking her away from Kalen. They hit the ground together. Kalen twisted, straining in his shackles. The metal cracked, but held. He let out a foul stream of curses.

Christine rolled atop Leanna, pinning her arms above her head and pressing her knee into the Sidhe's chest. Leanna's ribs were already restricted by the tight corset; the added pressure had her gasping for air. Christine pushed harder. "If you have any blood power at all over Culsu, use it. Get rid of her."

"You . . . make me . . . laugh."

"I'll make you do more than that," Christine muttered. She tightened her grip on Leanna's wrists as she gathered her magic. She sent a stream of blue energy flooding into the Sidhe's body. But something went wrong. The power recoiled, shooting back up Christine's arms. The jolt of the blast flung her backward.

Leanna jumped up. "That's a taste of your own medicine, witch."

Christine stared up at her. "What . . . what happened?"

"That oath of no harm? I modified it, right at the end. Added a recoil spell, on your side only. Anything you do to me reacts on you. But not the other way round." She gave an ugly smile. "You're useless here now. Crawl home before I decide to kill you."

"Bloody *hell*." Mac's curse was followed by a choking sound. Christine's eyes flew toward him. Tain had Mac in his grasp, his fingers bent like prongs of steel. Mac clawed at Tain's hand, gasping.

Culsu brushed a speck of dirt from her velvet dress.

"Oh, Culsu," Leanna called. The demon's brow rose. "I have your little human witch here."

"No." Kalen strained against his shackles. "Leanna, let Christine go."

"I was going to, Kalen, really I was, but she just wouldn't run. She loves you too much. Isn't that sweet? Now I have to give her to Culsu."

Leanna shoved Christine toward the demon. The odor of decay that clung to the elegant body turned Christine's stomach. Kalen gave a low curse; Mac gagged as Tain's fingers tightened.

Christine gathered every last scrap of courage she possessed and looked up into Culsu's red eyes. "I know you want my magic. You can have it. I'll give it to you freely. But first let Kalen and Mac go." With shaking fingers, she began unfastening the buttons of her blouse.

Culsu scoffed. "All three of you are mine. Why should I release the two demigods?"

"Because if you do, I won't fight." A willing victim was much sweeter to a demon than one taken by force. The last button slipped from its hole. Christine let the edges of the blouse part, revealing her naked breasts. "I'll come freely. I'll do . . . whatever you want. I know your kind prefers an eager . . ." She nearly choked on the word. ". . . *lover*. And I'm a muse, like Leanna. I'll give you my power freely. But only if you release them."

Kalen swore. "Pay her no mind. It's me you want, Culsu. This human witch's power is nothing."

Culsu didn't answer him. Eyes glinting, she reached out and drew a line from Christine's throat to her navel with one long red fingernail. The stroke was like fire, pure and painful, but with an underlying current of dark sensuality that caused Christine to close her eyes and let out a low moan.

"That's just a hint of what awaits you in hell, my dear."

Christine didn't resist. She felt Culsu grasp hold of her life magic, absorbing it into her soulless body. A measure of Christine's pure, shining power morphed into something dark and evil.

"So sweet," Culsu murmured. She glanced at Kalen, then at Mac, who was still struggling in Tain's grip. "I find I'm feeling unusually generous. Perhaps I'll let Mac Lir go." Her oily fingers snaked around Christine's wrist. "He was never part of my plan, and I don't need his parents' interference. But the Immortal . . . I'm sorry, my dear, but I just cannot accommodate you."

"That's not the bargain I offered you. Kalen must go free."

Culsu yanked on Christine's wrist. Christine pitched forward, her body coming flush against the demon's fetid, velvet-clad body. Culsu's arms tightened on Christine's ribs. "You think you can bargain with me? You little fool."

The rotting, putrid essence of Culsu's soul seeped into Christine's body. She choked, her mind reeling.

"Kalen," Culsu hissed, "will die. His life, and his brothers' lives, will end. The human world will be free."

"Free, free, free," parroted Tain. He rocked slowly forward and back, never loosening his viselike hold on Mac's neck.

"Feel me, my sweet," Culsu murmured. She stroked Christine's back, and smiled when her captive couldn't repress a cry. "Feel who I am. Feel my power, as ancient as the earth. And tremble."

There was a prickling like a million tiny needles on Christine's skin. The darts heated, burning through her flesh and into her soul. Christine gasped with horror when she understood—each tiny prick of pain was the essence of a human victim Culsu had fed on during the long millennia of her existence. The emotions of those doomed souls streamed into Christine's psyche. Despair. Impotence. Rage. Shame. The primitive anguish of a million souls, crushed and shaped and molded into one fathomless void of misery. Christine would be just one more anguished soul in Culsu's obscene collection. Unless she found a way to fight. Not from the outside, but perhaps from within . . .

She swallowed her panic and plunged her mind into the soulless void that was Culsu's essence. In the midst of darkness and hopeless evil, Christine found what she was looking for.

Light.

The life magic of Culsu's victims—it hadn't been completely obliterated. Christine caught flickers of light, so faint as to be almost invisible in the overwhelming darkness. But it was there, just out of reach.

If only she had water. Just a handful would be enough. With water, she could reach out with her magic, touch the souls of those long-dead victims. With water, she could command that power to . . .

A drop struck her nose.

She looked up. A cloud hovered overhead, low and angry. Christine had never seen such a beautiful sight. Her gaze snapped to Mac, still imprisoned by Tain. His eyes telegraphed a clear message: *whatever you've got up your sleeve, pull it out now.*

A second splash followed the first, striking her cheek. A spatter of big heavy drops laid a pockmarked pattern in the dirt. The storm intensified, bathing her face, neck, and arms. Christine closed her eyes, drawing power from the magic of the water on her skin. Searching Culsu's essence, she located the slumbering magic of damned souls. And awakened it.

Culsu gulped as the light grew within her. Her grip on Christine's wrist tightened. Her other hand found Christine's neck. "Stop it," she growled. "Stop it now."

Christine struggled for air. Her vision started to fade. Mac spat out a word, a spell of strengthening. The rain became a steady shower, then, suddenly, a torrential downpour.

And still Culsu's fingers tightened. Christine started to black out; dimly, she recognized a burst of elfshot from Mac's direction. Heard Kalen's angry roar and the sound of metal cracking. Leanna's cry was faint, a high, thin tone at the edge of her consciousness.

And then everything went black.

CHAPTER TWENTY-EIGHT

Rain poured from the sky, a sudden wind whipping through the glen, driving the pulsing torrents almost completely horizontal. Kalen, buoyed by the surge of energy Mac had sent in his direction, shattered the last of his restraints and sprang to his feet just as Christine collapsed. At the same moment, Tain gave an inhuman roar as a blast of Mac's elf-shot engulfed both their bodies in green fire. The Immortal drew his sword and swung it blindly; Mac ducked and sprang free.

Culsu fell back, arms raised for a duel. With a nod, she called Leanna and Tain to her side. Kalen willed his crystal spear to hand. It appeared the next instant, the white tip flaring dangerously. And yet, he dared not move. Christine lay unconscious at Culsu's feet.

"Leanna," Mac called. "You don't have to do this. You don't have to help Culsu."

"Ah, but she does," Culsu murmured. "Demonwhores have no choices."

Mac's eyes remained fixed on his sister. "Your soul is

Sidhe. We are creatures of life. We can't be enslaved by death."

Leanna lifted her chin. "You've done nothing for me. *Nothing.* Why should I help you now?"

"We're kin."

Leanna's mouth twisted. "No. We're nothing. *Nothing,* do you hear me?"

Pain flickered in Mac's eyes, but he gave a grim nod. "As you wish, then."

Culsu smiled. She turned toward Tain; some unspoken understanding passed between them. Casually, Tain angled the tip of his sword toward Christine's heart.

"And so it comes to this," Culsu said. Her outline wavered in the dark rain pouring over her. "Once again, Kalen, one of your own has betrayed you. Once again, someone you once loved will destroy the person you've pinned your future upon. Does it not grow tiresome?"

"You won't win this time, Culsu. I swear it."

"I will. And you, my old friend, will lose. Tain—kill the witch."

Tain's sword began a downward arc. Kalen sprang forward, deflecting the blow scant inches from Christine's chest. Mac's elfshot blistered the air, striking Tain in the back.

"No!" Tain spun and recovered, his sword now trained on Kalen.

Culsu summoned a ball of demonfire. Kalen blocked it with his shoulder. Pain smashed through him; he smelled burning flesh, saw blood running down his arm. The sight infuriated him.

Bloodlust exploded in his brain. His vision went red. Pain vanished as adrenaline pumped into his veins. A steely-minded sense of determination took hold. He *would* protect his own. And he would not fail.

"Kalen." Mac's warning note pierced the blood rushing in his ears. "Protect Christine. Let me fight."

"No," he snarled, raising his spear. White energy crackled

like lightning from the crystal tip. Culsu launched a barrage of demonfire. Kalen caught one missile after another, flinging them aside as he pressed his advance. Culsu faltered. For the first time, fear flickered in her eyes. Her hair whipped in frenzy.

"You wouldn't dare kill me."

"No? Watch me."

He leapt with a roar, knocking the demon to the ground. He pressed the crystal tip of his spear against her throat. Ice met heat with a hiss of steam. "The world will be a much better place without you."

"No!" Tain's anguished cry came from behind. "Don't hurt her! Kalen, you can't. Don't you see? She wants to help me. Help you."

"How? By killing us?"

"By setting us free."

"You'll be free," Kalen told Tain, "when I kill her."

Christine came awake to the electric sound of elfshot whizzing over her head. Rainwater streamed in cold rivulets, bathing her in mud. She gasped, inhaled a mouthful of water, and sputtered. Leanna and Mac were dueling over her prone body. Leanna's eyes glowed red; her elfshot was interspersed with red balls of demonfire. Mac's features were frozen into a mask of lethal intent. Digging her elbows into the mud, Christine dragged herself out of the line of fire. Her head was pounding, her stomach still weak. The misery of the souls lost to Culsu's evil still echoed in her heart.

"You'll be free when I kill her." Kalen's voice was low and deadly.

"No!" Tain sobbed. "You can't—"

"No," Christine cried.

Kalen's eyes flicked to hers and held her gaze. "Christine . . ."

Culsu took advantage of Kalen's hesitation. Demonfire

blasted from her hands; at the same time Tain, howling, lunged for Kalen. Kalen fell back, spear raised. His brother lifted his sword and roared.

"You traitor!" Tain sobbed. "You were going to kill her! I'll hack you to pieces! It will take months for your body to reform. By that time it won't matter. Life magic will be gone. We'll be free!"

Culsu appeared at her lover's side, a ball of demonfire rolling from her fingertips. Kalen reared up with a roar, catching it on his spear and flinging it away. Tain advanced and slashed, his blade hitting Kalen's spear shaft. Mac, still peppering Leanna with elfshot and ducking her heated return, tried to get off a shot at Culsu. The bolt went wide.

The battle continued, a standoff that slowly seemed to be turning for the worse. Culsu, Tain, and Leanna were herding Kalen and Mac slowly backward, toward the cairn, where the demon portal pulsed.

It was up to Christine to turn the tide. Fighting a spinning wave of vertigo, she struggled to her feet, bracing her spine against a standing stone. Spreading her arms, she took in as much of the rain as possible.

She gathered her magic. Focused on one simple thought. She brought it to form, tracing a rune in the air.

Eihwaz. Faith.

Like a dream, a blue mist descended, interweaving with the rain. Life magic. Water magic. It filled the circle, enveloping Mac and Kalen in a gentle blue glow. The same glow settled over Christine. Leanna's elfshot couldn't penetrate the shield. A ball of Culsu's demonfire struck the barrier and fizzled. Even Tain's sword recoiled with a dull clang.

But Mac and Kalen's missiles had no problem piercing the shield. Culsu dodged one blast, her lips twisting in a foul curse. She lunged toward the cairn, yanking Leanna behind her. Tain shadowed them closely.

"Don't let them reach the portal!" Mac cried.

Kalen cursed. He flung his spear at Culsu. Tain deflected

it with a stroke of his sword. Red fire spewed from the portal to hell, forming a nimbus around the demon and her lackeys. Mac drew up short before the barrier, cursing. Kalen called his spear to hand and slammed it into the fire. The crystal tip couldn't pierce it.

Culsu jerked her head at the fiery void. "Go," she commanded Leanna.

Leanna's face turned deadly white. "No! I called you with my blood! You have to fulfill your end of the bargain. I want to be immortal. . . ."

"And so you shall be, my sweet. In hell."

Culsu raised a hand. A dark mist passed over Leanna. Green sparks flew as the glamour on her features fell away. Her youthful form aged twenty years and beyond. Lines appeared on her face, her breasts sagged, her waist thickened. Leanna looked down at her body and let out a cry. *"No!"*

"Go," Culsu said. "Do not try my patience."

Leanna tried to resist; she could not. Her feet carried her inexorably toward the portal. At the threshold, she turned and gave a low moan. "Mac . . . please . . . help me."

Mac's features were hard, though his green eyes were fierce with emotion. Black smoke and fire swirled about Leanna's legs. Her sobs turned beseeching as Culsu grabbed her and thrust her toward the portal.

"Mac," Leanna sobbed. *"Bràthair!* Don't let her take me! *Ma's e do thoil e—"*

Flames shot from the shrinking passageway swallowing Leanna's body. Her cries faded to nothingness.

Mac stood motionless, staring at the void, his body rigid. Culsu's satisfied gaze flicked to Kalen.

"Now, Immortal," she said softly. "I will take what is most dear to you." Her gaze flicked to a point behind Christine.

A blur of movement snagged the corner of Christine's vision. In the next instant, Dougal's leering visage appeared before her. Before Christine could react, the half-breed lunged toward her circle of protection, his lead-gauntleted arms outstretched. A blast of demonfire exploded from Culsu's fingers, striking Christine's shield at the same time Dougal smashed into it.

It was too much. Christine scrambled to compensate for the double attack, but the burn of the toxic metal combined with the assault of the demonfire caused a fissure in her protective spell. Dougal fell on her, his thick fingers closing on her throat. His lead gauntlets seared her shoulders as his heavy body slammed her to the ground.

"Kill her," Culsu cried. "Now!"

"My pleasure," Dougal spat.

His fingers tightened on her throat. Suffocating blackness consumed her vision. Dimly, she heard Kalen's shout of fury.

A blast of white fire exploded behind Dougal. The half-breed went rigid, his head jerking back as pale lightning crackled around his body. With a guttural cry, he slumped forward onto Christine's body. Before she could react, someone was shoving the weight away.

Mac. Spitting curses, he hauled the body to one side. Christine sucked in a breath, her horrified gaze flying from Dougal's charred corpse to Kalen. The air rang with Culsu's manic laughter.

Oily smoke hissed through the demon portal, swirling about Tain's legs. At Culsu's nod, the Immortal disappeared into the void. The demon's human body twisted and melted, reforming into something dark and hideous. She slipped through the passage, her laughter a grating scratch on Christine's eardrums.

"Did you truly believe you could defeat me, Kalen? That, my ancient friend, was your downfall."

CHAPTER TWENTY-NINE

"Are you hurt?"

Kalen strode toward Christine. Her safety was all he could think of, and he knew he didn't have much time. He'd defied his Goddess Mother's will. Uni's temper was short. It would not be long before she sent him to his eternal punishment.

"Are you?" he repeated, reaching her side. She seemed to be in shock. He ran his hands over her body, reassuring himself that she was well.

Her gaze flicked to Dougal's charred corpse, then to him. Tears shimmered in her beautiful blue eyes. "You . . . killed him."

"Good riddance," he muttered.

"No . . . you shouldn't have killed him. You should have—"

"Let him kill you?" Kalen said harshly. "I'd rather rot in hell."

Anger flashed through the tears in Christine's eyes. "If you were so intent on sacrificing yourself, you should have done it while destroying Culsu, not Dougal! Culsu and Tain will be back stronger than ever. And you won't be here to fight them."

Kalen's lip twisted. "I'd prefer a simple thanks for your life."

Christine's rage crumpled. "Of course," she whispered, her expression stricken. "It's just that—I can't bear to think what will happen to you . . . because of me."

Kalen called his crystal spear to hand and ran his palm down its shaft. "Christine," he said gently. "I was created to be a warrior. See this weapon? It's mine to use for good, in defense of life. It matters not how many centuries have passed since I have acknowledged that duty. My people may be dead, but my vow to protect what they stood for—human civilization itself—remains. It was past time I returned to battle. I knew the price of saving your life, and I am not sorry to pay it. You mean everything to me."

Christine's shoulders started to shake as tears squeezed out of her closed eyes. Kalen slid his arm around her shoulders and pressed her body to his. He was acutely aware it would be the last time he embraced her. "Shh, love."

Mac spiked his fingers through his wet hair. "It will be my greatest pleasure to fight that demon bitch again. Next time, I will kill her for you, Kalen."

"I thought Lir summoned you to Annwyn."

"Do you think I bloody care? I'm not going through those Gates. Niniane will just have to deal with it." He looked at Christine. "I'm coming with you, love. To fight with your coven."

Christine nodded. "The Coven of Light will welcome—"

Her words were cut off by a gust of wind sweeping through the trees. Kalen went rigid as power swirled into the stone circle. As dawn broke over the horizon, a woman's clear voice drifted from the forest.

"Kalen. You have taken a life."

With a sense of fatal inevitability, Kalen turned to face the woods. "I have."

Uni emerged from the shelter of the oaks, cloaked in light. She stood as tall and proud and fierce as he remembered. Her long, dark hair was braided and wrapped around her head, accentuating the severity of her features. Her torso was draped in a shining white tunic, her luminous gold mantle pinned with starlight at her shoulders. Jeweled sandals shod her feet.

His mother was stunning and terrible. Light and fury melded. She advanced to the forest and raised a hand. Christine and Mac stood stunned as he went to her. Dropping to his knees on the muddy ground, he laid the crystal spear at her feet.

"Mother." He didn't dare look at her. "I have disobeyed your orders. I have taken up your spear and used it in anger."

Uni laid a firm hand on his head. "I've missed you, my son."

"As I have missed you." With a sense of wonder, he realized it was true. He'd felt the lack of Uni's blessing for seven long centuries.

"I've not been far. I've been watching you all these centuries."

His head came up. "You have?"

"Yes. I've watched you struggle. Watched you swallow your pride. Seen you piece together a new way of living in which killing had no part. You sought to know the spark of life and creation. Your compassion grew and your rash anger became tempered with true wisdom."

"I am not so wise, Mother. I've made many mistakes."

"Even the gods make mistakes, my son. Rise, Kalen."

He did so, slowly. When he stood fully erect, he was surprised to find the shaft of his spear held firmly in his right hand. He met Uni's gaze, a question in his eyes.

She inclined her head with regal grace. "Seven hundred years ago, you were arrogant and prideful. You fought fiercely, yes, but you did not understand what you protected. When faced with defeat, you manipulated the person you loved best, and in so doing, destroyed him."

Kalen bowed his head. "All you say is true."

"It was clear to me that you needed guidance. You needed to learn humility, and the true meaning of love and sacrifice." She pivoted slowly, her gaze coming to rest on Christine. "And now I see that you have."

Kalen looked up. "What do you mean?"

"This human woman. You were willing to exchange your life for hers."

"Yes."

"That, my son, is the lesson you needed to learn. I will not require more of you."

A violent hope unfurled in his chest. "You have not come to take me out of the world?"

"No, I have not. I have come to return you to it." She nodded to the weapon clutched in his hand. "Yes, Kalen, my crystal spear is once again yours to wield as you see fit. From this day on, guard the human race with wisdom. Respect all life, even that of your enemies. But do not yield before true evil. Those who love death must be destroyed."

It took several moments before he could recover his voice. When he did, his words wavered with heartfelt emotion. "I thank you, Mother. I will do as you say. I will protect humanity from all that is evil."

"One thing more," Uni added.

Kalen inclined his head. "Anything, Lady."

A smile touched her lips. "Guard your human witch well. She is a true treasure. Her love for you, and yours for her, is your true salvation."

"I . . . I will."

The goddess nodded once and vanished.

CHAPTER THIRTY

"Hey! You there! Quit your pushing. Show a bit of respect."

Mac shook his head in disgust as his charges mostly ignored his shouts as they jostled their way through the shimmering silver gates to Annwyn. Fifty thousand or so through, fifty thousand or so left to go. The way the refugees were fighting to cross the glittering threshold, you'd think the bloody Gates were going to disappear. Which they were. But not for a few hours. And magic was involved here. There was plenty of time to get everyone to the Otherworld before the Gates faded. Sighing, he looked across the water to the castle just visible in the mist. Kalen would have been a big help with the herding, but he'd taken Christine straight to the castle. He'd said she needed rest.

Mac grinned. Rest. Right. And afterward, maybe a little horizontal exercise. He'd never seen Kalen so hot for a woman. The Immortal had found love, and Mac was glad to see it. The question was, would Mac ever discover the emotion himself?

"Out of my way!"

Mac's thoughts were lost as a disgruntled Sidhe male—not one of Mac's own clan, he was happy to note—shoved through the midst of a halfling family, nearly trampling one of the smaller children. The little lad's mother launched an impassioned tirade at the ill-mannered bloke's back. Behind her, brownies, imps, and sprites grappled shamelessly, the larger ones yanking the smaller ones by the hair and depositing them farther back in the queue. Even the faeries and nymphs, usually the most polite of all the Celtic creatures, were landing well-placed elbows in their neighbors' ribs. As for the humans—well, frankly, Mac didn't even want to think about how badly the humans were behaving. Road rage, the Americans called it. It was not a pretty sight.

He'd had quite enough, thank you. He hated to do this, but . . .

"Cut. It. *Out!*"

He punctuated the command with a blast of elfshot aimed low over the refugees' heads. Then, just for good measure, he sent a lower, relatively mild bolt into a group of rowdy halfling teenagers, knocking them on their hairy asses.

"Take that, Frodo," he muttered.

Mac's tantrum gained an instant response. *Silence.* Blessed silence. Fifty thousand pairs of startled eyes turned toward him.

Now, *that* was more like it.

He nodded graciously. "Two at a time through the Gates, if you please."

The rest of the evacuation proceeded at a much calmer rate. A few hours later, Mac watched the last group, a pair of ill-tempered phookas, fly low through the archway. The uppermost section of the enchantment was already starting to fade. A few moments more and the portal would be gone. Mac paused, watching the swish of the phookas' white tails as the magical equines disappeared down the golden path. Trees arched over their heads, their silver branches scattered with leaves of crystal. Annwyn. The place was so beautiful, it hurt his eyes.

Which was probably why he hated it so much. When you came right down to it, perfection bloody sucked. The human world, with its craziness and its frantic vitality, was so much more interesting.

The portal was now little more than a network of glowing lines. Soon it would close, not to reopen unless Culsu and her minions were defeated. If they weren't, and the life magic of the human world was utterly destroyed . . . well, in that case, Mac wouldn't be around to worry about the Gates opening, would he?

He raised a hand, prepared to speak the final Words to seal the portal. The words died on his lips as an all-too-familiar figure appeared on the threshold.

"Mackie! What's the meaning of this?"

He shook his head, hoping the apparition would disappear. But no. Like a bad dream that wouldn't quit, Niniane remained standing before him, arms akimbo, looking more like Leanna than Mac cared to contemplate. The lines of her gauzy grass-green gown were exquisite, the points of the leaf-petal hem falling to midthigh. Her brilliant blond hair—the exact shade of Mac's own—was swept atop her head in an intricate braided arrangement.

And, man, was she pissed!

"Why haven't you been answering your cell?" Niniane demanded.

"Lost it," he replied. *Permanently.*

His mother pressed her ruby lips into a thin line of aggravation. "I could not believe my ears when Niall and Ronan told me you were planning to stay in this dung heap you call a world."

"Mum—"

"Are you *insane*, Mackie? How could you even think of doing something like this?"

"I—"

"Do you know, I haven't slept a wink in *decades*, worrying about you out here in this savage place. I absolutely *forbid* you to stay. I—"

Mac abruptly found his voice. "Forget it, Mother."

"Forget it? Oh no, not on your life. Don't you talk back to me, young man! No son of mine is going to throw away his life on a bunch of worthless humans. Get through this Gate this instant!"

With an effort, Mac squelched the volcano that was threatening to erupt inside his skull. "Sorry, Mum. No can do. I'm staying here on the outside. Culsu's a threat that has to be eliminated."

"Culsu? The Etruscan demon? The one with the eternal bad hair day? Mackie, that bitch is ancient! An Old One! She's nothing to fool around with. She'll eat you alive, suck out your soul, and save your bones to make soup! And *then* where will I be? Show a bit of sense for once. You're my only son, you belong in Annwyn, with me. Leave Culsu to the humans and come home."

"I can't do that, Mum." He paused. "She took Leanna."

"What?"

"Leanna didn't know what she was getting into. She thought she could control Culsu, but of course, she couldn't." He met his mother's gaze squarely. "She's in hell now."

Niniane blinked. "I can't imagine why you think I need to know this. That girl was nothing to me."

Mac sighed. "I know."

"Well, what *I* know is that you need to come home. For good. Settle down with one of your own kind. I have several girls in mind—"

"Whoa. Wait just a bloody minute. I'm only seven hundred and twelve! Way too young to be talking marriage."

"That's ridiculous. Why, I was barely four-fifty when I—"

"Mum. Give it up. I'm not coming home."

"Haven't you heard anything I've said? It's *dangerous* out there."

"Then may I suggest you take a giant step backward? Because I'm closing the Gates. Now." He lifted his hand and muttered the Words. The shimmering lines of the Gate faded into a spray of sparks.

Niniane's expression turned frantic. "But . . . what if all the life magic out there is destroyed? What if death *wins*?"

"Then I'll die," Mac said succinctly. "Any more questions?"

"You can't *do* this, Mackie! I'll tell your father!"

"He already knows," Mac muttered as the Gate gave its final shimmer and winked out of existence.

He stayed on the shore for a long time after, watching the pounding of the sea on the rocks.

Kalen sat with Christine on the couch in his bedchamber, rubbing her back. She buried her face in his chest and groaned. He just sighed. His little witch was never going to have the stomach for portal travel. Scooping her up in his arms, he carried her to the bed. It was a testament to how sick she was that she didn't utter even a murmur of a protest.

The castle was strangely quiet with Pearl and the brownies gone. For the moment, until Mac returned from ushering the refugees through the Gates, Christine and Kalen were alone.

Which was a very pleasing thought.

He left her sleeping while he went about preparing a bath. Without the brownies, he had to translocate both the tub and the water himself. He lit the fire and set the kettles on the grate to boil. As they heated, he added the contents of each one to the cold water in the tub.

Behind him, Christine stirred. He turned and noted with satisfaction that her color had improved. She opened one eye and watched his progress with a bemused expression.

"You could have heated that water magically," she said finally.

"I know. But I like doing it this way."

She laughed. "You're such a throwback."

He grinned. "Retro is in."

"Yeah. So I've heard."

He went to her and slipped her torn blouse from her shoulders. As he lowered her into the water, she cupped the side of his face. He turned his lips into her palm and kissed it.

"Thank you," she said.

He frowned. "For what?"

"You would have given yourself to Culsu to save me."

"And I would do it again. And again. Any number of times, for as long as I draw breath." He climbed into the tub behind her and settled her against his chest. Water sloshed over the sides of the tub and onto his parquet floor.

She gave a shaky laugh. "There's not going to be any water left."

He grinned. "Who cares? I'm getting used to tandem bathing." He stroked a hand down her back, his tone sobering. "I love you, Christine. You. Not your magic. If I never created another work of art, I would not regret it."

She turned and touched her finger to his lips. "I know," she said, smiling.

He washed and rinsed her hair, smiling as he tucked the long blue lock behind her ear. He lathered a bar of soap and massaged her shoulders, her back, her breasts. Her tense muscles relaxed under his fingers. When he'd finished, she turned and offered the same services to him.

She settled back into his arms with a sigh. "Water. It makes me feel . . . new. Alive. Like I've just awakened, ready for a new day."

"You make me feel that way," Kalen murmured. His hand slid over her breasts, her belly, dipped between her thighs. His phallus was hard. Lifting her hips, he eased her down on his erection. She grabbed the rim of the tub as she regained her seated position—but this time, with him inside her body.

It felt like home.

He wrapped his arms around her. She sighed. He held himself still, savoring the feeling of being within her. He kissed her shoulder, her neck. When he could stand his inaction no longer, he rocked, surging inside her. He smiled against her neck as a sexy moan dragged from her throat.

"I existed in a dream before you came to me," he told her seriously. "I lived my life in a fog, searching. But I didn't know what I was looking for."

She gasped as he stroked upward inside her. "It was . . . the same for me. I'd grown so used to holding myself apart—from people, from magic. From myself."

His fingers delved in the curls between her legs, seeking the pearl hooded by her sweet feminine flesh. "I wanted you from the first moment I saw you," he murmured. "When you put yourself into my arms with your scrying."

She blushed. "I told you. That was an accident."

"No. No accident. It was Uni's doing."

She twisted to look at him. "You think your *mother* sent me to you?"

"I'm sure of it. She's the only one who could have penetrated the magical defenses set on my castle." He smiled. "She must have recognized your potential as a daughter-in-law."

"Daughter-in—oh!" she moaned as he seated himself more deeply inside her.

"Be my wife, Christine," Kalen whispered fervently. "My mate. Bear my children. Accept Lir's gift of immortality. Once Culsu is defeated, we can be together always. We can live in Annwyn or here, in the human world. Wherever you wish."

She kissed him. There was moisture on her cheeks that he didn't think came from the bathwater. "Of course I'll marry you," she whispered. "If we both survive what's to come. If Culsu is defeated. If living magic survives. If the human world is still worth living in—"

Kalen's arms tightened. "Those things will happen."

"You can't know—"

He moved inside her, so deeply he felt as though he touched her very soul. "I promise you, my love, I'll do my best to make it so."

CHAPTER THIRTY-ONE

"Flight 1072 will board in just a few moments."

Christine glanced at Kalen, who'd somehow managed to wedge his immense body into a puny airport waiting area chair. His duffel and her backpack—retrieved from the Faerie Lights guesthouse—lay near his booted feet. Dark head buried in the sports pages of the *Scotsman*, he was oblivious of the attention he was attracting. Passersby stopped and stared, then glanced around nervously and moved on. The terminal was extremely crowded, but not a single passenger had attempted to occupy the free seat on Kalen's other side.

Dressed in snug black jeans and a black turtleneck sweater, a black leather jacket slung over the arm of his chair, the Immortal was far and away the most dangerous-looking creature, human or otherwise, in the airport. More than one armed security guard had given him second and third glances. So had every single female with eyes and a pulse.

Kalen closed his paper with an impatient sigh and flung it onto the empty seat beside him. He stared moodily at Christine's lumpy sweater and baggy jeans, then grimaced and looked away. Christine calmly ate the last salt and vinegar potato chip from the Walker's bag on her lap.

"Don't know how you can stand those things," Kalen grumbled. "They're the bane of the modern world."

"I thought that was plastic."

"That too." For about the thousandth time, he glanced at the huge overhead clock. "How much longer could it possibly be? We've been here for hours."

Christine smothered a laugh. Her big, bad lover sounded more like a petulant child than a lethal warrior. "They'll be calling our flight any minute."

"I can't believe I let you talk me into checking my spear with the baggage."

"Well, it certainly wouldn't have fit in the overhead compartment."

He made a sound of aggravation. "Sixteen hours from point A to point B. *With* layovers. I could've had us there in twelve minutes and forty-three seconds."

Christine's stomach turned completely over at the mere thought. Twelve minutes of Kalen's preferred mode of transport would have sent her to bed for a week. "The plane will be fine."

"That tin can with wings? I highly doubt it. You're lucky I'll be there to save you when the bloody thing takes a nosedive."

"Why, you're afraid, aren't you? Afraid of flying!"

"I am not," Kalen bit off, "*afraid.*" A faint tinge of color stained his cheekbones. "Translocation is more efficient, that's all."

"You *are* afraid!" Christine crowed. "Well, feel free to pop on over to Seattle without me. I'll be perfectly fine traveling with Mac."

Kalen snorted, then frowned. "Mac. Where is that kid, anyway? He should've been here by now."

Only Kalen would refer to a centuries-old demigod as a

kid. "He's got time yet," Christine said, settling back in her seat with a chuckle. She shook her head. "Kalen, Immortal Warrior. Afraid of flying. Who would have thought?"

"Imp." Kalen's dark eyes snapped as he leaned forward and silenced her laughter with a quick, hard kiss. Her magic sparked in response; he pulled away a fraction, looking down at her with darkening eyes.

"Salty," he murmured. He crumpled the empty crisp bag and tossed it toward the trash can at the end of the row. Then he dipped his head and kissed her again.

Christine held herself very still, fighting the sharp sensation of wanting—*needing*—that Kalen awakened in her so easily. A tightening of belly muscles, a heaviness in her breasts, a yearning in her heart. For a heartbeat, the airport melted away. She saw only Kalen. Felt only the magic of the love they'd created together.

He drew back, hesitating. An instant later, he groaned and captured her lips again, his mouth parting hers, his tongue tracing her lower lip until she opened fully. He swept inside; she drank him in on a sigh. Before she quite knew what had happened, she was in his lap, arms wrapped around his neck. Goddess, how she loved him. Loved touching him, loved making love to him. If she could've crawled inside his skin, she would've done it.

It had been like this for the last twenty-four hours, ever since she and Kalen had returned to his castle after the stalemated battle with Culsu. Poised as Christine was on a razor's edge between hope and dread, it seemed to her that every moment of her life was magnified. Sensations were more vivid, good and evil more pronounced. Time seemed to slow, but paradoxically, that only made her more acutely aware of its passing.

She'd spoken to Amber just the night before. The Immortal Darius, along with a witch named Lexi Corvin, had already arrived in Seattle after thwarting Tain and his demon lover in New York City. The last missing Immortal,

Hunter, was also waiting. And once all the brothers were assembled . . . a final battle would ensue, a war that could mark the end of life magic in the human world. The beginning of an eternity of death and slavery.

The realization brought home the fact that every second of life was a gift.

This here and now with Kalen . . . it was the seed from which eternity sprouted. Christine lost herself in the moment, in the feel of Kalen's lips on hers. She wanted the sensation to last forever. Kalen seemed to understand. He gripped her hips—hard—and rocked her against his erection. Hot pleasure spiraled through Christine's body. If only they weren't in a crowded airport terminal . . .

A familiar Scottish burr, thick with amusement, rolled over her head. "Get a bloody room, loves. You're embarrassing the old ladies and little children."

Oh, *Goddess*, they probably were. She wrenched her lips from Kalen's.

"Mac Lir," Kalen said with sardonic exasperation. "Your timing, as always, is impeccable."

Mac grinned. "I do try."

From her perch on Kalen's lap, Christine looked up at the demigod who was like a son to Kalen. Mac looked much as he had the day she'd first met him at King's Cross Station. Black leather motorcycle jacket, ragged jeans, ripped seagreen tee. Backpack on one shoulder, guitar case on the other.

He looked impossibly young. She had to keep reminding herself he had almost seven hundred years on her.

Reluctantly, Kalen released her and she slid back into her seat. "You certainly cut it close," he told Mac. "What took you so long?"

Mac's cheeks reddened. "A little divine message from Lir."

"Ah." Kalen shot him a look. "Everything all right?"

"No." He shrugged. "Mum's livid and she's making Da's life a living hell. He wants me to come home, but I told him no. He's not pleased, but he respects my decision." He shrugged. "I'll deal with Mum later. After we rid the world of Culsu."

Christine eyed him seriously. "Are you sure you want to be part of this battle? There's no guarantee we'll succeed."

"Don't need guarantees, love. You humans need me." He punched Kalen's arm. "This relic here needs me. Who better to watch his back than the lad who was his best pupil?"

Kalen blinked. His eyes were suspiciously moist.

Christine covered his hand with hers and he squeezed it tightly. "I'm glad to know you've got my back, Manannán."

"Glad to be there."

A voice crackled over the loudspeaker. "Flight 1072 is now ready for boarding. First-class passengers and those needing assistance please proceed to the gate."

"That's us," Kalen said, standing. He hoisted his duffel in one hand and Christine's backpack in the other.

"I'm all set," Mac said.

Christine rose, Kalen on her right, Mac on her left. Standing between them made her feel very, very safe.

And very, very hopeful.

"Okay," she said. "Let's roll."

Created at the dawn of time to protect humanity, the ancient warriors have been nearly forgotten, though magic lives on in vampires, werewolves, the Celtic Sidhe, and other beings. But now one of their own has turned rogue, and the world is again in desperate need of the

IMMORTALS

CHRISTINE FEEHAN

#1 *New York Times*
Bestselling Author

Savannah Dubrinski was a mistress of illusion, a world-famous magician capable of mesmerizing millions. But there was one—Gregori, the Dark One—who held her in terrifying thrall. With a dark magic all his own, Gregori—the implacable hunter, the legendary healer, the most powerful of Carpathian males—whispered in Savannah's mind that he was her destiny. That she had been born to save his immortal soul. And now, here in New Orleans, the hour had finally come to claim her. To make her completely his. In a ritual as old as time . . . and as inescapable as eternity.

DARK MAGIC

ISBN 13: 978-0-8439-6056-3

To order a book or to request a catalog call:
1-800-481-9191

This book is also available at your local bookstore, or you can check out our Web site **www.dorchesterpub.com** where you can look up your favorite authors, read excerpts, or glance at our discussion forum to see what people have to say about your favorite books.

Phantom

Every night at midnight Dax could start to feel the change. The curse that made him less human as the Phantom inside struggled to take over, reminding him that he was never safe. Nor were the ones he loved.

As a girl, Robyn had pledged herself to him. But that was a lifetime ago. Now she was a woman. Beautiful. Pure. Every time she was near—her soft skin, her delicate scent—the Phantom wanted to claim her, to bring her body to the greatest heights of pleasure. Then steal her soul. Dax couldn't allow that to happen. Deep down, he knew her love could save him. If the Phantom didn't get her first.

Lindsay Randall

AVAILABLE JUNE 2008

ISBN 13: 978-0-505-52765-3

KATHLEEN BACUS

In need of a break from her matchmaking mother and a score of hellish blind dates, to Debra Daniels the do-it-yourself boyfriend-in-a-box kit is a gift from Above.

Fiancé at Your Fingertips: Touted as the single woman's best defense against pitying looks and speculative stares, it comes with everything the single-and-slightly-desperate woman needs to convince friends, family and coworkers that she has indeed found Mr. Right. And "Lawyer Logan" is definitely that. Tall, handsome…and fictitious. Debra is going to have an absolute blast with her faux beau—until he shows up on her doorstep, acting as if he has every right to be there and in her arms.

Fiancé at Her Fingertips

ISBN 13: 978-0-505-52734-9

ENCHANTING THE LADY

In a world where magic ruled everything, Felicity Seymour couldn't perform even the simplest spell. If she didn't pass her testing, she'd lose her duchy—and any hope of marriage. But one man didn't seem to mind her lack of dowry: a darkly delicious baronet who had managed to scare away the rest of London's Society misses.

※

Sir Terence Blackwell knew the enchanting woman before him wasn't entirely without magic. Not only could she completely disarm him with her gorgeous lavender eyes and frank candor, but his were-lion senses could smell a dark power on her—the same kind of relic-magic that had killed his brother. Was she using it herself, or was it being used against her?

※

One needed a husband, and the other needed answers. But only together could they find the strongest magic of all: true love.

KATHRYNE KENNEDY

ISBN 13: 978-0-505-52750-9

MARJORIE M. LIU

THE LAST TWILIGHT

A *Dirk & Steele* Romance

A WOMAN IN JEOPARDY

Doctor Rikki Kinn is one of the world's best virus hunters. It's for that reason she's in the Congo, working for the CDC. But when mercenaries attempt to take her life to prevent her from investigating a new and deadly plague, her boss calls in a favor from an old friend—the only one who can help.

A PRINCE IN EXILE

Against his better judgment, Amiri has been asked to return to his homeland by his colleagues in Dirk & Steele—men who are friends and brothers, who like himself are more than human. He must protect a woman who is the target of murderers, who has unwittingly involved herself in a conflict that threatens not only the lives of millions, but Amiri's own soul...and his heart.

AVAILABLE FEBRUARY 2008!

ISBN 13: 978-0-8439-5767-9

Jade Lee

Dragonborn

ONE PROTECTOR

When dragon power flows through your veins, when dragon thoughts burn in your mind, you can accomplish anything. Natiya knows, for she carries one of the last eggs in the land disguised as a jewel in her navel. Day by day the Unhatched grows, and when at last it births they will be joined in a sacred and eternal bond.

ONE SLAYER

When dragon power flows through your veins, when dragon emotions trample your soul, you become a monster. So knows Kiril, for one destroyed his cousin. That is why Kiril vowed to destroy dragonkind—and he has almost succeeded. But there is an obstacle he did not foresee: love.

AVAILABLE MARCH 2008

ISBN 13: 978-0-505-52754-7

☐ **YES!**

Sign me up for the Love Spell Book Club and send my
FREE BOOKS! If I choose to stay in the club, I will pay only
$8.50* each month, a savings of $6.48!

NAME: _____

ADDRESS: _____

TELEPHONE: _____

EMAIL: _____

☐ I want to pay by credit card.

☐ **VISA**   ☐ **MasterCard.**   ☐ **DISCOVER**

ACCOUNT #: _____

EXPIRATION DATE: _____

SIGNATURE: _____

Mail this page along with $2.00 shipping and handling to:
Love Spell Book Club
PO Box 6640
Wayne, PA 19087
Or fax (must include credit card information) to:
610-995-9274
You can also sign up online at **www.dorchesterpub.com**.
*Plus $2.00 for shipping. Offer open to residents of the U.S. and Canada only. Canadian
residents please call 1-800-481-9191 for pricing information.
If under 18, a parent or guardian must sign. Terms, prices and conditions subject to
change. Subscription subject to acceptance. Dorchester Publishing reserves the right to
reject any order or cancel any subscription.